THREE EERIE TALES

JEREMIAS GOTTHELF

THE BLACK SPIDER

Translated by Mary Hottinger

ANNETTE VON DROSTE-HÜLSHOFF

THE JEWS' BEECH TREE

Translated by Michael Bullock

THEODOR STORM

THE RIDER ON THE WHITE HORSE

Translated by Muriel Almon

THREE EERIE
TALES *from*
19th Century German

INTRODUCTION BY *Edward Mornin*

FREDERICK UNGAR PUBLISHING CO. / NEW YORK

Copyright © 1975 by Frederick Ungar Publishing Co., Inc.
Printed in the United States of America
Designed by Irving Perkins

Library of Congress Cataloging in Publication Data
Main entry under title:
Three eerie tales from 19th century German.

    Translated from the German.
    CONTENTS: Gotthelf, J. The black spider—Droste-
Hülshoff, A. von. The Jew's beech tree.—Storm, T. The
rider on the white horse.
1.   Short stories, German—Translations into English.
2.   Short stories, English—Translations from German.
3.   German fiction—19th century—Translations into English.
4.   English fiction—Translations from German.
I.   Mornin, Edward.   II.   Bitzius, Albert, 1797-1854.
Die schwarze Spinne.   English.   1975.   III.   Droste-
Hülshoff, Annette Elisabeth, Freiin von, 1797-1848. Die
Judenbuche.   English.   1975.   IV.   Storm, Theodor,
1817-1888.   Der Schimmelreiter.   English.   1975.
PZ1.T369 [PT1327]   833'.01   75-2178
ISBN 0-8044-2637-6
ISBN 0-8044-6520-7 pbk.

CONTENTS

INTRODUCTION

The death of Goethe in 1832 marks the end of a literary period which, though not lacking in contrasts and contradictions, nevertheless possesses a fundamental uniformity. Its authors, whether Romantics or Classicists, were concerned with timeless rather than topical questions, and portrayed representative human types against a universal background rather than individuals involved in the specific circumstances of their own age.

Yet it would be true to state that from 1832 until the revolutionary new departures in content and style of the Naturalists in the 1880's, only a few writers like Heine, Büchner, and lesser authors virtually forgotten today, broke sharply with the literature of the past—and that usually for political or ideological reasons, rather than on esthetic grounds. Some writers, such as Grillparzer or Immermann, indeed felt themselves almost crushed by their burden of indebtedness to the past; most authors simply continued to draw on much that was conventional in the subject matter and form of the literature of the preceding period while contriving to look more closely at the world around them and to reproduce a greater wealth of its everyday detail and social reality—a tendency observable even in later Romantic works from about 1815 onward—in loose conformity with emergent scientific and materialistic views of man.

Though one cannot talk of a Realist movement in German literature—since no program was formulated and no group or

school was formed—the term Realism is generally applicable
to the works, particularly the prose works, of these more traditional of the post-Romantic writers. However, German
Realism is frequently qualified as "Poetic" Realism, to distinguish it from the mainstream of contemporaneous European
Realism, whose representatives—like Balzac, Dickens, Tol-
stoy, Flaubert, and Zola—were more often critical of society
and more concerned than writers in German with the burning social issues of modern mass societies, such as the impact
of materialism on the individual, the place of women in
society, the physical squalor and moral hopelessness of the
urban proletariat, etc. These themes may be adumbrated in
works of Poetic Realism but are not widely or systematically
discussed in German literature until Naturalism. Gotthelf,
Droste-Hülshoff, and Storm, as well as other Poetic Realists
like Stifter, Keller, Meyer, Ludwig, or Freytag, are—when
not historically oriented—firmly regional, not metropolitan in
their base and are strongly selective in their presentation of
reality, refining it poetically to highlight underlying patterns
of meaning. Of course, the serious political dislocation obtain-
ing in Germany until 1871—in addition to the severing of
Austria and Switzerland from Germany proper—spared it
many of the more grotesque excrescences of material progress
by hampering its industrial development and urban growth.
Life continued to be more old-fashioned and provincial—in a
word more "poetic"—in this pre-industrial society, which
was, of course, the everyday reality of authors writing in
German. It should be no surprise that the literary technique
which they employed to portray their surroundings should
have been more "poetic" too, synthesizing as it does realistic
description with symbolism and esthetic appeal.[1]

Though the lyric maintained its preeminence as the vehicle
for expressing subjective experience, the dominant literary
form for the depiction of everyday life during the Poetic
Realist period was the novella, or shorter prose narrative. In
contrast to England, France, and Russia, where the novel
thrived, in Germany the novel did not continue to enjoy the

high esteem in which it had been held during the Romantic period, when it had been valued as the modern literary genre *par excellence*. Stifter, Keller, Raabe, and Freytag wrote novels as well as tales, it is true, yet it was not until Fontane's novels of Berlin society in the 1880's that a German produced outstanding modern examples in this genre, and the German novel established an international reputation only with Thomas Mann in the twentieth century. It may be, as some literary historians have suggested, that German writers, handicapped by their provincialism, lacked the grand themes necessary for the production of great novels; yet it is certain that what their prose works lacked in length and scope they made good in the quality of their craftsmanship, in formal excellence, and in dramatic concentration. The form of the novella has received much attention from theoretically minded German scholars and authors[2]—including Goethe, Tieck, and Paul Heyse—and for that reason an attitude of caution is advisable on approaching this genre; for while theory has served as a valuable stimulant to discussion, readers should not overemphasize its importance in evaluating tales by writers like Gotthelf and Droste-Hülshoff, who either ante-dated such theorizing or wrote with indifference to it.

The Poetic Realists' overriding preoccupation with the day-to-day affairs of the provincial middle class, peasants, and artisans has given rise to censure of what some critics feel is a disregard for the really important political and social concerns of the nineteenth century. Charges of pettiness, narrowmindedness, and philistinism have been leveled, and the term *Biedermeyer*—originally the name of a fictitious Swabian schoolmaster in a parody on provincialism—has been applied to what is at best called their "love of things small," at worst their neurotic escapism. No unanimity exists, however, as to which authors or works are *Biedermeyer* in character, with inevitably confusing consequences. Some critics will apply the term only to minor writers or to writers whom they personally deprecate; others have attempted to

purge the label of its pejorative connotations, either by pointing to problematical or activist traits in writers so branded, or
by making of *Biedermeyer* a chronological designation (the
Biedermeyer Period) covering roughly the years 1815–48 and
so misleadingly embracing also both late Romantic authors
and the politically engaged writers of the 1830's and around
1848.[3] Gotthelf, Droste-Hülshoff, and Storm (at least in his
earlier writings, before 1870) have all at some time been clas-
sified *Biedermeyer*; yet despite the occasional usefulness of
this word as a designation for a certain outlook on the world,
its value as a *literary* term is more than doubtful when
applied to their works. What is valid for these three writers in
particular holds true also for the Poetic Realists in general,
whom they may be said fairly to represent.

Jeremias Gotthelf was the pseudonym of Albert Bitzius, a
pastor of the country parish of Lützelflüh in the Canton of
Berne, Switzerland. Born the son of a pastor in Murten in
1797, Gotthelf grew up and spent all of his life in the Canton
of Berne, except for one year spent at the University of Göttingen in 1821–22. Through his father—a man of progressive
social and political views—Gotthelf early developed an interest in politics, and he involved himself in the public affairs of
his parish from his first curacy onward. Never a friend of
abstract theological concepts, Gotthelf possessed a reforming
Christian zeal. He was aggressively devoted to the ideal of
universal education (in whose liberating value he firmly
believed) and was tireless in advancing the cause of orphans
and the rural indigent. As a pastor, Gotthelf was officially
responsible for the supervision of elementary education in his
parish, but his commitment extended far beyond this. In 1834
he founded a boarding school for poor children in Trachsel-
wald (about five miles from Lützelflüh), and he was more
than outspoken in his promotion of improved conditions for
teachers and in his advocacy of new methods of teacher-
training when he served for ten years as inspector of the
Bernese schools. He retired from this capacity in 1845 only

when forced to do so by the authorities because of his public criticism of the school system. It was inevitable that a man of Gotthelf's convictions should have become caught up in the Liberal movement of the age. When, however, Swiss Liberalism fell under the control of elements too radical for him and assumed an anti-clerical and materialistic stance, Gotthelf increasingly dissociated himself from the movement. His disenchantment came to a head in 1831 when the Liberal government of Berne barred ministers of religion from political office. An ineffective preacher on account of a defective speaking voice and now cut off from the possibility of open political activity, Gotthelf turned to writing as a vehicle for his Christian activism. His first book, *The Peasants' Mirror* (1837), was a frank exposure of social *misère* in rural Switzerland and suggested constructive approaches to the problems of poverty, unemployment, and the upbringing of orphans. A considerable success, it was followed by a series of twelve novels and about forty tales, which continued to appear until Gotthelf's death in 1854.

Most of the novels and stories following *The Peasants' Mirror* are likewise concerned with problems of the Swiss country folk, such as the living conditions of country teachers, alcoholism, quack-doctoring, the relationship of landowner to tenant-farmer, etc. Intended primarily for a Swiss readership, his writings contain much dialect, but though dialect use varies from work to work, in the main it adds local color without creating a serious impediment to understanding.[4] Gotthelf's Swissness is reflected not only in dialect and locale, however, but in his interest in national history and traditions. It was one of his ambitions to write a cycle of historical-legendary tales treating Bernese history from its beginnings until his own time. This cycle was never completed, but parts of it appeared, together with tales of country life in his own day, in *Pictures and Legends from Switzerland* (1842–46). It was in the first volume of these that *The Black Spider* appeared. Strangely, the tale attracted little notice on its appearance. In this century, however, it has come to be regarded as one of the masterpieces of German narrative prose and has been subjected to great depth and variety of interpretation.

The Black Spider consists of a framework story and two inset tales. In the framework (set on an Emmental farm not far from Lützelflüh) a grandfather explains to family and friends assembled for a christening why an old and charred wooden post has been incorporated into the structure of his new home. The two inset tales recount the history of this post and introduce the theme of the spider. Gotthelf has received high praise for his accurate and detailed portrayals of Bernese scenes and of Bernese customs and traditions in this work. Plague-legends of spiders, the Devil as a green huntsman, the imprisoning of evil spirits in a wooden post, pacts concluded with the Devil for the performance of impossible tasks, etc., were probably known to him from oral sources. Perfectly familiar to him as a pastor would be specifically baptismal practices: the superstitious observances, and the foods and dress appropriate to the occasion. Gotthelf's peasants, too, are as much part of the Emmental setting as are their language and traditions, and yet it is through this very circumstance, strangely, that a remarkable transformation is effected. So convincingly Bernese are they, that they become wholly human for us, as much representatives of humanity as are the country folk in the Scottish novels of Sir Walter Scott (whom Gotthelf greatly admired), and for the same reason: because both authors have depicted their characters as if they were living persons, in the round, and the reader recognizes himself not only in their strengths but, even more, in their characteristic humorous weaknesses. Except for the father (Benz), no character in the framework tale receives a personal name, but is marked as a type by the relationship which he bears to the baptized child. It is this universality—conspicuous also in the theme of the incorporated tales and in the work's overall structure—which raises Gotthelf's story above the level of realistic anecdote, making of it a work of art.

The mythical quality of the conflict in *The Black Spider* is suggested at the outset by the grandfather when, on commencing his narrative, he thinks it necessary to place events in their timeless context by harking back to the prehistoric past, when mankind had originated in the Orient and the first race of men had come to settle in the Emmental. The struggle (in the first enframed tale) between Hans von Stoffeln and the villagers, and between the villagers abetted by Christine and the child's mother assisted by the priest, and (in the second tale) between Christen and the villagers is a cosmic struggle between the forces of good and evil, whose almost obligatory accompaniment is the crashing of thunder and the flashing of lightening. The spider embodies evil itself and the revulsion which it arouses, and as the instrument both of the Devil's revenge for being deceived and of God's punishment for sin it suggests a monistic universe. In this universe, sin and suffering can be overcome only by a fearless and active Christian spirit, which, however, Gotthelf the realist shows is not always to be found where one might expect it: it is Hans von Stoffeln, a Christian knight, who first creates the occasion for evil to invade society; *Christ*ine and *Christ*en play quite contrasting roles; one priest is a hero of the Faith, girding up his loins to do battle with Satan, while another priest revels with debauched knights.

The tale also admits of interpretation on nonreligious levels. For instance, the sexual symbolism of the spider (which originates from the Devil's kiss) has been commented on,[5] though this interpretation cannot be applied very satisfactorily to the work as a whole. Of much greater import are the social implications of the conflict portrayed. Gotthelf wishes to enforce upon his readers the cardinal importance of responsible social attitudes. The villagers in the first inset tale compromise themselves irredeemably by their refusal to accept responsibility either for their inability to transport the beech trees from the Münneberg to Bärhegen Hill or for Christine's representations on their behalf. Ultimately, this leads to their readiness to connive at evil. Yet deny their guilt as they may, they must expiate their transgression by suffering. Christen, in the second tale, vindicates himself by accepting responsibility for his earlier want of moral courage, and by an act of selfless bravery rights the evil wrought by his indulged servant. The community, both as an anonymous collective and as a company of individuals, is shown to be accountable for even the least of its members—a theme which sounds a very modern note in *The Black Spider* and links it with works such as Dürrenmatt's *The Visit* (1956) and Frisch's *Andorra* (1961).

The structure of *The Black Spider* underscores Gotthelf's message and the universality of its application. The unchanging significance of the two inset tales, separated by a span of two hundred years, is emphasized through many parallelisms in their subject matter. The most obvious external links between these tales and the framework tale, with its contemporary setting, are the motif of baptism and the window post, but similarities go deeper than that. The theme of responsibility, for instance, recurs in the framework story in a more subtle form. Here the godmother is put to the test like the characters of the inset tales, albeit in a less terrifying manner. She, too, is tempted to expose an infant to danger: this time the danger of acquiring inquisitiveness, through asking what his name is to be. Yet she fulfills her responsibilities by remaining silent, even at the risk of losing face and of compromising her good name. The spider, as the godmother senses, is still alive, and it can become free again at any time if the inhabitants of the farm or the valley fail in their duties to God and their fellows.

As *The Black Spider* indicates, Gotthelf was a man of unassailable religious principle, concerned to lead his readers toward moral enlightenment, and disinclined to question the order of the universe. In contrast, self-doubt and metaphysical uncertainty pervade much of the work of Annette von Droste-Hülshoff, a close contemporary of Gotthelf's and Germany's greatest poetess. Born in the same year as Gotthelf, at Hülshoff Castle near Münster, Annette von Droste-Hülshoff was as attached to Westphalia and its people as Gotthelf was to Berne and the Bernese—though she did travel more widely than he did, visiting the Rhineland and Switzerland, and finally settling near a married sister at Meersburg on the Lake of Constance, where she died in 1848 after two years of residence. Though she was passionate and freedom-loving by nature, Droste-Hülshoff's life and, to a certain extent, her works—certainly her decision as to which works should be published during her lifetime—were circumscribed by convention, by the wishes of her family, and by what was expected of a respectable spinster descended from old country nobility. A Roman Catholic, she was yet uneasy in her faith, which was shaken, though not destroyed, in an emotional crisis precipitated by an unfortunate love experience in her early twenties. Her doubts and conflicts are perhaps most clearly reflected in *The Spiritual Year*, a cycle of poems written for each Sunday and each feast day of the church year. At first intended as a book of devotions for her pious grandmother, the work proved too complex and ambiguous to serve that purpose and too personal and revealing to be published until after the author's death. Metaphysical doubts also inform one level of *The Jews' Beech Tree*, where is to be found too the same interest in Westphalian scenery and in local lore and superstitions as in many of her poems, especially the *Heathland Pictures* (1841–42). Droste-Hülshoff is best known for her lyric poetry, which marks a departure from Romantic musicality (at the expense of good sense) and vague mysticism in favor of clarity and concision of expression and precise observation of the sights and sounds of nature. *The Jews' Beech Tree* (1842) is her only important finished prose work. Originally planned as part of an (uncompleted) series of sketches of Westphalian life (the subtitle "a Picture of Manners from Mountainous Westphalia" still suggests this), the tale was rounded out to stand as an independent work.

Like many of the outstanding works of Realism, *The Jews' Beech Tree* has a basis in a real occurrence. In 1782, the farm laborer Hermann Georg Winkelhagen, suspected of murdering a Jew who had publicly disgraced him, disappeared from the village of Bellersen, Westphalia. The Jewish community of the region obtained permission from the district magistrate to carve a Hebrew inscription on a tree in the wood in which their co-religionist had been killed. In 1806 Winkelhagen returned home after having spent twenty-four years as a slave in Algiers, and was pardoned for the murder because his enslavement was considered to have been adequate punishment. Nevertheless, he himself did not consider this to be adequate atonement and took further action. This story was known to the author from an early age, because her grandfather was the district magistrate who had handled the case, and her memory of it was refreshed by an account, *History of an Algeria Slave*, published in 1818 by her uncle, August von Haxthausen.

These events, expanded to include a (fictitious) account of the murderer's family background, are related by Droste-Hülshoff with extraordinary forcefulness and narrative concision and with considerable dramatic interest—seen, for instance, in her withholding the meaning of the Hebrew inscription until the end. Furthermore, she invests the bare facts with a moral and religious significance. Certainly, the story at first appearance seems to exemplify the Old Testament: "Eye for eye, tooth for tooth, hand for hand, foot for foot." (Exod. 21:24) Friedrich Mergel, though held to be innocent because another has confessed to the murder of Aaron the Jew, is nevertheless pursued by remorse and expiates his crime. Yet if the reader bears in mind the verse prologue to the tale, he will realize that illustration of the Old Testament injunction cannot alone have been the author's purpose:

> You, happy reader, born and raised secure
> Amid the light, by pious parents tended,
> Put by the scales to which you have no right!
> Put down the stone—your own head it will strike!

The reader is enjoined to cast no stone (John 8:7), nor to judge, lest he himself be judged (Matt. 7:1). Droste-Hülshoff shows herself to be a writer in advance of her day when she produces sociological reasons for the reader's compassion. Anticipating views which did not become current in Germany until the literature of Naturalism, she points to the extenuating circumstances of Friedrich's upbringing. Born and raised in a village whose chief magistrate even engages in timber thieving, and taught by his mother to distinguish between crimes not in accordance with their essential gravity, but according to the persons against whom they are committed—an offense against a Jew being deemed almost negligible—Friedrich Mergel can have little sense of right and wrong. It should be noted that this deterministic view of man is conveyed through the author's descriptions of milieu, which, except perhaps for the portrayal of the village wedding, do not occur as local color for its own sake, but rather in order to indicate the influences which shaped Friedrich's character—so providing an illustration also of Droste-Hülshoff's economy of style.

Yet *The Jews' Beech Tree* is considerably more equivocal than either Biblical or sociological readings suggest, and this ambiguity derives from the supernatural elements and the textual obscurities of the tale. How can one accommodate in a merely rational or moral interpretation the figures of Friedrich's uncle Simon and of his half-cousin and double Johannes Nobody, for instance? Simon, with flaming red hair, "the tails of his red coat trailing behind him like flames of fire," is a diabolical figure, an embodiment of evil rather than a real person, while Johannes—who mysteriously appears after Friedrich's innocence is imperiled through being entrusted to Simon and just as mysteriously disappears again after the murder of Aaron—is best understood not as his cousin in the flesh, but as an objectification of Friedrich's physically unattractive yet honest self.[6] The apparently magical influence of the Hebrew inscription also suggests a realm of the mystic and occult lying behind the world of outward appearances, though it is not clear whether the inscription functions as the medium of divine retribution or whether it is the instrument through which nature intervenes in the affairs of men.[7] The reader is also at a loss how to come to terms with Ragged Moises' supposed confession to the murder of Aaron. Has Moises perhaps killed another person altogether and been misunderstood? Nor is it even certain that the person who has returned from slavery is indeed Friedrich, and not Johannes, as he claims to be—for how trustworthy is the lord of the manor's identification of Friedrich by means of a scar of which the reader has had no previous knowledge? Some of the factual obscurities can be understood as arising from the author's predominantly objective standpoint. For instance, when Friedrich as a child is in bed and is disturbed by the unexplained entry of an uncle into his room, the reader shares Friedrich's perplexity because the narrator depicts the scene from the child's point of view. Other obscurities—concerning Friedrich's relationship to the timber thieves, for instance, or his complicity in the murder of the forester Brandis—have resulted from the author's concentration of the narrative in successive rewritings, as has been shown through manuscript comparisons.[8] Yet ultimately there is a level of meaning in this tale which defies all attempts at rational penetration—and, as Heinrich Henel[9] has pointed out, the stressing of the actuality of the events, the citing of dates, etc., emphasize this impenetrability of reality the more. It was Droste-Hülshoff's intention to suggest that life cannot be fully comprehended rationally at all, and that the known world borders on a region of the unfathomable, defying interpretation in terms of the Scriptures or of social forces alone.

In the general pattern of his life and works, Theodor Storm had much in common with Gotthelf and Droste-Hülshoff. He was born in 1817 into a prosperous middle-class family in an out-of-the-way part of the German speaking area, in Husum, Schleswig, which at that time was controlled by Denmark. After legal studies in Kiel and Berlin, he might well have settled in Husum for the rest of his life had he not been forced to leave as a consequence of the annexation of Schleswig-Holstein by the Danish crown in 1852. From 1853 until 1864 Storm lived in Potsdam and Heiligenstadt, Thuringia—returning to Husum as a lawyer and magistrate immediately after Schleswig-Holstein was wrested from Denmark by the combined forces of Austria and Prussia. After his retirement, he settled in Hademarschen, Holstein, where he died in 1888. So profoundly attached was Storm to his native province that he considered life in Prussia and Thuringia an exile, and he was bitterly opposed to the incorporation of Schleswig-Holstein into Prussia in 1866. It is Schleswig-Holstein, too, with its coastal towns and heathland villages, its dikes and polders, and its constant exposure to the violence of the sea, which provides the background for many of his most characteristic works. Though a lyricist of note, Storm is best known for his novellas, of which he wrote over fifty. After numerous early novellas in an excessively sentimental strain —which *Immensee* (1849) may be considered to typify— Storm turned after 1870 to a more starkly realistic portrayal of provincial life, and *The Rider on the White Horse* (1888), his last work, is generally held to be his masterpiece in his mature manner.

Storm's love of provincial background is evident in *The Rider on the White Horse* in his indulgence in genre painting for its own sake to a greater extent than either author of the other two stories. Storm lavishes attention on the interior of the dikemaster's home, devotes considerable space to the North German game of *Eisboseln*, describes a funeral and a wedding, mentions the traditional red stork or heron pattern on the stockings which Elke is knitting, etc. The landscape, too, is realistically depicted, particularly in its harsher moods, and the characters of the tale seem almost to be an extension of their surroundings, the more so since they express themselves in few words, more often through a mute gesture or a suggestive glance. Yet, as in *The Black Spider*, the more convincingly regional the characters are, the more representative of humanity they become. Also contributing to the haunting ambience of Fresia are the superstitions of its inhabitants. Foremost among these, of course, is the ghostly rider on the white horse himself—an authentic legendary figure familiar to Storm since his childhood. The eerie atmosphere of the landscape and the primordial, elemental quality of the tale are further heightened by unresolved mysteries: the wandering tinker and his disconcerting behavior, the enigma of the horse's skeleton, Trin' Jans's premonitions of disaster, and the fact that the dike when breached claims the living sacrifice which Hauke had earlier refused it.

The narrative technique of *The Rider on the White Horse*, which has attracted a great deal of critical attention[10] and which provides an elaborate and fitting frame for the picture of manners and of human conflicts painted in the nuclear tale, has a bearing on the reader's interpretation of the supernatural content. Storm is at a threefold remove from the events of Hauke's life, since these are originally recounted by a sceptical schoolmaster to the second narrator, who has retold the tale in a magazine, which the narrator proper claims to have read many years before as a boy. By such means, Storm maintains a stance of objectivity vis-à-vis the supernatural occurrences, yet so powerful is their aura that they radiate from the innermost tale, told by the disbelieving schoolmaster, and penetrate the second frame; for the rider on the white horse is seen both by the writer of the magazine article and by the officials responsible for dike maintainance, and the truth of the tradition of catastrophe associated with his appearance seems confirmed by the collapse of a dike in a storm. Though himself a religious agnostic, and believing that in some future age nature would yield up all her secrets to man's reason (as the supposed ghosts of drowned sailors are discovered by Hauke to be only birds), Storm gloomily acknowledged that nature cannot yet be fully comprehended. In Silz's words, Storm felt that "the Unknown and Unknowable . . . lurks outside our reasoned world, ready at all times to invade it."[11] Hence Storm refuses to dispel totally the atmosphere of mystery in this tale, though he makes it clear through the narrative structure that he himself cannot be held responsible for the veracity of what he relates.

Though the supernatural, then, constitutes an important ingredient of *The Rider on the White Horse*, the conflict of the tale can be understood on an altogether human level, involving an individual's struggles against society. In a letter to Gottfried Keller in 1881, Storm stated that his generation had lost its receptivity for tragic drama and that tragedy had been supplanted by the novella in his age. Calling the novella "the sister of the drama and the severest form of prose fiction," he required that it should treat the profoundest human problems in the form of a concentrated central conflict. Certainly, *The Rider on the White Horse* admits of interpretation as tragedy in these terms. Like some of Shakespeare's heroes, Hauke Haien is destroyed by an excess of his own best qualities. It is his very independence, shrewdness, and singlemindedness which, in distinguishing him before all other members of his community, also isolate him from them. Incapable of inspiring affection in his associates, envied by them, and suspect on account of his pride and ambition, Hauke cannot count upon them in a crisis. In a moment of physical weakness, he fails both himself and the community, and pays in full the price of his tragic failure.

These three tales, while retaining features which may broadly be classed as Romantic—a supernatural theme, an interest in custom and folklore, naive characters in a rural setting—surpass any Romantic work in their detailed depiction of everyday occurrences and commonplace objects and in their emphasis on the importance of social and environmental factors in shaping human behavior and morality. While in this way they expose very real problems in individuals' lives, they also, in their poetic function, go beyond the merely social and moral to illuminate man's place in the metaphysical universe. It is this regard for the demands of the real world, coupled with the acknowledgment that earthly existence is but an aspect of a wider reality, that constitutes the essential literary character and the most valuable contribution to man's understanding of himself in works of Poetic Realism.

EDWARD MORNIN

NOTES

1. For further discussion of the term Realism in the German context, see James M. Ritchie, "Realism," *Periods in German Literature,* ed. J. M. Ritchie (London, 1966), pp. 171–195.

2. For the theory and practice of the novella in Germany, see E. K. Bennett, *History of the German Novelle,* revised and continued by H. M. Waidson (Cambridge, England, 1965). See also, in German, Benno von Weise, *Novelle,* 2nd ed. (Stuttgart, 1963).

3. An enlightening discussion of the term *Biedermeyer* is to be found in M. J. Norst, "Biedermeyer," *Periods in German Literature,* pp. 147–168.

4. The success scored by *Uli the Farmhand* (1841) in Germany encouraged Gotthelf to rewrite the novel in a version free of Swiss dialect (1846), which, however, has never enjoyed the reputation of the original.

5. H. M. Waidson, *Jeremias Gotthelf: An Introduction to the Swiss Novelist* (Oxford, 1953), p. 183. This book is also to be recommended as the best and most comprehensive study of Gotthelf in English.

6. Benno von Wiese, *Die deutsche Novelle von Goethe bis Kafka,* I (Düsseldorf, 1963), 163.

7. Wiese, *Die deutsche Novelle,* I, 171.

8. For detailed textual commentary (and research report), see Heinz Rölleke, *Annette von Droste-Hülshoff: Die Judenbuche* (Bad Homburg, Berlin, and Zürich, 1970).

9. Heinrich Henel, "Annette von Droste-Hülshoff: Erzählstil und Wirklichkeit," *Festschrift für Bernhard Blume,* edited by Egon Schwarz et al. (Göttingen, 1967), pp. 150–151. Similar views, though less radically formulated, may be found also in the chapter on *The Jews' Beech Tree* in Walter Silz, *Realism and Reality* (Chapel Hill, 1954).

10. See, for example, Walter Silz in his chapter on *The Rider on the White Horse* in *Realism and Reality,* pp. 122–123, or A. Tilo Alt, *Theodor Storm* (New York, 1973), pp. 125–127. Alt's book also provides a good general introduction to Storm.

11. Silz, *Realism and Reality,* p. 125. See also Lee B. Jennings, " 'Shadows from the Void' in Theodor Storm's Novellen," *Germanic Review,* XXXVI (1961), 174–189.

JEREMIAS GOTTHELF

THE BLACK SPIDER

Translated by Mary Hottinger

◆
◆

The sun rose over the mountain tops, pouring its radiance into a smiling but narrow valley and wakening to joyous life the creatures whose sole end is to rejoice in their life's sunshine. From the golden fringe of the wood the morning song of the blackbird rang out, the quail's monotonous love call rose from among the sparkling flowers in the dew-pearled grass, mating rooks danced their marriage dance above dark pines or croaked tender lullabies over the thorny cradles of their unfledged young.

Full on the sunny hillside nature had marked out a fertile sheltered spot. In the middle of it there stood a farmhouse, broad and bright, set in a splendid orchard where a few apple trees still wore the bravery of a late blossom. Some of the lush grass watered by the farm fountain was still standing, the rest had gone the way of all grass. The house was bathed in the Sunday glory which no hurried sweeping between night and day of a Saturday can bestow, but stands witness to the precious heritage of that ancient cleanliness which, like the family honor, must be tended day by day lest, in one heedless hour, blots might come on it, and persist from generation to generation, like bloodstains that no paint can conceal.

There was good reason why the earth built by the hand of God and the house built by the hands of men should shine in purest beauty. Over both a star shone in the blue sky, for it was a solemn day. It was the day on which the Son had returned to the Father, a sign to all men that the ladder was still standing on which the angels had gone up, like the souls of men who have sought their salvation with the Father and not on earth. It was the day on which the whole vegetable creation strives upward toward Heaven in luxuriant bloom, a symbol, yearly renewed, of man's own destiny. The air was full of sweet ringing sounds which poured in over the hills on all hands. They came from the churches outside in the wide valleys, where the bells were calling that God's temples stand open to all whose hearts are open to the voice of God.

Round the stately house a great bustle was going on. By the fountain splendid horses were being groomed with special care—noble mares, their foals gamboling about them. Mild-eyed cows were drinking from the great trough by the fountain, and twice the farm lad had to take pan and brush to remove the lingering traces of their contentment. At the fountain, maids were scrubbing their faces with rough drill rags, their hair twisted in knots over their ears; others were hurrying through the open door with pails of water, while the dark column of smoke panted straight and high from the squat chimney into the blue air.

Leaning on the crook of his stick, the grandfather came slowly round the house, silently watching the farm hands and maids at their work, stroking a horse or warding off the lumbering advances of a playful cow, and pointing out to the heedless lad a forgotten wisp of straw here and there. Every now and then he took from his deep vest pocket the tinderbox to light his pipe, which he relished so much in the morning, though it drew so badly.

On a spotless bench in front of the house sat the grandmother, slicing fine bread into a huge dish, every piece very thin and just the right size, while hasty cooks and maids cut slices fit to choke a whale. Fat hens strutted at her feet, squabbling with stately pigeons for the crumbs, and if some timid pigeon was pushed out of its share, she would throw it a bit for itself with a kindly word to comfort it for the grossness of the others.

Inside the house, in the great shining kitchen, a vast fire of pine wood was crackling, coffee beans were dancing in a big flat pan, stirred with a wooden spoon by a fine upstanding woman. Beside her the coffee mill was creaking between the knees of a freshly washed maid, while in the open parlor door there stood a beautiful pale woman with an open bag of coffee in her hand.

"Listen, midwife," she said, "mind that the coffee isn't roasted so black today. They might think I wanted to skimp it. Half a pound more or less is no matter today. And mind you have the wine soup ready in time. Grandfather'd think it was no christening if we had no wine soup for the company before they go to church. Spare nothing—do you hear me? There's saffron and cinnamon in the dish on the dresser, and sugar on the table. Take as much wine as you think is half too much. There's little fear it won't be drunk up at a christening."

So that was it. There was a christening in the house and the midwife was doing her work as a cook as doughtily as she had done it as a midwife. But she would have her work cut out if she was going to be ready in time and cook on the old-fashioned stove all that custom required.

Out of the cellar came a broad-shouldered man carrying a huge piece of cheese; he took from the spotless dresser the first plate that came to his hand and was just on the point of taking it into the parlor to set on the brown walnut table.

"Benz, Benz," cried the beautiful pale woman, "how they'd laugh if we'd no better plate for the christening," and going to the polished cherry-wood dresser where the glories of the house were displayed behind glass doors, she took out one of the handsome plates with blue edges and nosegays in the middle, surrounded by such sayings as:

'Tis more than human heart can utter,
Three halfpence for a pound of butter!

In Hell 'tis hot,
The potter turns his pot.

As the cow eats grass,
Man's life must pass.

Beside the cheese, she laid the huge züpfe, the true Bernese loaf, plaited like the women's hair, brown and gold, made of fine white flour, eggs, and butter, big as a one-year-old and almost as heavy. Above and below it she set two more plates piled high with oatcakes and scones. Hot thick cream stood in a covered flowered jug on the stove and the coffee was simmering in the shining three-legged pot with the yellow lid. A breakfast was awaiting the company such as princes never have on earth and no farmers but the Bernese.

"If only they'd come, it's all ready," sighed the midwife. "It'll take time for them to eat it all up and for everyone to have his share, and parson's terrible strict and as sharp-tongued as he can be if anyone's late."

"And Grandfather'd never let us take the gocart," said the young mother. "It's his belief that a child that rides to its christening'll grow up lazy and never be able to use its legs properly. If only Godmother would come! She takes longest. The men eat quicker. Besides, they could run."

The worry spread through the house. "Aren't they here yet?" was heard at every turn, from every corner eyes were on the watch, and Turk barked with might and main as if to hurry them on. But the grandmother said: "In my time it wasn't like this. People knew they had to rise betimes on such a day and that the Lord waits for nobody."

At last the farm lad rushed into the kitchen—the god-mother was in sight.

She arrived, bathed in sweat and laden like a Christmas tree. In one hand she held the black strings of a huge flowered bag with a vast züpfe, wrapped in a fine white towel, sticking out of it—a present for the young mother. In the other she carried another bag with an outfit for the baby and some finery for herself, in particular beautiful white stockings, and under one arm she held a box with her wreath and the lace cap with the magnificent black silk ribbons.

A chorus of joyful "God welcomes" greeted her. She could hardly find time to set down one of her loads to shake the hands stretched out to her. Eager helpers stood round to

relieve her of her burdens, while the young wife stood in the
doorway and it all began over again until the midwife warned
them into the parlor—they could say what custom required
in there.

And, mannerly but firm, the midwife got the godmother
settled down at table, and the housewife came in with the
coffee, though the godmother declared she'd had some
already. Her aunt would never let her leave the house without bite nor sup, it was bad for young girls. But her aunt was
an old woman, and the maids wouldn't get up in the morning
and that was why she was late. If it hadn't been for them
she'd have been here long ago. The thick cream went into the
coffee, and though the godmother protested and vowed she
didn't like it a lump of sugar went in too. And for a long time
the godmother wouldn't hear of the züpfe being cut on her
account, but all the same she had to let a large piece be cut
and set before her. As for cheese, she would have none of it.
But the housewife said she must be thinking it was only half
cream, and that was why she wouldn't eat it, so the godmother had to give way. But she wouldn't touch the cakes,
she wouldn't know where to put them, she said. But then
there must be something wrong with the cakes, she was told,
of course she was used to better, so what was she to do but
eat cakes? While all this urging was going on she had drunk
her first bowl of coffee in steady sips, and now a real dispute
arose, for the godmother turned her bowl upside down,
declared she hadn't any room left for any more good things
and that they should leave her in peace. And this time she
wasn't going back on it. Then the housewife said she was
sorry the coffee was so bad, she'd given the midwife strict
orders to make it as good as she could, she really couldn't
help it if it was so bad nobody could drink it, it couldn't be
the cream, she'd skimmed the milk with her own hands, and
that was a thing she didn't do every day. So what was the
poor godmother to do but submit to another bowl?

For a long time past the midwife had been bustling about
impatiently, and at last she burst out:

"If there's anything I can do to help, just say so. I've got time."

"Why, there's no hurry," said the housewife.

But the poor godmother, who was steaming like a boiler, took the hint, swallowed the hot coffee as fast as she could, and, in the pauses forced on her by the scalding drink, remarked:

"I'd have been finished this long while if I hadn't had to take more than I can do with. But now I've finished."

She stood up, unpacked her bags, handed over the züpfe, the clothes, and the christening gift—a bright new thaler wrapped up in a beautifully painted christening text—with many an excuse that it was all so poor. But the young wife broke in upon her time and again, crying that it was a sin and shame to spend so much, she could hardly take it all, and if they'd known, they wouldn't have dared to bid her to the christening.

But now the girl set to work, helped by the midwife and the housewife, and did her best to make herself a bonny godmother from her shoes and stockings to the wreath on her precious lace cap. Everything had to be just so, in spite of the midwife's impatience, and the godmother always found something out of place. Then the grandmother came in, saying: "I must have a look at our bonny godmother." But she dropped a hint that the second bell had already rung and that both godfathers were already waiting in the outer parlor.

There indeed sat the two godfathers, the elder and the younger, scorning the newfangled coffee they could have any day, with the wine soup steaming in front of them, that old, traditional Bernese drink made of wine, toast, eggs, sugar, cinnamon, and saffron, that ancient spice that no christening must lack in the soup, in the stew, in the sweet tea. They smacked their lips over it, and the elder godfather, whom they called Cousin, cracked many a joke with the young father, telling him they would eat him out of house and home that day, but to judge from the wine soup he wouldn't grudge it them.

Now the godmother appeared like a bright rising sun, and the two godfathers bade her God welcome, and she was dragged to table and a huge plate of wine soup set in front of her; she was to drink it up, there was time enough while they were getting the baby ready. The poor girl warded it off with hands and feet, declaring she had had enough for many a day to come, she could hardly breathe. But it was all no good. Old and young set upon her, gravely or gaily, till she took up her spoon and, strange to say, one spoonful after the other found a bit of room somewhere.

But there was the midwife again with the baby in its fine swaddling clothes. She tied the embroidered cap with its pink silk ribbon on its head, laid it on its cushion, put its sweetened comforter in its mouth, then said she hadn't wanted anyone to be kept waiting, so she thought she would get the baby ready, then they could go when they liked.

All stood round the child, praising it duly, and indeed it was a wonderfully fine boy. The mother rejoiced in the praise, and said: "I'd have been glad to go to church and help to commit him to God. You can remember what you've promised so much better if you've been at the christening yourself. Besides, it frets me not to be able to go beyond the eaves for a whole week, just when we're so busy with the planting."

But the grandmother said they hadn't come to that yet, that her own daughter-in-law should have to go to church in the first week, and the midwife put in that she didn't at all like to see young wives going to church for the christening. They were always worriting less something should go wrong at home, and hadn't their minds on what was going on in church, and on the way home they hurried for fear something should be forgotten, and got overheated, and many a one had taken ill of it and nearly died.

Then the godmother took the baby on its cushion in her arms, the midwife laid the fine white christening veil with the black tassels at the corners over its face, taking care not to brush against the nosegay on the godmother's breast, and said: "Now go, in God's holy name." Grandmother folded her hands and offered up a silent prayer for a blessing on them, but the young mother followed the procession to the door, saying: "My little one, my little one! Three whole hours without you! How shall I bear it?" And the tears rushed into her eyes. Hastily wiping them away with her apron, she turned into the house.

The godmother stepped briskly down the hill and along the road to the church with the sturdy baby in her arms, followed by the godfather, the young husband, and the grandfather. None thought of relieving her of her burden, though the younger godfather wore a huge nosegay on his hat as a sign that he was single, and there was in his eyes something like great good will toward the godmother, all masked, of course, by a show of complete indifference.

Grandfather told them about the terrible storm there had been when he had been carried to church: what with hail and lightning the churchgoers hardly thought they would escape with their lives. Afterward people had prophesied all manner of things on account of the storm, some a dreadful death, others that he would make his fortune at war. And after all he had had a quiet life of it like anyone else, and at seventy-five he would hardly die young or make his fortune at war.

They were more than halfway when the maid came running after them who was to carry the baby home as soon as it was christened, while the family and the rest of the company stayed for the sermon in the good old fashion. The maid, determined to make the best of herself that day, had forgotten the time. She offered to take the baby, but though the others urged her, the godmother would not give it up. It was too good a chance to show the young godfather how strong her arms were and how much she could carry. A proper countryman takes more pride in the strength of his wife's arms than in useless little sticks which the north wind can blow to bits at the first gust. A mother's strong arms have been the saving of many a child whose father had died, and she has had to heave the wagon of home out of all the ruts that threatened it.

Suddenly the sturdy godmother leapt backward as if somebody had tugged her plaits or clouted her over the head. She gave the baby to the maid, waited for the others to come up, and pretended to be in difficulties with her garter. Then she joined the men, interrupted their talk, and tried to distract the grandfather, now with this, now with that, from what he was saying. But as old people will, he stuck to his point and steadfastly picked up the broken thread of his talk. Then she set on the young father and tried to inveigle him into talking to her, but he was quiet and unresponsive. Perhaps he was busy with his own thoughts, as every father must be when his child is carried to its christening, especially the first son. The nearer they came to the church, the more people joined them. Some were already waiting in the road, their hymn books in their hands; others were hurrying down the narrow footpaths, and in a great procession they advanced on the village.

Next the church stood the inn, side by side as they often are in life, sharing joy and sorrow, in the good old fashion. There the company sat down, the baby was changed, and the father ordered wine, though the others protested—he shouldn't do it, they had just had all their hearts desired and needed neither bite nor sup. But once the wine was there they all fell to, especially the maid, thinking, most likely, that she had better drink wine when it was offered, for that didn't happen often the long year through.

Only the godmother resisted, in spite of endless urging, till the landlady told them they should stop, the girl was turning quite pale and a few drops of hartshorn would do her more good than wine. But the godmother wanted none of that either, could hardly be persuaded to drink a glass of plain water, but had to submit to a few drops of hartshorn on her handkerchief; innocent as she was, many a suspicious look was cast upon her and she could not help herself. For she was half dead with fear. No one had told her what the baby's name was to be, and it was an old custom for the godmother to whisper the child's name to the pastor as she handed it over; when there were many children to be christened, he might easily confuse the registered names.

In their hurry over all that had to be thought of and their

anxiety not to be late, nobody had told her the name, and her aunt had once for all strictly forbidden her to ask, if she didn't want to make the child unhappy for life, for if a godmother asks the child's name it will be inquisitive its life long.

So she didn't know the name and mustn't ask, and if the pastor had forgotten too and were to ask her in front of all the people, or, in his hurry, to christen the boy Anni or Babi, all the people would laugh, and she would be put to shame for all her life. She sat in mounting terror, her sturdy legs quivering like bean poles in the wind and the sweat pouring in streams from her pale face.

The landlady now came to warn them that it was time to move if she wasn't going to be scolded by the pastor, but to the godmother she said: "You'll never go through with this, my girl. You're as white as a fresh-washed sheet."

It was only the hurry, declared the godmother, she'd feel better in the fresh air. But she didn't feel better. The people in the church turned black before her eyes, and now the baby began to scream, louder and louder. The poor godmother rocked it in her arms, and the louder it screamed the higher she rocked it, till the petals rained down from the nosegay at her breast. And there was a tightness in her throat and all the people could hear her labored breathing. As her breast surged higher the child rocked higher, and the higher it rocked the more thunderous grew the pastor's prayers, till the voices re-echoed from the church walls. The godmother no longer knew where she was, there was a roaring in her ears like the waves of the sea and the church began to dance round in the air with her. At last the pastor said Amen, and now the dire moment had come, now she would know whether she was to be a laughingstock to children and children's children, now she had to raise the christening veil, give the child to the pastor and whisper its name into his right ear. In fear and trembling she raised the veil and held out the child; the pastor took it but never so much as looked at her, asked her no stern question but, dipping his hand in the water, let fall a drop on the forehead of the suddenly silent baby and chris-

tened it neither Anni nor Babi but Hans Uli, a good honest
Hans Uli.

Then the godmother felt as if not only all the hills of the
Emmental had fallen from her heart, but the sun, moon, and
stars too, as if she had been carried from a fiery furnace into
a cooling bath, but all through the sermon she trembled in
every limb and could not keep still. The pastor gave a beautiful and moving sermon, all about how the life of man should
really be an ascension all the time, but the godmother could
not really feel moved, and by the time they left the church
she had forgotten the text. She could hardly wait to tell the
others about her secret terrors and the reason for her pale
face. There was great laughter and many a joke about inquisitiveness, and how women fear it but all the same pass it on
to their daughters, while it does no harm to the boys. So she
might have asked after all.

Rustling fields of oats, pretty patches of flax, glorious
growth in field and pasture, however, soon drew all eyes and
occupied all minds. They found many a reason for lingering
on the way. But the brilliant rising sun of May was hot, and
when they reached home a glass of cooling wine did them all
good, protest as they might. Then they sat down outside the
house, while busy hands worked in the kitchen and the fire
set up a great crackling. The midwife was glowing like Shad-
rach, Meschach, and Abednego. Before eleven there was a call
to dinner, but only for the servants. They were to have their
dinner first, and a good one too, but the people were glad
when they were out of the way, especially the farm hands.

Outside the house the talk trickled in a thin stream, but
did not dry up. Before dinner the stomach thwarts the mind,
though no one will admit it and all pass it off with casual
remarks on whatever comes into their heads. The sun was
already past noon when the midwife, her face flaming but her
apron still spotless, appeared on the threshold with the welcome news that dinner was ready if everybody was there. But
most of the bidden guests had not arrived, and the messen-
gers sent to fetch them, like those in the Gospel, brought

back many answers, though in this case everybody was coming, but not yet. One had workmen in, another had business on hand, the third some errand to go, but nobody was to wait; dinner was to go on. The company soon agreed, for if they were to wait for everybody, they would be sitting there at moonrise. The midwife grumbled a bit; there was nothing more vexatious than to keep everything waiting, she declared. In their hearts they all wanted to come, but didn't want to show it. And she'd have the trouble of putting everything back to keep warm and wouldn't know if there was enough and would never get done.

But although they had soon reached an agreement about the absentees, there was more trouble with those present. It took a vast amount of urging to get them into the parlor and make them sit down, for nobody wanted to be the first to do this or that. When they had at last all got settled down, the soup was brought in, a rich broth colored and spiced with saffron and so full of the fine white bread the grandmother had cut that not much liquid was to be seen. Then every head was bared, hands were folded, and a long and solemn grace was offered up to the giver of all good gifts. Only then did they take up their pewter spoons, wipe them carefully on the fine white tablecloth, and fall to on the soup, and many a compliment was paid—if there was broth like this every day nobody would want anything else. When the soup was finished the spoons were carefully wiped on the tablecloth again, the loaves were sent round, everyone cut his own slice and watched the stew in saffron gravy being brought in—a stew of brains, mutton, and pickled liver. When that had been dealt with in leisurely fashion, the beef appeared, piled high in dishes, fresh and smoked, and each took what he liked best; then there were dried beans and stewed pears and a gammon of bacon and magnificent loins of pork from three-hundredweight pigs, red and white and juicy.

All these things followed each other in slow succession, and when a new guest arrived, everything was brought in again from the soup on, and everyone had to begin again; not a dish was spared them. Benz, the young father, poured wine out of the beautiful white flagons which were richly ornamented with crests and mottoes. Where his arms were too short to reach, he bade others be his cupbearers, and urged all to drink, saying over and over again: "Drink up, that's what it's there for"; and every time the midwife brought in a new dish he gave her another glass, so that if she had drunk them all there might have been curious scenes in the kitchen.

The younger godfather had to put up with a good deal of banter for not being able to persuade the godmother to do more justice to the wine. If he didn't do better than that, they said, he'd never get a wife. Oh! Hans Uli didn't want one, opined the godmother, unmarried lads these days had other things in their heads than marrying and most of them couldn't even afford to.

"You're right there," saids Hans Uli. "Slovens as most girls are these days make terrible spendthrift wives and most of them think that to make a good wife all she needs is a blue silk kerchief on her head, gloves in summer, and embroidered slippers in winter. If you've got no cows in the byre, things are bad, but you can change them, but if you've got a wife who's costing you hearth and home, the law says you've got to keep her. So a man does better for himself if he's got other things in mind than marrying and leaves the girls alone."

"And that's a fact," put in the elder godfather, a small nondescript man whom they treated with great respect and called Cousin, for he was childless and had a farm of his own and a hundred thousand Swiss francs out at interest. "A fact it is," he went on. "It's a poor showing the women make today. I'm not saying there isn't one here and there who's the pride of the home, but they're few and far between. Most of them have nought in their heads but pride and folly. They dress like peacocks, strut about like storks, and if they have to do an honest day's work they take to their beds with a headache for three days after. When I went courting my old woman things were different. You didn't have to worry about getting a fool or a fury instead of a good manager."

"Nay, nay, Godfather Uli," said the godmother, who had been struggling to get a word in edgeways for a long time past. "Anyone'd think there'd been no good farmer's daughters since your time. You don't know the girls, and that's right and proper for an old man, but there's as good girls now as when you went courting. Self-praise is no recommendation, but Father's often said that if I go on as I'm going I'll be as good a housewife as my mother that's dead, God rest her soul, and she was a rare housewife. Father never took such fat pigs to market as he did last year, and the butcher often said he'd like to see the lass that fattened those pigs. But there'd be plenty to say about the young men nowadays—what in Heaven's name is the matter with them? Smoking, sitting in the sun with their hats on the side of their heads and staring like the town gates of Berne, and skittles and shooting and running after the wenches—that's about all they can do. But if they've got to milk a cow or plow a field they're done for, and with a tool in their hands they're as clumsy as a gentleman or a clerk. Often enough I've sworn I'll never take a husband till I know for certain how I'd get on with him, and even if one here and there does turn out to be a good farmer, you never can tell if he'll turn out a good husband."

The others laughed, the girl blushed, they chaffed her without mercy. How long would a man have to be on trial before she knew for certain he'd be a good husband?

And so, with laughter and joking, they put away a good deal of the meat, until the elder godfather said it seemed to him they'd had enough for the present, they should stretch their legs a bit, and a pipe never tasted so well as on top of meat. This advice was received with general applause, though the young wife and husband begged them again and again not to go. Once they'd gone there'd be no getting them back.

"Don't you trouble, Cousin," said the elder godfather. "Put something good on the table and you'll soon see us back and if we stretch our legs a bit we'll be handier at the eating after."

Then the men made the round of the stables, had a look into the hayloft to see if there was any old hay lying about, praised the fine grass, and looked up into the trees to see what kind of fruit crop they could hope for.

Under one of the trees which was still in bloom the cousin called a halt, saying that this was the best place for a rest and a pipe, it was cool, and when the women had got something tasty ready they wouldn't have far to go.

Soon they were joined by the godmother and the other women, who had inspected the garden and the vegetables. One after another they sat down in the grass, carefully lifting the hems of their gay jackets, but exposing their bright red petticoats to stains from the lush grass.

The tree round which the company had settled stood above the house just where the gentle slope began. In the foreground was the new house; beyond, the view spread to the other side of the valley, over many a fine rich farmstead and yet farther to green hills and other dark valleys.

" 'Tis a fine house you've got here, and everything ship-shape," said the cousin. "And now you can live with room for all of you. I never could tell how you could live in that poor old house when you'd money and wood enough to build a new one like this."

"Nay," returned the grandfather. "There's none too much of either and building's a bad thing. You know where you start but you never know where you'll stop, and now one thing stood in the way and now another."

"It's a wonderful house to my thinking," said one of the women. "We should have had a new one this long while, but we're afraid of the cost. As soon as my man's here he'll take a good look at this one. If I had one like it I'd think myself in Heaven. But there's one thing I'd like to know, and no offense meant in asking. What's that old black window post doing there next to the new one? It spoils the whole look of the house."

Grandfather looked very grave and puffed away still more vigorously at his pipe, then said there wasn't enough wood for the building, they'd had nothing else at hand, and in their haste they'd taken some wood from the old house.

"But look," said the woman, "that black window post was too short; you've had to piece it together above and below, and any neighbor'd have given you a new post."

"Well we just didn't think of it and we couldn't go on plaguing the neighbors, they'd helped us enough as it was with wood and the loan of their carts."

"Come, come, Granddad," said the cousin. "Don't beat about the bush. Tell the whole story just as it was. I've heard plenty of talk and never could get to the bottom of it. And now it'd be the very thing to while away the time till the womenfolk have the roast ready. So out with it!"

Grandfather took a deal of persuading, but the cousin and the women gave him no peace till he promised, though with a warning that what he told should be kept among themselves and go no further. Things like that set a lot of people against a house, and he wouldn't like to do ill by his own folk at his age.

Whenever I look at that post, began the venerable old man, I can't help wondering how it happened that men came from far away in the East, where the human race is said to have come into being, and found this nook here in this narrow valley, and I think how much those who found their way or sought refuge here must have suffered and who they can have been. I've asked and asked again, but never could find out anything but that there were men in these parts in very early times, indeed that Sumiswald was a township before our Saviour was born, though that's written down nowhere. But one thing we do know, and that's that the castle which used to stand where our hospital is was there six hundred years ago, that most likely there was a house here too at that time, which belonged to the castle along with most of the neighborhood, and had to pay tithes and rent to the castle, and do labor for it. Indeed, the men were serfs and not men in their own right, as every man is these days when he comes of age.

Very different were the lives of men at that time, and side by side there lived serfs who made a fine living and others who were sorely, maybe unbearably oppressed and went in fear of their lives. It all depended on their overlords; they could do as they liked with the men, while the men had no one they could complain to without fear or with any hope of redress. It's said that the serfs who belonged to this castle were worse off at times than most of the others. The other castles mostly belonged to a single family and were handed down from father to son; the lord and his men knew each other in their boyhood and many a lord was a father to his serfs. But in early days this castle came into the hands of knights called the Teutons, and the lord who commanded here was called the Comthur. Now these overlords changed from time to time. Once there would be a Swabian, the next time a Saxon, and no love could grow up and each brought his own ways with him from his own country.

Their real business was to fight the heathen in Poland and Prussia, and although they were really spiritual knights, they lived more in heathen fashion and treated their serfs as if there were no God in Heaven, and when they came back to live here carried on as if they were still in heathen lands. Those who preferred a life of ease to fighting bloody battles, and those who had wounds to heal or needed to restore their strength were sent to the estates which the Teutonic Order, for that was the name given to the company of knights, possessed in Germany and Switzerland, and each one of them went his own way and did as he pleased. One of the worst of them, they say, was called Hans von Stoffeln, and it was under him that there happened what you want to know, and has been handed down in our family from father to son.

It came into this Hans von Stoffeln's head to build a great castle up there in Bärhegen Hill, where even today, when a storm is brewing, you can see the castle demons sunning their treasures. Generally the knights built their castles overlooking the roads, just as innkeepers do today, and both so as to make it easier to rob passers-by, though in a different way.

But why the knight wanted a castle up there on that wild ugly hill in the wilderness we don't know. Anyway, he wanted it and the peasants who belonged to the castle had to build it. The knight never troubled his head about any work the season required, whether haymaking, or harvest, or sowing. So many loads must be carried, so many hands must work, at such and such a time the last tile must be on the roof and the last nail driven home. And he would not let them off a single sheaf of tithes corn, not a doit of rent, not a carnival hen, nor even a carnival egg. There was no mercy in him; and he knew nought of the needs of poor men. In his heathen fashion he drove them on with blows and curses, and when one was tired, slackened in his work or sat down to rest, the bailiff was after him with the whip, and neither age nor weakness was spared. When the savage knights were up there they loved to hear the whip crack, and they plagued the laborers in many other ways too. If they could double their labor for pure sport, they did so with a will, and then made merry over the serfs' sweat and toil.

At last the castle was finished; five ells thick were the walls, nobody knew why it was up there, but the peasants were glad it was standing at last where it had to stand and that the last nail had been driven in and the last tile was on the roof.

They wiped the sweat from their brows and looked round their own fields with heavy hearts, sighing to see how far behind the accursed building had put them. But a long summer lay before them, God was above them, and they took heart and laid strong hands to the plow, speaking comfort to their wives and children who had so nearly starved and now saw only fresh torment in work.

But hardly was the first furrow driven when a message came that all the serfs were to appear at a certain time in the castle at Sumiswald. They trembled and hoped. True, they had never known kindness, but only hard and bitter cruelty from the present inmates of the castle, but it seemed to them only right that their lords should do something to reward their terrible labors, and because they thought so, many a one thought that the knights must think so too, and make them some present, or promise some respite that evening.

They arrived at the castle in good time and with beating hearts, but were kept waiting a long time in the courtyard, a laughingstock to the castle servants. These men had been in heathen lands too. Besides, it was most likely the same then as now, when any half-baked squire thinks he has the right to mock and despise the old farmers who have tilled the soil for centuries.

At last they were summoned to the banqueting hall. The heavy door opened before them. Inside, round the huge ash table, sat the swarthy knights, their savage dogs at their feet, and at the head of the table sat Stoffeln, a big fierce man with a head like a double quart pot, eyes like plow wheels, and a beard like an old lion's mane. None of the men wanted to be the first to go in, and everyone pushed his neighbor. Then the knights laughed till the wine splashed out of the tankards and the dogs dashed out in fury, for when dogs see trembling legs, they scent good quarry. The men's hearts sank, they wished themselves back home again, and each tried to hide behind his neighbor. When silence had at last been restored among the dogs and the knights, Stoffeln spoke, and his voice was like the roaring of a century-old oak.

"My castle is built, but one thing is lacking. Summer is coming and there is no shady walk up there. Within a month you must plant one for me. Take a hundred fullgrown beeches from the Münneberg with boughs and roots and plant them on Bärhegen Hill, and if a single beech is lacking you shall pay for it with land and limb. There is food and drink for you below, but see to it that the first beech is standing on Bärhegen Hill tomorrow."

One of the peasants, hearing the words food and drink, thought the knight was in gracious mood and good humor, and began to speak of the work they had to do, and of their hungry wives and children, and of winter when the thing would be easier to do. Then the knight's head swelled up high with rage, and his voice bellowed out of it like thunder echoing from a mountain wall, telling them that he only had to show them a little kindness and they must needs turn stubborn. In Poland, if a man had his bare life he would kiss your feet for it, and here they had children and cattle, house and home, and were not content.

"But you shall learn to obey and quit your fat living, and if the beeches are not standing up beyond in a month, you shall be shipped till there is not a finger's breadth whole on you and your wives and children shall be thrown to the dogs."

Then none dared to say another word, neither did anyone touch the food and drink. Once the furious command had been given, they crowded out of the door, each trying to get out first, and the knight's thundering voice, the laughter of his fellows, the jeering of the servants, and the snarling of the dogs followed them far on their way.

When a turn in the road hid them from the castle, they sat down and wept bitterly. None could find a word of comfort for the other, none had even the heart to feel a righteous anger, for want and torment had quenched their courage till there was no room in their hearts for anger, but only for grief. Three hours' distance they would have to cart the beeches, with boughs and roots, over rough ways and up the steep hill, while close by the hill fine beeches grew in plenty, yet they must not touch them. Within a month the work was to be done, on two days three beeches, the third day four, to be dragged through the long valley and up the steep hill by their weary beasts. And above all it was May month, when the farmer must be at work in his fields from morning till night, must hardly leave them if he wants bread and food for the winter.

As they sat there helplessly weeping, none daring to look at the other and see his grief because each was drowning in his own, and none daring to go home with the tidings, none daring to carry his trouble home to wife and child, there suddenly appeared before them—they did not know from where —a green huntsman, tall and lean. A red feather waved on his

jaunty cap, a little red beard flamed in his swarthy face, and
between his arched nose and pointed chin, almost invisible,
like a cave under overhanging rocks, a mouth opened to say:

"What's your trouble, goodmen all, that you sit there howling till the stones burst out of the earth and the boughs from
off the trees?"

Twice he asked the question and twice no answer came.

Then the Green Man's swarthy face grew blacker still, his
red beard redder till it seemed to crackle and sparkle like fire
in pine logs, his mouth pursed up as sharp as an arrowhead,
then it opened again to ask quite graciously and mildly:

"But, goodmen all, what good is it to sit there howling?
You can howl a new flood down or burst the stars out of the
sky, but little will it help you. When a man who means well
by you and might help you in your trouble asks you what it
is, it would be better to speak sense than to howl. It would
help you far more."

Then an old man shook his white head and said:

"We mean no offense, but no green huntsman can relieve our
trouble, and when the heart is swollen with grief, no words
can rise from it."

Then the Green Man shook his head and said:

"There's truth in what you say, father, but that's not the
way of it. You can beat what you will, stone or tree, it com-
plains. And a man should complain too, tell all his trouble,
tell it to the first man he meets, for maybe the first man he
meets can help him. I am but a plain huntsman, but who
knows if I haven't a stout team of horses at home to cart wood
and stones or beeches and firs."

When the poor peasants heard the word team, it dropped
into every heart, turning to a spark of hope, and all eyes were
fixed on the Green Man, and the old man's tongue was loos-
ened. It wasn't always best, he said, to tell the first man you
met the trouble in your heart, but since they could see that
he meant well by them and maybe could help, they would
hide nothing from him. For two years they had had troublous
times with the building of the new castle, and not a home in

the domain but was sadly in want. And just when they had taken fresh heart, thinking their hands were free at last for their own work, the Comthur had commanded them to plant beside his castle an avenue of beeches from the Münneberg, and all in a month. How they were to do it with their worn-out beasts they did not know, and even if they did, what good would it be? They could sow nothing and must die of hunger if the work did not kill them first. And they dared not carry the tidings home and bring fresh trouble on top of the old.

Then the Green Man looked very compassionate, shook a long thin dark hand at the castle, and swore dire revenge for such tyranny. But he was ready to help them. His team, and there was not its like in the world, would cart all the beeches from the church hill on this side of Sumiswald—as many as they could bring—up to Bärhegen, for love of them and in defiance of the knights, and all for a small reward.

All the men pricked up their ears at this unexpected offer. If they could come to an agreement about the pay, they were saved, for they could cart the beeches to the church hill without delaying their work in the fields and so perishing. So the old man said: "Then name your reward and we'll make a bargain of it."

A sly look came into the Green Man's face, his beard crackled, and his eyes glittered at them like the eyes of snakes, and a grisly smile curled the corners of his lips as he parted them to say:

"I told you, it's little that I ask for, just an unbaptized child."

The word flashed through the men like lightning, the scales fell from their eyes and they scattered like chaff in the wind.

Then the Green Man laughed aloud till the fish hid in the waters, and the birds sought the thickets, while his little red beard wagged up and down.

"Take counsel among yourselves, or ask it from your womenfolk. The third night from now you'll find me here," he called to them as they fled, in a sharp ringing voice which made his words stick in their ears like barbed arrows in the flesh.

Pale, trembling in heart and limb, the men rushed home.
None looked round for the others. They would not have
turned their heads for all the riches in the world. When the
men came hurrying home in their plight like doves frightened
from the dovecote by a hawk, terror entered every home, and
all feared to hear the tidings which had turned the men's
knees to water.

Agog with curiosity, the women crept after the men until
they had got them in some quiet spot where they could speak
undisturbed. Then every man had to tell his wife what had
been spoken in the castle, and the women listened with rage
and curses. Then the men had to tell who had met them and
the offer he had made. A nameless dread seized the women, a
cry of woe rose over hill and dale, and every woman felt as if
it were her child that must be given to the being who knew
no mercy.

Only one woman did not lament with the others. She was a
terrible valiant woman; they say she came from Lindau and
lived on this farm. She had fierce black eyes and feared neither God nor man. She had already fired up because the men
hadn't simply refused to obey the knight's command. If she'd
been there she'd have spoken her mind to him, she said. When
she heard of the Green Man and his offer, and how the men
had fled before him, she raged and upbraided the men for
their cowardice and for not standing up to the Green Man
more boldly. Perhaps he would have been satisfied with some
other reward, and since the work was for the castle, it'd do no
harm to their souls if the Devil did it. She raged to the very
depths of her soul that she hadn't been there, if only to see
the Devil and find out what he looked like. And so this
woman shed never a tear, but in her anger spoke bitter words
against her husband and all the other men.

The next day, when the lamentation had died down into
quiet weeping, the men sat together, seeking counsel and
finding none. First they thought of a fresh petition to the
knight, but none was willing to carry it, for none held life or
limb cheap. One said they should send the women, weeping
and wailing, but he soon fell silent when the women began to

speak, for even in those days, when the men sat in council, the women were not far off. In the end they could see no way but to obey in the name of God, to have masses said to obtain God's help; they would ask neighbors to help in secret and at night, for their lords would never suffer it by day. They would divide into two companies, one working with the beeches, the other sowing the oats and tending the cattle. In this way they hoped, with God's help, to cart at least three beeches a day up to Bärhegen Hill. Not a word was said about the Green Man. Whether any man thought of him is not written.

So they divided into two companies, made their tools ready, and at sunrise on May Day they assembled on the Münneberg and set to work with a quiet courage. A side trench was dug round each beech, sparing the roots, and the trees were carefully lowered to the ground so as to take no harm. Morning was not yet high in the sky when three lay ready to go, for they were to be carted three by three, so that all the men could help on the hard road with their work and their oxen. But the sun rose to noon, and they still had not left the wood with the three beeches. It had sunk behind the mountains, and the teams were not yet beyond Sumiswald, and not till the new day had dawned did they reach the foot of the castle hill on which the beeches were to be planted. The stars in their courses seemed to fight against them. Disaster followed disaster; traces snapped, axles broke, horses and oxen stumbled or turned stubborn. The next day was worse. Fresh troubles brought fresh work, the poor creatures panted in unremitting toil, yet not a single beech stood on the hill, nor was the fourth carted beyond Sumiswald.

Stoffeln raged and cursed; the more he raged and cursed, the heavier grew their hearts and the more stubborn their beasts. The other knights mocked and jeered and took their pleasure in the peasants' struggles and Stoffeln's fury. They had laughed at his new castle on the bare hilltop. He had sworn that within a month a shady walk should stand there. So the knights laughed and the peasants wept.

A terrible discouragement overcame them. Not a cart was
whole, not a team unharmed; in two days they had not
brought three beeches to their place and all their strength
was gone.

Night had fallen, black clouds were rising, the first lightning of the year was flashing. The men sat down by the wayside at the very turn in the road where they had sat three
days before, though they did not know it. There sat the
farmer of Hornbach, the Lindau woman's husband, with two
farm hands, and others sat beside them. They were waiting
for the beeches which were to come from Sumiswald, and
they took time there to brood over their misery and give their
aching limbs a rest.

Suddenly, with a noise like the whistling of the wind, a
woman approached with a basket on her head. It was Christine, the Hornbach farmer's wife. He had come by her when
he had followed his overlord to the wars. She was not the
kind of woman to take pleasure in staying at home, going quietly about her work and caring only for her house and children. Christine had to know all that was going on, and where
she had no say in a matter, it must go wrong, or so she
thought.

Therefore she had not sent a maid with the food, but had
loaded the heavy basket onto her own head, and had sought
the men for a long time in vain. When she found them, she
upbraided them bitterly. But she did not stand idle; she
could talk and work at the same time. She set down her
basket, took the lid off the porridge pail, set the bread and
cheese out, stuck a spoon in the porridge opposite each man
and each farm hand, and bade even those who had nothing to
eat to join in. Then she asked about the day's work and what
had been done these two days. But the men had lost both
their hunger and their desire to speak, and none took up his
spoon nor did any give her an answer. Only one lad, who did
not care whether it rained or shone at harvest time if only
the year went round and wage day came and there was food
on the table at mealtimes, took up his spoon and told Chris-

tine that not a beech was planted—it seemed as if the Devil was in it.

Then Christine said it was all idle fancy, and the men were no more good than women in childbed. Not a beech would be carted up to Bärhegen with working and weeping, with sitting and wailing. It would serve them all right if the knight vented his rage on them, but for their wives' and children's sakes they must set about it in another fashion. Then over the woman's shoulder there came a long, swarthy hand and a shrill voice cried: "She has spoken well." And there among them stood the Green Man, grinning, with the feather waving on his cap. Then fear drove the men away; they scattered down the hill like chaff in a whirlwind.

But Christine could not flee, for now she was to know what it means to face the Devil himself. She stood rooted to the spot, her eyes fixed on the red feather on his cap and on the red beard merrily wagging in his swarthy face. He sent a shrill laugh after the men, but on Christine he bent a loving look and took her hand graciously. Christine tried to pull it away, but she could no longer escape the Green Man; it was as if her flesh were hissing between red-hot tongs. Then he began to speak courteously to her, and as he spoke his little red beard wagged with desire. Not for a long time had he seen so fine a woman, he said; his heart was laughing within him. Besides, he liked a bold woman, and above all, he liked women who stood their ground when the men ran away.

And as he spoke, he seemed less terrible to Christine. This was a man you could talk to, she thought, and she didn't see why she should run away—she had seen far uglier men in her day. More and more she came to feel that this was a man you could drive a bargain with, and if she set about it the right way, he would do her a favor after all, or she might outwit him, as she had outwitted the other men. But the Green Man went on to say that he couldn't understand why they were all so terrified of him; he meant well by all men, and if they treated him so scurvily, they could hardly wonder if he refused to do what they wanted.

Then Christine plucked up courage and said that he frightened people out of their wits. Why had he asked for an unbaptized child? He might have asked for something else; it looked so suspicious. After all, a child was a human being and no Christian would hand one over unbaptized.

"That's the reward I'm used to nor will I stir a finger for any other. Who troubles about a child that knows nobody? It's just when they're young that people are most willing to give them away, before they've had any joy of them or trouble with them. But the younger they are, the better they suit me, and the earlier I can set about bringing up a child in my own way the more I can do with it. But I need no baptism and I'll have none either."

Then Christine knew that he would not be put off with any other reward, and it came home to her that this was a man who could not be tricked.

So she said that if a man wanted to earn a reward, he must be content with what could be given him, and at the moment there wasn't a single unbaptized child in any home, and none expected within a month, and by that time the beeches had to be planted. Then the Green Man said, with a most polite wag of his head:

"I'm not asking for a child in advance. As soon as I have the promise of the first one to be born, unbaptized, I shall be content."

Christine was highly delighted. She knew that no child was to be born in her lord's domain for a long time to come. Once the Green Man had kept his promise and the beeches were planted, they need give him nothing, neither a child nor anything else. They could have masses said and laugh at the Green Man boldly, or at any rate she thought so. So she thanked him heartily for his good offer, said it was worth thinking over and she would see what the men had to say.

"Gently there," said the Green Man. "The time for thinking and talking is over. I told you to be here today, and now I want my answer. I've got plenty to do elsewhere—I'm not here only for you. Yea or nay I must have, then I want to hear no more about the whole matter."

Christine tried to put him off, for she was unwilling to take everything on herself. She even made as if to caress him in order to gain time. But the Green Man was not in the mood and made no move. "Now or never," he said. As soon as the bargain for the child was struck, he would carry as many beeches up to Bärhegen as the men would bring to the bottom of the hill before midnight. He would wait for them there.

"And now, my beauty, no more shilly-shallying," he said, patting her cheek kindly. Her heart beat fast, and she would have been glad of the men to push in front of her and take the blame. But time was passing, there was no man there to be the scapegoat, and she still believed she was more cunning than the Green Man and would find a way to outwit him after all.

So she said that as far as she was concerned she would agree, but if, later on, the men would not, she couldn't help it and hoped she wouldn't have to pay for it. But the Green Man said that he was quite satisfied with her promise to do what she could. Then Christine shuddered, soul and body, for now, she thought, the dreadful moment had come when she would have to sign the pact with the Green Man in her own blood. But he made it easy for her and said he never asked a handsome woman to sign. A kiss was all he wanted. And therewith he pursed up his lips against Christine's face, and again she could not flee and again she stood rooted to the spot.

Then the sharp mouth touched her face, and it seemed to her as if the heat from a red-hot spit were pouring through her veins, and yellow lightning flashed between them, showing Christine the Green Man's face in a devilish grin, and thunder rolled over her as if Heaven had burst.

The Green Man had vanished, and Christine still stood there as if turned to stone, as if her feet had struck roots deep in the earth at that dreadful moment. At last the use of her limbs came back to her, but there was a roaring in her head as if a mighty river were plunging overtowering black rocks into a black gulf beneath. And just as we cannot hear our own voices in the thunder of the waters, Chrstine could not hear her own thoughts through the din in her soul.

She fled down the hill, and where the Green Man's lips had touched her, there was a fire which grew. She rubbed, she washed, but the fire would not die down.

It was a wild night. The storm raged and howled in the heavens and in the valleys as if the demons of night were holding their wedding in the black clouds, the winds playing savage tunes to their dancing, with lightning for marriage torches and thunder for the marriage blessing. Never had such a night been seen at that season.

In the dark valley, the men were crowding round a large house, many taking shelter under its spreading roof. As a rule, fear for his own cattle drives the countryman under his own roof in a storm, and as long as the storm rages in Heaven, he watches over his own house. But now the need of all was greater than the fear of the storm, and that was what had brought them to this house, which was on the way both for those who had been driven from the Münneberg by the storm and for those who had fled from Bärhegen. Forgetting the terrors of the night in their own wretchedness, they loudly lamented their evil plight, and nature's rage merely swelled their own misery. Horses and oxen had shied in terror, had kicked the carts to pieces and fallen down precipices, and many a wounded man was groaning in his pain, and loud were the cries of those whose torn limbs were being set and bound.

Into this misery there rushed, in deadly fear, those who had seen the Green Man, and trembling they told how he had come again. Trembling the crowd listened, came huddling out of the dark corners of the room to the fire where the men were sitting, and when the wind roared through the rafters, or thunder rolled over the house, a cry went up and the people seemed to see the Green Man breaking through the roof into their presence. But when no Green Man came, when the dread of him waned, when the old misery remained and the groans of the sufferers rose again, there slowly entered into their minds the thoughts that can so easily cost a man his soul. They began to reckon how much more worth they were than one unbaptized child, forgetting that the guilt of one soul's destruction weighs far heavier than the saving of thousands and thousands of human lives.

Slowly these thoughts found a voice, and began to mingle, in words that all could understand, in the groans of the wounded. The people began to ask about the Green Man, complained that he had not been given a better answer. He had made away with nobody, and the less they feared him, the less harm he could do them. If their hearts had been in the right place they might have helped the whole valley. Then the men began to make excuses. They did not say that there is no tricking the Devil, and that whoever gives him an inch must soon give him an ell, but they spoke of the Green Man's fearful shape, of his flaming beard and the fiery feather on his cap, and of the frightful smell of sulphur that had robbed them of their senses. But Christine's husband, who always turned to his wife for support, said they should ask her, she could tell them whether anyone could have borne it, for she was a bold woman and everybody knew it.

Then they all turned to look for Christine, but she was nowhere to be seen. Every single one of the men had thought only of his own safety, and not of the others', and once he was safe, imagined the others must be safe too. Only now did they realize that Christine had not been seen since that ghastly moment and had not come into the house. Then her husband began to complain, and the others with him, for now it seemed to all as if Christine alone could help.

Suddenly the door opened and there was Christine in their midst; her hair was streaming, her cheeks blazing, and her eyes glowing darker than ever in unholy fire. She was bidden welcome with unwonted kindness, and every man tried to tell her what he had thought and how great had been his fear for her. But Christine soon saw through it all, and, in order to conceal the fire within her, taunted them bitterly for taking to their heels and having no thought for a poor woman, nor so

much as casting a look behind them to see what the Green
Man was doing to her. Then the storm of curiosity broke, and
everyone wanted to be the first to hear what the Green Man
had done to her, and those at the back stood up to hear and
see better the woman who had been so close to the Green
Man. By rights, Christine went on, she should hold her
tongue, they didn't deserve anything from her, they had
made her life a burden to her here in the valley because she
came from foreign parts, and the women had given her a bad
name, and the men had never stood up for her, and if she
weren't better and braver than them all there'd be no comfort and no hope for them. For a long time she went on, calling the women hard names because they wouldn't believe her
when she said that Lake Constance was bigger than the
castle fish pond, and the more they begged the harder she
seemed to grow, and again and again she told them that it
was no use talking, they'd only take it ill, whatever she said,
and if things turned out well, small thanks she'd get for it,
and if they turned out badly, she'd get all the blame to bear.

When at last the whole assembly was almost on its knees
before Christine, and the groans and prayers of the wounded
came to swell the prayers of the others, she seemed to be mol-
lified and began to tell how she had stood her ground and
made a pact with the Green Man, but she said nothing about
the kiss, nor of the burning in her face nor the roaring in her
mind. But she told them what she had planned in her own
crafty thoughts. The beeches had to be carted up to Bärhegen, that was the first thing. Once they were up there, the
men would have plenty of time to see what was to be done
next, for what really mattered was that, as far as she knew,
no child was to be born among them till then.

Many a man's flesh crept as she spoke, but they were all
glad to think that there was plenty of time for them to decide
what was to be done later.

But one poor young woman wept so bitterly that they
could have washed their hands at her eyes, though she said
nothing. Then an old and venerable woman, tall of stature

and with a face to bow to or flee from, stepped into the midst of them and spoke: to do this would be to forget God, to stake the sure on the unsure, to play with eternal life. The man who parleys with the Evil One will never be rid of him, and to give him a finger means to give him the whole body. Nobody could help them out of their plight but God, but the man who abandoned God in his time of troubles would drown in his troubles. But this time they scorned the old woman's words, and bade the young one cease her weeping; howling and crying would help nobody. What they needed was help of another kind.

They soon agreed to try the plan. Even at the worst, no great harm could come to them. It wasn't the first time that men had tricked the most evil of spirits, and if there was no other way out, the priest would give them counsel. But in the dark depths of his heart many a man thought, as he confessed later, that he would risk little money or trouble to save an unbaptized child.

At the moment when they made up their minds to take Christine's advice, it was as if all the whirlwinds had broken loose over their heads, as if the ranks of the wild huntsmen were galloping past. The pillars of the house quivered, the rafters bent, and trees were splintered against the house like spears against a knight's armor. Inside the house, the people turned pale and fear entered into them, but they did not give up their plan. In the gray of dawn they put it into action. The morning was clear and bright, the storm and devilry were past, the axes struck deep, the soil was light and free, every beech fell just as it should, not a trace broke, the animals were strong and willing and the men protected from all mishaps as if by an invisible hand.

There was only one strange thing about it all. Below Sumiswald no road led into the valley at that time. It was all swamp watered by the wild river. They had to ride up through the village and past the church. In the same way as on the other days, they drove three teams at a time so that they could stand by each other with advice, strength, and

THE BLACK SPIDER 51

beasts. All they had to do was to ride through Sumiswald, and down the church hill outside the village where a little chapel stood. But as soon as they were up the hill and on the flat road leading to the church, the weight of the carts did not ease off. It grew heavier and heavier, they had to bring fresh horses and oxen, as many as they had, and lash them without mercy, or even lay hold of the spokes themselves, and even the quietest horses shied as if an invisible presence from the churchyard stood in their way, and the muffled toll of a bell, almost like a wandering death knell, rang from the church, a nameless dread overcame even the strongest of them, and every time the men and beasts reached the church, they trembled. Once past the church, they could drive on in peace, unload in peace, and return in peace for a fresh load.

That day they unloaded six beeches side by side at the appointed place, and in the early morning six beeches stood on Bärhegen Hill, and throughout the valley no one had heard the creaking of an axle on its hub, nor the shouting of carters, nor the steady lowing of oxen. But six beeches were standing there for all to see, and they were the beeches the men had unloaded at the bottom of the hill, and no others.

Then there was great wondering in the valley, and many a one was agog to know how it had happened. Above all, the knights were curious to know what bargain the peasants had made and how the beeches had been brought to their place. They tried, with their heathen ways, to squeeze the truth out of the peasants, who they soon saw knew nothing themselves and were half terrified. Besides, Stoffeln forbade them to go on. He was not merely indifferent as to how the beeches had come to Bärhegen. On the contrary, if only they were there, he was glad if he could spare the peasants. He knew quite well that his knights' taunts had tempted him into folly, for if the peasants perished and there was no one to work in the fields, it was the master who had to pay for it. But what Stoffeln had once said he abode by. So he was quite pleased that the peasants had found help, and cared little whether they had sold their souls for it, for what were the peasants' souls to

him once death had taken their bodies? So now he laughed at
the knights and shielded the peasants from their mockery. All
the same, the knights wanted to find out what was behind it
all; they sent out squires to keep watch, but they were found
next day half dead in the ditches where an invisible hand had
flung them.

Then two knights came up to Bärhegen; bold men they
were, and whenever a deed of daring was to be done in
heathen lands they had done it. In the morning they were
found senseless on the ground, and when they had recovered
the use of speech, they said that a red knight had ridden
them down with a flaming lance. Here and there some
curious woman could not resist peeping through a slit or a
crack when midnight had descended on the world. But at
once a poisonous wind blew on her, her face swelled, for
weeks neither nose nor eyes could be seen, and her mouth
hardly at all. Then the people gave up spying and not an eye
looked down the valley when midnight lay over it.

One night a man felt his last hour draw near, and lay in
need of extreme unction, but no one dared go for the priest.
Only his son, an innocent boy, dear to God and man, in his
fear for his father ran unbidden to Sumiswald. As he
approached the church hill, he saw how the beeches on it rose
from the ground, each carried by two fiery squirrels, and
beside them he saw a green man riding a black goat, with a
fiery whip in his hand, a flaming beard in his face, and on his
hat a fluttering feather, glowing red. Then they rose high up
in the air over all the hills and as swift as a moment of time.
So much the boy saw, but no harm was done him.

Not three weeks had passed when ninety beeches stood on
Bärhegen Hill, making a beautiful walk, for all flourished gloriously and not a single one withered. But the knights, and
even Stoffeln himself, seldom walked there, for every time a
nameless dread overcame them. They would have been best
pleased to put an end to the whole thing, but no one put an
end to it, and each took comfort to himself, saying: "If evil
comes of it, the other will be to blame."

But with every beech that stood on Bärhegen the peasants' hearts grew lighter, for with each one their hope grew that they might please their overlord and cheat the Green Man. The Green Man had no pledge from them, and when the hundredth beech stood on the hill, who was going to trouble his head about green men at all? Yet they were not quite sure in their hearts. Every day they dreaded that he would play some trick on them and leave them in the lurch. On St. Urban's day, they brought the last beeches to the church hill, and neither old nor young slept much that night. They could hardly believe that he would finish the work without child or pledge.

Next morning, long before sunrise, young and old were afoot, all moved by the same evil curiosity, but a long time passed before they ventured to the place where the beeches had lain. Would no trap be waiting there for men who had in mind to trick the Green Man?

In the end, a wild young goatherd who had brought the cheese from the pasture took heart, ran on ahead, and found the beeches gone from the church hill and no devilry to be seen anywhere. The people were still suspicious; they sent the young herd on to Bärhegen ahead of them. There everything was as it should be; a hundred beeches stood in ranks, none had withered, and no man had a swollen face or an aching limb. Then the men's hearts leaped within them, and they mocked the Green Man and the knights. For the third time they sent out the wild young goatherd, this time to tell Stoffeln that the work on Bärhegen Hill was finished, he could come and count the beeches. But his soul shrank within him and he sent to tell them to get away home. He would have preferred to order them to clear the whole walk away, but he dared not on account of his knights. They were not to say he was afraid, yet he knew nothing of the bargain and of who might have taken a hand in it.

When the goatherd brought the tidings, the people's hearts leapt within them, the young men and women danced madly in the beech walk, fierce yodels rang from gorge to gorge,

from hill to hill, echoing from the walls of the castle at Sumiswald. Grave elders warned and prayed, but hard hearts have
no ears for the warnings of grave elders, yet when trouble
comes, it is the elders who have brought it upon them with
their fears and warnings. The time is not yet come for men to
realize that it is their own hard hearts that bring the trouble.
The jubilation spread over hill and dale into every home, and
wherever a handsbreadth of meat still hung on the rafters, it
was boiled, and wherever a spoonful of butter was still in the
jar, it went on fritters.

The meat was eaten, the fritters had gone, the day had
passed, and once more the sun rose over Sumiswald. Nearer
and nearer came the day when a woman was to bear a child,
and the nearer the day came, the greater grew their terror.
The Green Man would come again, demand his due or set
some trap for them.

But who shall measure the grief of the young wife whose
child it was? The house was filled with her lamentations and
all who lived in it were moved, but none could tell what to do,
though all knew that it was folly to trust their partner to the
pact. The nearer her hour came, the closer the young wife
clung to God's holy Mother, not only with her arms, but with
her body, soul and spirit, beseeching protection for her
blessed Son's sake. And day by day she grew stronger in the
faith that in life and death, in every sorrow, the greatest comfort is in God, for where He is the Demon cannot be and has
no power.

Day by day she came to see more clearly that if the priest
of the Lord were present at the birth with the Holy of Holies,
the blessed body of the Redeemer, and armed with powerful
exorcisms, no evil could come near, and the priest could at
once bestow on the child the sacrament of baptism, as custom
then permitted; then the poor child would be wrested forever
from the danger which the foolhardiness of the fathers had
brought upon it. The others began to believe it too, and the
grief of the young wife went to their hearts, but they shrank
from confessing their pact with Satan to the priest, and no
one had been to confession since that day and no one had

told him the truth. A very devout man he was; even the knights at the castle played none of their pranks on him, while he, for his part, told them the truth. Once the thing was done, the peasants had thought, no one could prevent it, yet now nobody was willing to tell him about it, their consciences knew why.

At last one of the women could bear it no longer. She went and told the priest about the pact, and what the young wife wished. The good man's soul was seized with terror, but he wasted no time in vain words. Boldly he took up the struggle with his mighty adversary for the sake of one poor soul. He was a man who feared not the most grievous battle because he looked to be crowned with the crown of eternal life, and knew that none shall be crowned who has not fought lawfully.

Round the house where the woman lay awaiting her hour he traced with holy water the circle which evil spirits dare not enter. He blessed the threshold and the whole room, and the young wife bore her child in peace and the priest baptized it unmolested. Outside all was peace, the bright stars glittered in the sky, and the breeze played softly in the trees. Some declared they had heard a neighing laughter, but the others said it was only the owls at the edge of the wood.

Then all rejoiced; fear had vanished, they thought forever. If once they had cheated the Green Man, they could do it again.

A great feast was prepared and guests bidden from far and near. In vain the priest warned them against feasting and revelry, exhorted them to tremble and pray, for the adversary was not overcome, nor was their peace made with God. He felt in his soul that it was not for him to lay penance on them, as if a huge and grievous penance were coming from God's own hand. But they would not listen, and tried to silence him with food and drink, and he went sadly away, prayed for those who did not know what they did, and armed himself with prayer and fasting to fight like a good shepherd for his flock.

Christine too sat among the revelers, but she was unwontedly silent, with her burning cheeks and gloomy eyes. There was a strange twitching to be seen in her face. As an experienced midwife she had been present at the birth and had stood godmother at the hasty christening, with pride, but no fear, in her heart. But when the priest sprinkled the child with holy water and baptized it in the three Holy Names, she felt as if a red-hot iron were being driven into the spot where the Green Man had kissed her. She had started in sudden dread, nearly dropping the child, and since then the pain had not abated, but had burned more fiercely hour by hour. At first she had sat still, stifling the pain and mutely revolving her heavy thoughts in her awakening mind, but her hand kept moving to the burning spot; it was as if a venomous wasp were sitting there, plunging its glowing sting into the very marrow of her bones. But as there was no wasp to brush away, and the smarting grew fiercer with the horror in her mind, she began to show her cheek to the people and ask if there was anything to be seen on it. But nobody could see anything, and soon nobody was willing to waste the merry time with searching her cheek. In the end she induced an old woman to look; the cock was crowing, the day dawning, when the old woman spied an almost invisible spot on Christine's cheek. It was nothing bad, she declared, it would go away again, and she went on her way.

Christine tried to take comfort; it was nothing bad, it would go away again soon, but the pain did not abate and the little spot spread until all saw it and asked what the black thing in her face was. They meant no harm, but their questions stung her to the heart, bringing back her grievous thoughts, and she could not forget that the Green Man had kissed her on that very spot, and that the fire which had flashed through her limbs like lightning now sat fast there, burning and destroying. Sleep fled from her, her food tasted like glowing embers, ceaselessly she hurried hither and thither, seeking comfort and finding none, for the pain still grew and the black spot spread and spread, dark stripes crawled out of it, and near her mouth a little swelling seemed to be rising on the spot.

So Christine suffered and roamed about for many a long day and many a long night, but she had not confided to anyone the dread in her heart nor what she had received from the Green Man on that spot. Yet if she had known how to rid herself of the pain, she would have sacrificed anything in heaven and on earth. She was by nature a bold woman, but now, in her raging pain, she was like a wild beast.

Then it came about that a woman was again with child. This time there was no great fear among the people and they were in good spirits; provided they sent for the priest in good time, they thought, they could laugh at the Green Man.

Christine alone knew better. The nearer the day of the birth came, the fiercer grew the fire in her cheek and the huger grew the black spot. Distinct legs ran out of it, short hairs grew on it, gleaming spots and stripes came out on its back, and the little swelling turned into a head which glittered venomously as if from two eyes. When the people saw the evil Spider on Christine's face they screamed aloud and fled in fear and trembling, for they saw how firm it sat on the face it had grown out of. They talked, one advised this, another that, but all were content that whatever was to come should fall on Christine, and all shunned her and fled before her whenever they could. The more they fled, the more Christine was driven to follow them; she ran from house to house. She knew only too well that the Devil was reminding her of the promised child, and in her determination to make the people speak openly of the sacrifice, she pursued them in mortal dread.

But the others cared little, Christine's anguish caused them no pain; what she suffered, they thought, she had deserved, and when they could escape her no longer, they said to her: "Now listen. Nobody promised a child, so nobody will give one."

She set furiously on her own husband. He fled like the others, and when he could escape her no longer, said cooly that it would get better; it was a mole such as many people had, and once it was full grown they could tie it at the root and it would fall off.

But the pain did not cease, every bone was like the fires of Hell, and when the woman's hour came, it seemed to Christine as if there were a wall of flame round her, as if glowing knives were burrowing in the marrow of her bones, as if fiery whirlwinds were rushing through her head. But the Spider grew, and reared, and between the bristles, malignant eyes swelled up. When Christine, in her burning anguish, found no comfort anywhere, and saw the woman in childbirth well guarded, she rushed like a madwoman along the path the priest was to take.

Striding manfully, he mounted the slope, his burly sexton by his side. Neither the hot sun nor the steep hillside could check him, for there was a soul to be saved, an eternal wrong to be righted, and, coming from a distant sickbed, he trembled lest he should come too late. In despair, Christine threw herself in his path, embraced his knees, prayed for rescue from her hell, for the sacrifice of the child who had not yet known life, and the Spider swelled yet higher and more hideous in Christine's flushed face, and glared on the priest's holy vessels with baleful eyes. But he swiftly thrust Christine aside, making the sign of the cross; he could see the enemy, but abandoned the battle to save a soul. Then Christine started up and rushed after him, straining all her strength, but the sexton's strong hand held the raving woman from the priest, and the priest was in time to protect the house and to receive in his consecrated hands the child which he committed into the hands of Him whom death could not overcome.

Outside the house Christine had fought a desperate battle. She wanted the child unbaptized in her hands, and struggled to reach it, but the hands of strong men prevented her.

Gusts of wind smote the house, pale lightning licked round it, but the hand of the Lord was upon it, the child was christened, and Christine roamed about the house in vain. A prey to yet more mortal anguish, sounds came from her such as no human throat can utter; the cattle shuddered in the byres and tore at their tethers, and the oaks in the forest rose rustling in horror.

Inside the house the people began their rejoicing over this new victory, the powerlessness of the Green Man and the vain struggles of his accomplice, but outside Christine lay on the ground in agony, and in her face pains began such as no woman in childbirth has known on this earth, and the Spider in her face swelled yet higher and burned through her bones more fiercely than ever.

Then Christine felt as if her face had burst, as if red-hot coals were being born and coming to life in it; she felt a crawling over her face, over all her limbs, as if everything in her were coming to life and crawling in fire over her body. Then, in the livid light of the lightning, she saw, long-legged, poisonous, and countless, black spiders hurrying over her limbs and away into the night, to be followed by others, long-legged, poisonous, and countless. At last no more came, the fire in her face died down, the Spider settled and shrank into an almost invisible spot, gazing with dying eyes at the infernal brood it had borne and sent forth as a sign that there was no jesting with the Green Man.

Weak as a woman in childbed, Christine crept home. Though the fire no longer burned so fiercely in her face, the fire in her heart was burning still. Though her weary limbs craved for rest, the Green Man left her no peace. That is his way with those who have once become his.

Inside the house the people rejoiced and were glad, so that a long time passed before the lowing of the cattle in the byre came to their ears. Then they started up, and some men went to see. White with terror, they came back to say that the finest cow lay dead and the others were raging and plunging as had never been seen before. Something was wrong, some strange thing was afoot. Then the revelry ceased, all hurried to the cattle whose lowing rang over hill and dale, but none knew what to do. They tried to break the spell by exorcisms, spiritual and temporal, but in vain; before day had dawned, death had laid low all the cattle in the byre. But when silence came there, the lowing rose again, now here, now there, and those who were in the house heard, by the piteous cries of the cattle for their masters in their fear, how the calamity had descended on their own byres.

The men hurried away as if their homes were on fire, but they brought no help with them. On all hands, death struck down the cattle, the cries of man and beast reechoed far and wide, and the sun, which set on their rejoicings, rose upon terrible woe. In the light of the risen sun, the people saw how, in the byres where the cattle had fallen, countless black spiders were crawling. They crawled over the cattle and the fodder, poisoning whatever they touched, and any beast that was still alive began to plunge and was soon laid low in death. Once the spiders had entered a byre, it could never be rid of them; they seemed to grow out of the ground. Nor could any byre that had not been attacked be protected; they crawled out of the walls and fell in heaps from the ceiling. The men drove the cattle to pasture, but only drove them into the jaws of death. For as soon as a cow set foot on a pasture, the earth came to life, long black spiders sprouted up like hideous Alpine flowers, and crawled up the cattle, and a piteous cry of pain echoed from the mountain to the valley. And all the spiders were as like the Spider on Christine's face as children are like their mother, and the like of them had never been seen before.

The cries of the poor beasts were heard in the castle too, and soon cowherds came with the news that their cattle had died of the poison, and with growing anger Stoffeln learned how herd after herd had been lost, learned of the pact with the Green Man, how he had been cheated a second time, how the spiders were as like the Spider on Christine's face as children are like their mother, and how the Lindau woman had made the pact alone with the Green Man and never told the truth about it. Then Stoffeln rode up the hill, grim with anger, and thundered at the poor men that he was not going to lose herd after herd for their sakes, that they would have to make good all he lost, whatever happened, and whatever they had done they must bear the consequences. He was not going to suffer loss by them, or, should he suffer, they would

pay for it a thousandfold. Such was his manner of speech to
them, careless of the burden he was laying on their shoulders,
nor did he think that it was he himself who had driven them
to it; what they had done he laid at their own doors.

Most of them had slowly come to understand that the spiders were a pest sent by the Evil One to remind them that
the bargain must be kept; they felt too that Christine must
know more about it and had not told them of all her dealings
with the Green Man. But now they shuddered at the thought
of the Green Man, ceased mocking at him and trembled
before their temporal lord, for if they made their peace with
him, what would their spiritual lord have to say; would he
allow it and would he lay no penance on them? In their fear,
the most respected of them assembled in a lonely barn and
sent for Christine to come and tell them openly what bargain
she had really driven.

Christine came, savage and revengeful, again a prey to the
growing Spider.

She looked at them and saw their fear, saw too that none of
the women were present. Then she told them exactly what had
happened, how the Green Man had promptly taken her at her
word and, as a pledge, given her a kiss she had paid no more
attention to than any other. How on that very spot the Spider
had grown in mortal agony from the moment the first child
was born. How the Spider, when they had christened the second child and tricked the Green Man, had given birth in agony
to a countless brood, for he would not be fooled for nothing,
and how she had felt that in her mortal pain. And now the
Spider was growing again, and the pain with it, and if the next
child was not given to the Green Man, nobody could tell how
deadly the pestilence would be and how grim the knight's
revenge.

Thus Christine spoke, and the men's hearts trembled
within them, and for a long time none would speak. Then,
little by little, broken sounds came from their oppressed
breasts, and when the sounds were put together, they meant
what Christine meant, yet no single one of the men had agreed

to her advice. Only one of them stood up and spoke briefly and to the point. The best thing, he said, would be to kill Christine; once she was dead the Green Man would rest content with the dead, but he would have no more hold on the living.

Then Christine broke out into savage laughter, strode up to him, face to face, and told him to strike. She would not complain, but what the Green Man wanted was not her, but an unbaptized child, and the mark he had put on her he could just as well put on the hand that did her harm.

Then the man who had spoken felt his hand twitch, he sat down and listened to the others. With no man saying all, and each something which mattered little, they agreed to sacrifice the next child, but none would put his hand to it, and none carry the child to the church hill where the beeches had been laid. None feared to make use of the Devil for the good of all but none would have dealings with him in his own person. Then Christine said she would do it, for if anyone has had to do with the Devil once, the second time cannot do much harm. They knew who was to bear the next child, but none spoke the name and the father was not there.

Having agreed, with and without words, they parted.

The young wife who had trembled and wept without knowing why that dreadful night when Christine had come back with her tale of the Green Man was now awaiting her next child. She could draw neither comfort nor confidence from what had happened. A nameless dread lay upon her heart which neither prayer nor confession could dispel. A suspicious silence seemed to surround her. Nobody spoke of the Spider now; the eyes that rested on her looked wary, and seemed to be calculating the hour when they could get possession of her child and pacify the Devil.

And so she felt lonely and helpless. There was no one to stand by her but her mother-in-law, a devout woman, but what can one old woman do against a savage crowd? She had her husband, and he had comforted her with promises, but how he complained about his cattle and how little he thought about his poor wife's fears! The priest had promised to come as quickly as he could and as soon as they sent for him, but what might happen when he was on the way? And the poor woman had no trusted messenger but her own husband, who should have been her watch and ward. Besides, she lived in the same house as Christine, their husbands were brothers. She had no kin of her own, and had come to the house an orphan. There is no telling how great was the poor woman's terror. Her only comfort was prayer with the pious mother, and that died away when she looked in the wicked eyes.

And all the time the pestilence went on, keeping fear alive. True, it was only now and then that a cow died, and the spiders were seldom to be seen. But as soon as the horror quitted one farm, as soon as anyone said that the pestilence would disappear of itself and that they should think well before sinning against a child, Christine's agony returned, the Spider in her face swelled up high, and death came upon the herd of the man who had thought or spoken. The nearer the expected hour came, the greater grew the calamity, and they saw that they must at last settle how to get possession of the child. It was the husband they feared most, yet it went against the grain to do him violence. Then Christine undertook to win him over, and she did. He was willing to shut his eyes, to do his wife's will and fetch the priest, yet not hurry on the way and ask no questions about what had happened in his absence, and so he set his conscience at rest. He would settle his account with God by masses, and perhaps something could be done for the poor child's soul. Perhaps the pious priest could win it back from the Devil, then they would be shut of the whole matter, would have done all they could and yet fooled the Evil One. So the man thought, and in any case he felt he would be guiltless, whatever happened, if he did not put his hand to it.

And so the poor wife was sacrificed and knew nothing about it, hoped in fear and trembling that she might be saved while the council of the men had pronounced her death blow, but what He above had resolved was hidden in the clouds that veil the future.

It was a thundery year and harvest time had come. All hands were at work to bring the corn into safety as long as the sun shone. It was a hot afternoon, the clouds stretched black heads over the dark mountains, the swallows fluttered anxiously round the roof, and the poor young wife, alone in the house, felt cramped and afraid, for even the old grandmother was out helping in the field, though more with will than with deed. Then pain struck through her like a two-edged sword, the place turned black before her eyes, she felt her hour approach and she was alone. Fear drove her out of the house, heavily she moved toward the distant field; she struggled to call, but her voice died in her throat. Beside her was her little boy, who was just learning to walk and had never yet been to the field on his own legs. And this little boy was the only messenger the poor woman had at hand, not knowing if he could find the field or his little legs carry him to it. But the staunch little lad saw his mother's fear and ran and fell and stood up again; his lamb ran after him, gamboling and butting, the cat ran after his rabbits, doves and hens ran under his feet. But the boy paid no heed, would not be stayed, and loyally delivered his message.

Panting, the grandmother came, but the husband delayed. He had just one more load to bring in, they said. An eternity passed, at last he came, another eternity passed, at last he set out slowly on his way, and in mortal fear the poor woman felt her hour approach on hurrying feet.

Christine had watched all this from the field, rejoicing. The sun shone hot on her labors, but the Spider hardly burnt at all, and in the next few hours her steps were light. She worked merrily and made no haste to go home, for she knew how slow the messenger would be. Not until the last sheaf was loaded and gusts of wind were heralding the coming storm did she hasten to her prey, which, she thought, was hers this time for sure. And as she went home she nodded meaningly to many a one she met, they nodded back and hurried home with the tidings. Then many a knee turned to water and many a soul strove to pray in unwilling dread, but could not.

Inside the house, the poor wife moaned, the minutes dragged out to eternity and the grandmother could not soothe her anguish with prayer and consolation. True, she had bolted the door and piled heavy furniture behind it. As long as they were alone in the house they could bear it, but when they heard Christine come home, heard creeping foot-steps at the door, when more and more footsteps crowded round, with muffled whisperings, when no priest appeared, and the moment women wait for so eagerly came ever nearer, there is no telling the dread which closed over the women like boiling oil as they sat there without help and without hope. They heard Christine keeping guard at the door. The poor young wife felt the fierce eyes of her sister-in-law burning through her, body and soul. At last a child's first whimpering cry came through the door, stifled at once, but too late. With one well-prepared thrust the door flew open, and like a tiger on its prey Christine fell on the mother. The old woman, who had thrown herself in the way of the onslaught, was hurled aside. In the holy dread of motherhood the young wife dragged herself up, but her weakened body failed her, a scream of agony broke from her heart, then the blackness of a swoon wrapped her round.

When Christine appeared with the child, the men shrank back in fear. The premonition of a terrible future came to them, but none had the courage to say nay, and the fear of the Devil's torments overcame the fear of God. Christine alone did not waver. Her face glowed like a victor's after battle. The Spider seemed to caress her cheek with a soft and pleasant itching. The lightning which forked round her on her way to the church hill were gleams of joy, the thunder a tender growl, the revenge-snorting storm a sweet rustling.

Hans, the poor woman's husband, had kept his promise only too well. He had gone slowly on his way, mustering every field at his leisure, watching every bird, waiting for the fish to rise before the coming storm. Then again he would start forward, mend his pace, begin to run. There was some-thing in him that drove him on and made the hair rise on his head: it was his conscience, warning him of what a father deserved who betrays his wife and child; it was the love he still bore his wife and the fruit of her body. But then another and stronger power held him back; it was the fear of men, the fear of the Devil, and the love of what the Devil could take from him. Then he would slacken his pace again and walk as slowly as a man on his way to execution. No man knows, when he sets out, whether it is for the last time or no. If he did, he would go otherwise or not at all.

And so it had grown late by the time he reached Sumiswald. Black clouds were driving over the Münneberg, heavy drops fell hissing in the dust, and the muffled toll of the church bell was warning men to think of God and beseech Him not to make His thunder a judgment on them. The priest was standing in front of his house, ready for any call if his Lord, striding over his head, should call him to a deathbed, a burning house, or anywhere else. When he saw Hans coming, he knew it was a summons to a grievous errand. He girded up his loins and sent to tell his sexton to find someone to take his place at the bell so that they might set out together.

Meanwhile he set wine before Hans to refresh him after his hurried walk through the sultry air. But Hans did not need it; the good priest knew nothing of the malice of men. Hans refreshed himself at his leisure. The sexton came unwillingly and was glad to take the share of the wine which Hans offered him. The priest stood waiting beside them, disdaining to drink; he had no need of it for such an errand and such a battle. He was loath to order them away from the flagon he had set before them, for all guests have privileges, but he knew a law which stood above hospitality, and anger at their sloth boiled up in him in waves.

At last he told them he was ready, an afflicted woman was waiting with a terrible wrong hanging over her head, and it was his duty to avert that wrong with holy weapons; therefore they should not delay, but come. There would be drink enough when they arrived for any whose thirst had not been already quenched. Then Hans, the woman's husband, spoke:

there was no great hurry, his wife always had a long labor. At that moment a flash of lightning blazed through the room, dazzling them all, and a roll of thunder pealed over the house till every post and wall in it quivered.

Then the sexton, having said his grace, spoke:

"Hark to the weather. Heaven itself is saying what Hans has said. We should wait. What good would it be for us to go? We should never reach the top of the hill alive, and he himself said there was no hurry about his wife."

It is true that a thunderstorm was moving toward them such as had not often been seen in mortal memory. From every gorge and hollow it rolled, racing in on all hands, swept together by all the winds over Sumiswald, and every cloud became a host of war, and every cloud stormed the next, was out for the blood of the next, and a battle of clouds began and the storm stood still and, flash after flash, the lightning struck the earth as if to blast its way through to the other side. Relentlessly the thunder rolled, the storm howled in rage, the womb of the clouds burst, the floodgates were opened, and the priest delayed for his companions' sake. But when the cloud battle had broken out, huge and sudden, he had given the sexton no answer. He had sat down, with rising dread in his heart. He felt he must fling himself into the raging elements. Then, through the dreadful voice of the thunder, he seemed to hear the piercing scream of a woman in childbirth, the thunder became God's terrible chiding for his delay, he set out in spite of the others. Out he strode into the flaming storm, into the rage of the cloudburst, armed against whatever might come. Slowly and unwillingly the others followed.

The storm screamed and howled and raged as if it were gathering itself together for the Last Trump which heralds the end of the world, and flame fell on the village in sheaves as if to set every house on fire, but the servant of Him who gives the thunder its voice and whose servant is the lightning has nothing to fear from that fellow servant of God, and he who walks in the ways of God can safely leave the thunder to rage. Therefore the priest strode undaunted through the

storm to the church hill. But there was no faith in the hearts
of them that followed him, for their hearts were not where his
was. They did not want to go down the church hill, not in
such weather and at that hour of night, and Hans had his
own reasons for not wanting to go. They begged the priest to
turn back, to take other paths; Hans knew shorter ones, the
sexton better ones, and Hans warned him of the swollen
Green Water in the valley. But the priest would not listen
and paid no heed to what they said. Driven on by a wonderful power he hastened toward the church hill on the wings of
prayer; his foot struck against no stone, no lightning dazzled
him. Trembling, far behind, guarded, as they thought, by the
Holy of Holies in the priest's own hands, Hans and the sexton
followed.

But as they left the village, where the hill drops to the
valley, the priest stopped short, his hand shading his eyes.
Below the chapel a red feather gleamed in the lightning and
the priest's sharp eyes discerned a black head with a red
feather on it rising above the green hedge. As he looked, he
saw on the opposite slope a wild figure flying at full speed
toward the dark head on which the red feather waved like a
pennant.

Then the lust of holy battle flamed up in the priest, that
lust which enters into such as have, in the presence of the
Evil One, dedicated their lives to God, as growth enters into
the corn seed, pierces the bud when the flower is to unfold,
and inflames the hero when the enemy draws his sword. And
as the hart plunges into the cooling stream and the hero into
battle, the priest rushed down the hill, hurled himself into
the boldest battle of all, thrust himself between the Green
Man and Christine, who was laying the child in his arms,
thundered the three Holy Names into the Green Man's face,
and the holy water he sprinkled on the child fell on Christine
too. Then the Green Man fled with a howl of pain, flashing
away like a crimson streak till the earth swallowed him up.
At the touch of the holy water, Christine shrank together in
a rain of sparks with a horrible hiss like wool in fire, like

chalk in water, shrank down to the black, huge, swollen, hideous Spider in her face, shrank with it, hissed into it, leaving the Spider on the child's very body, bursting with defiance and venom and darting evil looks at the priest. He flung holy water at it; it hissed like well water on a hot stone. The Spider swelled and swelled, stretched its black legs over the child and glared yet more venomously at the priest, who, in the holy wrath of his faith, laid hold of it with a valiant hand. It was as if he had plunged his hand into red-hot thorns, but he grasped unshakably fast, flung the creature away, snatched up the child, and hurried on to the mother.

And when his battle was over, the battle in the clouds died down and they hurried back to their gloomy chambers. Where but a short time before the fiercest fight had raged, the valley now lay glimmering in the quiet starlight, and almost at the end of his breath, the priest reached the house where the unholy deed had been wrought on mother and child.

There the mother still lay senseless; her senses had left her with her wild scream. Beside her the old woman sat praying. She trusted in God to be stronger than the Devil was evil. With the child, the priest restored the mother to life. When, awaking, she saw her child again, a warmth streamed through her such as only the angels in Heaven can feel, and in her arms the priest baptized the child in the name of the Father, Son, and Holy Ghost. And now it was wrested from the power of the Devil till it would yield itself up to him of its own free will. But God guarded it from that, while its body was poisoned by the Spider.

Soon its soul took flight again, and the little body was branded as if with fire. The poor mother wept indeed, but when each part returns to its appointed place, the soul to God, the body to earth, comfort will come, sooner to one, later to another.

As soon as the priest had performed his holy office, he felt a strange itching in the hand and arm which had hurled away the Spider. His hand came out in little black spots; they spread and swelled under his very eyes, and the fear of death trickled through his heart. He blessed the women and hurried home. Like a faithful soldier, he wished to restore his holy weapons to their proper place so that they should stand ready to the hand of his successor. His arm swelled high, black boils swelled yet higher on it, he struggled with the weariness of death but did not yield.

When he reached the church hill, he saw Hans, the Godforsaking father, whose fate no one had known, lying on his back across the path. His face was swollen and black with burning and on it there sat, bloated, black, and grisly, the Spider. When the priest approached it blew itself up, the hairs on its back bristled venomously, and its eyes glared and flashed poison; it might have been a cat gathering itself together to spring in its archenemy's face. Then the priest pronounced holy words and raised his holy weapons, and the Spider shrank away, crawled long-legged from the blackened face and was lost in the hissing grass.

Then at last the priest went home, and set the Holy of Holies in its place, and while fierce pains racked his body, his soul awaited in sweetest peace its God, for whom it had fought a good fight in God's holy warfare, and God did not keep it waiting long.

But the sweet peace which waits patiently upon the Lord was to be found neither below in the valley nor up in the mountains.

From the moment when Christine had rushed down the hill with the child to meet the Devil, a terrible dread had overcome all hearts. As the huge storm raged, the people shuddered in the fear of death, for in their hearts they knew only too well that, if God's destroying hand was upon them, they had more than deserved it. When the storm had passed, the tidings spread from house to house of how the priest had brought back the child, but neither Hans nor Christine had been seen.

When the gray of dawn came, it rested on livid faces, and the radiant sun restored no color to them, for all knew that the greatest horror was yet to come. Then they heard that the priest lay dead with black boils; Hans was found, his face distorted; and strange, confused tidings were spread of the Spider which was Christine.

It was a fine harvest day, but no man lifted his hand to work; the people gathered in knots, as they do on the morrow of some great disaster. Now in truth they felt in their shuddering souls what they had done in striving to buy themselves free of earthly pain and toil at the cost of an immortal soul, felt that there was a God in Heaven who took fearful vengeance for all wrong done to poor defenseless children. So they gathered together and stood lamenting, and no man who came to join them could tear himself away again, though there was strife and dissension among them and each blamed his neighbor, and declared that his had been the warning voice.

None minded punishment falling on the wrongdoers, but each was resolved that he and his house should go free. And if, in their dreadful loitering and strife, they had known of another innocent victim, not one but would have raised his hand against it to save himself.

Then one in their midst howled as if he had trodden on red-hot iron, as if his foot were nailed to the ground with a red-hot nail, as if fire were streaming through the marrow of his bones. They scattered, and all eyes turned to the man who had howled and on the hand which grasped his foot. But on the foot there sat, black and huge, the Spider, casting evil looks upon them. The blood froze in their veins, the breath in their throats, while, in unhurried malevolence, the Spider sat gloating, and the foot turned black and in the man's body, fire and water seemed to hiss and fight. Terror burst the bonds of fear, the group scattered. But in ghastly haste the Spider had left its first resting place and crept over one man's foot and another's heel, and fire coursed through their bodies and their dreadful cries lent wings to the feet of those who fled. On the wings of the wind, in the terrors of death, like the ghostly quarry before the ghostly hunt, they scattered to their homes, each feeling the Spider behind him. Then they bolted their doors and could not stop shuddering in mortal dread.

One day the Spider vanished. No cries of death were heard, and the men had perforce to leave their bolted houses to seek food for their cattle and themselves. But where was the Spider? Could it not be lying in wait, invisible, to appear unawares on a man's foot? And he who set down his foot most cautiously, and spied about him most keenly, suddenly saw the Spider sitting on his hand or foot; it crawled over his face, sat black and huge on his nose, glaring into his eyes, and red-hot strings burrowed into his bones, and the fires of Hell closed over him till death laid him low.

Thus the Spider was now nowhere, now here, now there, now down in the valley, now up in the hills. It hissed through the grass, fell from the ceiling, rose from the ground. In broad daylight, as the people sat at their midday porridge, it sat gloating at the foot of the table, and before they could scatter in their fear, it had run over their hands, was sitting at the top of the table on the father's head, glaring gleefully over the table and the blackening hands. It fell on their faces at night, met them in the woods, sought them out in the byre. No man could avoid it; it was nowhere and everywhere. Awake or asleep, they could not ward it off. When they felt most safe, in the open air or up in a tree, fire crept up their backs, fiery feet were plunged into their necks, and the Spider glared at them over their shoulders. It spared neither the child in the cradle nor the old man on his deathbed. It was a dying such as had never been heard of before, and the death of it was more dreadful than had ever been known, and still more dreadful than death was the nameless horror of the Spider, which was everywhere and nowhere and which, when they thought themselves in safety, suddenly glared, death-dealing, into their eyes.

The tidings of the horror had, of course, soon reached the castle, and had stirred up fear and strife there too, insofar as might be within the rule of the Order. Stoffeln trembled lest the visitation should come upon them too, as it had come upon their cattle, and the dead priest had said many things which now disquieted his soul. For the priest had told him more than once that all the suffering he inflicted on the peasants would be paid home to him, but he had never believed it, thinking that God would know the difference between a knight and a serf, having created them so different.

But now he was afraid all the same lest things might be as the priest had said, and gave his knights hard words and told them that their wanton speech would be bitterly avenged. But the knights would not take the blame either; each blamed the other, and though none said so, thought it concerned Stoffeln alone, for, looked at properly, it was he who had brought the whole thing about. And beside him their eyes rested on a young Polish knight who had jested most wantonly about the castle and had been most zealous in egging Stoffeln on to its building and to the planting of the flaunting avenue. He was very young, but the fiercest of all, and when a deed of daring was to be done, he was the first. He was no better than a heathen, for he feared neither God nor Satan. He soon saw what was in the others' minds, and marked their secret dread. Therefore he taunted them, saying that if they feared a spider, what would they do against a dragon? Then he armed himself well and rode up the valley, boasting that he would not return until his thrust had laid the Spider low and his fist crushed it. Savage dogs leaped round him, his hawk sat on his wrist, his horse reared spiritedly. Half in fear, half in malice, the others watched him ride out of the castle, and they thought of the night watch at Bärhegen, where earthly weapons had availed so little against such an enemy.

He rode along the edge of a pine wood to the nearest farm, keeping a sharp lookout around and above him. When the house came into sight, with people standing round it, he called to his dogs and unhooded his hawk, while his dagger rattled loose in its sheath. As the hawk turned its dazzled eyes to the knight, awaiting his signal, it suddenly flung itself from his wrist and soared up into the air, the dogs howled aloud and fled, their tails between their legs. In vain the knight galloped and called, he saw his creatures no more. Then he rode toward the people to ask for tidings. They stood still till he was near them, then a hideous cry arose, they fled to wood and gorge, for on the horseman's helmet there sat, unnaturally huge, the Spider glaring with baneful malice over the countryside. What the knight sought he bore unwittingly with him. Afire with rage he rode after the people, calling ever more fiercely, till he and his horse fell over a precipice into the valley. There they found his helmet and his body, and the Spider's feet had burned into the knight's brain, where it had raged in dreadful fire till he could die.

Then indeed fear entered the castle. They locked themselves in, but could not feel safe. They sought for spiritual weapons, but a long time passed before they could find a priest who would and dared to be their leader. He came, and summoned them to sally forth with holy vessels and holy water against the enemy. But he did not strengthen himself in prayer and fasting; he sat at table early in the morning with the knights, did not count the goblets he drank, and lived well on venison and bear flesh. Between times he would talk of his valorous spiritual deeds, while the knights talked of their worldly ones, and no man counted the goblets and the Spider was forgotten.

Then, in a moment, life was paralyzed, the hands stiffened round fork or goblet, mouths hung open and all eyes were fixed on one spot. Stoffeln alone drank on, telling a tale of a deed of daring in heathen lands, but on his head there throned the Spider, glaring round the banqueting table, and the knight did not feel it. Then the fire began to course through his brain and blood. Raising his hand to his head he uttered a dreadful cry, but the Spider was no longer there, had, in its hideous speed, crawled over all their faces, and one after the other they screamed aloud, devoured by the fire, and from the priest's tonsure it gloated over the horror. The priest strove to quench with the goblet in his hand the fire which flamed through his bones. But the Spider defied his weapon and sat upon its throne gloating on the horror till the last knight had uttered his last cry and drawn his last breath.

Of all that lived in the castle only a few servants were spared who had never scorned the peasants; they told the dreadful tale. But the feeling that the knights had got what they deserved was little comfort to the peasants; the horror grew and spread and was more dreadful day by day. Some set out to leave the valley, but it was just they whom the Spider fell upon. Their bodies were found by the wayside. Others fled to the high mountains, but the Spider was there before them, and when they thought themselves in safety, there was the Spider sitting on their necks or faces. Day by day the creature grew more malevolent, more devilish. It no longer took them by suprise, no longer burnt death into them unawares; it sat in front of them in the grass, hung over them in the trees, glaring at them with venomous eyes. But if any man who had taken flight slackened his pace, then only did it crawl toward him and strike him down.

Many, in their despair, tried to kill the Spider, dropped hundredweight-heavy stones on it as it sat in the grass in front of them, or struck at it with clubs or axes, but it was all in vain. The heaviest stone could not crush it nor the sharpest axe wound it, and there it was sitting on their faces or crawling unharmed toward them. To flee was as vain as to fight. All hope was at an end and despair filled the valley and sat on the heights.

Till then the creature had spared one single house and had never appeared in it. It was the house where Christine had lived and from which she had stolen the child. She had attacked her own husband on a lonely pasture; they found his body more horribly mutilated than any other, his features wrung with unspeakable pain. She had wreaked her most dreadful anger on him, preparing an awful reunion with her husband. But no man had seen it happen.

She had not yet come to the house. Whether she wished to save it to the last, or whether she shunned it, no one could guess. But dread housed there as in every other place.

The good young wife had recovered. She had no fear for herself, but only for her staunch little boy and his sister. Day and night she watched over them, and the grandmother watched with her. Together they prayed that God would keep their watching eyes open, and give them light and strength to save the innocent children.

It often seemed to them, as they kept watch through the long nights, as if they could see the Spider glimmering and glittering in the dark corner, or glaring in through the window, and then their fear was great, for they knew of no way to shield the children from it, and they prayed all the more fervently to God for His counsel and help. They had laid all kinds of weapons ready, but when they heard that stones lost their weight and axes their edge, they put them away again. Then a thought began to take shape in the mother's mind, and grew clearer day by day. If anyone dared to grasp the Spider in their hand, it could be overcome. She had heard too that some of the people, when stone proved powerless, had striven to crush it in their hand, but in vain. A stream of fire pulsing through hand and arm swept all their strength away and carried death to their hearts.

She did not think she could crush the Spider, but she could lay hold of it, and God would give her the strength to put it where it would be harmless. She had often heard how wise men had imprisoned spirits in a hole in rock or wood, which they had then shut fast with a nail, and as long as no one drew out the nail, the demon remained in the hole.

More and more the spirit moved her to attempt a like deed. She bored a hole in the window post nearest her right hand as she sat by the cradle, prepared a plug which exactly fitted it, sprinkled it with holy water, and laid a hammer ready, then prayed day and night to God for strength to carry out the deed. But at times the flesh overcame the spirit, heavy sleep pressed her eyes shut, and in dreams she saw the Spider

glaring at her boy's golden hair. Then she would start up out
of her dream and stretch out her hand to her boy's curls. But
no spider was sitting there, and there was a smile on his face
such as children smile when they see their angel in a dream,
but the mother saw the Spider's venomous eyes glittering in
every corner, and sleep left her for many a long day.

Once more, as she kept strict watch, sleep had overcome
her, hanging her round with black veils. Then it seemed to
her that the priest who had died to save her child came rushing toward her from far distances, crying: "Woman awake!
The enemy is at hand!" Three times he called, and not until
the third time did she cast off the clinging bonds of sleep. But
as she toilsomely opened her heavy eyelids, she saw the
Spider, bloated with venom, moving over the cot to her boy's
face. Then she thought of God and with a swift hand seized
the Spider. Streams of fire flowed from it, through the faithful mother's hand and arm into her heart, but her faith and
love pressed her hand together and God gave her the strength
to endure. In a thousandfold agony of death she pressed the
Spider into the hole with one hand, pressed in the plug with
the other, and drove it home with the hammer.

Inside the room there was a roaring as when whirlwinds
fight with the sea, the house rocked to its foundations, but
the plug held, the Spider was a prisoner.

The faithful mother had time to rejoice that her child was
saved and to thank God for His grace, then she died the same
death as the others, but her mother-love quenched the pain
and the angels led her soul to the throne of God, where all
the heroes stand who have given their lives for others and
dared all for God and their loved ones. Now the Black Death
was over. Peace and life returned to the valley, and the
Spider was seen no more at that time, for it sat a prisoner in
that hole where it sits now.

"What, in that black post there!" screamed the godmother,
leaping up from the ground as if she had sat on an anthill.
Her back smarted, she turned round on herself, looked down

her back, felt herself all over, but could not shake off the fear that the Spider was sitting on her neck.

The hearts of the others were oppressed too, but the grandfather sat silent. An awed silence had fallen on all. None dared to jest, yet none would yield easily to belief. Each thought it better to listen to what the others might say; it was the best way not to go wrong.

Then the midwife, who had called more than once without getting an answer, came running, her face flaming as if the Spider had crawled over it. She began to scold, telling them that no matter how loud she might call, nobody would come. She had cooked the dinner and now nobody wanted to come to table, and when everything was spoilt, she would get the blame, it was always the way. Nobody could eat meat as fat as was waiting for them if it had got cold; besides, it would be bad for them.

So they came, but very slowly, and nobody would go through the door first, and Grandfather had to lead the way. But this time it was not out of respect for the old custom of hanging back so as not to seem too eager. It was the shrinking which befalls all men at the entrance to a place of dread, and yet there was nothing dreadful to be seen. On the table the refilled wine bottles shone bright, two brave hams glistened, huge roasts of veal and mutton smoked, fresh züpfen lay between, plates of fruit tarts and three kinds of cakes were squeezed in between, and the pots of sweet tea had not been forgotten. It was a fine sight, but they paid little heed to it all and looked round anxiously to make sure that the Spider was not glittering in some corner or fixing venomous eyes on them from the top of a ham. It was nowhere to be seen, yet no one paid the customary compliments—whatever could the housewife have been thinking of to load the table that way?—anyone who ate all that would soon have too much, and so on. They huddled together at the foot of the table and none would go up higher.

In vain the guests were urged to move up, and empty chairs were pointed out. They stood as if nailed to the ground. In vain the young father poured out wine and called on them to come and drink healths; the glasses remained full.

Then he took the godmother by the arm, saying: "Come, Godmother, show your wits and set an example." But the godmother fended him off with might and main, crying: "I wouldn't sit there, no, not for a thousand pounds. My whole back is creeping and crawling as if someone were stroking it with nettles. And if I were to sit there in front of that window post I'd feel that dreadful spider in my neck."

"It's all your fault, Grandfather," said the grandmother. "Why do you rake up such things? Nobody believes them nowadays, and they might bring discredit on the house. The day the children come crying home from school, complaining that the other children have cast it up at them that their grandmother was a witch and is shut up in that window post, you'll see."

"Quiet there, Grandmother," said the grandfather. "People have short memories these days. They don't keep things in their minds as they used to long ago. The company wanted to hear about it all from me, and it's better for folk to know the truth just as it is rather than make things up for themselves. The truth can bring no dishonor on our house. But come and sit down, all of you. Look, I'll sit in front of the post myself. After all, I've sat there thousands of days without fear or trembling and then there's no danger. It was only when ill thoughts rose in me which might give the Devil a handle that I seemed to hear something purring behind me like a cat when you stroke its stomach. Then the goose flesh crawled up my back. But the rest of the time it sits in there as still as a mouse and as long as God is not forgotten here outside it'll have to wait inside."

Then the guests plucked up courage and sat down, but nobody moved up to sit by the grandfather. Now at last the young husband could curve. He laid a huge slice of roast on his neighbor's plate, stripping it off with his thumb. The slice went the rounds until one of the company said thanks, he'd keep it, there was more where that came from, then another slice was sent round. While the husband filled the glasses and the guests told him he'd have his work cut out that day, the midwife went round with the tea, strongly spiced with saffron and cinnamon, offering it to all and saying that anyone who liked it need only say so, there was plenty. And when anyone made an offer she poured the tea into the wine and said she was fond of it too, the wine lay better on the stomach and there was no fear of headaches.

They ate and drank, but hardly had the noise subsided which means that fresh dishes have made their appearance when silence fell again, faces grew grave, and it was easy to see that all thoughts were busy with the Spider. Furtive eyes sought the plug behind the grandfather's back, yet everybody was afraid of raising the subject again. Then suddenly the godmother screamed and nearly fell off her chair.

A fly had crawled over the plug; she seemed to see the Spider's black legs scrabbling out of the hole, and she was quivering in every limb from the shock. They hardly laughed at her. Her shock was a welcome pretext to begin again about the Spider, for once a thing has really gone home to people's minds, it is no easy matter to put it aside again.

"Now listen, Cousin," said the elder godfather. "Hasn't the Spider ever been out again? Has it stayed in there all these hundreds of years?"

"Ah!" said the grandmother. "It'd have been better not to bring the whole thing up at all. You've been talking about nothing else the whole afternoon."

"Now, Mother," said the cousin. "Let the old man have his say. He's kept us quiet and nobody's going to cast it up at you. After all, you're no kin of Christine's. But you won't stop us thinking about it, and if you won't let us talk about it we'll talk about nothing else and there'll be nothing to pass the time. Go on, Grandfather, your old woman won't grudge it us."

"Well, if you will have it then have it, as far as I'm concerned, but it'd have been better to start about something else, especially now night's coming on," said the grandmother.

Then the grandfather began again, and all faces turned toward him expectantly.

I don't know much more to tell, but I'll tell you what I do know. Somebody might take an example by it even today. In any case, there's plenty of people who'd come to no harm by it if they did.

When the people knew that the Spider was a prisoner and their lives safe again, it's said that they felt as if they were in Paradise, with the Lord God in His blessedness in the midst of them, and for a long time all was well. They walked in God's ways and shunned the Devil, and even the new knights who had come to the castle respected the hand of God and treated the people kindly, and helped them to prosper.

But all looked on this house with awe, almost as if it had been a church. It's true they shuddered at first when they looked at it and saw the Black Spider's dungeon and thought how easily it could break out and the calamity begin all over again by the Devil's power. But they soon saw that God's power was greater than the Devil's, and as a token of their gratitude to the mother who had died for them they looked after her children and worked the farm for nothing until the children were able to work for themselves. The knights would have let them build a new house so that they might get rid of the fear of the Spider, or in case it might get out again in a house that was lived in, and they'd have had help in plenty from the neighbors who couldn't shake off their dread of the creature they had so mortally feared. But the old grandmother wouldn't hear of it; she taught her grandchildren that here the Spider would be kept prisoner by God the Father, Son, and Holy Ghost. As long as the three Holy Names were venerated in that house, as long as food and drink were taken at that table in the three Holy Names, so long would they be safe from the Spider in its hole and no chance could change that. Here, at this table, with the Spider behind them, they would never forget their fear of God nor the greatness of His power, and so the Spider would turn

their minds to God in spite of the Devil. But if they abandoned God, were it a hundred miles away, the Spider or the
Devil himself would find them. The children understood and
grew up in the fear of God, and God's blessing was upon the
house.

The little boy who had stood so staunchly by his mother
grew up to be a fine upstanding man, who was beloved of God
and found favor with the knights. He was blessed with
worldly goods, but never forgot God on their account nor
closed his hand upon them. He helped others in need as he
desired that others should help him in his last need, and
when he grew too weak to help himself, he became all the
more powerful an advocate with God and man. He was
blessed with a wise wife, and between them was the peace
that passeth understanding; therefore their children bloomed
in piety and man and wife were granted a peaceful death.
And after them the family continued to prosper in the fear of
God and in righteous ways.

Yes, the blessing of God lay upon the whole valley, and
there was plenty in field and byre and peace among men.
They had taken the dreadful lesson to heart; they clung close
to God, what they did they did in His name, and where one
could heep his neighbor he did so without delay. At the castle,
no evil and much good was done them. The number of
knights dwindled as the war with the heathen raged more
fiercely and the need of every hand that could wield a
weapon grew greater. But to those who remained in the
castle, the great hall of death, where the Spider had vented
its rage on knights and serfs alike, was a daily warning that
God's power ruled equally over every man who abandoned
Him, be he knight or serf.

Thus many years of happiness and blessing passed, and the
valley was renowned above all others. The houses were
stately, their storerooms rich, their money chests well-filled.
Their cattle were the finest up hill and down dale, their
daughters were famous far and wide and their sons welcome
everywhere. And their fame did not wither overnight like

Jonas's gourd, but endured from generation to generation, for the sons remained God-fearing and respected of men from generation to generation.

But just as it is the best-watered and most vigorous pear tree that the worm gnaws and blasts, it also happens that when the stream of God's blessing pours most abundantly over men, the worm enters the blessing, making them proud and blind, so that in the midst of God's blessing they forget Him who bestowed it, and become like the Israelites who, when God had succored them, forsook Him for golden calves.

And so, after many generations had passed away, pride and vanity entered the valley, and foreign wives came too, increasing both. More and more splendid grew their clothes, jewels glittered, and the vainglory spread even to the holy things, for instead of raising their eyes to God in prayer, they let them rest proudly on the gold beads of their rosaries. Then God's divine service became a show of pride, while their hearts hardened toward God and men. None troubled to keep God's commandments, all mocked His service and His servants, for where there is great pride or great wealth, men soon come to believe that their appetites are their wisdom, which is higher than God's. They, who had been so sorely oppressed by the knights in olden times, turned hard and cruel toward their own servants, and as the knights had built before them, they built now, and as the knights had once plagued them, they now spared neither man nor beast once the building devil had entered into them. The change had come over this house too, while the old plenty remained.

Nearly two hundred years had passed since the Spider had been shut in its hole. A clever and valiant woman was master here. She was not from Lindau, as Christine had been, but in many ways she was like Christine. She too came from foreign parts and was much given to show and pride. She had an only son; her husband had died under her rule. This son was a fine lad, kindly and gentle to man and beast, and she loved him, though she would not show it. Every step he took was ruled by her, and nothing he did was right unless she had allowed it. Though he was long since a grown man, he could not be with the other young men, or as much as go to the fair unless his mother went with him. When at last she thought he was old enough she gave him a wife from among her own kin and after her own mind. So now he had two masters instead of one, and because both were proud as peacocks they meant Christen to be like them. When he was kind thoughtful for others, as was his true nature, he had to learn who was master.

The house had long been a thorn in their flesh. They were ashamed of it, for the neighbors, even though they were not so rich, had new houses. The memory of the Spider, and of what the grandmother had said, still lived in the minds of all, otherwise the old house would have been pulled down long before. But all the people forbade it. For their part, all the women could see in the ban on a new house was the envy that grudged it to them. Besides, they were growing uneasy in the old house. When they sat at this table, it was as if the cat were placidly purring behind their backs, or as if the hole had gently opened and the Spider were aiming at their necks. Theirs was not the spirit which had plugged the hole, and so their fear that the hole might open grew. Thus they found good reasons for building a new house where they would need to fear the Spider no longer; or so they thought. They decided to leave the old house to the servants, who so often stood in the way of their pride.

With a heavy heart, Christen consented. He remembered what the old grandmother had said; he believed that the family blessing was bound up with the family house, and his prayers were never so heartfelt as when he sat at the head of this table. He said what he thought, but his womenfolk bade him be silent, and because he was their slave he did so, but when he was alone he often wept bitterly.

Above the tree where we sat they planned to build a house such as nobody in the whole parish possessed.

In the impatience of their pride, because they knew nothing about building and could hardly wait to show off their new house, they drove men and beasts without mercy while the building was going on. They would not let them keep the holy feast days and even grudged them their sleep at night. And there was no neighbor whose help pleased them, and they wished them all ill when, having given their help freely, as men did even in those days, they went home to look after their own needs.

When the roof was on and the first peg was driven into the threshold, smoke poured from the hole as it does when damp straw is fired. Then the workmen shook their headsgravely and said, in secret and aloud, that the new house would never be old, but the women laughed and paid no heed to the sign. When at last the house was finished they settled in with unbelievable splendor, and for the house-warming they gave a feast which children and children's children still spoke of in the Emmental.

But the whole three days long there was heard all over the house a strange noise like a cat purring with pleasure when its stomach is stroked. But search as they might, no cat could be found in the house. Then many a one grew uneasy and in spite of the splendor ran away in the midst of the revelry. The women alone heard nothing or paid no heed. They thought their battle won with the new house.

Yes, the blind man cannot see the sun, and the deaf man cannot hear the thunder. Therefore the women rejoiced in the new house, grew prouder every day, never thought of the Spider, but led, in their new house, an idle life of gluttony and finery. No one was a match for them, and of God they thought not at all.

In the old house the servants remained by themselves, living as they pleased, and when Christen tried to take them in hand, the women would not have it and scolded him, the mother chiefly from pride, the wife from jealousy. And so there was an end to all decent living among them, and with that all fear of God vanished, as is always the way where there is no master. When no master sits at the head of the table, no master holds the reins inside the house and out, he who behaves worst counts himself the greatest, and he who speaks most evilly the best.

So it went on in the old house and the servants soon came to look like a troop of wild cats. They had forgotten how to pray, and so they had no respect for God's will or His gifts. As the pride of their mistresses lost all bounds, the bestial wantonness of the servants knew no restraint. They outraged the bread without fear, threw the porridge at each other's faces across the table, and even fouled the food to spoil each other's appetites. They teased the neighbors, tormented the animals, mocked at Holy Mass, denied all higher power, and plagued to the top of their bent the priest who had warned them of retribution to come. In short, they forgot all fear of God and man and grew worse every day. Man and maid vied with each other in evil living, yet they plagued each other whenever they could, and when the men could find no new way of tormenting the maids, one of them hit on the idea of cowing them with the Spider in its hole. He threw a spoonful of porridge and milk at the plug, crying that the prisoner must be hungry in there after all those centuries of fasting.

Then the maids set up a terrible screaming and promised him everything. Even the other men were afraid. But since the game was repeated with impunity, it soon palled, the maids stopped their screaming and the other men began in their turn. Then the first farm hand began to brandish his knife at the hole, declaring with most hideous oaths that he would take the plug out and see what was inside, for they must have something new to see for once. That was the signal for a fresh outburst, and the man who did it was the master of all and could get what he wanted, especially from the maids.

He was, indeed, a strange creature, people say, and no one knew where he came from. He could be as meek as a lamb and as savage as a wolf. When he was alone with a woman he was as meek as a lamb, but in front of the other men he was as savage as a wolf, as if he hated them all and only wanted to be their master in wickedness. And so, in front of the other men, the maids were terrified of him, but, people say, he was their favorite when they could get him alone. His eyes did not match, but no one really knew what color they were, and one eye hated the other and never looked the same way, though he managed to conceal it with his long hair and downcast looks. His hair curled beautifully, but no one knew whether it was red or golden. In the shade it was a perfect gold, but when the sun shone on it no squirrel ever had a redder coat. He ill-treated the beasts more than all the others, and they hated him accordingly. Each of the men believed he was his friend, but he only stirred up strife among them. He was the only one who could please the mistresses; he alone was often at the upper house. Then the maids misbehaved down below, and as soon as he noticed it, he would stick his knife into the plug and threaten till the maids cringed before him.

Yet they soon tired even of this game. The maids got used to it and said at last: "Do it if you dare, but you daren't."

Christmastide and the Holy Night were approaching. They had no thought for all that hallows it to us. They planned to make a merry night of it. In the castle there was only one old knight left, and he cared little for the things of this world. A rascally bailiff managed everything to his own profit. The servants had bargained with him for some fine Hungarian wine in exchange for some roguery or other, but they knew nothing of its strength and fire. A terrible storm broke out, with lightning and wind such as is seldom seen at that season. Not a dog would have been driven from the fireside that night. It was not the wild weather that kept them from church, but it was a good excuse for them to stay alone in the old house with the noble wine.

Christmas Eve began with cursing and dancing, with wicked and worse things, then they sat down to a meal. The maids had cooked meat, white pudding, and whatever other dainties they had managed to steal. More and more bestial grew their doings. All the food was outraged, every holy thing blasphemed. The strange farm hand mocked at the priest, distributed bread and wine as if presiding at Holy Mass, baptized the dog by the fire, and carried on till the others, wild as they were, were terrified. Then he stuck his knife into the plug and vowed he would show them far worse things.

When they would not be afraid because he had done the same thing so often, and the plug in any case resisted his knife, he snatched up an awl and, half raving, swore in most unholy fashion that they should see what he could do and pay for their laughter till the hair rose on their heads, and with a savage thrust he screwed the awl into the plug. Screaming shrilly the others rushed on him, but before they could stop him, he laughed like the Devil himself and gave a vigorous tug at the awl.

Then a huge clap of thunder struck the house to its foundations, the evildoer fell on his back, a red stream of flame burst out of the hole, and in the midst of it, huge, black, and bloated with the venom of centuries, sat the Spider, gloating balefully at the rabble who stood paralyzed with fear, unable to move a limb to escape from the hideous monster, which crawled with slow glee over their faces, stinging them to fiery death. Then the house shook with dreadful cries of pain such as a horde of a hundred starving wolves could not utter.

Soon a like scream was heard from the new house. Christen, who was just coming uphill from Mass, thought robbers had broken in and, trusting to his strong right arm, rushed to his family's help. He found no robbers, but death. His wife and mother were in their death throes, and no voice issued from their black and swollen faces. His children were sleeping peacefully, their bright faces flushed with health. A dreadful premonition came to Christen. He hurried down to the lower house; there he found all the servants lying dead, the parlor a death chamber, the grisly hole in the window post open, and in the hand of the hideously distorted man the awl with the dreadful plug on its point.

Then he knew what had happened. He raised his hands in horror and if the earth had opened and swallowed him up he would have been glad. Then something crawled out from behind the fireplace. He started away in fear, but it was not the Spider. It was a poor little boy he had taken in for God's sake and left among the savage servants. The child had taken no part in the servants' doings. He had fled in terror behind the stove, and he alone had been spared by the Spider and could tell the dreadful tale.

But even as he spoke, cries of fear from the other houses rang through wind and weather. In century-old glee the Spider sped through the valley, choosing first the finest houses, whose inmates thought least of God and most of worldly things, and were therefore least prepared to think of death.

Day had not yet dawned when the tidings were in every home. The Spider had broken out and was roaming through the parish, dealing death on its way. Many, it was told, lay dead already, and up the valley scream after scream was rising to Heaven from those already marked by death. No need to tell of the woe in the countryside, the dread in all hearts, or the kind of Christmas that was at Sumiswald. None could think of the joy it brings, and the affliction came from the evildoing of men. The calamity grew from day to day, for the Spider was bigger, swifter, and more deadly than before. Now it was at one end, now at the other, of the valley, and appeared in the valley and on the mountain tops at one and the same time. While before it had marked down one here, another there, for death, it seldom left a house now before poisoning all the inmates. Not until all were in their death agony would it settle on the threshold to gloat over its work, as if to say: Here I am, I have come back, however long I was a prisoner.

It seemed to know that its time was short, or perhaps it simply wished to save trouble. Wherever it could lay low many at a blow, it did so. For that reason it would lie in wait for the processions which carried the dead to church. Now here, now there, but most often at the foot of the church hill, it would suddenly appear in the midst of the company or sit on the coffin, glaring down on the men. Then a hideous cry rose from all, man by man they fell till the whole procession lay on the road in the throes of death, till no life was left in them and a heap of dead lay round the coffin as brave heroes lie round their banner when a greater power has struck them down.

Then the people ceased carrying the dead to church; none would carry and none go with them. The dead were left to lie where death had struck them down.

Despair filled the valley. Every heart was boiling with rage, and hideous curses were launched against poor Christen. He was to blame for it all.

Suddenly everyone knew that Christen should never have left the old house nor abandoned the servants. Suddenly it came home to them that the master is answerable for his servants, that he should keep watch over them at prayer and at table, should prevent them living a godless life, with godless speech and the outraging of God's gifts. All at once the people had enough of pride and vainglory. They banned them to the lowest parts of Hell and would hardly have believed God Himself if He had told them how shamelessly they had indulged in them but a few days before. Suddenly they were all devout again, wore their poorest clothes, took their old forgotten rosaries up again, and persuaded themselves they had always been devout, and if they could not make God believe it, it was not for want of trying.

Christen alone was the godless one among them, and on all hands curses as high as the hills were heaped on him. Yet he was perhaps the best of them all, but his will lay chained in the will of his womenfolk, and to be so bound is a grievous punishment for any man, nor can he escape his burden of responsibility for not being what God meant him to be. Christen's eyes were opened too; therefore he did not turn on the people and rend them, but took more guilt upon himself than was his by rights. But that did not pacify them, for now more than ever they screamed at each other how great his guilt must be, since he took so much upon himself and freely confessed his unworthiness.

Meanwhile Christen besought God day and night to avert

the evil, but it grew more grievous every day. It came home to him that he must atone for his sin, must be the sacrifice himself, must do the deed his ancestress had done before him. He prayed to God till his heart was fired with the resolve to save the valley, and his resolution was strengthened by the steadfast courage that never fails, but is always ready for the one deed, morning and evening.

Then, with his children, he moved down into the old house, cut a new plug for the hole, had it consecrated with holy water and sacred words, placed the hammer beside the plug. and sat down by his children's bedside to wait for the Spider.

There he sat, watching and praying, and with a good courage fought against sleep and did not falter. But the Spider did not come, though it was everywhere else, for death spread day by day and the rage of the survivors grew fiercer. In the midst of the terror, a woman was to bear a child. Then the old dread came over the people that the Spider would fetch the child unbaptized as the pledge of their ancient pact. The woman was beside herself. With no faith in God, she had all the more hatred and revenge in her heart.

They knew how their forefathers had warded off the Green Man long ago when a child was to be born, and that the priest was the shield they had set up between themselves and the eternal adversary. They resolved to send for the priest, but who was to be the messenger? The road was barred by the unburied dead whom the Spider had struck down on the funeral processions, and would any messenger who took the path over the wild heights be able to escape the Spider? At last the woman's husband said that if the Spider meant to have him it would get him at home as easily as on the way. If he was marked for death, he could escape it nowhere.

He set out, but hour after hour passed and no messenger returned. As the hour of birth approached, the woman's rage and lamentation mounted. In the frenzy of despair she tore herself from her bed and rushed to the house of Christen, the thousandfold accursed, who sat beside his children, praying and waiting for the Spider. From far off her cries were heard,

her curses thundered at Christen's door long before she flung
it open. When she came rushing in with her terrible face, he
started up, not knowing at first whether it was Christine herself. But in the doorway pain checked the woman's onrush,
she writhed against the doorpost, pouring her curses over
poor Christen. If he was not to be accursed by children and
children's children, let him be the messenger. Then pain overcame her, and on Christen's threshold she bore a son. All who
had followed her scattered far and wide, dreading the final
horror.

Christen stood with the innocent child in his arms. In her
riven face the woman's eyes glared piercing, wild and venomous, till he seemed to see the Spider itself crawling out of
them.

Then God gave him strength, and a more than human will
was born in him. Casting a look of love at his children, he
wrapped the newborn child in his warm cloak, sprang over
the glaring woman, and ran down the hill and along the
valley to Sumiswald. It was he himself who would carry the
child to the holy sacrament as an atonement for the guilt
that was upon him, the head of his house. The rest he committed to God. The dead lay in his path. He had to place his
feet with care. Then a light footstep caught up with him; it
was the poor little boy who had feared the wild woman and
had followed his master with childish trust. Christen's heart
was wrung by the thought that his children were alone with
the frantic woman, but his foot stayed not and he hastened
on to his holy goal.

He had already reached the foot of the church hill, and the
chapel was in sight, when suddenly fire barred his way, a red
feather waved in the bushes, and the Spider sat before him,
rearing high to leap.

Then Christen called upon the Holy Trinity with a loud
voice, and a savage cry echoed from the bushes. The red
feather vanished, Christen laid the child in the boy's arms
and, commending his spirit to the Lord, laid hold of the
Spider with a strong hand, for it had sat motionless as if

spellbound by the holy words. Fire streamed through his bones but he held fast, the way was open, and understanding was given to the little boy, who hurried on to the priest with the child.

But Christen, fire in his strong hand, ran home as if on wings. The fire in his hand was agony, the blood seemed to freeze in his veins and his breath to stop, but he prayed unceasingly with God steadfastly before him, and so the pains of Hell could not overcome him.

His house came in sight, his hope grew with his pain, the woman stood in the doorway. When she saw him coming without her child, she rushed on him like a tigress robbed of her young, believing in a most shameful treachery. She paid no heed to his signals, was deaf to the words which came from his panting breast, fell into his outstretched hands and clung to him. In the fear of death he had to drag the raving woman into the house and struggle himself free before he could push the Spider into the hole and hammer it in with his dying hands.

With God's help it was done. His dying eyes rested on his children; they were smiling sweetly in their sleep. Then a lightness entered into him, a higher hand seemed to quench his fire, and praying aloud he closed his eyes in death. Those who came creeping anxiously to see what had happened to the woman saw peace and joy in his face. Amazed, they saw the hole plugged, but the woman lay singed and distorted in death. She had taken the fiery death from Christen's hand.

The people were still standing, not knowing what had happened, when the little boy returned with the child and the priest, who had quickly baptized it according to the custom of those times. He was ready, well armed and of a good courage, to plunge into the very battle in which the priest of old had won victory with his life. But God required no such sacrifice of him. Another had already won the battle.

It was a long time before the people grasped the great deed that Christen had done. When at last belief and understanding came to them, they prayed joyfully with the priest, thanked God for the life He had restored to them and for the strength He had bestowed on Christen. But to the dead Christen they prayed for forgiveness for the wrong they had done him, and resolved to bury him with great honor, and his memory was enshrined in their hearts as gloriously as that of any saint.

When the hideous terror which had never ceased to quiver through their limbs suddenly vanished, and they could look up to the blue sky with joy, not fearing that the Spider was crawling over their feet, they could hardly believe their senses. They resolved to have many masses said and to make a general procession to church. First of all they wished to bury the two bodies, those of Christen and his savage besieger; then they would bury the other dead, as far as room could be found.

It was a solemn day when the whole valley moved to church; there was a solemn feeling in many a heart, many a sin was confessed and many a vow made, and from that day on there was little vainglory to be seen in faces or clothing.

When, in church and the graveyard, many tears had been shed, many prayers offered up, all those who had come to the burying—and all who could move their limbs had come—went to the inn for the funeral meal. According to custom, the women and children sat apart at one table, but all the grown men found room at the famous round table that can still be seen at the Bear Inn at Sumiswald. It was kept there to remind people that once there were only two score men where now nearly two thousand live, and as a warning that even the lives of two thousand are in the hands of Him who had saved two score. They did not linger long over that meal. Their hearts were too full for meat or drink. When they came out of the village onto the open height, they saw a glow in the sky, and when they reached home they found the new house burned to the ground. How it happened they never knew.

But the people never forgot what Christen had done for them and paid their debt to his children. They were brought up in piety and strength in the most devout homes. No hand touched what was theirs, and though no account of it was ever seen, it was well tended and multiplied, and when the children grew up, not only were they not cheated of their possessions, they were not cheated of their souls. They became godly and righteous men, who found favor with God and good will among men, who were blessed in this life and still more blessed in Heaven. And so it remained in the family, and no man feared the Spider because all feared God, and as it was then, so may it remain, if God will, as long as a house stands here, as long as children follow in the ways and thoughts of their forefathers.

There the grandfather stopped, and for a long time all were silent, some thinking over the story, others waiting for him to go on.

At last the elder godfather spoke:

"I've sat at that round table many a time myself, and I've heard of the dying and how after it there was room at the table for all the grown men in the village. But how exactly everything came about nobody could tell me. Some guessed this and some that. Now tell us how you came to know all about it."

"Ah!" said the grandfather. "It was handed down among us from father to son, and when the memory of it faded among the people in the valley, the family kept it secret and would not let it be known. Only the family spoke of it, so that no member of it should forget what builds a house and what destroys a house, what brings a blessing and what drives it away. You heard how unwilling our old grandmother was to hear it spoken of. But to my mind, the more time passes, the more it should be spoken of, so that men may know where pride and vanity can lead them. That's why I won't keep it all a secret, and it's not the first time I've told the story to friends. I always think that what has preserved the fortunes of my family for so many years will bring no harm to anybody, and it's not right to make a secret of what we can call ours by good luck and God's blessing."

"You're right there, Cousin," answered the godfather. "But there's one more question. Was the house you pulled down seven years ago the old one?"

"Nay," said the grandfather. "The house was nearly falling down three hundred years ago, and God's gifts from field and pasture could long since find no room in it. Yet the family did not want to leave it, and they dared not build a new one. They could not forget what had happened to that other new one so long ago. And so they were hard put to it, and at last turned for counsel to a wise man. He answered, so they say, that they might well build a new house in the same place as the old one, but nowhere else, and two things they must keep, the old window post where the Spider lived and the old spirit which had thrust the Spider into the old wood. Then the blessing would again rest on the house.

"They built the new house, and with care and prayer built the old window post into it, and the Spider did not stir, and the old spirit and the blessing did not forsake them.

"But even the new house grew old and cramped, and its wood was devoured of worms and rotten. Only the window post stayed firm and hard as iron. My father ought to have built. He put it off, then my turn came. I thought a long time, then I ventured. As my fathers had done before me, I built the old wood into the new house, and the Spider did not stir. But I will confess, never in my life have I prayed as I prayed when I held that dreadful post in my hands. My whole body was on fire, and I couldn't help looking to see if there were any black spots coming out on my hands or anywhere else on me, and a load fell from my heart when at last everything was in its place. And I was strengthened in my faith that neither I nor my children and children's children had anything to fear from the Spider as long as we feared God."

Then the grandfather was silent, but they still felt the shudder that had crept up their backs when they heard that he had held the post in his hands, and they wondered what they would feel if they had to take it in theirs.

Then the cousin spoke:

"It's only a pity that nobody knows how much truth there is in such things. You can't believe the whole story, and all the same there must be something in it or else the old post wouldn't still be there."

"However that may be, there's still plenty to learn from it," said the younger godfather, and went on that time had passed so quickly, it seemed as if they had only just come out of church.

But the grandmother said they shouldn't talk too much or her old man would be beginning another story. They should eat and drink now; nobody would eat and drink, it was a disgrace. It must all be uneatable, though they had done what they could, as far as in them lay.

So then they fell to, there was a great eating and drinking and many a wise remark was passed, till the moon stood high and golden in the sky, and the stars issued from their majestic chambers to warn men it was time for them to seek their humble ones.

The company saw the mysterious warners, but they sat so contentedly together, and the hearts of all beat so strangely in their breasts at the thought of going home, that though nobody said so, nobody wanted to be the first to go.

At last the godmother stood up and made herself ready to go with trembling hands, but there was no lack of doughty protectors to go with her, and the whole company left the hospitable house with many thanks and good wishes, though the family pressed them hard to stay—it wasn't dark yet.

Soon the house lay still, and inside too was silence. Peacefully it stood there, shining pure and beautiful down the valley in the moonlight. With care and tenderness it guarded good people in quiet sleep, as those sleep who carry the fear of God and an untroubled conscience in their hearts, and will never be awakened from sleep by the Black Spider, but only by the kindly sun. But what power is the Spider's if their spirit should change is known only to Him who knows all, and bestows on all His power, on spiders as on men.

ANNETTE VON DROSTE-HULSHOFF

THE JEWS' BEECH TREE

A Picture of Manners from Mountainous Westphalia

Translated by Michael Bullock

◆
◆

Where is the hand so soft that undeterred
It can sort out the troubled mind's confusion,
So firm that without trembling it can hurl
The stone at some poor wretched wasted life?
Who dares to judge the urge of boastful blood,
To weigh each word that unforgotten
Put out in some young breast tenacious roots
Of secret, soul-destroying prejudice?
You, happy reader, born and raised secure
Amid the light, by pious parents tended,
Put by the scales to which you have no right!
Put down the stone—your own head it will strike!

Friedrich Mergel, born in 1738, was the only son of a so-called
sharecropper or minor landowner in the village of B, which,
badly built and smoky though it was, nevertheless caught
every traveler's eye by the picturesque beauty of its situation
in the green-wooded ravine of an important and historically
noteworthy mountain range. The district to which it belonged
was at that time one of those out-of-the-way corners with
no factories or trade, no military roads, where a strange face
still attracted attention, and a journey of thirty miles made
even the more prosperous individual the Ulysses of his region.
In short, it was one of those spots of which there were so
many in Germany at one time, with all the shortcomings
and virtues, all the originality and narrow-mindedness that
flourish in such circumstances. Under extremely simple and
frequently inadequate laws, the inhabitants' ideas of right
and wrong had become somewhat confused; or rather, along-
side legal justice a second justice had grown up, a justice of
public opinion, and custom, of a law of prescription established by neglect. The landowners, who dispensed justice at

the lower levels, punished and rewarded as they saw fit—in most cases honestly. The underling did what seemed to him practicable and acceptable to a rather permissive conscience. Only those who had lost their suit occasionally thought of leafing through dusty old documents.

It is difficult to view those times with an unprejudiced eye. Since their disappearance they have either been arrogantly censured or foolishly praised, as those who lived through them are blinded by too many fond memories, while those born later do not understand them. This much may, however, be asserted: the outward form was weaker, the inner kernel firmer, lawbreaking was more frequent, lack of conscience rarer. For he who acts according to his convictions, no matter how faulty they may be, can never go entirely to the dogs, whereas nothing is more soul-destroying than to invoke the letter of the law against one's own inner sense of right and wrong.

A particular human species, more restless and more enterprising than all its neighbors, made everything stand out more blatantly in the little state of which we are speaking than anywhere else under the same circumstances. Thefts of timber and the poaching of game were the order of the day, and after the frequent fights everyone had to console himself for his own bruised pate. Nevertheless, since extensive and profitable forests were the region's main source of wealth, a sharp watch was kept over the woodlands; but they were protected not so much by legal means as by ever renewed attempts to overcome force and cunning by the same weapons.

The village of B was considered the most arrogant, the craftiest, and boldest community in the whole principality. Its situation in the proud solitude of the surrounding forest may have nourished the inborn stubbornness of its inhabitants from early times. The proximity of a river that flowed into the sea and carried vessels large enough to bear shipbuilding timber out of the country did much to incite the natural audacity of the timber thieves, and the fact that the whole area was seething with foresters only served as an added incentive, since in the frequent skirmishes the peasants usually came off best. Thirty or forty carts would drive out together into the beautiful moonlit night, manned by about double that number of individuals of all ages, from half-grown boys to the seventy-year-old chief magistrate, who, as an experienced bellwether, led the column with the same proud self-confidence as he took his seat in the law court. Those left behind listened unperturbed as the creaking and bumping of the cartwheels died away in the gorges, and went peacefully back to sleep. An occasional shot or a low cry may have caused a young wife or sweetheart to sit up with a start; no one else took any notice. At first light the column would return as silently as it had left, the faces of the men glowing like bronze, and here and there a bandaged head, to which no one paid any attention; while a few hours later the whole region was full of the misfortune of one or more foresters who had been carried out of the forest, battered and bruised, blinded with snuff and for a time incapable of carrying on with their job.

In these surroundings Friedrich Mergel was born, in a house which, by the proud addition of a chimney and tiny windowpanes, bore witness to the ambitions of its builder, just as its present state of dilapidation proclaimed the wretched circumstances of its current owner. The earlier railing around the yard and garden had been replaced by a neglected fence; the roof leaked; someone else's cattle were grazing in the pastures; someone else's corn was growing in the field beside the yard; and the garden, apart from a few woody rose trees from better days, contained more weeds than flowers. Naturally, misfortune had done much to bring about this state of affairs; but muddle and bad management had played their part. In his bachelor days Friedrich's father, old Hermann Mergel, had been a so-called moderate drinker, that is to say, one who lay in the gutter only on Sundays and feast days and the rest of the week was as well-behaved as anyone else. Thus no obstacles were put in the way of his courtship of a very pretty and well-to-do girl. There was great merrymaking at the wedding. Mergel was not too terribly drunk, and the bride's parents went home content. But next Sunday the young woman ran through the village to her parents screaming and covered in blood, abandoning all her good clothes and household utensils. Naturally this caused a scandal and was a great vexation to Mergel, who needed consolation. Thus by the afternoon not one windowpane in his house remained unbroken and he could be seen till late that night lying on his doorstep, bringing the broken neck of a bottle to his mouth from time to time, cutting his face and hands horribly. The young woman remained with her parents, where she soon pined away and died. Whether or not Mergel was tormented by remorse or shame, he seemed to have an ever greater need of his consolation and soon began to be numbered among the totally depraved.

The farm went to rack and ruin; maids from outside brought trouble and loss; years passed. Mergel was and remained a helpless and, in the end, rather pitiful widower, until he suddenly appeared once more in the role of bridegroom. If this was unexpected in itself, the personality of his bride increased everyone's surprise still more. Margreth Semmler was a worthy, respectable person in her forties, who had been a village beauty in her youth and was still considered very intelligent and thrifty and was not without means. Hence no one could understand what had prompted her to take this step. We believe that the reason may be sought precisely in her self-confident maturity. On the eve of her wedding she is reputed to have said: "A woman who is badly treated by her husband is either stupid or useless. If things go badly with me, you can say it's my fault." Subsequent events unfortunately prove that she overestimated her strength. To begin with, she intimidated her husband. When he had had one too many, he either did not come home or crawled into the barn. But the yoke was too heavy to be borne for long, and soon he could be seen often enough staggering across the street into the house, from which his brutal shouting echoed until Margreth hurriedly closed the doors and windows. On one such day—no longer a Sunday—she was seen to rush out of the house in the evening, without bonnet or scarf, her hair hanging in disorder, throw herself down beside a herb bed in the garden and grub in the earth with her hands, then look fearfully over her shoulder, quickly break off a bunch of herbs and walk slowly back toward the house; she did not enter it, however, but went into the barn. People said that on this day Mergel first struck her, although this admission never crossed her lips.

The second year of this unhappy marriage saw the birth of a child—we cannot say was blessed with a child, since Margreth is reported to have wept bitterly when the baby was presented to her. Nevertheless, although he had been carried under a heart filled with grief, Friedrich was a healthy, pretty child who flourished mightily in the fresh air. His father was very fond of him and never came home without bringing him a roll of the finest white bread or something of the sort. People even said that since the birth of the boy he had started to behave better; in any case, there was less noise in the house.

Friedrich was in his ninth year. It was around the time of the feast of the three Magi, a harsh, stormy winter's night. Hermann had gone to a wedding, leaving early, because the bride's house was three-quarters of a mile away. Although he had promised to return in the evening, Frau Mergel did not count on this, the less so since at sunset a heavy snowstorm had begun. Around ten she scraped the ashes together in the hearth and prepared for bed. Friedrich was standing beside her, already half undressed, listening to the howling of the wind and the rattling of the downstairs windows.

"Mother, isn't Father coming back today?" he asked.

"No, child, tomorrow."

"Why not, Mother? He promised to."

"Oh God, if he did everything he promised. Hurry up and get undressed."

They had barely got into bed when a gust of wind shook

the house as though about to carry it away. The bedstead trembled and there was a rattling in the chimney like a goblin.

"Mother, someone's knocking at the door."

"Quiet, Fritzchen. That's the loose plank in the gable being shaken by the wind."

"No, Mother, it's at the door."

"It doesn't shut. The latch is broken. Heavens, do go to sleep. Don't prevent me from getting my wretched little bit of a night's sleep."

"But suppose Father comes?"

The mother turned violently over in bed. "The Devil is holding him tight enough."

"Where is the Devil, Mother."

"Just wait, you fidget. He's at the door and will take you away with him if you don't keep quiet."

Friedrich stopped talking. He listened for a little while longer, then fell asleep. A few hours later he woke up. The wind had turned and was now hissing like a snake through the frame of the closed window by his ear. His shoulder was stiff. He crept further under the feather bed and lay quite still out of fear. After a while he noticed that his mother was not asleep either. He heard her crying, and every now and then: "Hail Mary," and "Pray for us poor sinners." The beads of the rosary slid past his face. He uttered an involuntary sigh.

"Friedrich, are you awake?"

"Yes, Mother."

"Child, pray a little—you know half the Lord's Prayer— pray to God to preserve us from fire and flood."

Friedrich thought about the Devil and wondered what he looked like. He was amazed by all the various noises in the house. He thought there must be something alive inside, and outside too.

"Listen, Mother. I'm sure someone is knocking."

"No, child, there's no one. But there isn't a single old plank in this house that doesn't rattle."

"Listen. Don't you hear? Someone's shouting. Listen."

His mother sat up. The roaring of the storm subsided for a moment. Someone could be clearly heard knocking at the shutter and several voices cried: "Margreth. Frau Margreth, hey there, open up."

Margreth groaned loudly. "They've brought the pig back home again."

The rosary flew onto the wooden chair with a clatter. She seized her clothes and went to the fireplace. Soon afterward Friedrich heard her walking with sullen steps across the threshing floor. Margreth did not return; but from the kitchen came much murmuring and the sound of unknown voices. Twice an unknown man came into the bedroom and seemed to be anxiously looking for something. Suddenly a lamp was brought in. Two men led in Friedrich's mother. She was as white as chalk and her eyes were closed. Friedrich thought she was dead and let out a frightful yell. Someone boxed his ears, which silenced him, and now he learned bit by bit from the conversation of the bystanders that his mother's brother, Franz Semmler, and a man named Hülsmeyer had found his father dead in the forest and he was now lying in the kitchen.

As soon as Margreth had recovered her senses, she tried to get rid of the strangers. Her brother stayed with her, and during the rest of the night Friedrich, who had been told to remain in bed on pain of severe punishment, heard the fire crackling in the kitchen and a sound like furniture being pushed to and fro and things being brushed. There was little talking and then in low voices, but from time to time Friedrich heard sighs that cut him to the quick, young though he was. Once he made out the words as his uncle said: "Margreth, don't take it to heart. We will each have three Masses said and at Easter we'll make a pilgrimage together to Our Lady of Werl."

When, three days later, the body was taken away, Margreth sat by the fireplace, her face hidden in her apron. After a few minutes, when everything was quiet, she said to herself: "Ten years, ten crosses. But we bore them together and now I'm alone." Then out loud: "Fritzchen, come here."

Friedrich came slowly over. His mother looked uncanny to him with the black ribbons and her distracted expression. "Fritzchen," she said, "are you going to be a good boy now and bring me joy, or are you going to be bad and tell lies, or drink and steal?"

"Mother, Hülsmeyer steals."

"Hülsmeyer? God preserve us! Do you want a thrashing? Who told you such a dreadful thing?"

"The other day he beat Aaron up and stole six groschen from him."

"If he took money from Aaron, the damned Jew must have cheated him out of it in the first place. Hülsmeyer is a respectable, well-established man, and Jews are all rascals."

"But, Mother, Brandis also says he steals wood and deer."

Margreth remained silent for a while. Then she said: "Child, Brandis is a forester."

"Mother, do foresters tell lies?"

"Listen, Fritz. God makes wood grow freely and game wanders from one gentleman's estate to another. They can't belong to anyone. But you don't understand all that yet. Go and fetch me some brushwood from the barn."

Friedrich had seen his father lying in the straw, drunk and looking terrible. But he never talked about this and seemed not to want to think about it. The memory of his father had left behind a feeling of tenderness mixed with horror—nothing takes greater hold on us than the love and care of a being who seems callous toward everyone else, and in Friedrich's case this feeling grew with the years, intensified by the frequent rejections he suffered at the hands of others. He was extremely sensitive as a child to unflattering comments on the dead man; and the neighbors' tact did nothing to spare him such grief. It was usual in that region to deny peace to the dead. Old Mergel had become the ghost of the Breder Wood. As a will-o'-the-wisp he led a drunken man by his hair into the pond; the herd boys, when they cowered around their fires at night and the owls were screeching in the valleys, from time to time clearly heard him repeating in broken tones: "Just listen to me, fine Lieseken"; and an "unlicensed woodcutter," who had fallen asleep under the broad oak and been overtaken by night, woke to see his blue, swollen face peering through the branches. Friedrich was forced to listen to a lot of this from the other boys. Then he would howl and strike out. Once he stabbed one of them with his little knife and received a dreadful beating as a result. After this he drove his mother's cows off to the other end of the valley, where he could often be seen all alone lying for hours in the same position in the grass tearing up thyme from the earth.

He was twelve years old when his mother received a visit from her younger brother, who lived in Brede and since his sister's foolish marriage had not crossed her threshold. Simon Semmler was a small, restless, skinny man with protruding fish's eyes and a face altogether like a pike, a weird fellow in whom boastful reserve alternated with an equally contrived ingenuousness; a man who posed as an enlightened mind, but was actually considered by everyone an objectionable fellow always on the lookout for a business deal profitable to himself. As he advanced in years people became increasingly anxious to have nothing to do with him—like all those with a restricted mentality his demands grew as his usefulness diminished. Nevertheless poor Margreth, who now had no other living relatives, was glad to see him.

"Simon, is that you?" she said, trembling so that she had to hold onto a chair. "Have you come to see how things are going with me and my ragamuffin boy?"

Simon looked at her seriously and shook her hand. "You have grown old, Margreth."

Margreth sighed. "Things have gone badly at times with all that has happened."

"Yes, girl, late to marry, bound to be sorry. Now you're old and the child is still young. There's a time for everything. But when an old house burns there's no putting out the fire."

A flame as red as blood passed across Margreth's careworn face.

"But I hear your lad is sharp and smart," Simon continued.

"Oh, pretty fairly, and pious with it."

"H'm, pious is as pious does. But he is quiet and thoughtful, isn't he? He doesn't run around with the other lads?"

"He's a solitary child," said Margreth, as though to herself. "That isn't good."

Simon laughed loudly. "Your boy is shy because the others have beaten him up a few times. He'll pay those fellows back for it one day. Hülsmeyer came to see me the other day; he says the boy is like a young deer."

What mother's heart does not grow warm when she hears her child praised? Poor Margreth rarely had that pleasure. Everyone called her son spiteful and withdrawn. Tears came to her eyes. "Yes, thank God, he has straight limbs."

"What does he look like?" continued Simon.

"There's a great deal of you about him, Simon, a great deal."

Simon laughed. "He must be a fine fellow then. I get better looking every day. I don't suppose he's too keen on school. You send him out to herd the cows? That's just as good. So there's not much truth in what the schoolmaster says. But where does he herd them? In the Telgen valley? In the Roder Wood? In the Teutoburg Forest? Even at night and in the early morning?"

"Right through the night. But what do you mean?"

Simon seemed not to have heard the question. He turned his head toward the door. "Hey, here he comes. Like father like son. He swings his arms just like your late husband used to. And just look, he really does have my fair hair."

A secret, proud smile crept over the mother's features. Her Friedrich's fair curls and Simon's red bristles! Without answering, she broke a branch from the nearby hedge and went to meet her son; ostensibly to drive along a lazy cow, but really to whisper a few quick, half threatening words to him. For she knew his obstinate nature, and Simon's manner intimidated her more than ever today. But everything went unexpectedly well. Friedrich was neither sulky, nor impertinent, perhaps a trifle timid and very anxious to please his uncle. So it came about that after half an hour of conversation Simon proposed an arrangement resembling adoption, according to which he would not remove the boy entirely from his mother but would have the main claim on his time. In return for this Friedrich would inherit the old bachelor's property, which, of course, was bound to come to him in any case. Margreth patiently allowed Simon to explain to her how great were the advantages of this arrangement and how small the sacrifice on her part. She knew best the sacrifice an ailing widow was making in giving up the help of a twelve-year-old boy whom she had already accustomed to taking the place of a daughter. But she kept silent and agreed to everything. Only she stringently enjoined her brother not to treat the boy harshly.

"He's a good boy," she said, "but I'm all on my own. He is not like a child that has had a father's discipline."

Simon nodded slyly. "Just let me do it my way, we'll get along fine, and you know something? Let me take the lad along right away; I have a couple of sacks to fetch from the mill; the smaller one will be just right for him; that way he will learn to give me a hand. Come on, Fritzchen, put your wooden shoes on."

Soon Margreth watched the two of them walking away, Simon in front cutting through the air with his face, the tails of his red coat trailing behind him like flames of fire. He looked rather like a fiery man doing penance under a stolen sack. Friedrich was following behind him, fine and slender for his age, with delicate, almost noble features and long, fair curls that were better looked after than the rest of his outward appearance would have led one to expect; apart from this he appeared ragged, neglected, and with a certain rough melancholy in his expression. Nevertheless, a great family likeness between the two of them was unmistakable. As Friedrich followed slowly in the footsteps of his guide, his gaze firmly attached to this man who attracted him precisely by his strange appearance, he inescapably called to mind someone looking aghast at his future revealed in a magic mirror.

Now the two of them were approaching the part of the Teutoburg Forest where the Breder Wood runs down the mountainside and fills a very dark ravine. Up to now they had spoken little. Simon seemed thoughtful, the boy abstracted, and both of them were panting under their sacks. Suddenly Simon asked: "Do you like brandy?"

The boy did not answer. "I asked you if you like brandy? Does your mother give you some sometimes?"

"My mother doesn't have any herself," said Friedrich.

"Aha, so much the better. Do you know this wood in front of us?"

"That's the Breder Wood."

"Do you know what happened there?"

Friedrich remained silent. Meanwhile they were coming closer and closer to the gloomy ravine.

"Does your mother still pray so much?" Simon started off again.

"Yes, two rosaries every evening."

"So? And do you pray with her?"

The boy laughed half in embarrassment and with a crafty side glance. "My mother tells her beads for the first time in the dusk before supper, then I'm usually not back with the cows yet, and for the second time in bed, then I usually fall asleep."

"So that's how it is!"

These last words were spoken under the umbrella of a wide beech tree that arched over the entrance to the ravine. It was now quite dark. The first quarter of the moon hung in the sky, but its faint gleam only served to give a strange appearance to the objects that it occasionally fell upon through a gap in the branches. Friedrich kept close behind his uncle. He was breathing fast, and anyone who could have made out his features would have perceived the expression of a tremendous tension which, however, sprang more from stimulated imagination than fear. The two of them strode vigorously forward, Simon with the firm step of the hardened wanderer, Friedrich swaying and as though in a dream. It seemed to him as though everything were moving and the trees in the single rays of the moon swaying now together, now apart. Tree roots and slippery patches, where water had gathered on the path, made his steps uncertain. Several times he almost fell. Then the darkness seemed to be broken a little way ahead, and soon the two of them stepped out into a fairly large clearing. The moon shone into it clearly, revealing that not long before the ax had ravaged it pitilessly. Everywhere the stumps of trees rose up, some of them several feet above the ground, to the point where it had been easiest to cut them in haste. The illegal work must have been unexpectedly interrupted, for a beech lay right across the path, its foliage intact, its branches rising high into the air and its still fresh leaves whispering in the nightwind. Simon stopped for a moment and looked attentively at the felled tree. In the center of the clearing stood an old oak, wider than it was high. A pale moonbeam falling on its trunk through the branches revealed that it was hollow, which had probably saved it from the general destruction. Here Simon suddenly grasped the boy's arm.

"Friedrich, do you know that tree? That's the Broad Oak."

Friedrich started and clung with his cold hands to his uncle.

"Look," went on Simon, "this is where Uncle Franz and Hülsmeyer found your father after he had gone to the Devil in a drunken state and without penance and extreme unction."

"Uncle, Uncle," sobbed Friedrich.

"What's the matter with you? You're not scared, surely? Damn you, boy, you're pinching my arm! Let go, let go!" He tried to shake the boy off. "Anyhow, your father was a good fellow. God won't be too hard on him. I loved him like my own brother."

Friedrich let go of his uncle's arm. The two of them walked the rest of the way through the wood in silence and the village of Brede stood before them, with its mud cottages and the few better dwellings of brick, of which Simon's house was one.

The following evening Margreth had been sitting with her distaff outside the door for an hour waiting for her son. It had been the first night she had spent without hearing her child's breathing beside her, and still Friedrich did not come. She was angry and anxious and knew that both feelings were groundless. The clock in the tower struck seven, the cattle returned home. He was still not there, and she had to get up and look after the cows. When she came back into the dark kitchen, Friedrich was standing by the fireplace. He was bending forward warming his hands at the coals. The firelight was playing on his features, giving them a repulsive look of emaciation and frightened twitching. Margreth stood still in the doorway, so strangely altered did her son look to her.

"Friedrich, how is your uncle?"

The boy muttered a few unintelligible words and huddled up against the fire wall.

"Friedrich, have you forgotten how to talk? Open your mouth, boy. You know I can't hear well with my right ear."

The child raised his voice and began to stammer so badly that Margreth could understand him no better than before.

"What did you say? Greetings from Master Semmler? He's gone again? Where to? The cows are already in the barn. Damn boy, I can't understand you. Wait, I must see if you have a tongue in your mouth."

She took a vigorous step forward. The child looked up at her with the miserable expression of a poor, half-grown dog learning to stand guard, and in his fear began to stamp his feet and rub his back up against the fire wall.

Margreth stood still. She looked at him, frightened. The boy seemed to her shriveled; his clothes were not the same either; no, that was not her child, and yet . . . "Friedrich, Friedrich," she called.

A closet door banged shut in the bedroom and Friedrich emerged, carrying in one hand a so-called sabot-violin, that is to say, an old wooden shoe strung with three or four wornout violin strings, in the other a bow entirely worthy of the instrument. He went up to his stunted mirror image with a demeanor of conscious dignity and independence which, at this moment, made the difference between the two boys, in other respects strikingly similar, stand out clearly.

"Here, Johannes," he said, handing him the work of art with the air of a Maecenas. "Here's the violin I promised you. My playing days are over; now I have to earn money."

Johannes cast another shy glance at Margreth, then slowly stretched out his hand until he had a firm grip on the proffered object and slipped it furtively under the wing of his wretched jacket.

Margreth stood quite still and let the children go on with what they were doing. Her thoughts had taken a different, very serious direction and she looked with disquieted eyes from one to the other. The strange boy had bent over the coals again with an expression of momentary comfort bordering on idiocy, while about Friedrich's features there played a sympathetic expression that was more self-satisfied than truly benevolent, and for the first time the look in his eyes revealed with almost glassy clarity that unrestrained ambition and tendency to ostentation which was to appear later as the chief motive for all his actions. His mother's call had disturbed him from thoughts that were as new to him as they were pleasant. She sat down again at the spinning wheel.

"Friedrich," she said hesitantly, "tell me . . ." and then fell silent. Friedrich looked up and then, hearing no more, turned back to his protégé.

"No, listen . . ." and then, in a low voice: "Who is that boy? What is his name?"

Friedrich answered in an equally low voice: "That's Uncle Simon's swineherd. He has a message for Hülsmeyer. Uncle gave me a pair of shoes and a drill waistcoat. The boy carried them for me on our way here and I promised him a violin as a reward. He's just a poor child; his name is Johannes."

"Well?" said Margreth.

"What is it, Mother?"

"What's his other name?"

"He hasn't got one, no, wait a minute, it's Nobody, Johannes Nobody. He has no father," he added in an undertone.

Margreth rose and went into the kitchen. After a while she came out with a hard, somber expression. "Listen, Friedrich," she said, "let the boy go and run his errand. Boy, what are you lying around in the ashes for? Haven't you anything to do at home?"

The boy jumped up so quickly, like a startled fugitive, that he fell over himself and the sabot violin very nearly fell in the fire.

"Wait, Johannes," said Friedrich proudly. "I'll give you half my bread and butter. It's too big for me anyway; Mother always cuts up the whole loaf."

"Let him be," said Margreth. "He's going home."

"Yes, but he won't get anything now. Uncle Simon eats at seven."

Margreth turned to the boy. "Won't they keep something for you? Speak, who looks after you?"

"Nobody," stammered the child.

"Nobody?" she repeated. "Then take it, take it," she added vehemently. "You're called Nobody and nobody looks after you. That cries out to heaven. Now go! Friedrich, don't go with him, do you hear, don't walk together through the village."

"I just want to fetch some wood from the shed," answered Friedrich.

When the two boys had gone, Margreth dropped onto a chair and clapped her hands together with an expression of the deepest grief. Her face was as white as a sheet. "A false oath, a false oath!" she groaned. "Simon, Simon, how will you answer before God?"

She sat like this for a while, rigid with pursed lips, as though her mind were elsewhere entirely. Friedrich stood before her and had already spoken to her twice.

"What is it? What do you want?" she cried, starting up.

"I've brought you money," he said, more surprised than frightened.

"Money? Where?" She straightened up and the small coins fell tinkling to the ground. Friedrich picked them up.

"Money from Uncle Simon, because I helped him with the work. I can earn money myself now."

"Money from Simon? Throw it away, throw it away! No, give it to the poor. No, no, keep it," she whispered almost inaudibly. "We're poor ourselves. Who knows if we shall manage without having to beg."

"I'm to go back to Uncle on Monday and help him with the sowing."

"Go back to him? No, no, never again!" She threw her arms around her child. "Yes," she added, and a flood of tears suddenly poured down over her hollow cheeks, "go, he's my only brother and the calumny is great! But keep God before your eyes and don't forget your daily prayers."

Margreth laid her face against the wall and wept loudly. She had borne many a heavy load, her husband's maltreatment and his even harsher death, and it was a bitter hour when the widow had to hand over the last piece of arable land for the use of a creditor and the plow stood still outside the house. But she had never felt like this. Nevertheless, after she had wept all night, she came around to thinking her brother Simon could not be so godless, the boy surely wasn't his, likeness proved nothing. Forty years ago she herself had lost a little sister who looked exactly like the foreign peddler. What will people not believe, when they have so little and by not believing would lose the little they have!

From this time on, Friedrich rarely came home. Simon seemed to have directed all the warm feelings of which he was capable toward his sister's son. At least he missed him a great deal and kept sending messages when some domestic business kept him with his mother for a time. Meanwhile the boy was as though transformed; his dreamy ways had vanished completely; he bore himself confidently and began to pay heed to his outward appearance, soon gaining the reputation of a good-looking, adroit lad. His uncle, who could not live without projects, occasionally undertook rather important public works, for example road-building, in which Friedrich was considered one of his best workers and everywhere his right-hand man. For although his physical strength had not yet reached its full extent, no one could easily match him in staying power. Up to now Margreth had merely loved her son; now she began to be proud of him and even to feel a kind of respect for him, as she saw the young man developing entirely without her help and even without her advice, which, like most people, she considered priceless and therefore could not rate highly enough the abilities that could dispense with such a precious aid.

In his eighteenth year Friedrich had already assured himself of a considerable reputation among the young people of the village by winning a wager that he would carry a newly killed boar over two miles on his shoulders without putting it down. Meanwhile a share in his fame was just about the only advantage Margreth derived from these favorable circumstances, since Friedrich spent more and more on his appearance and gradually began to find it hard to tolerate when lack of money caused him to fall short of anyone in the village in this respect. Moreover, all his energy was directed toward earning outside; at home, quite contrary to his reputation elsewhere, any continuous occupation seemed to him burdensome and he preferred to undertake some hard, but brief exertion that soon allowed him to return to his former task of herding the cows, which was already beginning to be unsuited to his age and occasionally earned him mockery, which, however, he quickly silenced by using his fists. Thus people became accustomed to seeing him at one moment spick and span, the acknowledged village dandy, at the head of the young people, and then again as a ragged herdboy wandering along lonely and dreamy behind the cows, or lying in a forest clearing, apparently without a thought in his head, and plucking the moss from the trees.

Around this time the slumbering laws were to some extent shaken awake by a band of timber thieves who, under the name of the Blue Smocks, so far surpassed all their predeces-

sors in cunning and impudence that even the most patient
could not help feeling it was time to call a halt. Contrary to
the usual situation, where the ringleaders could always be
pointed out, it had so far proved impossible, despite the general alert, to name a single individual. They had got their
name from the identical costume worn by all of them, which
made recognition difficult when a forester caught sight of a
few stragglers disappearing in the undergrowth. They spread
devastation like processionary caterpillars; whole stretches of
forest were felled and carried away in a night, so that next
morning there was nothing to be found but chips and deso-
late piles of lopped-off branches. And the fact that the cart
tracks never led to a village, but always from the river and
back, proved that they were working under the protection,
and perhaps with the aid, of shipowners. The band must have
included very skillful spies, for the foresters could lie in wait
for weeks in vain; the first night, no matter whether it was
stormy or moonlit, on which they relaxed their vigil from
exhaustion, destruction descended. It was a strange fact that
the local population seemed to be as ignorant and on edge as
the foresters themselves. It was said with certainty of some
villages that they did not belong to the Blue Smocks, but
none of them could be described as under immediate suspicion, since the most suspicious of all, the village of B, had to
be exonerated. This had been established through a coinci-
dence: a wedding at which almost all the inhabitants of this
village were well known to have spent the night, at precisely
the time when the Blue Smocks were carrying out one of
their most massive expeditions.

Meanwhile the damage in the forest became just too great,
so that the preventive measures were intensified to a hitherto
unheard-of-degree. Patrols were active day and night, plowmen and houseboys armed with guns and enlisted in the for-
estry service. Nevertheless, success was small, and often the
guards had barely left one end of the forest when the Blue
Smocks moved into the other. This lasted longer than a
whole year, guards and Blue Smocks, Blue Smocks and

guards, like the sun and the moon, alternately in possession of the terrain and never meeting.

It was in July, 1756, at three in the morning. The moon hung clear in the sky, but its light was beginning to dim and in the east a thin yellow strip was already showing that edged the horizon and closed the entrance to a narrow gorge with a gold band. Friedrich was lying in the grass in his usual manner, carving a willow wand to whose knotty end he was trying to give the shape of a clumsy animal. He looked tired, yawned, occasionally rested his head on the weatherbeaten trunk of a tree and cast sleepy glances at the entrance to the gorge, which was almost overgrown with brush and the shoots of young trees. A few times his eyes lit up and assumed the glassy gleam peculiar to them, but immediately afterward he half closed them again and yawned and stretched as is only permitted to lazy herdsmen. His dog lay a little way away close to the cows which, unconcerned about the forest laws, munched away at the young tree shoots as often as at the grass and snorted into the fresh morning air. From time to time a dull crash rang out from the forest; the sound lasted a few seconds only, accompanied by a long echo from the walls of the mountain and was repeated every five to eight minutes or so. Friedrich took no notice of it. Only from time to time, when the sound was unusually loud or persistent, did he raise his head and let his eyes glide over the various paths that run into the gorge.

The first light was getting considerably brighter. The birds were beginning to twitter softly and the dew could be felt rising from the ground. Friedrich had leaned back against the trunk and was staring into the slowly advancing dawn with his hands behind his head. Suddenly he sat up. A flash of light passed across his face; for a few seconds he listened, bending forward from the waist like a hunting dog who has caught a scent on the wind. Then he quickly thrust two fingers into his mouth and gave a long, shrill whistle. "Fidel, you damned animal!" He threw a stone that struck the unconcerned dog in the side. Startled out of its sleep, the dog

first snapped around it and then hopped howling on three
legs to seek consolation in the very place from which the
harm had come. The same moment the branches of a neighboring bush were parted almost without a sound and a man
stepped out, wearing a green huntsman's coat with a silver
scutcheon on the sleeve and carrying a cocked gun. He
glanced quickly over the ravine and then looked particularly
sharply at the boy, stepped forward and beckoned in the
direction of the bush. Gradually seven or eight men came into
view, all dressed in the same manner, with hunting knives in
their belts and carrying cocked guns.

"Friedrich, what was that?" asked the first man to appear.

"I wish the wretch would die on the spot. As far as he's
concerned the cows can eat the ears from my head."

"The scum have seen us," said another man.

"Tomorrow you can set out on a journey with a stone
around your neck," Friedrich went on, giving the dog a kick.

"Friedrich, don't pretend to be an idiot. You know me and
you understand me too." The look accompanying these words
took quick effect.

"Herr Brandis, think of my mother."

"I am. Didn't you hear anything in the forest?"

"In the forest?" The boy glanced at the forester's face.
"Your woodcutters, nothing else."

"My woodcutters!"

The forester's naturally dark complexion darkened still
more to a deep brownish-red. "How many of them are there,
and where are they working?"

"Where you sent them. I don't know."

Brandis turned to his companions. "Go on ahead; I'll follow
in a minute."

When they had disappeared one after the other into the
thicket, Brandis came up close to the boy. "Friedrich," he
said in a tone of suppressed rage, "my patience is at an end.
I'd like to beat you like a dog, and that's all you're worth.
You trash that don't own a single tile on your roof! Thank
God, it won't be long before you have to go begging, and your

old witch of a mother won't get one mouldy crust of bread at my door. But I'll have you both in jail before then!"

Friedrich clutched convulsively at a branch. He was deathly pale and his eyes seemed about to jump out of his head like crystal balls. But only for an instant. Then the greatest calm, bordering on lethargy, returned.

"Sir," he said firmly, in an almost gentle voice, "you said things you cannot answer for, and perhaps so did I. We will let one cancel out the other. And now I will tell you what you want to know. If you didn't send for the woodcutters yourself, they must have been the Blue Smocks; because no carts came from the village; the road passes in front of me and there were four carts. I didn't see them, but I heard them going along the hollow way." He hesitated for an instant. "Can you say that I ever cut down a tree in your district? That I ever cut anything anywhere except on orders? Just think whether you can say that."

An embarrassed mutter was the only answer from the forester who, like most rough people, was quick to feel remorse. He turned crossly and started off toward the bushes.

"No, sir," called Friedrich, "if you want to join the other foresters, they went up over there by the beech."

"By the beech?" said Brandis doubtfully. "No, over there, toward the Master Valley."

"I tell you they went to the beech tree. Tall Heinrich's gun strap caught in the crooked branch. I saw it."

The forester set off in the direction indicated. All this time, Friedrich had not changed his position; half-lying, his arm around a dead branch, he stared after the departing forester as he slipped through the half overgrown path with the cautious, long step of his trade, as soundlessly as a fox climbing the ladder to a hen coop. Here a branch sank down behind him, there another. The outlines of his figure grew fainter and fainter. There was one last flash through the foliage; it was one of the steel buttons on his hunting jacket; then he was gone. As the forester gradually disappeared Friedrich's face lost its cold expression and finally his features seemed to be in restless motion. Did he perhaps regret not having asked the forester to keep quiet about the information he had given him? He walked a few paces, then came to a stop. "It's too late," he said to himself and picked up his hat. There was a low tapping sound not twenty paces away. It was the forester sharpening his flint. Friedrich listened. "No," he said then in a resolute tone, gather his things together and hurriedly drove the cattle along the ravine.

Toward the middle of the day Frau Margreth was sitting by the fireplace making tea. Friedrich had come home sick; he complained of a headache and in reply to her worried question told her how very angry he had been over the forester; in short, he related the whole incident described above, apart from a few details he considered it better to keep to himself. Margreth stared silent and gloomy into the boiling water. She was used to hearing her son complain from time to time, but today he looked more unstrung than ever before. Was he about to fall ill? She sighed deeply and dropped a block of wood she had just picked up.

"Mother," cried Friedrich from the bedroom.

"What is it?"

"Was that a shot?"

"No, no, I don't know what you mean."

"It must have been the pounding in my head," he answered.

Their neighbor entered and whispered some insignificant piece of gossip, which Margreth listened to without interest. Then she left.

"Mother," cried Friedrich.

Margreth went in to him.

"What was Frau Hülsmeyer telling you?"

"Oh, nothing, lies, empty chatter." Friedrich sat up.

"About Gretchen Siemers. You know the old story. And there isn't a word of truth in it."

Friedrich lay back again. "I'll see if I can get to sleep," he said.

Margreth sat by the fire thinking depressing thoughts. The

village clock struck half pass eleven. The door opened and clerk of the court Kapp entered. "Good day, Frau Mergel," he said. "Can you give me a drink of milk? I've just come from M."

When Frau Mergel brought him the milk, he asked: "Where is Friedrich?"

She was just busy getting out a plate and did not hear the question. He drank hesitantly and at short intervals. Then he said: "Did you know that last night the Blue Smocks wiped a whole stretch of the Master Wood as bare as my hand?"

"Heavens above," she replied indifferently.

"The rascals ruin everything," continued the clerk of the court. "If they would just spare the young timber, but they cut down oak saplings no thicker than my arm that wouldn't even make the shaft of an oar. It's as though they were just as keen on damaging other people as on making a profit themselves."

"That's a pity," said Margreth.

The clerk of the court had finished his milk, but he still did not go. He seemed to have something on his mind. "Haven't you heard about Brandis?" he asked suddenly.

"No, nothing. He never comes here."

"So you don't know what has happened to him?"

"No. What has happened to him?" asked Margreth with interest.

"He is dead."

"Dead?" she cried. "Merciful heaven. This very morning he walked past here in perfect health with his gun on his back."

"He's dead," repeated the clerk of the court, gazing at her intently. "Murdered by the Blue Smocks. His body was brought into the village a quarter of an hour ago."

Margreth clapped her hands together. "God in heaven, do not judge him, he knew not what he was doing!"

"Do not judge him?" cried the clerk of the court. "You meant the accursed murderer?"

From the bedroom came the sound of groaning. Margreth hurried in, followed by the clerk of the court. Friedrich was sitting up in bed, his face in his hands, groaning like a dying man.

"Friedrich, what's the matter?" said his mother.

"Oh, my belly, my head," he moaned.

"What's the matter with him?"

"Oh, God knows," she replied. "He came home with the cows at four this morning because he felt so ill. Friedrich—Friedrich—answer me, shall I fetch the doctor?"

"No, no," he moaned. "It's only a colic, it will be better soon."

He lay back. His face twitched convulsively with pain. Then the color returned to it.

"Go," he said dully. "I must sleep, then it will pass."

"Frau Mergel," said the clerk of the court seriously. "Are you sure Friedrich came home at four and didn't go out again?"

She stared at him. "Ask any child in the street. And as for going out again, would to God he could."

"Didn't he tell you anything about Brandis?"

"In God's name, yes, that he abused Friedrich in the forest and reproached him with our poverty, the scoundrel. But God forgive me, he is dead. Go," she went on vehemently. "Did you come here to insult honest people? Go." She turned back to her son. The clerk of the court left.

"Friedrich, how do you feel?" she asked. "Did you hear? Terrible, terrible! Without confession or absolution."

"Mother, mother, in heaven's name let me sleep. I'm all in."

At this moment Johannes Nobody entered the bedroom, thin and tall as a bean pole, but as ragged and shy as we saw him five years ago. His face was even paler than usual. "Friedrich," he stammered, "you must come to your Uncle at once; he has work for you; but at once."

Friedrich turned to the wall. "I'm not coming," he said gruffly. "I'm ill."

"But you must come," panted Johannes. "He told me I had to bring you with me."

Friedrich laughed scornfully. "I'd like to see you do it!"

"Leave him in peace," sighed Margreth. "You can see the state he is in."

She left the room for a few minutes. When she came back Friedrich was already dressed.

"What are you thinking of?" she cried. "You can't, you mustn't go."

"What must be, must be," he retorted and was already outside the door with Johannes.

"Oh God," sighed his mother, "when children are little they kick us in the womb, when they are big they kick us in the heart."

The legal investigation had already begun. The deed was as clear as daylight, but there was so little information about the doers that, although all the circumstances cast strong suspicion on the Blue Smocks, it was impossible to do more than speculate. There was *one* clue, but with good reason little was expected of it. The absence of the lord of the manor compelled the clerk of the court to deal with matters on his own. He was sitting at the table. The room was packed with peasants, some there out of curiosity, others because it was hoped that, in the absence of any real witnesses, some information might be extracted from them. Herdsmen, who had been watching over their herds that night, plowmen, who had been plowing nearby. They all stood stiffly erect, their hands in their pockets as though as a mute declaration that they refused to be involved. Eight foresters were questioned. Their statements were all identical: on the evening of the tenth Brandis had ordered them all to take part in a patrol, because he must have heard news that the Blue Smocks were plotting something. But he had spoken of this only very vaguely. At two o'clock at night they had set out and come across many signs of destruction, which had put the head forester in a very bad mood. Otherwise all was quiet. Around four Brandis had said: "We've been fooled. Let's go home." As they were rounding the Bremer Mountain the wind changed and they clearly heard the sound of felling in the Master Wood and from the rapid sequence of blows deduced that the Blue

Smocks were at work. For a while they discussed whether it was wise to attack the audacious band with such a small force; then, without having come to a definite decision, they walked slowly in the direction of the sounds. Then followed the incident with Friedrich. Then, after Brandis had sent them off without any instructions, they had walked on for a while until they noticed that the noise in the wood, which was still quite a long way off, had ceased. Thereupon they stopped and waited for the head forester. Irritated by standing around doing nothing, they went on to the site of the devastation. It was all over. There was not a sound in the forest. Of twenty felled trees eight were still there; the remainder had already been taken away. They could not understand how this had been done, since there were no cart tracks to be found. Also, the dryness of the season and the pine needles covering the soil made it impossible to distinguish any footprints, although the ground all around had been trampled hard. Since they considered it pointless to wait for the head forester, they quickly walked across to the other side of the forest, in the hope of catching sight of the thieves. Here, as they were leaving the wood, one of them had caught the strap of his water bottle in the brambles; when he turned around he saw something flash in the undergrowth. It was the head forester's belt buckle and they had found Brandis lying behind the brambles, stretched out, his right hand clamped around the barrel of his gun, the other clenched and his forehead split with an ax.

These were the foresters' statements. Then it was the peasants' turn, but there was nothing to be got out of them. Many asserted that at four o'clock they were still at home or busy elsewhere. No one admitted to having noticed anything. What could be done? They were all men of some substance and beyond suspicion. The Court had to rest content with their negative testimony.

Friedrich was called in. He entered with a mien in no way different from usual, neither tense nor impudent. The interrogation was pretty long and some of the questions rather craftily worded. But he answered them all frankly and unhesitatingly and related the incident between himself and the head forester more or less truthfully, apart from the end, which he considered it wiser to keep to himself. His alibi at the time of the murder was easily proved. The forester was lying at the way out of the Master Wood, over three-quarters of an hour from the gorge in which he had spoken to Friedrich at four o'clock and from which the latter had driven his herd into the village ten minutes later. Everyone had seen this. All the peasants present were quick to bear witness to it: he had spoken to this one, nodded to that.

The clerk of the court sat there disgruntled and at a loss. Suddenly he reached behind him with one hand and flashed something in front of Friedrich's eyes.

"Whose is this?"

Friedrich jumped back three paces. "Lord Jesus, I thought you were going to smash in my skull!"

His eyes had run quickly over the deadly implement and seemed to rest for a moment on a splinter broken off the shaft.

"I don't know," he said firmly.

It was the ax that had been found wedged in the head forester's skull.

"Look at it closely," continued the clerk of the court.

Friedrich took hold of it, looked it up and down, turned it around. "It's an ax like any other," he said, laying it down on the table indifferently. A patch of blood was visible; he seemed to shudder, but reiterated very positively: "I've never seen it before."

The clerk of the court sighed with annoyance. He knew no more himself and had merely hoped to find out something by the effect of surprise. There was nothing for it but to close the hearing.

I must tell those who may be waiting expectantly for the outcome of this incident that it was never cleared up, although great efforts were made to get to the bottom of it and this hearing was followed by others. The Blue Smocks seemed to have been scared off by the attention this episode aroused and the stricter measures that followed it. Thereafter it was as though they had vanished, and although many timber thieves were subseqently caught there was no apparent reason to believe that they belonged to the notorious band. The ax lay for twenty years as a useless piece of material evidence in the court archives, where it may still be lying with its patches of rust. In a made-up story it would be wrong to disappoint the reader's curiosity in this way. But all this really happened; I cannot add or subtract anything.

Next Sunday Friedrich rose very early to go to confession. It was the Feast of Assumption, and the parish priests were in the confessional before daybreak. After dressing in the dark, Friedrich left the narrow partition set aside for him in Simon's house with as little sound as possible. His prayer book must be lying on the kitchen shelf and he hoped to be able to find it by the pale moonlight. It was not there. He looked around in search of it and started with fright: in the bedroom door stood Simon, almost without clothes; his gaunt figure, uncombed, disheveled hair, and the pallor of his face caused by the moonlight made him look horribly changed.

"Is he walking in his sleep?" thought Friedrich and kept quite still.

"Where are you going, Friedrich?" whispered the old man.

"Uncle, is it you? I'm going to confession."

"That's what I thought. Go in God's name, but confess like a good Christian."

"I certainly will," said Friedrich.

"Think of the Ten Commandments: thou shalt not bear witness against thy neighbor."

"False witness!"

"No, no witness at all; you've been misinformed; he who accuses another in confession is not worthy to receive the sacrament."

They were both silent.

"Uncle, what makes you think of that?" said Friedrich, then: "Your conscience is not clear; you have lied to me."

"Have I?"

"Where is your ax?"

"My ax? In the barn."

"Have you fitted a new shaft to it? Where is the old one?"

"You can find it in the woodshed any day. Go," he added contemptuously. "I thought you were a man, but you're an old woman who thinks the house is on fire when her warming pan begins to smoke. Look," he went on, "if I know any more about the matter than that doorpost there, may I be forever damned. I was at home long before," he added.

Friedrich stood oppressed and in doubt. He would have given a lot to see his Uncle's face. But while they were whispering the sky had clouded over.

"I bear a heavy burden of guilt," sighed Friedrich, "for sending him the wrong way—although—no, I certainly didn't think that would happen, I certainly didn't. Uncle, I have you to thank for a heavy conscience."

"Then go and confess," whispered Simon, his voice quivering. "Dishonor the sacrament by talebearing and hang a spy around the neck of honest people, who will find a way to snatch the bread from their teeth if he doesn't get a chance to speak right away—go!"

Friedrich stood irresolute; he heard a low sound; the clouds passed, the moonlight fell on the bedroom door again: it was closed. Friedrich did not go to confession that morning.

The impression this incident had left upon Friedrich unfortunately faded all too soon. Who can doubt that Simon did everything to guide his adopted son into the same paths he himself was treading? And there were characteristics in Friedrich that made this all too easy: frivolity, excitability, and above all a limitless arrogance that did not always disdain mere appearances and then staked everything on making the false claims true so as to avoid the possibility of being put to shame. His nature was not lacking in nobility, but he grew accustomed to preferring inward shame to outward. We can only say that he got used to preening himself while his mother suffered want.

This unfortunate change in his character was the work of several years, during which time it was noticed that Margreth spoke less of her son and gradually sank into a state of demoralization that in the past no one would have thought possible. She became timid, negligent, even untidy, and many people thought her brain had suffered. Friedrich meanwhile became all the louder; he never missed a village feast or wedding, and since a very touchy sense of honor did not allow him to overlook the secret disapproval of many people, he was constantly up in arms, so to speak, not so much to offer opposition to public opinion as to guide it in the channel that pleased him. He was outwardly respectable, sober, and apparently guileless, but crafty, boastful, and often brutal, a man whose company no one enjoyed, least of all his mother, and who had nevertheless gained a certain dominance in the village through his feared audacity and even more feared cunning, a dominance that was all the more acknowledged the more people realized that they did not know him and could not predict what he might be capable of. Only one lad in the village, Wilm Hülsmeyer, dared to defy him in the consciousness of his strength and good position. And since he was quicker with his tongue than Friedrich, and when he had wounded Friedrich always managed to hold him up to ridicule as well, he was the only one Friedrich preferred not to encounter.

Four years had passed; it was October; the mild autumn of 1760, which had filled all the barns with corn and all the cellars with wine, had spread its riches over this corner of the earth too, and one saw more drunken people and heard of more fights and foolish pranks than ever. There was merrymaking everywhere; the holiday Monday came into fashion, and anyone who had a few thaler to spare immediately wanted to find a woman to help him eat today and starve tomorrow. A good solid wedding as to be celebrated in the village, and the guests could expect more than an out-of-tune fiddle, a glass of brandy, and whatever high spirits they brought with them. From early morning everybody was up; outside every door clothes were being aired and throughout the day B looked like a second-hand store. Since many guests from outside were expected, everyone wanted to uphold the honor of the village.

It was seven in the evening and everything in full swing; gaiety and laughter on all sides, the downstairs rooms filled to suffocation with blue, red, and yellow figures, like pounds into which too many animals have been squeezed. There was dancing on the threshing floor, that is to say, anyone who had conquered two square feet of space kept turning around and around, trying to make up by jubilant shouts for what was lacking in movement. The orchestra was brilliant, the first violin played by a recognized musician predominated, while the second violin and a large bass viol with three strings were played *ad libitum* by amateurs. There were brandy and coffee in plenty. All the guests were dripping with sweat. In short, it was a splendid party. Friedrich strutted around like a cock in a new sky-blue coat, exercising his rights as the village dandy. When the party from the manor arrived, he was sitting behind the bass fiddle bowing the deepest string with great vigor and decorum.

"Johannes," he cried imperiously, and his protégé came over from the dance floor, where he too had been trying to swing his clumsy legs and let out a few lighthearted shouts. Friedrich handed him the bow, communicated his wishes with a proud nod and joined the dancers. "Let it go, musicians: the Papen van Istrup!"

The popular dance was played, and Friedrich made such leaps before the eyes of his masters that the cows in the barn drew in their horns and the jingling of chains and the sound of lowing ran around their stalls. A foot above everyone else's his fair head rose and fell, like a pike jumping out of the water. On all sides girls screamed as he flicked his long flaxen hair in their faces with a quick movement of his head as a sign of homage.

"That's enough," he said at last and dripping with sweat stepped up to the buffet. "Long live the lord and lady of the manor and all the noble princes and princesses, and if anyone refuses to drink to their health I'll give him such a box on the ears he will hear the angels singing!"

A loud *vivat* greeted this gallant toast.

Friedrich bowed. "No offense, ladies and gentlemen. We are only ignorant peasants."

At this moment uproar broke out at the far end of the barn, shouting, scolding, laughter all intermingled. "Butter thief, butter thief," cried a few children and Johannes Nobody pushed his way forward—or rather, was pushed by others—his head between his shoulders, trying as hard as he could to get to the door.

"What's going on? What are you doing to our Johannes?" cried Friedrich imperiously.

"You'll find out soon enough," panted an old woman wearing an apron and carrying a wiping cloth.

Shame! Johannes, the poor devil for whom at home the worst was good enough, had tried to secure himself half a pound of butter for the coming drought, and forgetting that he had put it in his pocket neatly wrapped in his handkerchief he had gone close to the kitchen fire and now the fat was running ignominiously down his coattails. General turmoil. The girls jumped back, for fear of getting dirty, or pushed the delinquent forward. Others made way, out of pity as well as caution.

But Friedrich stepped forward. "Ragamuffin," he shouted, slapping his patient protégé hard in the face several times. Then he pushed him to the door and helped him on his way with a vigorous kick.

He returned dejectedly. His dignity was injured; the general laughter cut him to the quick, and though he tried to get himself back into the mood with a courageous shout of huzza! he did not quite manage it. He was on the point of taking refuge behind the bass viol when he tried one more startling effect: taking out his silver pocket watch, at that time a rare and costly ornament, he announced: "It's almost ten. Now for the bridal minuet. I'll play the music."

"That's a splendid watch," said the swineherd, pushing his face forward in reverent curiosity.

"How much did it cost?" cried Wilm Hülsmeyer, Friedrich's rival.

"Do you want to pay for it?" asked Friedrich.

"Have *you* paid for it?" retorted Wilm.

Friedrich cast a proud glance at him and with silent majesty picked up the fiddle bow.

"Well, well," said Hülsmeyer, "it's not the first time that has happened. You know, Franz Ebel had a fine watch too, until the Jew Aaron took it away from him again."

Friedrich did not answer, but nodded proudly to the first violin, and they began to play for all they were worth.

The lord and lady of the manor had meanwhile gone into the bedroom, where the neighbor women were just decking out the bride with the sign of her new status, the white headband. The young girl was weeping bitterly, partly because custom demanded it, partly out of real anguish. She was to take charge of a chaotic household, under the eyes of a surly old man whom, on top of everything else, she was supposed to love. He was standing beside her, in no way like the bridegroom in the *Song of Songs*, who "enters the bedchamber like the morning sun."

"You've cried enough," he said with annoyance. "Just remember, it's not you who make me happy, it's I who make you happy."

She looked up at him humbly and seemed to feel that he was right.

The business was finished. The young woman had drunk to her husband; young jokers had looked through the tripod to see if the headband was on straight, and everyone crowded back to the barn again, whence echoed constant laughter and noise. Friedrich was no longer there. He had suffered great, unbearable shame, since the Jew Aaron, a butcher and occasional dealer in second-hand goods from the neighboring small town, had suddenly appeared and after a brief, unsatisfactory dialogue had loudly demanded, before all those present, the sum of ten thaler for a watch delivered the previous Easter. Friedrich had left in utter dejection and the Jew had followed him crying:

"Oh, woe is me! Why didn't I listen to sensible people!

They told me a hundred times everything you own is on your
back and you haven't a loaf of bread in the closet!"

The barn rocked with laughter. Many crowded out into the
yard. "Grab the Jew! Weigh him against a pig," shouted
some. Others had grown grave.

"Friedrich looked as white as a sheet," said an old woman,
and the crowd parted as the lord of the manor's carriage
drove into the yard.

On the way home Herr von S was in an ill humor, as
always happened when the desire to maintain his popularity
led him to attend such festivities. He was gazing out of the
carriage in silence. "Who are those people?" he pointed to two
dark figures who ran in front of the carriage like ostriches.
Then they slipped into the castle. "A couple of blessed pigs
from our own pigsty," sighed Herr von S.

When he reached home he found the entrance hall occupied by all the sevants, standing around two farm laborers
who had sat down pale and breathless on the staircase. They
asserted that they had been pursued by old Mergel's ghost as
they were returning home through the Breder Wood. First,
there had been a soughing and rustling overhead; then a
clapping high in the air like two sticks being banged together;
suddenly a shriek and quite clearly the words: "Oh, woe is
me, my poor soul," from high above. One claimed to have also
seen glowing eyes flashing between the branches, and both
had run as fast as their legs would carry them.

"Stuff and nonsense," said the lord of the manor with vexation, and went to the bedroom to change his clothes.

Next morning the fountain in the garden refused to send
up its jet of water and it turned out that someone had dis-
lodged a pipe, apparently searching for the skull of one of
four horses buried here many years ago—a horse's skull being
considered a reliable protection against witchcraft and ghosts.

"H'm," said the lord of the manor, "what the rogues don't
steal the fools damage."

Three days later a terrible storm raged. It was midnight,
but everyone in the castle was out of bed. The lord of the

manor stood at the window looking out into the darkness, worried about his fields. Leaves and twigs went flying past the panes. At one point a tile fell and shattered on the cobbles of the courtyard.

"Terrible weather," said Herr von S.

His wife looked frightened. "Is the fire quite safe?" she said. "Gretchen, go and look at it again; you'd better pour water on it and put it right out. Come, let us pray from the Gospel according to St. John."

Everyone kneeled down and the lady of the house began: "In the beginning was the Word and the Word was with God and the Word was God."

There was a terrible clap of thunder. Everyone started. Then frightful cries and tumult broke out on the stairs.

"In heaven's name, is the house on fire?" cried Frau von S and sank down with her face buried in the chair.

The door was flung open and in rushed the wife of the Jew Aaron, as pale as death, her hair tangled and dripping with rain. She threw herself on her knees before the lord of the manor.

"Justice," she cried. "Justice! My husband has been murdered." Then she collapsed unconscious.

It was only too true, and the subsequent investigation showed that the Jew Aaron had lost his life through a single blow on the temple with a blunt instrument, probably a staff. There was a blue patch on his left temple; no other injury could be found. The statement by the Jewess and her servant Samuel ran as follows: Aaron had gone out three days ago in the afternoon to buy cattle, saying that he would probably stay away overnight, since there were a few bad debtors in B and S to be reminded of their debts. In this case, he would spend the night with the butcher Salomon. When he did not come home next day, his wife had become very worried and finally had set out at three in the afternoon in the company of her servant and the big butcher's dog. At the Jew Salomon's house no one knew anything about Aaron; he had not been there. Then they went to all the peasants with whom they knew that Aaron had intended to do business. Only two of them had seen him, and that was on the day he left. Meanwhile, it had grown very late. Her great fear drove the woman home, where she had a faint hope of finding her husband waiting. They had been overtaken by the storm in the Breder Wood and had sought shelter under a large beech tree growing on the mountainside. The dog had snuffed around in a striking manner and finally, despite all their efforts to restrain it, had run off. Suddenly, during a flash of lightning, the woman saw something white beside her in the moss. It was her husband's staff, and at almost the same moment the dog burst through the bushes carrying something in its mouth. It was her husband's shoe. Soon afterwards they found the Jew's body in a ditch filled with dead leaves.

This was the statement made by the servant, only supported in general terms by the woman. Her wild excitement had now given way to a state of confusion, or rather apathy. "An eye for an eye, a tooth for a tooth!" These were the only words she blurted out from time to time.

That same night the police were ordered to arrest Friedrich. No accusation was necessary, since Herr von S had himself witnessed an occurrence that was bound to cast the most serious suspicion upon him. Furthermore, there was the story of ghosts on the evening, the clashing of staves in the Breder Wood, and the cry from up above. Since the clerk of the court happened to be absent, Herr von S saw to everything himself more quickly than would otherwise have been the case. Nevertheless, dawn was already beginning to break before the police, as silently as possible, had surrounded poor Margreth's house. The lord of the manor himself knocked at the door. It was scarcely a minute before the door was opened and Margreth appeared fully clothed in the doorway. Herr von S started back: he almost failed to recognize her, so pale and stony-faced did she look.

"Where is Friedrich?" he asked uncertainly.

"Look for him," she answered, sitting down on a chair.

The lord of the manor hesitated a moment. Then he said

gruffly to his men: "Come in, come in, what are we waiting for?"

They went into Friedrich's bedroom. He was not there, but the bed was still warm. They climbed up into the loft, went down into the cellar, prodded the straw, looked behind every barrel, even in the oven. Some of them went out into the garden and looked behind the fence and up into the apple trees. He was not to be found.

"He's got away," said the lord of the manor with very mixed feelings; the sight of the old woman affected him deeply.

"Give me the key to that chest."

Margreth did not reply.

"Give me the key," repeated the lord of the manor and only then noticed that the key was in the lock. The contents of the chest appeared: the fugitive's best Sunday clothes and his mother's shabby things; then two shrouds with black ribbons, one for a man, the other for a woman. Herr von S was deeply shaken. Right at the bottom of the chest lay the silver watch and some papers in a very legible hand, one of them signed by a man who was under strong suspicion of connections with the timber thieves. Herr von S took them with him for scrutiny and they left the house, without Margreth's giving any other sign of life than incessantly biting her lips and blinking her eyes.

Back at the castle, the lord of the manor found the clerk of the court, who had returned the previous evening and claimed to have slept through the whole affair, since the lord of the manor had not sent for him.

"You always come too late," said Herr von S in vexation. "Wasn't there some old woman in the village who told your maid about it? And why didn't someone wake you?"

"Sir," rejoined Kapp, "it's true my Anne Marie heard about the matter an hour before I did; but she knew Your Honor had taken charge of it yourself, and also," he added with a plaintive expression, "that I was dead tired."

"A splendid police force," muttered the lord of the manor. "Every old bag in the village knows all about things, when they're supposed to be kept secret." Then he added vehemently: "Only a really stupid criminal would ever let himself get caught!"

They both remained silent for a while.

"My coachman lost his way in the dark," the clerk of the court began again. "We stopped for over an hour in the forest; it was dreadful weather; I thought the wind was going to blow the carriage over. Finally, when the rain eased off we drove as fast as we could, further into the Zeller Plain, still unable to see our hands before our faces. Then the coachman said: 'I only hope we don't come too close to the stone quarries.' I was scared myself. I stopped the coach and struck fire, in order at least to draw some comfort from my pipe. All of a sudden, quite close and directly beneath us, we heard the bell ringing. Your Honor can imagine what a shock that was. I jumped out of the carriage, because you can trust your own legs, but not those of the horses. So I stood still, in the mud and the rain, without moving, until thank God day soon began to break. And where were we? Right beside the Heerse Gorge with the Heerse Tower just below us. If we had driven on another twenty paces we should all have been dead ducks."

"That was really no joke," replied the lord of the manor, half placated.

Meanwhile he had looked through the papers he had brought back with him. They were dunning letters concerning borrowed money, most of them from usurers.

"I never realized the Mergels were in so deep," he muttered.

"Yes, and that it has come to light like this," added Kapp, "will be no small embarrassment to Frau Margreth."

"Oh, God, she's not thinking about that now." With these words the lord of the manor rose and left the room in order to carry out the legal inquest with Herr Kapp.

The investigation was brief, violent death proven, the probable culprit fled, the evidence against him very strong but without a personal confession not conclusive, though his flight was very suspicious. Thus the case had to be closed without adequate success.

The Jews of the district had shown great sympathy. The widow's house was never empty of people wailing and giving advice. Never within living memory had so many Jews been seen together in L. Extremely embittered by the murder of their coreligionist, they had spared neither trouble nor money to track down the culprit. One of them, generally known as Joel the Usurer, is even said to have offered one of his customers, who owed him several hundred thaler and whom he considered particularly crafty, a release from the whole of his debt if he assisted in Mergel's arrest; for it was generally believed among the Jews that the culprit had only escaped with the aid of others and was probably still in the district. When all these efforts came to nought, however, and the case was declared closed, a number of the most prominent Israelites appeared next morning at the castle to make the Baron an offer. The offer concerned the beech tree under which Aaron's staff had been found and the murder probably committed.

"Do you want to cut it down? Now, while it's in full leaf?" asked the lord of the manor.

"No, Your Honor, it must remain standing winter and summer as long as a single splinter is left."

"But if I have the wood felled it will damage the young growth."

"We're willing to pay more than the normal price."

They offered 200 thaler. The deal was concluded and all the foresters strictly forbidden to damage the Jews' beech in any way. One evening thereafter some sixty Jews, led by their Rabbi, were seen making their way into the Breder Wood silently and with downcast eyes. They remained in the wood for over an hour and then returned just as gravely and solemnly through the village of B to the Zeller Plain, where they scattered and went each his own way. Next morning the following line was found cut into the beech tree with an ax:

אִם תַּעֲמוֹר בַּמְקוֹם הַזֶּה יִפְבַּע בָּךְ כַּאֲשֶׁר אַתָּה עָשִׂיתָ לִי

And where was Friedrich? Without doubt gone, far enough to have no further fear of the short arms of such a weak police force. Soon he was lost and forgotten. Uncle Simon rarely spoke of him, and then badly. The Jewish woman was finally consoled and took a new husband. Only poor Margreth remained uncomforted.

About half a year later the lord of the manor was reading some newly arrived letters in the presence of the clerk of the court.

"Strange, strange," he said. "Just imagine, Kapp, Mergel may be innocent of the murder. The President of the Court in P had just written to me: 'Le vrai n'est pas toujours vraisemblable. I frequently discover that in my profession and now I have done so again. Do you know that your faithful servant Friedrich Mergel may be no more guilty of murdering the Jew than you or I? Unfortunately there is no proof, but it is extremely probable. A member of the Schlemming Gang (most of whom, by the way, we now have under lock and key), known as Ragged Moises, stated at the last interrogation that he regretted nothing so much as the murder of a coreligionist called Aaron, whom he slew in the forest and then only found six groschen on him. Unfortunately the hearing was interrupted by the noon break, and while we were at table the dog of a Jew hanged himself with his garter. What do you say to that? It's true that Aaron is a common name, etc.'

"What do you say to that?" reiterated the lord of the manor. "And in that case, why did the idiot of a boy run away?"

The clerk of the court pondered. "Well, perhaps because of the timber thefts we were just investigating. Isn't it said: The evildoer runs from his own shadow? Mergel's conscience was stained enough without that spot."

This thought pacified them. Friedrich was gone, vanished

—and Johannes Nobody, poor, neglected Johannes, on the same day with him.

A good long time had passed, twenty-eight years, almost half a human life. The lord of the manor had become very old and gray; his good-natured helper Kapp was long since in his grave. People, animals, and plants had come into being, matured, and passed away; only the castle of B still looked down, equally gray and noble, on the cottages which, like old, consumptive people always seemed on the point of falling but were still standing. It was Christmas Eve, December 24, 1787. Snow lay in the sunken paths up to twelve feet deep, and penetrating frosty air froze the windowpanes in the heated room. Midnight was near, but dim lights were everywhere flickering from the snowy hills and in every house the occupants were on their knees, waiting with prayers for the commencement of the holy festival of Christ, as is the custom in Catholic countries, or at least was then, when a figure came slowly down toward the village from the Breder Heights. The wanderer seemed very weary or sick; he groaned heavily and dragged himself with great difficulty through the snow.

Halfway down the slope he stopped, leaned on his crutched staff and stared fixedly at the points of light. It was so quiet everywhere, so dead and cold; it was impossible not to think of jack-o'-lanterns in churchyards. Then the clock in the tower struck twelve. The last stroke slowly died away, and in the nearest house a low singing began that gained volume from house to house and spread over the whole village:

> A little child so good and gay
> Was born to us this holy day.
> His mother was a virgin pure;
> His name forever shall endure.
> If this child had ne'er been born
> The world would be a place forlorn.
> He brought salvation to us all.
> Oh, Jesus Christ, from evil's thrall
> Set us free and by your grace
> Grant us everlasting peace.

The man on the hillside had fallen to his knees and was trying with trembling lips to join in. All he managed was a loud sob, and heavy, hot drops fell in the snow. The second stanza began; he prayed softly along with it; then the third and the fourth. The song came to an end and the lights in the houses began to move. The man rose to his feet with an effort and crept slowly down into the village. Panting, he passed several houses, then he stopped in front of one and knocked at the door.

"What's that?" said a woman's voice inside. "The door is banging and the wind won't stop."

He knocked louder. "In the name of God, let in a half-frozen man who comes from slavery in Turkey!"

Whispering in the kitchen. "Go to the inn," replied another voice. "The fifth house from here."

"For the love of God, let me in. I have no money."

After some hesitation the door opened and a man shone out a lamp.

"Come in," he said. "You won't cut our throats."

In the kitchen, apart from the man, there were a woman of middle age, a grandmother, and five children. All of them gathered around the new arrival and scrutinized him with shy curiosity. A wretched figure, with a crooked neck, and bent back, his whole form broken and feeble. Long snow-white hair hung around his face, which wore the twisted expression of long suffering. The woman went without a word to the fire and put on fresh brushwood.

"We can't give you a bed," she said. "But I'll put a pile of good straw down here. You'll have to make do with that."

"May God reward you," replied the stranger. "I'm used to worse than that."

The homecomer was recognized as Johannes Nobody, and he himself confirmed that he was indeed that Johannes who had fled with Friedrich Mergel.

Next day the village was full of the adventures of the man who had disappeared for so long. Everyone wanted to see the man from Turkey and they were almost surprised that he still looked like other people. The young, to be sure, had no memory of him, but the old still clearly recognized his features, miserably altered though he was.

"Johannes, Johannes, how gray you have become," said an old woman. "And how did you get that crooked neck?"

"From carrying wood and water as a slave," he replied.

"And what happened to Mergel? You ran away together, didn't you?"

"Yes, of course; but I don't know where he is; we got separated. When you think of him, pray for him," he added. "I'm sure he needs it."

People asked him why Friedrich had made off, since he hadn't murdered the Jew.

"He didn't?" said Johannes, and listened intently as they told him what the lord of the manor had industriously spread abroad, in order to remove this stain from Mergel's name.

"So it was all for nothing," he said thoughtfully. "So much suffering all for nothing." He sighed deeply and in his turn asked after various people.

Simon was long since dead, but before his death he had sunk into poverty, through lawsuits and bad debtors, against whom he could not take legal proceedings because, it was said, his dealings with them were not above board. In the end he had begged his bread and died on the straw in someone else's barn. Margreth had lived longer, but in a state of complete mental apathy. Because she allowed everything she was given to go to rack and ruin, the villagers had soon grown tired of helping her, as people always abandon the most helpless, those with whom the help has no lasting effect and who remain in constant need of further help. Nevertheless, she had not actually suffered want. The people from the castle had looked after her, sending her food daily and arranging for medical attention when her wretched state had degenerated into total emaciation. Her house was now occupied by the son of the former swineherd who, on that unhappy evening, had so admired Friedrich's watch.

"Everyone gone, everyone dead," sighed Johannes.

In the evening, when darkness had fallen and the moon

was shining, he was seen hobbling about in the snow in the churchyard. He did not pray beside any grave, nor did he go close to any, but his eyes seemed to be fixed upon several from a distance. This was how he was found by the forester Brandis, the son of the man who had been murdered, whom the lord of the manor had sent to bring him to the castle.

On entering the living room he looked around shyly, as though dazzled by the light, and then at the Baron, who was sitting in his armchair, very shrunken but still with the same bright eyes and the little red cap on his head as twenty-eight years before. Beside him sat his lady wife, also grown old, very old.

"Well, Johannes," said the lord of the manor, "tell me clearly and in proper order about your adventures. But," he scrutinized him through his eyeglasses, "you've been badly knocked about in Turkey!"

Johannes began, telling him how Mergel had called him from the herd in the middle of the night, saying he had to run away with him.

"But why did the foolish fellow run away at all? You know he was innocent, don't you?"

Johannes stared at the floor. "I don't really know. I have an idea it had something to do with timber. Simon was engaged in all sorts of business. No one told me anything, but I don't believe everything was as it should be."

"Then what did Friedrich tell you?"

"Nothing, just that we had to run, they were after us. So we ran as far as Heerse. It was still dark there and we hid behind the big cross in the churchyard until it was a bit lighter, because we were afraid of the stone quarries in the Zeller Plain; and after we had been sitting there for a while we suddenly heard snorting and stamping overhead and saw long streaks of fire in the air just above the Heerse church tower. We jumped up and ran straight ahead as fast as our legs would carry us, and when dawn broke we actually were on the right road for P."

Johannes seemed to shudder at the memory, and the lord

of the manor thought of the now dead Kapp and his adventure on the Heerse slope.

"Strange," he laughed, "you were so close to each other. But go on."

Then Johannes told him how they had managed to pass through P and get to the frontier. From there on they had begged their way to Freiburg im Breisgau as itinerant journeymen.

"I had my haversack with me," he said, "and Friedrich a bag, so people believed us."

In Freiburg they had allowed themselves to be recruited by the Austrians. They didn't want to take him, but Friedrich had insisted. So they found themselves in the army.

"We spent the winter in Freiburg," he went on, "and things weren't too bad; even for me, because Friedrich often told me what to do and helped me when I made mistakes. In spring we had to march, to Hungary, and in autumn war with the Turks broke out. I can't tell you much about that, because I was taken prisoner in the first bit of fighting and after that I was a slave in Turkey for twenty-six years!"

"Heavens above, how dreadful," exclaimed Frau von S.

"It was pretty bad. The Turks treated us Christians no better than dogs; but the worst thing was that as a result of the hard labor I lost my strength; I grew older too and was still supposed to do the same work as years earlier."

He fell silent for a while. "Yes," he said then, "it was beyond human strength and human patience. From there I came aboard a Dutch ship."

"How did that happen?" asked the lord of the manor.

"They fished me out of the Bosphorus," replied Johannes. The Baron looked at him in surprise and raised his finger warningly; but Johannes went on with his story. Things had not been much better on the ship.

"Scurvy broke out. Anyone who was not completely sick had to do the work of two, and the rope's end ruled just as strictly as the Turkish whip. At last," he concluded, "when we came to Holland, to Amsterdam, I was set free, because I was no use, and also the merchant to whom the ship belonged felt sorry for me and wanted to make me his doorkeeper. "But," he shook his head, "I preferred to beg my way here."

"That was pretty stupid," said the lord of the manor.

Johannes sighed deeply. "Oh, sir, I have had to spend my life among Turks and heretics; shall I not at least lie in a Catholic churchyard?"

The lord of the manor had taken out his purse. "Here, Johannes, now go and come back soon. You must tell me the story in greater detail. Today it was all a bit confused. I suppose you are still very tired?"

"Very tired," replied Johannes. "And," he pointed to his forehead, "my thoughts are so odd at times, I can't really tell what's happening."

"I know," said the Baron. "I remember from the old days. Go now. I'm sure the Hülsmeyers will keep you overnight. Come back tomorrow."

Herr von S felt most sincerely sorry for the poor fellow. By the following day he had decided where he could rent lodgings for him. He was to take his meals daily at the castle and clothing would also be found for him.

"Sir," said Johannes, "I can also do something in return. I can carve wooden spoons, and you could also send me out as a messenger."

Herr von S shook his head compassionately. "That wouldn't work out very well."

"Oh, yes, sir, once I've got going—I'm not very fast, but I would get there eventually, and it won't be as much of an effort as you might think."

"Well," said the Baron doubtfully, "do you want to try? Here is a letter for P. There's no particular hurry."

Next day Johannes moved into his little room with a widow in the village. He carved spoons, ate at the castle, and ran errands for the Baron. On the whole things went tolerably well for him; the people at the castle were kind, and Herr von S often chatted with him at length about Turkey, the Austrian army, and the sea.

"Johannes could tell us a lot," he said to his wife, "if he wasn't so completely simple-minded."

"More melancholic than simple-minded," she rejoined. "I'm always afraid he will go crazy."

"Not a chance!" replied the Baron. "He has been a simpleton all his life; simple people never go mad."

Some time later it happened that Johannes was away on an errand longer than he should have been. The good Frau von S was very worried about him and was on the point of sending people to look for him, when he was heard stumping up the stairs.

"You've been gone a long time, Johannes," she said. "I was beginning to think you had lost your way in the Breder Wood."

"I went through the Pine Hollow."

"That's a long detour. Why didn't you go through the Breder Wood?"

He looked up at her gloomily. "People told me the wood had been felled and there were now so many paths running this way and that; I was afraid I wouldn't find my way out again. I'm getting old and muddle-headed," he added slowly.

"Did you see the strange look in his eyes?" Frau von S asked her husband afterward. "I tell you seriously, that's going to end badly."

Meanwhile September drew near. The fields were empty; the leaves began to fall, and many consumptives felt the scissors at their life's thread. Johannes also seemed to be suffering under the approaching equinox. Those who saw him during those days say he looked strikingly troubled and constantly talked to himself in a low voice, which in any case he did from time to time, but rarely. Finally, he failed to come home one evening. It was thought that the people at the castle had sent him off somewhere. He did not return on the second day either. On the third, his landlady became worried. She went to the castle and made inquiries.

"No, no," said the lord of the manor, "I know nothing whatever about him. But quick, call the huntsmen together,

and forester Wilhelm. If that poor cripple has merely fallen
into a dry ditch he won't be able to get out again. Who knows
if he hasn't broken one of his crooked legs! Take the dog with
you," he called out to the huntsmen just as they were leaving. "And look especially in the ditches. Look in the stone
quarries," he called out more loudly.

The huntsmen returned a few hours later. They had found
nothing. Herr von S was very upset.

"Just think of it, he may be lying there like a stone, unable
to move. But he may be still alive. A man can probably live
for three days without food."

He went out himself. Inquiries were made at every house;
people went around blowing horns and shouting; dogs were
urged on to search for him, in vain. A child had seen him sitting at the edge of the Breder Wood carving a spoon. "But he
cut it right in two," said the little girl. That had been two
days ago. In the afternoon they found another clue: again a
child who had caught sight of him on the other side of the
wood, sitting with his face on his knees as if sleeping. That
was the previous day. It seemed he had been wandering
around in the Breder Wood.

"If the damned bushes weren't so thick! It's impossible to
get through," said the lord of the manor.

The dogs were driven into the new growth. The searchers
blew their horns and shouted and finally returned home disgruntled, when they were sure the animals had hunted
through the whole wood.

"Don't give up! Don't give up!" besought Frau von S.
"Better a few steps in vain than to leave something undone."

The Baron was almost as anxious as she. His disquiet
actually drove him to Johannes' lodgings, although he was
sure he would not find him there. He had the missing man's
room opened up for him. There stood his bed still unmade, as
he had left it; there hung his good coat, which Frau von S
had had made for him from the Baron's old hunting jacket;
on the table stood a bowl, six new wooden spoons, and a box.
The lord of the manor opened it; inside were five groschen,

neatly wrapped in paper, and four silver waistcoat buttons. The lord of the manor examined them closely. "A memento from Mergel," he murmured and went out, for he felt quite constricted in the narrow, stuffy little room. The search was continued until everyone was certain Johannes was no longer in the district, at least not alive. So he had disappeared for the second time. Would he ever be found?—perhaps years later his bones would come to light in a dry ditch. There was little hope of ever seeing him again alive—certainly not after twenty-eight years.

Two weeks later, young Brandis was coming home one morning through the Breder Wood after inspecting his area. It was an unusually hot day for the time of year. The air quivered, no birds were singing, only the ravens croaked tediously from the branches and held their open beaks up to the air. Brandis was very tired. At one moment he removed his cap, heated through by the sun, at the next he put it back on again; either way was equally unbearable. Working his way through the knee-high undergrowth was very laborious. All around not a tree was standing except the Jews' Beech. He forced his way over to it with all the energy he could muster and dropped down exhausted on the shaded moss beneath it. "Filthy toadstools," he muttered half in his sleep. There is in that region a very juicy toadstool that stands for only a few days, then collapses and emits an intolerable stench. Brandis thought he could detect some such unpleasant neighbors; he turned this way and that a few times, but could not bring himself to stand up. Meanwhile his dog was jumping up and down, scratching at the trunk of the beech tree and barking up into the air. "What have you got there, Bello? A cat?" murmured Brandis. He half opened his eyes and caught sight of the Jewish inscription, very overgrown but still quite recognizable. He closed his eyes again; the dog went on barking and finally put his cold nose against his master's cheek. "Leave me alone! What's the matter with you?" As he said this Brandis, still lying on his back, looked up aloft. Then he jumped to his feet with one bound and ran into the undergrowth like a man possessed.

Deathly pale, he reached the castle. There was a man hanging in the Jews' Beech, he said. He had seen his feet dangling just above his face.

"And you didn't cut him down, you donkey?" cried the Baron.

"Sir," panted Brandis, "if Your Honor had been there you would know that the man was no longer alive. At first I thought it was the toadstools." Nevertheless, the lord of the manor called for the greatest possible speed and even went along himself.

They were standing under the beech tree. "I can't see anything," said Herr von S.

"You must come over here."

That was quite right. The lord of the manor recognized his own wornout shoes. "God, it's Johannes! Put the ladder up against the tree. Right. Now take him down. Gently, gently, don't drop him. Heavens above, the worms are already at work. Undo the noose and his neckerchief."

A broad scar came into sight. The lord of the manor recoiled. "My God," he said, bending down over the corpse again and examining the scar intently. For a while he remained silent, deeply shocked. Then he turned to the foresters.

"It is not right for the innocent to suffer for the guilty. Tell everyone: that man," he pointed to the body, "was Friedrich Mergel."

The corpse was buried in the saddle maker's yard.

All this happened exactly as related in September of the year 1788. The Hebrew characters on the tree read:

"If you approach this place, you will suffer what you inflicted upon me."

THEODOR STORM

THE RIDER ON THE WHITE HORSE

Translated by *Muriel Almon*

The story that I have to tell came to my knowledge more
than half a century ago in the house of my great-grand-
mother, the wife of Senator Feddersen, when, sitting close up
to her armchair one day, I was busy reading a number of
some magazine bound in blue cardboard, either the *Leipziger*
or *Pappes Hamburger Lesefrüchte*, I have forgotten which. I
still recall with a tremor how the old lady of more than eighty
years would now and then pass her soft hand caressingly over
her great-grandchild's hair. She herself, and that day, have
long been buried and I have sought in vain for those old
pages, so I can just as little vouch for the truth of the facts as
defend them if anyone should question them. Only one thing
I can affirm, that although no outward circumstance has
since revived them in my mind they have never vanished
from my memory.

On an October afternoon, in the third decade of our
century—thus the narrator began his tale—I was riding in
very bad weather along a dike in northern Friesland. For
more than an hour I had been passing, on the left, a bleak
marsh from which all the cattle had already gone, and, on
the right, uncomfortably near, the marsh of the North
Sea. A traveler along the dike was supposed to be able
to see islets and islands; I saw nothing however but the
yellow-gray waves that dashed unceasingly against the dike
with what seemed like roars of fury, sometimes splashing
me and the horse with dirty foam; in the background eerie
twilight in which earth could not be distinguished from
sky, for the moon, which had risen and was now in its
second quarter, was covered most of the time by driving

clouds. It was icy cold. My benumbed hands could scarcely hold the reins and I did not blame the crows and gulls that, cawing and shrieking, allowed themselves to be borne inland by the storm. Night had begun to fall and I could no longer distinguish my horse's hoofs with certainty; not a soul had met me; I heard nothing but the screaming of the birds, as their long wings almost brushed against me or my faithful mare, and the raging of wind and water. I do not deny that at times I wished myself in some secure shelter.

It was the third day of the storm and I had allowed myself to be detained longer than I should have by a particularly dear relative at his farm in one of the northern parishes. But at last I had to leave. Business was calling me in the town which probably still lay a few hours' ride ahead of me, to the south, and in the afternoon I had ridden away in spite of all my cousin and his kind wife could do to persuade me, and in spite of the splendid home-grown Perinette and Grand Richard apples which were yet to be tried. "Just wait till you get out by the sea," he had called after me from the door, "you will turn back then; we will keep your room ready for you!"

And really, for a moment, as a dark layer of clouds made it grow black as pitch around me and at the same time a roaring gust threatened to sweep both me and my horse away, the thought did flash through my head: "Don't be a fool! Turn back and sit down in comfort with your friends." But then it occurred to me that the way back was longer than the one to my journey's end, and so, drawing the collar of my cloak closer about my ears, I trotted on.

But now something was coming along the dike towards me. I heard nothing, but I thought I could distinguish more and more clearly, as a glimmer fell from the young moon, a dark figure, and soon, when it came nearer, I saw that it was riding a long-legged, lean white horse. A dark cloak fluttered about the figure's shoulders and as it flew

past two burning eyes looked at me from a pale countenance.

Who was it? Why was it here? And now I remembered
that I had heard no sound of hoofs nor of the animal's
breathing, and yet horse and rider had passed close
beside me.

Wondering about this I rode on. But I had not much
time to wonder; it was already passing me again from
behind. It seemed to me as if the flying cloak brushed
against me and the apparition shot by as noiselessly as
before. Then I saw it farther and farther ahead of me and
suddenly it seemed to me as if its shadow was suddenly
descending the land-side of the dike.

With some hesitation I followed. When I reached the
spot where the figure had disappeared I could see close to
the dike, below it and on the land-side, the glistening of
water in one of those water-holes which the high tides bore
in the earth during a storm and which then usually remain
as small but deep-bottomed pools.

The water was remarkably still, even stiller than the
protection of the dike would account for. The rider could
not have disturbed it; I saw nothing more of him. But I
did see something else that I greeted with joy; below me,
on the reclaimed land, a number of scattered lights shone.
They seemed to come from the long, narrow Friesian
houses that stood singly on mounds of different heights;
while close before me, halfway up the inside of the dike,
stood a large house of the same sort. All its windows on
the south side, to the right of the door, were illuminated;
behind them I could see people and even thought I could
hear them, in spite of the storm. My horse had already
turned of its own accord onto the path down the side of the
dike that would lead me to the house. It was evidently a
public house, for in front of the windows I could see the
beams, resting on two posts and provided with iron rings,
to which the cattle and horses that stopped there were tied.

I fastened mine to one of the rings and then commended

it to the care of the hostler who came to meet me as I stepped into the hall. "Is there a meeting here?" I asked him, hearing distinctly the sound of voices and the clatter of glasses through the open door of the room.

"Something of the kind," he replied in Low German, and I learnt later that this dialect in the place had been current, together with the Friesian, for over a hundred years. "The dikegrave and commissioners and some of the others interested! It's on account of the high water!"

Entering I saw about a dozen men sitting at a table which ran along under the windows; on it stood a bowl of punch over which a particularly stately man seemed to preside.

I bowed and asked to be allowed to sit down with them, which request was readily granted. "You are keeping watch here, I suppose," I said, turning to the stately man; "it is dirty weather outside; the dikes will have all they can do!"

"Yes, indeed," he replied; "but we here, on the east side, think we are out of danger now; it is only over on the other side that they are not safe. The dikes there are built, for the most part, after the old pattern; our main dike was moved and rebuilt as long ago as in the last century. We got chilled out there a little while ago, and you are certainly cold too," he added, "but we must stand it here for a few hours longer; we have our trustworthy men out there who come and report to us." And before I could give the publican my order a steaming glass was pushed towards me.

I soon learnt that my friendly neighbor was the dikegrave. We got into conversation and I began to tell him my singular experience on the dike. He grew attentive and I suddenly noticed that the conversation all around us had ceased. "The rider on the white horse!" exclaimed one of the company and all the rest started.

The dikegrave rose. "You need not be afraid," he said across the table; "that does not concern us alone. In the

year '17 too it was meant for those on the other side; we'll
hope that they are prepared for anything!''

Now the shudder ran through me that should properly
have assailed me out on the dike. ''Pardon me,'' I said,
''who and what is this rider on the white horse?''

Apart from the rest, behind the stove, sat a little lean
man in a scant and shabby black coat. He was somewhat
bent and one of his shoulders seemed to be a little crooked.
He had taken no part whatever in the conversation of the
others, but his eyes, which in spite of his sparse gray hair
were still shaded by dark lashes, showed clearly that he
was not sitting there merely to nod off to sleep.

The dikegrave stretched out his hand towards him.
''Our schoolmaster,'' he said, raising his voice, ''will be
able to tell you that better than any of the rest of us here—
only in his own way, to be sure, and not as correctly as
Antje Vollmers, my old housekeeper at home, would do it.''

''You're joking, Dikegrave,'' came the somewhat thin
voice of the schoolmaster from behind the stove, ''to put
your stupid dragon on an equality with me!''

''Yes, yes, Schoolmaster!'' returned the other; ''but tales
of that kind you know are said to be best preserved among
the dragons!''

''To be sure,'' said the little man. ''We are not quite
of the same opinion in this matter,'' and a smile of superi-
ority passed over his delicately formed face.

''You see,'' the dikegrave whispered in my ear, ''he is
still a little haughty. He studied theology once, in his
youth, and stuck here in his home as schoolmaster only on
account of an unfortunate betrothal.''

In the meantime the schoolmaster had come forward
out of his corner and seated himself beside me at the long
table. ''Go on Schoolmaster, let us have the story,'' called
a few of the younger ones in the party.

''To be sure,'' said the old man turning to me, ''I am
glad to oblige you; but there is much superstition inter-

woven with it and it requires art to tell the tale without including that.''

"Please don't leave that out," I replied, "trust me to separate the chaff from the wheat myself.''

The old man looked at me with a smile of understanding. ''Well, then,'' he said, ''in the middle of the last century, or rather, to be more exact, before and after the middle, there was a dikegrave here who understood more about dikes, drains and sluices than peasants and farmers usually do; yet even so it seems hardly to have been enough, for he had read but little of what learned experts have written about such things, and had only thought out his own knowledge for himself from the time he was a little child. You have probably heard, sir, that the Friesians are good at figures and undoubtedly you have heard some talk too about our Hans Mommsen of Fahretoft, who was a peasant and yet could make compasses and chronometers, telescopes and organs. Well, the father of this dikegrave was a bit like that too; only a bit, to be sure. He had a few fields in the fens where he planted rape and beans, and where a cow grazed. Sometimes in autumn and spring he went out surveying, and in winter when the northwester came and shook his shutters, he sat at home sketching and engraving. His boy generally sat there with him and looked up from his reader or his Bible at his father measuring and calculating, and buried his hand in his blond hair. And one evening he asked his father why that which he had just written had to be just like that and not otherwise, and gave his own opinion about it. But his father, who did not know what answer to give, shook his head and said: ''I can't tell you why, it is enough that it is so; and you yourself are mistaken. If you want to know more go up to the attic tomorrow and hunt for a book in the box up there. The man who wrote it was called Euclid; you can find out from that book.''

The next day the boy did go up to the attic and soon found the book, for there were not many in the whole house; but his father laughed when the boy laid it down before him on the table. It was a Dutch Euclid, and Dutch, although after all it is half German, was beyond them both. "Yes, yes," he said, "the book was my father's, he understood it. Isn't there a German one there?"

The boy, who was a child of few words, looked quietly at his father and only said: "May I keep it? There is no German one there."

And when the old man nodded he showed him a second little volume, half torn. "This one too?" he asked again.

"Take them both," said Tede Haien; "they won't do you much good."

But the second book was a little Dutch grammar, and as most of the winter was still to come it did help the lad enough so that finally when the time came for the gooseberries to bloom in the garden he was able to understand nearly all of the Euclid, then very much in vogue.

"I am not unaware, Sir," the narrator interrupted himself, "that this same incident is told of Hans Mommsen; but, here with us, people used to tell it of Hauke Haien— that was the boy's name—before Mommsen was born. You know how it is, when a greater man arises, he is credited with everything that his predecessors may have done, in earnest or in fun."

When the old man saw that the lad cared nothing about cows or sheep and scarcely even noticed when the beans were in blossom—which after all is the joy of every man from the marshlands—and that his little place might indeed get on with a peasant and a boy, but not with a semi-scholar and a servant, and also because he himself had failed of prosperity, he sent his big boy to the dike, where from Easter till Martinmas he was to wheel his barrow of earth with the other laborers. "That will cure him of Euclid!" he said to himself.

And the lad pushed his wheelbarrow, but he kept the Euclid in his pocket all the time, and when the workmen ate their lunch or stopped for a bite in the late afternoon he sat on the bottom of a wheelbarrow with the book in his hand. And in autumn when the tides began to be higher, and the work had sometimes to be stopped he did not go home with the others, but stayed, and sat on the slope of the dike, his hands clasped round his knee, and watched for hours how the gray waves of the North Sea dashed up higher and higher towards the grass-line of the dike. Not until the water came in over his feet and the foam spattered in his face did he move up a few feet higher and then sit on there. He heard neither the splashing of the water nor the screaming of the gulls and shore-birds that flew above and around him, almost touching him with their wings, and flashing their black eyes into his; nor did he see how night came and enveloped the broad, wild desert of water in front of him. All that he saw was the hem of the water outlined by the surf which, when the tide was in, struck again and again with its heavy beat on the same spot in the dike and washed away the grass-line on its steep side before his very eyes.

After staring at it long he sometimes nodded his head slowly, or, without looking up, drew a soft line in the air with his hand as if he would thus give the dike a gentler slope. When it grew so dark that all earthly things vanished from his sight and only the tide continued to thunder in his ears, he got up and trotted home half wet through.

One evening when he came home in this state, his father, who was cleaning his measuring instruments, looked up and turned on him. "What have you been doing out there so long? You might have been drowned; the water is eating right into the dike today."

Hauke looked at him stubbornly.

"Don't you hear what I say? You might have been drowned."

"Yes," said Hauke; "but I didn't get drowned."

"No," replied the old man after a time and looked at him absent-mindedly—"not this time."

"But," went on Hauke, "our dikes are no good!"

"What's that, boy?"

"The dikes, I say!"

"What about the dikes?"

"They're no good, Father."

The old man laughed in his face. "Is that so, boy? I suppose you are the child prodigy of Lübeck!"

But the lad would not allow himself to be confused. "The water-side is too steep," he said; "if it should happen again as it has already happened more than once we may all drown in here, behind the dike too."

The old man pulled his tobacco out of his pocket, twisted off a piece and pushed it in behind his teeth. "And how many barrows did you wheel today?" he asked crossly, for he saw that working at the dike could not cure the boy of working with his mind.

"I don't know, Father; about the same as the others; perhaps half a dozen more. But—the dikes must be built different."

"Good," said his father with a laugh; "you may get to be dikegrave; then, build them different."

"Yes, Father," returned the boy.

The old man looked at him and swallowed once or twice; then he went out. He did not know what answer to give the lad.

When, at the end of October, work on the dike came to an end Hauke Haien still continued to find more pleasure in a walk out towards the north, to the sea, than in anything else. Just as the children of today look forward to Christmas, he looked forward to All Saints' Day, when the equinoctial gales burst over the land, an occasion for lamentation in Friesland. In spite of wind and weather he was certain to be found at the time of the high spring tides lying out on the dike all by himself; and when the gulls shrieked, when the waves dashed high against the dike, and in rolling back washed out whole pieces of sod into the sea, Hauke's angry laughter was something worth hearing.

"You can't do anything right," he shouted out into the noise, "just as people don't know how to do anything!" And at last, often when it was quite dark, he would turn away from the broad, bleak expanse and trot home along the dike till he reached the low door under his father's thatch, and his tall, overgrown figure slipped through and into the little room beyond.

Sometimes he brought a handful of clay with him. Then he sat down beside his father who had begun to let him go his own way, and, by the light of the thin tallow candle, kneaded all kinds of dike-models, laid them in a shallow dish of water and tried to imitate the way in which the waves washed out the bank. Or he took his slate and drew on it profiles of dikes on the water-side as he thought they ought to be.

It never entered his head to associate with the boys who had been his companions in school, and apparently they cared nothing about such a dreamer. When it came winter again and the frost had taken hold he wandered out along the dike farther than he had ever been before to where the ice-covered surface of the shoals stretched before him as far as the eye could reach.

In February, during continuous frost, dead bodies were found washed up on the shore; they had lain out by the open sea on the frozen shoals. A young woman who had seen them being carried into the village stood and chattered to old Haien: "Don't think that they looked like people," she exclaimed, "no, they looked like sea-devils! Big heads like this," and she held up her hands with the fingers stretched out, far apart from each other, "black and wrinkled and shiny like freshly baked bread! And the crabs had nibbled them; the children screamed when they saw them."

Such a description was not exactly new to old Haien. "They have probably been washing about in the sea since November," he said indifferently.

Hauke stood beside them in silence. But as soon as he

could he crept away out to the dike; no one could say
whether he wanted to hunt for more corpses or whether
the horror that still hung about the now deserted spots
where the others had been found attracted him. He ran on
farther and farther till he stood all alone in the bleakness
where only the winds swept across the dike and where there
was nothing but the plaintive voices of the great birds as
they wheeled quickly by. On his left lay the wide empty
marsh, on the other side the never-ending shore with the
great expanse of shoals now glistening with ice; it seemed
as if the whole world lay in white death.

Hauke remained standing on the dike and his keen
eyes glanced far in all directions; but there were no more
dead to be seen; only where the invisible currents moved
under it the ice field rose and sank like a stream.

He ran home; but on one of the following evenings he
was out there again. The ice was now broken in places:
clouds of smoke seemed to rise out of the cracks and above
the whole surface of the shallows was spread a net of
steam and fog that combined strangely with the dusk of the
evening. Hauke gazed at it with fixed eyes, for dark figures
moved up and down in the fog, and as he watched them they
seemed to be as large as men. There, far away on the edge
of the smoking fissures, they walked back and forth, full of
dignity but with long noses and necks and odd, terrifying
gestures; suddenly they began to jump up and down in an
uncanny way, liks imps, the big ones over the little ones
and the little ones towards the others; then they spread
out and lost all form.

"What of them? Are they the spirits of those who were
drowned?" thought Hauke. "Ahoy!" he shouted loudly
into the night; but the forms heeded him not, merely continued their strange doings.

Then he suddenly thought of the fearful Norwegian sea-
ghosts about whom an old captain had once told him, who
instead of a head and face had only a tuft of sea-grass
on their necks; he did not run away however, but dug the

heels of his boots deep into the clay of the dike and gazed at the weird antics that went on before his eyes in the growing dusk. "Are you here with us too?" he asked in a hard voice. "You shall not drive *me* away."

Not till the darkness had covered everything did he start for home, walking with a stiff, slow step. But from behind him there seemed to come the whirring of wings and resounding laughter. He did not look round, neither did he quicken his step, and it was late when he reached home, but he is said never to have spoken to his father or anyone else of this experience. Only many years later, after God Almighty had laid the burden of an half-witted child upon him, he took the girl out on the dike with him at the same time of day and of the year and the same thing is said to have happened again out on the shallows. But he told her not to be afraid, those creatures were only herons and crows that looked so big and dreadful in the fog as they caught fish in the open cracks.

"God knows, Sir!" the schoolmaster interrupted himself; "there are all kinds of things in the world that may confuse an honest Christian's heart; but Hauke was neither a fool nor a dunce."

As I did not reply he was about to go on, but suddenly there was a stir among the other guests who hitherto had listened in silence, only filling the low room with dense tobacco smoke. First one or two, then nearly all of them turned towards the window. Outside—we could see through the uncurtained windows—the wind was driving the clouds, and light and darkness were madly intermingled; but it seemed to me, too, as if I had seen the haggard rider shoot by on his white horse.

"Wait a bit, Schoolmaster," said the dikegrave softly.

"You need not be afraid, Dikegrave," replied the little story-teller. "I have not slandered him and have no reason to do so," and he looked up at him with his wise little eyes.

"Well, well," said the other, "just let me fill your glass again." And after that had been done and the listeners,

most of them with disconcerted faces, had turned to him
again the schoolmaster continued:

"Thus keeping to himself and loving best to live only
with the wind and water and the images that solitude
brings, Hauke grew up to be a tall, lean fellow. He had
been confirmed for more than a year when things began to
change with him, and that was owing to the old white
Angora tom-cat which had been brought home from a
Spanish sea voyage to old Trien' Jans by her son, who later
perished on the flats. Trien' lived a good distance out on
the dike in a little cottage and when she was working about
in her house this monster of a cat used to sit in front of
the door and blink out at the summer day, and the lap-
wings that flew by. When Hauke passed the cat mewed
at him and Hauke nodded; they both knew what was going
on between them.

Once, it was spring, and Hauke often lay out on the
dike as was his habit, farther down nearer the water, among
the shore-pinks and the sweet-smelling sea-wormwood, and
let the sun, which was already strong, shine down on him.
The day before, when he was on the uplands, he had filled
his pockets with pebbles and when the low tide had laid
bare the flats and the little gray sand-pipers hopped over
them, piping as they went, he suddenly took a stone out of
his pocket and threw it at the birds. He had practised this
from childhood and generally managed to bring one down;
but just as often it was impossible to go out on the mud
after it; Hauke had often thought of bringing the cat with
him and teaching it to retrieve. Here and there, however,
there were firm spots in the mud or sandbanks and then
he could run out and fetch his plunder himself. If the cat
was still sitting in front of the door as he passed on his
way home it mewed wild with rapacity until Hauke threw
it one of the birds he had killed.

On this particular day as he went home, his jacket on
his shoulder, he only had one bird, of a kind unknown to
him but which was covered with beautiful plumage that

looked like variegated silk and burnished metal. The cat
looked at him and begged loudly as usual. But this time
Hauke did not want to give up his prey—it may have been
a kingfisher—and paid no attention to the animal's desire.
"Turn and turn about," he called to him, "my turn today,
yours tomorrow; this is no food for a tom-cat!" But the
cat crept up cautiously towards him; Hauke stood and
looked at him, the bird hanging from his hand and the cat
stopped with its paw raised. But Hauke seems not to have
understood his friend thoroughly, for, as he turned his
back on him and prepared to go on his way he felt his
plunder torn from his grasp with a jerk, and at the same
time a sharp claw dug into his flesh. A sudden fury like
that of a beast of prey surged in the young fellow's blood;
he grabbed madly about him and had the robber by the
neck in a moment. Holding up the powerful creature in
his fist he strangled it till its eyes obtruded from the rough
hair, not heeding the strong hind claws that were tearing
the flesh from his arm. "Ho, ho!" he shouted and gripped
it still tighter; "we'll see which of us can stand it longest!"

Suddenly the hind legs of the great cat dropped lifelessly
from his arm and Hauke went back a few steps and threw
it towards the cottage of the old woman. As the cat did
not move he turned and continued his way home.

But the Angora cat had been its mistress's treasure; it
was her companion and the only thing that her son, the
sailor, had left her when he came to his sudden end on
the coast hard by, while trying to help his mother catch
prawns in a storm. Hauke had scarcely taken a hundred
steps, sopping up the blood from his wounds with a cloth as
he went, when a loud outcry and lamentation from the
direction of the cottage struck on his ear. He turned and
saw the old woman lying on the ground in front of it while
the wind blew her gray hair about the red handkerchief
that covered her head. "Dead!" she shrieked, "dead!"
and stretched out her thin arm threateningly towards him:
"you shall be cursed! You killed him, you useless vaga-

bond; you weren't worthy to stroke his tail." She threw
herself on the animal and gently wiped away with her
apron the blood that flowed from its nose and mouth. Then
she again began her loud lamentation.

"Will you soon be through?" called Hauke to her, "then
let me tell you this: I will get you a tom-cat that is satisfied with the blood of rats and mice!"

With this he went on his way, not apparently paying heed
to anything. But the dead cat must have confused his head
all the same, for when he came to the village he went on
past his father's house and all the others too, out a long
way on the dike towards the south, where the town lies.

In the meantime Trien' Jans too wandered out in the
same direction; she carried a burden in her arms wrapped
in an old blue-checked pillow slip, holding it carefully as if
it had been a child; and her gray hair blew about in the
gentle spring breeze. "What are you carrying there,
Trina?" asked a peasant who met her. "More than your
house and home," she replied and went on eagerly. When
she came near to old Haien's house, which stood down
below, she turned down the "Akt" as we call the cattle-
paths and footways that run up or down the side of the
dike.

Old Tede Haien was just standing out in front of the
door looking at the weather. "Well, Trien'!" he said as
she stood before him, panting and digging the point of her
stick into the ground. "What have you got new in your
bag?"

"First let me come in, Tede Haien! Then I'll show you,"
she said with an odd gleam in her eyes.

"Come in then," said the old man. Why should he
bother about the foolish woman's eyes?

And when they were both inside she went on: "Take the
old tobacco box and writing things away from the table—
what do you want to be always writing for? There! And
now wipe it off nice and clean!" And the old man, who
was beginning to be curious, did everything that she told

him. Then she took the blue pillow slip by the corners and shook the body of the great cat out on the table. "There you have him," she cried, "your Hauke has killed him." Whereupon she began to cry bitterly. She stroked the thick fur of the dead animal, laid its paws together, bowed her long nose over its head and whispered indistinct words of endearment into its ear.

Tede Haien watched the scene. "So," he said, "Hauke killed him?" He did not know what to do with the blubbering woman.

She nodded grimly: "Yes, by God, he did it!" and she wiped away the tears from her eyes with her gnarled gouty hand. "No child, nothing alive any more!" she sobbed. "And you know yourself how it is with us old ones, after All Saints' Day 's over our legs freeze at night in bed and instead of sleeping we listen to the northwester rattling at the shutters. I don't like to hear it, Tede Haien, it comes from where my lad went down in the mud."

Tede Haien nodded and the old woman stroked her dead cat's coat. "And this one here," she began again, "in the winter when I sat at my work and the spinning wheel and hummed he sat beside me and hummed too and looked at me with his green eyes! And when I was cold and crept into bed—it was not long before he sprang up too and laid himself on my shivering legs and then we slept warm together!" And the old woman looked at the old man standing beside her at the table with smouldering eyes as if she wanted his assent to this memory.

But Tede Haien said slowly: "I know a way to help you, Trien' Jans." He went to his strong box and took a silver coin out of the drawer. "You say that Hauke has robbed you of your pet and I know that you don't lie; but here is a crownpiece of Christian IV.; go and buy yourself a dressed lambskin to keep your legs warm. Besides, our cat will soon have kittens and you may pick out the largest of them. The two together ought to make up for an Angora tom-cat that is weak with old age. And now take the creature and

carry it into town to the knacker, for aught I care, and
hold your tongue about its having lain here on my respectable table!''

While he was speaking the woman had taken the crown
and hidden it in a little bag that she wore under her skirts;
then she stuffed the cat back into the pillow-case, wiped the
spots of blood from the table with her apron and stumped
out of the door. ''Don't forget about the young kitten,''
she called back as she went.

Some time later, as old Haien was walking up and down
in the little room, Hauke came in and threw his bright bird
onto the table; but when he saw the blood-stains which were
still recognizable on its white, scoured top he asked with
apparent carelessness, ''What's that?''

His father stood still. ''That is the blood that you
shed!''

The boy flushed hotly. ''Oh, has Trien' Jans been here
with her cat?''

The old man nodded. ''Why did you kill it?''

Hauke bared his torn arm. ''That's why,'' he said; ''he
snatched my bird away from me.''

The old man said nothing. He began to walk up and
down again for some time; then he stopped in front of his
son and looked at him absently. ''I have settled the matter
of the cat,'' he said after a moment, ''but you see Hauke,
this cottage is too small; two masters can't *hold* it—it is
time now, you must get yourself something to do.''

''Yes, Father,'' replied Hauke; ''I have thought the
same myself.''

''Why?'' asked the old man.

''Well, a fellow boils within, if he has not enough to do
to work it off.''

''So,'' said the old man, ''and that's why you killed the
Angora? That might easily lead to something worse!''

''You may be right, Father; but the dikegrave has sent
his servant-boy off; I could do that work.''

The old man began to walk up and down again and

squirted a stream of black tobacco-juice from his mouth. "The dikegrave is a dunce, as stupid as an owl! He is only dikegrave because his father and grandfather were dikegraves before him and because of his twenty-nine fens. When Martinmas comes round and the dike and sluice accounts have to be made up he feeds the schoolmaster on roast goose and mead and wheat-cracknels, and just sits there and nods when the other man runs over the columns of figures and says: "Yes, indeed, Schoolmaster, may God reward you! What a man you are at figures!" But if at any time the schoolmaster can't or won't, then he has to do it himself and he sits and writes and crosses out again, and his big stupid head grows red and hot and his eyes stand out like glass balls as if what little brain he has was trying to get out there."

The boy stood up straight before his father and was amazed that he could make such a speech; he had never heard him talk like that before. "Yes, he is stupid enough, God knows," he said; "but his daughter Elke, she can figure!"

The old man looked at him sharply. "Oh ho, Hauke!" he exclaimed, "what do you know of Elke Volkerts?"

"Nothing, Father; only the schoolmaster told me so."

The old man made no answer to this; he merely shifted his tobacco quid slowly from one cheek to the other. "And you think," he said then, "that when you're there you will be able to help figure too."

"Oh, yes, Father, I could do that all right," answered the son and his mouth quivered with earnestness.

The old man shook his head: "Well, as far as I am concerned, you may try your luck!"

"Thank you, Father!" said Hauke, and went up to the attic where he slept. There he seated himself on the side of the bed and thought and wondered why his father had questioned him about Elke Volkerts. He knew her of course, the slender eighteen-year-old girl with the narrow, brown-skinned face and the dark brows that met above the

defiant eyes and narrow nose; but he had scarcely spoken
a word to her till now. Well, if he should go to work for
old Tede Volkerts he would look at her more closely to
see what kind of a girl she was. And he would go right
away so that no one else should get the place ahead of
him, for it was still quite early in the evening. And so he
put on his Sunday suit and best boots and started on his
way in good spirits.

The long low house of the dikegrave could be seen from
far away, for it stood on a high mound, and the highest tree
in the village, a mighty ash, stood near it. In his youth the
grandfather of the present dikegrave, the first one in the
family, had planted such a tree to the east of the front
door; but the first two saplings died and so, on his wedding morning, he had planted this tree which with its ever
wider-spreading top still murmured in the unceasing wind,
as it seemed, of by-gone days.

When, some time later, Hauke's tall, overgrown form
ascended the high mound, the sides of which were planted
with turnips and cabbages, he saw above him, standing
beside the low door, the daughter of the master of the house.
One of her somewhat thin arms hung loosely at her side, her
other hand seemed to be feeling behind her for an iron ring,
two of which were fastened to the wall, one on either side of
the door, so that a rider coming to the house could tie up his
horse. She seemed to be looking out over the dike to the
sea where, in the still of evening, the sun was just sinking
into the water and sending its last ray to gild the brown-
skinned girl who stood there watching.

Hauke slackened his steps and thought to himself: "She
does not look half bad that way!" And then he had already
reached the top. "Good evening," he said going up to her,
"what are your big eyes looking at now, Jungfer Elke?"

"At something that happens here every evening," she
replied, "but which cannot always be seen every evening."
She let the ring drop from her hand so that it fell back

clanging against the wall. "What do you want, Hauke Haien?" she asked.

"Something that I hope won't displease you," he said. "Your father has turned out his servant-boy so I thought I might get the place."

She looked him over from head to foot. "You still look rather too slight to be strong, Hauke," she said, "but two good eyes would serve us better than two good arms." She looked at him with an almost lowering glance as she spoke, but Hauke did not falter. "Come along then," she went on, "the master is in the house, let us go in."

The next day Tede Haien and his son entered the large room of the dikegrave. The walls were covered with glazed tiles on which to please the eye, there was here a ship under full sail or an anchor on the shore, there a recumbent ox before a peasant's house. This durable wall-covering was broken by an immense wall-bed, the doors of which were now closed, and a cupboard through the glass doors of which all sorts of china and silverware might be seen. Beside the door leading into the adjoining parlor a Dutch clock was let into the wall behind glass.

The stout, somewhat apoplectic, master of the house sat in an armchair on a bright-colored woolen cushion at the end of a table that had been scoured until it shone. His hands were folded over his stomach and his round eyes were contentedly fixed on the skeleton of a fat duck; knife and fork lay on a plate in front of him.

"Good day, Dikegrave," said Haien and the dikegrave slowly turned his head and eyes towards him. "Is it you, Tede?" he replied, and the fat duck he had just eaten had had its effect on his voice. "Sit down, it's a long way over here from your house to mine!"

"I've come," said Tede Haien, sitting down at right angles to the dikegrave on a bench that ran along the wall. "You've had trouble with your servant-boy and have agreed to take my boy in his place!"

The dikegrave nodded: "Yes, yes, Tede; but—what do you mean by trouble? We people from the marsh have something to take for that, thank God!" And he picked up the knife that lay before him and tapped the skeleton of the poor duck caressingly. "That was my favorite bird," he added with a comfortable laugh; "it would eat out of my hand!"

"I thought," said old Haien not hearing the last words, "that the fellow did a lot of mischief in the stable."

"Mischief? Yes, Tede; mischief enough, to be sure! The lazy mutton-head had not watered the calves, but he lay dead drunk in the hayloft and the creatures mooed with thirst the whole night, so that I had to lie in bed till noon to make up my sleep. No farm can go on that way!"

"No, Dikegrave, but there is no danger of that where my son is concerned."

Hauke stood against the door-post with his hands in his side pockets; he had thrown his head back and was studying the window casing opposite him.

The dikegrave raised his eyes and nodded to him: "No, no, Tede," and now he nodded to the old man too, "your Hauke will not disturb my night's rest; the schoolmaster has already told me that he would rather sit before a slate and reckon than over a glass of spirits."

Hauke did not listen to this speech of encouragement for Elke had come into the room and was clearing away the remains of the food from the table with her light, quick hands, glancing at him furtively with her dark eyes, as she did so. Now his glance too fell upon her. "By God," he said to himself, "she does not look half bad that way either."

The girl had left the room. "You know, Tede," the dikegrave began again, "God has denied me a son."

"Yes, Dikegrave, but do not let that trouble you," answered the other. "For the brains of a family are said to come to an end in the third generation; your grandfather, as we all still know today, was the man who protected the land!''

After thinking for some moments the dikegrave looked almost puzzled. "How do you mean that, Tede Haien?" he asked, and sat upright in his armchair; "I am in the third generation myself."

"Oh, that's so! No offence, Dikegrave; that's just what people say." And Tede Haien with his lean form looked at the old dignitary with somewhat mischievous eyes.

The latter went on unconcernedly: "You must not let old women's talk put such foolishness as that into your head, Tede Haien; you don't know my daughter, she can figure two or three times as well as I myself! I only wanted to say that besides his work in the field your Hauke can gain considerable here in my room with pen or pencil and that won't do him any harm!"

"Yes, indeed, Dikegrave, that he will; there you're quite right!" said old Haien and began to arrange for several benefits to be included in his son's contract which had not occurred to the boy the evening before. Thus besides the linen shirts that Hauke was to receive in the autumn in addition to his wages, he was also to have eight pairs of woolen stockings; then he was to help his father with the work at home for a week in the spring and so on. The dike-grave agreed to everything; Hauke Haien seemed to be just the right man for him.

"Well, God have mercy on you, my boy," said the old man as soon as they left the house, "if you are to learn from him how the world goes!"

But Hauke answered quietly: "Let it be, Father; everything will turn out all right."

And Hauke was not wrong; the world, or what the world meant to him, did grow clearer to him the longer he stayed in that house. This was more the case perhaps, the less a superior judgment came to his aid, and the more he was obliged to depend on his own strength, on which he had been

accustomed to rely from the beginning. There was one
person in the house to be sure whom he did not suit at all
and that was Ole Peters, the head man, a capable workman
but a fellow with a very ready tongue. The former lazy
and stupid but stocky second man on whose back he had
been able to load a whole barrel of oats and whom he could
knock about as he chose had been more to his liking. He
could not get at Hauke, who was much quieter and mentally
far superior to him, in this way; for Hauke had such a very
peculiar way of looking at him. Nevertheless he managed
to find work for him which might have been dangerous to
his body as it was not yet firmly knit, and when he said:
"You should have seen fat Niss; it was all play to him!"
Hauke took hold with all his strength and managed to do
the job even though he had to overexert himself. It was
fortunate for him that Elke was generally able to counter-
mand such orders either herself or through her father. We
may well ask ourselves what it is that sometimes binds perfect strangers to each other; perhaps—they were both born
mathematicians and the girl could not bear to see her comrade ruined by doing rough work.

The breach between the head man and his subordinate
did not grow better in winter when, after Martinmas, the
different dike accounts came in to be examined.

It was on a May evening, but the weather was like November; inside the house the surf could be heard thundering
out beyond the dike. "Here, Hauke," said the master of
the house, "come in here; now you can show whether you
can figure!"

"I have got to feed the yearlings first, Master," replied
Hauke.

"Elke," called the dikegrave, "where are you, Elke? Go
to Ole and tell him to feed the yearlings; Hauke must come
and figure!"

And Elke hurried to the stable and gave the order to the
head man, who was just occupied in putting away the har-
ness that had been used that day.

Ole Peters took a snaffle and struck a post near which he was standing as if he would smash it to bits: "The devil take the damned scribbling farm-hand!" She overheard the words as she closed the stable-door behind her.

"Well?" asked her father as she came back into the room.

"Ole is going to do it," she answered biting her lips a little, and sat down opposite Hauke on a coarsely carved wooden chair such as at that time the people here used to make in their own homes during the winter evenings. She took out of a drawer a white stocking with a red-bird pattern on it and went on knitting; the long-legged creatures in the pattern might have been herons or storks. Hauke sat opposite her deep in his calculations, the dikegrave himself rested in his armchair, blinking now and then sleepily at Hauke's pen. As always in the dikegrave's house, two tallow-candles burned on the table and in front of the windows with their leaded glass the shutters were closed outside and screwed tight from within; the wind might bluster as it would. At times Hauke raised his head from his work and glanced for a moment at the stockings with the birds on them or at the narrow, quiet face of the girl.

All at once a loud snore came from the armchair and a glance and a smile flew back and forth between the two young people; then followed gradually quieter breathing; one might have begun a little conversation, only Hauke did not know how. But as she stretched out her knitting and the birds became visible in their entirety he whispered across the table:

"Where did you learn that, Elke?"

"Learn what?" the girl asked back.

"To knit birds?" asked Hauke.

"Oh, that? From Trien' Jans, out at the dike, she can do all sorts of things; she served here once in my grandfather's time."

"But you weren't born then, were you?" asked Hauke.

"No, I hardly think I was; but she often came to the house afterwards."

"Is she so fond of birds? I thought she only liked cats."

Elke shook her head. "She raises ducks, you know, and sells them; but last spring after you killed her Angora, the rats got at the ducks in the back of the duck-house. Now she wants to build another one at the front of the house."

"Oh!" said Hauke and gave a low whistle, drawing his breath in through his teeth, "That is why she has dragged all that clay and stone down from the upland. But if she does that she will build on the road on the inside of the dike; has she got a permit?"

"I don't know," said Elke; but Hauke had spoken the last word so loud that the dikegrave started up out of his slumber. "What permit?" he asked and looked almost wildly from one to the other. "What is the permit for?"

But when Hauke had explained the matter to him he tapped him on the shoulder laughing. "Well, well, the inside road is wide enough; God have mercy on the dikegrave if he has got to bother about every duckhouse as well!"

It made Hauke's heart heavy to think that he had been the means of delivering the old woman's ducklings up to the rats and he allowed himself to let the dikegrave's excuse stand. "But Master," he began again, "there are some that would be better off for just a little nip and if you don't want to do it yourself just give the commissioner a nudge who is supposed to see that the dike regulations are carried out."

"How, what's the lad saying?" and the dikegrave sat perfectly upright while Elke let her elaborate stocking fall and listened.

"Yes, Master," Hauke went on, "you have already had the spring inspection; but all the same Peter Jansen has not harrowed out the weeds on his piece till today. In summer the goldfinches will play merrily about the red thistle-blossoms there! And close beside it there's another piece —I don't know whom it belongs to—but there's a regular hollow in the dike on the outside. When the weather's fine its always full of little children who roll about in it, but—God preserve us from high water!''

The old dikegrave's eyes had grown steadily bigger.

''And then,'' began Hauke again.

''Well, and what else, young man?'' asked the dikegrave; ''haven't you done yet?'' and his voice sounded as if his second man had already said too much to please him.

''Yes, and then, Master,'' went on Hauke, ''you know that fat girl Vollina, the daughter of Harders, the commissioner, who always fetches her father's horses home from the fens,—once she's up on the old yellow mare with her fat legs then it's: 'Cluck, cluck! Get up!' And that's the way she always rides, right up the slope of the dike!''

Not till this moment did Hauke notice that Elke's wise eyes were fixed on him and that she was shaking her head gently.

He stopped, but the blow that the old man gave the table with his fist thundered in his ears. ''The devil take it!'' he roared, and Hauke was almost frightened at the bellow that filled the room. ''She shall be fined! Make a note of it, Hauke, that the fat wench is to be fined! Last summer the hussy caught three of my young ducks! Go on, make a note of it,'' he repeated when Hauke hesitated; ''I think she really got four!''

''Oh, come, Father,'' said Elke, ''don't you think it was the otter that took the young ducks?''

''A giant otter!'' the old man shouted snorting. ''I think I know that fat Vollina from an otter! No, no, it was four ducks, Hauke. But as for the other things you've chattered about, last spring the chief dikegrave and I lunched together here in my house and then we went out and drove past your weeds and your hollow and we didn't see anything of the sort. But you two,'' and he nodded significantly towards his daughter and Hauke, ''may well thank God that you are not a dikegrave! A man's only got two eyes and he's supposed to use a hundred. Just run through the

accounts of the straw work on the dike, Hauke; those fellows' figures are often altogether too careless.''

Then he lay back again in his chair, settled his heavy
body once or twice and soon fell into a contented sleep.

Similar scenes took place on many an evening. Hauke
had keen eyes and when he and the dikegrave were sitting
together he did not fail to report this or that transgression
or omission in matters relating to the dike, and as his
master was not always able to shut his eyes, the management gradually became more active before anyone was
aware of it, and those persons who formerly had kept on in
their accustomed sinful rut, and now unexpectedly received
a stroke across their mischievous or lazy fingers, turned
round annoyed and surprised to see where it came from.
And Ole, the head man, did not fail to spread the information far and near and thus to turn those circles against
Hauke and his father, who, of course, was also responsible;
but the others, on whom no hand descended or who were
actually anxious to see the thing done, laughed and rejoiced
that the young man had succeeded in poking the old one
up a bit. ''It is only a pity,'' they said, ''that the fellow
hasn't the necessary clay under his feet; then later on he'd
make a dikegrave like those that we used to have; but the
couple of acres that his father has would never be enough!''

When in the following autumn the chief dikegrave, who
was also the magistrate for the district, came to inspect, he
looked old Tede Volkerts over from top to toe while the
latter begged him to sit down to lunch. ''Upon my word,
Dikegrave,'' he said, ''it's just as I expected, you've grown
ten years younger; you've kept me busy this time with all
your proposals; if only we can get done with them all
today!''

''We'll manage, we'll manage, your Worship,'' returned
the old man with a smirk; ''this roast goose here will give
us strength; yes, thank God, I am always brisk and lively
still!'' He looked round the room to see if Hauke might

not perhaps be somewhere about; then he added with dignity; "and I hope to God to be spared to exercise my office a few years longer."

"And to that, my dear Dikegrave," replied his superior rising, "let us drink this glass together!"

Elke, who had arranged the lunch, was just going out of the room door with a soft laugh as the two men clinked their glasses together. Then she fetched a dish of scraps from the kitchen and went through the stable to throw them to the fowls in front of the outside door. In the stable she found Hauke Haien just pitching hay into the cows' cribs, for the cattle had already been brought in for the winter owing to the bad weather. When he saw the girl coming he let his pitchfork rest on the ground. "Well, Elke!" he said.

She stopped and nodded to him. "Oh, Hauke, you ought to have been in there just now!"

"Should I? Why Elke?"

"The chief dikegrave was praising the master!"

"The master? What has that got to do with me?"

"Well, of course, he praised the dikegrave!"

A deep red spread over the young man's face. "I know what you are driving at," he said.

"You needn't blush, Hauke; after all it was you whom the chief dikegrave praised!"

Hauke looked at her half smiling. "But it was you too, Elke," he said.

But she shook her head. "No, Hauke; when I was the only one that helped he didn't praise us. And all I can do is to figure; but you see everything outside that the dikegrave ought to see himself; you have cut me out!"

"I didn't mean to, you least of all," said Hauke shyly, pushing aside one of the cows' heads. "Come, Spotty, don't eat up my fork; I'll give you all you want!"

"Don't think that I am sorry," said the girl after thinking a minute; "after all it's a man's business!"

Hauke stretched out his arm towards her. "Give me your hand on it, Elke."

A deep scarlet shot up under the girl's dark brows. "Why? I don't lie," she cried.

Hauke was about to answer, but she was already out of the stable, and standing with the pitchfork in his hand he could only hear the ducks and hens outside quacking and cackling around her.

It was in January of the third year of Hauke's service that a winter festival was to be held. "Eisboseln" (winter golf) they call it here. There had been no wind along the coast and a steady frost had covered all the ditches between the fens with a firm, smooth crystal surface so that the divided pieces of land now formed an extensive course over which the little wooden balls filled with lead, with which the goal was to be reached, could be thrown. A light northeast breeze blew day after day. Everything was ready. The uplanders from the village lying to the east across the marsh and in which stood the church of the district, who had won the previous year, had been challenged and had accepted. Nine players had been picked out on each side. The umpire and the spokesmen had also been chosen. The latter, who had to discuss disputed points when a doubtful throw was in question, were generally men who knew how to present their case in the best light, usually fellows who had a ready tongue as well as common sense. First among these was Ole Peters, the dikegrave's head man. "See that you throw like devils," he said, "I'll do the talking for nothing."

It was towards evening of the day before the festival. A number of the players had gathered in the inside room of the parish tavern on the uplands, to decide whether or not a few applicants who had come at the last minute should be accepted. Hauke Haien was among the latter. At first he had decided not to try, although he knew that his arms were well trained in throwing. He feared that Ole Peters, who held a post of honor in the game, would succeed in having him rejected and he hoped to spare himself such a defeat. But Elke had changed his mind at the eleventh hour. "He wouldn't dare to, Hauke," she said; "he is the son of a day laborer; your father has a horse and cow of his own and is the wisest man in the village as well."

"Yes, but what if he should do it in spite of that?"

She looked at him half smiling with her dark eyes. "Then," she said, "he'll get turned down when he wants to dance with his master's daughter in the evening." Thereupon Hauke had nodded to her with spirit.

Outside the tavern the young people, who still wanted to enter the game, were standing in the cold, stamping their feet and looking up at the top of the church-tower, which was built of stone and stood beside the public-house. The pastor's pigeons, which fed in summer on the fields of the village, were just coming back from the peasants' yards and barns where they had sought their grain and were now disappearing into their nests under the eaves of the tower. In the west, above the sea, hung a glowing evening crimson.

"It'll be good weather tomorrow!" said one of the young fellows walking up and down stamping, "but cold, cold!" Another, after he had seen the last pigeon disappear, went into the house and stood listening at the door of the room through which there now came the sound of lively conversation; the dikegrave's second man came and stood beside him. "Listen, Hauke, now they're shouting about you," and within they could distinctly hear Ole Peters' grating voice saying, "Second men and boys don't belong in it."

"Come," said the other boy and taking Hauke by the sleeve he tried to pull him up to the door. "Now you can hear what they think of you."

But Hauke pulled himself away and went outside the house again. "They didn't lock us out so that we should hear what they said," he called back.

The third applicant was standing in front of the house. "I'm afraid I shan't be taken without a hitch," he called to Hauke, "I am hardly eighteen years old; if only they don't ask for my baptismal certificate! Your head man will talk you up all right, Hauke!"

"Yes, up and out!" growled Hauke and kicked a stone across the way, "but not in."

The noise inside increased; then gradually it grew still; those outside could hear again the gentle northeast wind as it swept by the top of the church tower. The boy who had been listening came back to the others. "Who were they talking about in there?" asked the eighteen-year-old boy.

"Him," the other answered and pointed to Hauke; "Ole Peters tried to make out he was still a boy, but they were all against that. And Jess Hansen said, 'and his father has land and cattle.' 'Yes, land,' said Ole Peters, 'land that could be carted away on thirteen barrows!' Finally Ole Hensen began to speak: 'Keep still there,' he called, 'I'll put you straight; tell me, who is the first man in the village?' They were all quiet a minute and seemed to be thinking, then someone said 'I suppose it's the dikegrave!' And all the others shouted, 'Well, yes; it must be the dikegrave!' 'And who is the dikegrave?' asked Ole Hensen again; 'and now think carefully!' Then one of them began to laugh softly and then another until at last the whole room was just full of laughter. 'Well, go call him then,' said Ole Hensen; 'you surely don't want to turn away the dikegrave from your door!' I think they're still laughing; but you can't hear Ole Peters' voice any more!" the boy finished his report.

Almost at that moment the door of the room inside was flung open and loud, merry cries of "Hauke! Hauke Haien!" rang out into the cold night.

So Hauke went into the house and did not stop to hear who the dikegrave was; what had been going on in his head during these moments nobody ever knew.

When, some time later, he approached his master's house he saw Elke standing down at the gate of the carriage-drive. The moonlight glistened over the immeasurable white-frosted pasture-land. "Are you standing here, Elke?" he asked.

She only nodded: "What happened?" she said. "Did he dare?"

"What would he not do?"

"Well, and?"

"It's all right, Elke. I can try tomorrow."

"Good-night, Hauke!" and she ran lightly up the mound and disappeared into the house.

Hauke followed her slowly.

On the following afternoon a dark mass of people was seen on the broad pasture-land that ran along towards the east on the land side of the dike. Sometimes the mass stood still, then, after a wooden ball had twice flown from it over the ground which the sun had now freed from frost, it moved gradually forward away from the long, low houses that lay behind it. The two parties of winter golfers were in the middle, surrounded by all the young and old who were living or staying either in these houses or on the uplands. The older men were in long coats, smoking their short pipes with deliberation, the women in shawls and jackets, some of them leading children by the hand or carrying them in their arms. Out of the frozen ditches which were crossed one after another the pale shine of the noonday sun sparkled through the sharp points of the reeds; it was freezing hard. But the game went on uninterruptedly, and all eyes followed again and again the flying wooden ball, for the whole village felt that on it hung the honor of the day. The spokesman of the home side carried a white staff with an iron point, that of the upland party a black one. Wherever the ball ceased rolling this staff was driven into the frozen ground amid the quiet admiration or the mocking laughter of the opposing party and whoever first reached the goal with his ball won the game for his side.

There was very little conversation in the crowd; only when a capital cast was made the young men or women sometimes broke into a cheer, or one of the old men took his pipe out of his mouth and tapped the thrower with it on the shoulder, saying, "That was a throw, said Zacharias, and threw his wife out of the attic window," or "That's how your father used to throw, may God have mercy on his soul!" or some other pleasant words.

The first time he cast luck had not been with Hauke; just as he threw his arm out behind him to hurl the ball a cloud which had covered the sun till then passed away from it and the dazzling rays struck him full in the eyes; his cast was too short, the ball fell on a ditch and stuck in the uneven ice.

"That doesn't count! That doesn't count! Throw again, Hauke!" shouted his partners.

But the uplanders' spokesman objected: "It must count. What's cast is cast."

"Ole! Ole Peters!" shouted the men from the marsh. "Where is Ole? Where the devil can he be?"

But he was there already. "Don't shout so! Is there something wrong with Hauke? That's just how I thought it would be."

"Oh, nonsense! Hauke must throw again; now show that you've got your mouth in the right place."

"I certainly have that!" shouted Ole, and he went up to the other spokesman and made a long harangue. But the sharp cuts and witty points that usually filled his speech were lacking this time. At his side stood the girl with the enigmatical brows and watched him sharply with angry eyes; but she might not speak for the women had no voice in the game.

"You're talking nonsense," shouted the other spokesman, "because reason is not on your side. Sun, moon and stars treat us all alike and are in the sky all the time; it was a clumsy cast and all clumsy casts count!"

Thus they talked at each other for a while, but the end of it was that, according to the umpire's decision, Hauke was not allowed to repeat his cast.

"Forward!" cried the uplanders and their spokesman pulled the black staff out of the ground and the next player took his stand there when his number was called and hurled the ball forward. In order to see the throw the dikegrave's head man was obliged to pass Elke Volkerts. "For whose sake did you leave your brains at home today?" she whispered to him.

He looked at her almost fiercely and all trace of fun disappeared from his broad face. "For your sake," he said, "for you have forgotten yours too."

"Oh, come! I know you, Ole Peters!" answered the girl drawing herself up, but he turned his head away and pretended not to hear.

And the game and the black staff and the white one went on. When Hauke's turn to throw came again his ball flew so far that the goal, a large whitewashed hogshead, came plainly into sight. He was now a solidly built young fellow and mathematics and throwing had occupied him daily since he was a boy. "Oh ho! Hauke!" the crowd shouted; "the archangel Michael could not have done better himself!" An old woman with cakes and brandy made her way through the crowd to him; she poured out a glass and offered it to him: "Come," she said, "let us be friends; you are doing better today than when you killed my cat!" As he looked at her he saw that it was Trien' Jans. "Thank you, Mother," he said; "but I don't drink that stuff." He felt in his pockets and pressed a newly coined mark-piece into her hand. "Take that and drink this glass yourself, Trien'; then we shall be friends again!"

"You're right, Hauke!" returned the old woman obeying him. "You're right; it is better for an old woman like me than for you!"

"How are you getting on with your ducks?" he called after her as she was going away with her basket; but she only shook her head without turning round and clapped her old hands in the air. "It's no good, Hauke; there are too many rats in your ditches; God have mercy on me! I must find some other way of earning my bread." And with this she pushed her way into the crowd again, offering her spirits and honey-cakes as she went.

At last the sun had sunk behind the dike and in its place had left a reddish violet glow that flamed up into the sky; now and then black crows flew by and seemed for the moment to be of gold; it was evening. On the fields however the dark crowd of people kept on moving farther and farther away from the black houses in the distance behind them towards the hogshead; an exceptionally good cast might reach it now. It was the marsh party's turn and Hauke was to throw.

The chalky hogshead stood out white in the broad shadows that now fell from the dyke across the course. "You'll have to leave it to us, this time!" cried one of the uplanders, for the contest was hot and they were at least ten feet in advance.

Hauke's tall, lean figure stepped out of the crowd; the gray eyes in his long Friesian face were fixed on the hogshead; his hand, which hung at his side, held the ball.

"The bird's too big for you, eh?" came the grating voice of Ole Peters close to his ear, "shall we exchange it for a gray pot?"

Hauke turned and looked at him steadily. "I'm throwing for the marsh," he said. "Where do you belong?"

"To the marsh too, I imagine; but you are throwing for Elke Volkerts, eh?"

"Stand aside!" shouted Hauke and took his position again. But Ole pressed forward with his head still nearer to him. Then suddenly, before Hauke himself could do anything, a hand gripped the intruder and pulled him backwards so that he stumbled against his laughing comrades. It was not a large hand that did so, for as Hauke hastily turned his head he saw Elke Volkerts beside him pulling her sleeve to rights, and her dark brows were drawn angrily across her hot face.

The power of steel shot into Hauke's arm; he bent forward a little, weighed the ball in his hand once or twice, then he drew his arm back and a dead silence fell on both sides; all eyes followed the flying ball, it could be heard whistling through the air; suddenly, far away from the spot where it was thrown, the silver wings of a gull hid it as, shrieking, the bird flew across from the dike. But at the same moment it was heard in the distance striking against the hogshead. "Hurrah for Hauke!" shouted the marshlanders and the news ran loudly through the crowd: "Hauke! Hauke Haien has won the game!"

But Hauke himself as they all crowded about him had only felt for a hand at his side and even when they called again: "What are you waiting for, Hauke? Your ball is lying in the hogshead!" he only nodded and did not move from the spot; not until he felt the little hand clasp his firmly did he say: "I believe you're right; I think I've won!"

Then the whole crowd streamed back and Elke and Hauke were separated and swept along by the crowd towards the tavern on the road that turned up by the dike-grave's mound towards the uplands. But here they both escaped and while Elke went up to her room Hauke stood at the back, in front of the stable door and watched the dark mass of people wandering up to the tavern, where a room was ready for the dancers. Night gradually fell over the open country; it grew stiller and stiller about him, only behind him he could hear the cattle moving in the stable; he fancied he could already catch the sound of the clarinets in the tavern on the uplands. All at once he heard the rustle of a gown round the corner of the house and firm little steps went down the footway that led through the fens up onto the uplands. Now, in the dusk, he could see the figure swinging along and he knew that it was Elke; she too was going to the dance in the tavern. The blood rushed up into his throat; should he not run after her and go with her? But Hauke was no hero where women were con-

cerned; weighing this question he remained standing till
she had disappeared from his sight in the dark.

Then, when the danger of overtaking her had passed, he
too went the same way till he reached the tavern up by the
church, and the talking and shouting of the crowd before
the house and in the passage, and the shrill tones of the
violins and clarinets within, surrounded him with a deafen-
ing noise. Unnoticed he made his way into the "guild-
hall." It was not large and was so full that he could
scarcely see a step in front of him. In silence he stood
leaning against the door-jamb and watched the moving
throng; the people seemed to him like fools; he did not need
to fear either that anyone would think of the struggle in
the afternoon or of who had won the game an hour ago.
Each man had eyes only for his girl and turned round and
round with her in a circle. He was seeking for one only
and at last—there she was! She was dancing with her
cousin, the young dike commissioner—but she had already
disappeared again and he could see only other girls from
the marsh and the uplands for whom he cared nothing.
Then suddenly the violins and the clarinets ceased and the
dance was at an end; but already another was beginning.
The thought passed through Hauke's mind whether Elke
would really keep her word, if she might not dance past
him with Ole Peters. He almost screamed at the idea; then
—well, what would he do then? But she did not seem to
be dancing this dance at all and at last it came to an end
and another, a two-step, which was just beginning to be
popular then, followed. The music started with a mad
flourish, the young fellows rushed up to the girls, the lights
on the walls flared. Hauke nearly dislocated his neck trying to distinguish the dancers; and there, the third couple,
was Ole Peters and—but who was the girl? A broad fellow
from the marsh stood in front of her and hid her face.
But the dance went on madly and Ole and his partner cir-
cled out where he could see them. "Vollina! Vollina
Harders!" Hauke almost shouted aloud and gave a sigh of

relief. But where was Elke? Had she no partner or had she refused them all because she did not want to dance with Ole? The music stopped again and then a new dance began but still he did not see her. There was Ole, still with his fat Vollina in his arms! "Well," said Hauke to himself, "it looks as if Jess Harders with his twenty-five acres would soon have to retire! But where is Elke?"

He left the door and pushed his way further into the room; suddenly he found himself standing before her as she sat with an older friend in a corner. "Hauke!" she exclaimed, raising her narrow face to look at him; "are you here? I didn't see you dancing!"

"I haven't danced," he replied.

"Why not, Hauke?" and half rising she added: "Will you dance with me? I wouldn't with Ole Peters; he won't come again!"

But Hauke made no move to begin. "Thank you, Elke," he said, "but I don't know how well enough; they might laugh at you; and then * * *" he broke off suddenly and looked at her with feeling in his gray eyes as if he must leave it to them to finish what he would say.

"What do you mean, Hauke?" she asked softly.

"I mean, Elke, that the day can have no happier ending for me than it has had already."

"Yes," she said, "you won the game."

"Elke!" he said with scarcely audible reproach.

A hot red flamed up into her face. "There!" she said, "what do you want?" and dropped her eyes.

A partner now came and claimed her friend and after she had gone Hauke spoke louder. "I thought I had won something better, Elke!"

Her eyes searched the floor a few seconds longer; then she raised them slowly and a glance, filled with the quiet strength of her being, met his and ran through him like summer warmth. "Do as your feeling tells you, Hauke," she said; "we ought to know each other!"

Elke did not dance again that evening and when they

went home they went hand in hand; from the sky above the
stars sparkled over the silent marsh; a light east wind blew
and made the cold severe, but the two walked on without
many wraps as if spring had suddenly come.

Hauke had thought of something, to be used perhaps
only in the uncertain future, but with which he hoped to
celebrate a secret festival. Accordingly he went to town
the next Sunday to the old goldsmith Andersen and ordered
a thick gold ring. "Stretch out your finger till I measure
it," said the old man and took hold of Hauke's third finger.
"It's not as big as most of you people have," he went on.
But Hauke said: "I'd rather you measured my little
finger," and he held it out to him.

The goldsmith looked at him somewhat puzzled; but what
did he care what the whim of a young peasant might be.
"We'll probably find one among the ladies' rings," he
said, and the blood mounted into Hauke's cheeks. But
the ring fitted his little finger and he took it hastily and
paid for it with bright silver. Then, with his heart beating loudly and as if it were a solemn act, he put it into
his waistcoat pocket. And from then on he carried it there
day by day with a restless yet proud feeling, as if his
waistcoat pocket were made only to carry a ring in.

So he carried it for years, in fact, the ring had to leave
that pocket for a new one; no opportunity to escape presented itself. It had indeed passed through Hauke's head
to go straight to his master; after all, his father belonged
in the village and held land there. But in his calmer
moments he knew well that the old dikegrave would have
laughed at his second man. And so he and the dikegrave's
daughter lived on side by side, she in girlish silence, and
yet both as if they walked hand in hand.

A year after the winter festival Ole Peters had left the
dikegrave's service and married Vollina Harders; Hauke
had been right; the old man had retired and instead of his
fat daughter his brisk son-in-law now rode the yellow mare

to the fens and on his way back, it was said, always up the side of the dike. Hauke was now head man and a younger fellow had taken his former place. At first the dikegrave had not wanted to advance him. "He's better as second man," he had growled, "I need him here with my books!" But Elke had said, "Then Hauke would leave, Father!" That frightened the old man and Hauke had been made head man but he still kept on as before helping in the administration of the dike.

After another year had passed he began to talk to Elke about his father's growing feeble, and explained that the few days that the master allowed him in summer in which to help at home were no longer enough; the old man was overworking himself and he, Hauke, could not stand by and see it go on. It was a summer evening; the two were standing in the twilight under the great ash in front of the door of the house. For a time the girl looked up in silence at the bough of the tree; then she answered, "I did not want to say it, Hauke; I thought you would find the right thing to do yourself.

"Then I must go away out of your house," he said, "and cannot come again."

They were silent for a time and watched the sunset glow that was just sinking into the sea over behind the dike. "You must know best," she said; "I was at your father's this morning and found him asleep in his armchair; he had a drawing-pen in his hand and the drawing-board with a half finished drawing lay before him on the table. Afterwards he woke and talked to me for a quarter of an hour but only with difficulty, and then, when I was going, he clung to my hand as if he were afraid that it was for the last time; but * * *"

"But what, Elke?" asked Hauke, as she hesitated to go on.

A few tears ran down over the girl's cheeks. "I was only thinking of my father," she said; "believe me, it will be hard for him to lose you." And with an effort she

added: "It often seems to me as if he too were preparing
for his end."

Hauke did not answer; it seemed to him as if the ring
in his pocket suddenly moved but before he could suppress
his indignation at this involuntary stir Elke went on: "No,
don't be angry, Hauke! I trust and believe that even so
you will not forsake us!"

At that he seized her hand eagerly and she did not draw
it away. For some time longer the two stood there together
in the growing dusk till their hands slipped apart and they
went their different ways. A gust of wind struck the ash-
tree and rustled through its leaves, rattling the shutters
on the front of the house; but gradually the night fell and
silence lay over the vast plain.

The old dikegrave yielded to Elke's persuasion and allowed Hauke to leave his service although the latter had
not given notice at the proper time. Two new men had
since been engaged. A few months later Tede Haien died,
but before he died he called his son to his bed: "Sit down
here beside me, child," he said in a feeble voice, "close beside me! You need not be afraid; the one who is with me
is only the dark angel of the Lord who has come to call
me."

And the grief-stricken son sat down close to the dark
wall-bed: "Speak, Father, tell me all that you still have to
say!"

"Yes, my son, there is still something," said the old
man and stretched out his hands on the counterpane.
"When you, only a half-grown boy, went into the dikegrave's service you had it in your mind to be a dikegrave
yourself some day. You infected me with the idea and
gradually I too came to think that you were the right
man for that. But your inheritance was too small for you
to hold such an office. I have lived frugally during the
time you were in service. I thought to increase it."

Hauke pressed his father's hands warmly and the old
man tried to sit up so that he could see him. "Yes, my

son,'' he said, ''the paper is there in the top drawer of the strong chest. You know, old Antje Wohlers had a field of five and a half acres; but in her crippled old age she could not get on with the rent from it alone; so every Martinmas I gave the poor creature a certain sum and more too, when I had it; and for that she made over the field to me; it is all legally arranged. Now she too is lying at the point of death; the disease of our marshes, cancer, has over-taken her; you will not have anything more to pay!''

He closed his eyes for a time; then he added: ''It isn't much; but still you will have more than you were accus-tomed to with me. May it serve you for your life in this world!''

Listening to his son's thanks the old man fell asleep. He had nothing more to attend to, and a few days later the angel of the Lord had closed his eyes forever, and Hauke came into his paternal inheritance.

On the day after the funeral Elke came to his house. ''Thank you for looking in, Elke!'' was Hauke's greeting.

But she answered: ''I am not just looking in; I want to tidy the house a little so that you can live in comfort. With all his figures and drawings your father had not time to look about him much and death too brings confusion; I'll make it a little homelike for you again!''

He looked at her with his gray eyes full of trust: ''Tidy up, then,'' he said; ''I like it better too.''

And so she began to clear up the room. The drawing-board which still lay there was dusted and put away in the attic. Drawing-pens, pencils and chalk were carefully locked away in a drawer of the strong chest. Then the young servant was called in and helped to move the furni-ture of the whole room into a different and better posi-tion so that there seemed to be more light and space. ''Only we women can do that,'' said Elke, smiling, and Hauke, in spite of his grief for his father, looked on with happy eyes and helped too when it was necessary.

And when, towards twilight—it was at the beginning of

September—everything was as she wanted it for him, she took his hand and nodded to him with her dark eyes. "Now come and have supper with us; I had to promise my father to bring you back with me; then when you come home later everything will be ready for you."

When they entered the spacious living-room of the dike-grave, where the shutters were already closed and the two lights burning on the table, the old man started to get up out of his armchair but his heavy body sank back again and he contented himself with calling out to his former servant: "That's right, Hauke, I'm glad you've come to look up your old friends again! Just come nearer, nearer!" And when Hauke came up to his chair he took his hand in both his podgy ones and said: "Well, well, my boy, don't grieve too much, for we must all die and your father was not one of the worst! But, come, Elke, bring the roast in; we need to strengthen ourselves! There is a lot of work ahead of us, Hauke! The autumn inspection is coming on; the dike and sluice accounts are piled as high as the house; then there's the recent damage to the dike on the western koog—I don't know which way to turn my head; but yours, thank God, is a good bit younger; you are a good lad, Hauke!"

And after this long speech in which the old man had laid bare his whole heart, he fell back in his chair and blinked longingly at the door through which Elke was just entering with the roast. Hauke stood beside him smiling. "Now sit down," said the dikegrave; "we mustn't waste time; this dish doesn't taste good cold."

And Hauke sat down; it seemed to him a matter of course that he should share in Elke's father's work. And when later the autumn inspection came and a few months more had been added to the year, he had really done the greater part of it.

The narrator stopped and looked about him. The shriek of a gull had struck the window and outside in the entrance the stamping of feet was heard as if someone were shaking off the clay from his heavy boots.

The dikegrave and the commissioners turned their heads towards the door. "What is it?" exclaimed the former.

A stout man with a sou'wester on his head entered. "Sir," he announced, "we both saw it, Hans Nickels and I: the rider of the white horse has thrown himself into the water-hole!"

"Where did you see that?" asked the dikegrave.

"There is only the one hole; in Jansen's fen where the Hauke Haien Koog begins."

"Did you only see it once?"

"Only once; and it only looked like a shadow; but that doesn't mean that it was the first time."

The dikegrave had risen. "You will excuse me," he said, turning to me, "we must go out and see where the mischief is brewing." He went out with the messenger and the rest of the company rose too and followed him.

I was left alone with the schoolmaster in the large bare room; we now had a clear view through the uncurtained windows which were no longer hidden by people sitting in front of them, and could see how the wind was driving the dark clouds across the sky. The old man still sat in his place, a superior, almost compassionate smile on his lips. "It has grown too empty here," he said, "will you come upstairs with me to my room? I live here in the house, and, believe me, I know the weather here near the dike; we have nothing to fear for ourselves."

I accepted gratefully; for I too was beginning to feel chilly there, and after taking a light we climbed the stairs to an attic-room which did indeed look towards the west like the other, but whose windows were now covered with dark woolen hangings. In a bookcase I saw a small collection of books and beside it the portraits of two old professors; in front of a table stood a large easy-chair. "Make yourself at home," said my friendly host and threw a few pieces of peat into the still faintly burning stove,

on the top of which stood a tin kettle. "Just a few minutes! It will soon begin to sing and then I will brew a
glass of grog for us; that will keep you awake."

"I don't need that," I answered; "I don't grow sleepy
following your Hauke on his way through life."

"Really?" and he nodded to me with his wise eyes after
I had been comfortably settled in his easy chair. "Let me
see, where were we?—— Oh yes, I know. Well then!"

Hauke had come into his paternal inheritance, and as old
Antje Wohlers had also succumbed to her illness, her field
had increased it. But since the death, or, rather, since the
last words of his father, something had grown up in him,
the seed of which he had carried in his heart since his boyhood; more than often enough he repeated to himself that
he was the right man when there should have to be a new
dikegrave. That was it. His father who surely understood
it, who, in fact, had been the wisest man in the village, had,
as it were, added these words to his inheritance as a final
gift; Antje Wohlers' field, which he also owed to him,
should form the first stepping-tone to this height. For, to
be sure, a dikegrave must be able to point to far more
extensive property than this alone. But his father had
lived frugally for lonely years and had bought this new
possession with the money thus saved; he could do that too,
he could do more than that; for his father's strength had
been gone, while he could still do the hardest work for
years to come. Of course, even if he did succeed in that
way, yet the keen edge that he had put on his old master's
administration had not made friends for him in the village,
and Ole Peters, his old antagonist, had lately come into an
inheritance and was beginning to be a well-to-do man. A
number of faces passed before his inward vision and they
all looked at him with unfriendly eyes; then wrath against
these people took hold of him and he stretched out his arms
as if he would seize them; for they wanted to keep him
from the office to which he alone was suited. And these
thoughts did not leave him; they were always there and so

side by side with honor and love there grew up ambition and hatred in his young heart. But he hid them deep within him; even Elke did not suspect their existence.

With the coming of the New Year there was a wedding. The bride was a relative of the Haiens, and Hauke and Elke were both there as invited guests; in fact they sat side by side at the wedding breakfast owing to the failure of a nearer relative to come. Only the smile that passed over both their faces betrayed their joy at this. But Elke sat listless in the noise of the conversation and the clatter of glasses that went on about them.

"Is there something the matter?" asked Hauke.

"Oh, no, not really; there are only too many people here for me."

"But you look so sad!"

She shook her head; then they were both silent again.

Gradually a feeling as if he were jealous because of her silence grew in him and he took her hand secretly under cover of the tablecloth; it did not start but closed confidingly round his. Had a feeling of loneliness taken hold of her as she watched her father growing older and weaker day by day? Hauke did not think of putting this question to himself but he ceased to breathe now as he drew the gold ring from his pocket. "Will you leave it there?" he asked, trembling as he slipped it onto the third finger of her slender hand.

The pastor's wife was sitting opposite them at the table; suddenly she laid down her fork and turned to her neighbor: "Good gracious, look at that girl!" she exclaimed, "she's pale as death!"

But the blood was already coming back into Elke's face. "Can you wait, Hauke?" she asked softly.

The prudent Friesian stopped to think for a moment. "For what?" he said then.

"You know well; I don't need to tell you."

"You are right," he said; "yes, Elke, I can wait—if only the time's within reason!"

"Oh God, I'm afraid it's near! Don't speak like that, Hauke, you are talking of my father's death!" She laid the other hand on her breast: "Till then," she said, "I will wear the ring here; never fear, you will never get it back as long as I live."

Then they both smiled and his hand pressed hers so that at any other time the girl would have screamed aloud.

During this time the pastor's wife had been looking steadily at Elke's eyes which now burned as with dark fire beneath the lace edging of her little gold-brocaded cap. But the increasing noise at the table had prevented the older woman from understanding anything that was said; she did not turn to her neighbor again either, for budding marriages—and that is what this looked like to her—even if it were only because of the fee that budded for her husband at the same time, she was not in the habit of disturbing.

Elke's premonition had come true. One morning after Easter the dikegrave Tede Volkerts had been found dead in his bed; his countenance bore witness to a peaceful end. He had often spoken in the previous months of being tired of life and had had no appetite for his favorite dish, a roast joint, or even for a young duck.

And now there was a great funeral in the village. In the burying ground about the church on the upland, lying towards the west, was a lot surrounded by an iron fence. In it the broad, blue grave-stone had been lifted up and was now leaning against a weeping ash. A figure of Death with a very full and prominent set of teeth had been chiseled on the stone and below stood in large letters:

> Dat is de Dot, de allens fritt,
> Nimmt Kunst un Wetenschop di mit;
> De kloke Mann is nu vergån
> Gott gäw em selik Uperstån.

> This is Death who eats up all,
> Art and science go at his call;
> The clever man has left us forlorn
> God raise him on resurrection morn!

This was the resting place of the former dikegrave, Volkert Tedsen. Now a new grave had been dug in which his son, the dikegrave Tede Volkerts, was to be laid. The funeral procession was already coming up from the marsh below, a throng of carriages from all the villages in the parish; the one at the head bore the heavy coffin, the two glossy black horses from the dikegrave's stables were already drawing it up the sandy slope to the uplands; the horses' manes and tails waved in the brisk spring breeze. The churchyard was filled to the walls with people, even on top of the brick gate boys squatted with little children in their arms; all were anxious to see the burying.

In the house down on the marsh Elke had prepared the funeral repast in the living-room and the adjoining parlor; old wine stood at every place; there was a bottle of Langkork for the chief dikegrave—for he too had not failed to come to the ceremony—and another for the pastor. When everything was ready she went through the stable out to the back door; she met no one on her way; the men had gone with the carriages to the funeral. There she stood, her mourning clothes fluttering in the spring breeze, and looked across to the village where the last carriages were just driving up to the church. After a while there was a commotion there and then followed a dead silence. Elke folded her hands; now they were probably lowering the coffin into the grave: "And to dust thou shalt return!" Involuntarily, softly, as if she could hear them from the churchyard she repeated the words; then her eyes filled with tears, her hands which were folded across her breast sank into her lap; "Our Father, who art in heaven!" she prayed with fervor. And when she had finished the Lord's prayer she stood there long, immovable, she, from now on the owner of this large lowland farm; and thoughts of death and of life began to strive within her.

A distant rumble roused her. When she opened her eyes she saw again one carriage following the other in rapid succession, driving down from the marsh and coming to

wards her farm. She stood upright, looked out once more
with a keen glance and then went back, as she had come,
through the stable and into the solemnly prepared living
rooms. There was no one here either, only through the
wall she could hear the bustle of the maids in the kitchen.
The banquet table looked so still and lonely; the mirror
between the windows was covered with white cloth, so were
the brass knobs of the warming-oven; there was nothing to
shine in the room any more. Elke noticed that the doors
of the wall-bed in which her father had slept for the last
time were open and she went over and closed them tight;
absently she read the words painted on them in gold letters
among the roses and pinks:

> "Hest du din Dågwerk richtig dan
> Da kommt de Slåp von sülvst heran."

> If you have done your day's work right
> Sleep will come of itself at night.

That was from her grandfather's time! She glanced at
the cupboard; it was almost empty but through the glass-
doors she could see the cut-glass goblet which, as he had
been fond of telling, her father had won once in his youth
tilting in the ring. She took it out and stood it at the
chief dikegrave's place. Then she went to the window, for
already she could hear the carriages coming up the drive.
One after another stopped in front of the house, and, more
cheerful than when they first came, the guests now sprang
down from their seats to the ground. Rubbing their hands
and talking, they all crowded into the room; it was not long
before they had all taken their places at the festive table on
which the well-cooked dishes were steaming, the chief dikegrave and the pastor in the parlor; noise and loud conversation ran along the table as if the dreadful silence of death
had never hovered here. Silently, her eyes on her guests,
Elke went round with the maids among the tables to see
that nothing was missing. Hauke Haien too sat in the
living-room besides Ole Peters and other small landowners.

After the meal was over the white clay pipes were fetched out of the corner and lighted and Elke was busy again passing the coffee cups to her guests, for she did not spare with that either today. In the living-room, at her father's desk, the chief dikegrave was standing in conversation with the pastor and the white-haired dike commissioner Jewe Manners. "It is all very well, Gentlemen," said the former, "we have laid the old dikegrave to rest with honors; but where shall we find a new one? I think, Manners, you will have to take the dignity upon you!"

Smiling, the old man raised the black velvet cap from his white hair: "The game would be too short, Sir," he said; "when the deceased Tede Volkerts was made dikegrave, I was made commissioner and I have been it now for forty years!"

"That is no fault, Manners; you know the dike affairs so much the better and will have no trouble with them!"

But the old man shook his head: "No, no, your Grace, leave me where I am and I can keep on in the game for another few years yet!"

The pastor came to his aid. "Why," he said, "do we not put into office the man who has really exercised it in the last years?"

The chief dikegrave looked at him. "I don't understand you, pastor."

The pastor pointed into the parlor where Hauke seemed to be explaining something to two older men in a slow earnest way. "There he stands," he said, "the tall Friesian figure with the clever gray eyes beside his lean nose and the two bumps in his forehead above them! He was the old man's servant and now has a little piece of his own; of course, he is still rather young!"

"He seems to be in the thirties," said the chief dikegrave, measuring Hauke with his eyes.

"He is scarcely twenty-four," returned Commissioner Manners; "but the pastor is right; all the good proposals for the dike and drain work and so on that have come from the dikegrave's office during the last years have come from him; after all, the old man didn't amount to much towards the end.''

''Indeed?'' said the chief dikegrave; ''and you think that he would be the man now to move up into his old master's place?''

''He would be the man,'' answered Jewe Manners; ''but he lacks what we call here 'clay under his feet'; his father had about fifteen, he may have a good twenty acres; but no one here has ever been made dikegrave on that.''

The pastor opened his mouth as if he were about to speak, when Elke Volkerts, who had been in the room for some little time, suddenly came up to them. ''Will your Grace allow me a word?'' she said to the chief officer, ''it is only so that an error may not lead to a wrong!''

''Speak out, Miss Elke!'' he answered; ''wisdom always sounds well from a pretty girl's mouth.''

''—It is not wisdom, your Grace; I only want to tell the truth.''

''We ought to be able to listen to that too, Jungfer Elke.''

The girl's dark eyes glanced aside again as if she wanted to reassure herself that no superfluous ears were near. ''Your Grace,'' she began then, and her breast rose with strong emotion, ''my godfather, Jewe Manners, told you that Hauke Haien only possesses about twenty acres, and that is true for the moment; but as soon as is necessary Hauke will have as many more acres as there are in my father's farm which is now mine; this with what he now has ought to be * * *''

Old Manners stretched his white head towards her as if he were looking to see who it was that spoke. ''What's that?'' he said, ''what are you saying, child?''

Elke drew a little black ribbon out of her bodice with a shining gold ring on the end of it. ''I am engaged, Godfather,'' she said; ''here is the ring, and Hauke Haien is my betrothed.''

"And when—I suppose I may ask since I held you at the font, Elke Volkerts—when did this happen?"

"It was some time ago, but I was of age, Godfather Manners," she said; "my father was already growing feeble and, as I knew him, I did not want to trouble him with it; now that he is with God he will see that his child is well cared for with this man. I should have said nothing about it till my year of mourning was over, but now, for Hauke's sake and on account of the koog, I have had to speak." And turning to the chief dikegrave she added: "Your Grace will pardon me, I hope!"

The three men looked at one another. The pastor laughed, the old commissioner contented himself with murmuring "Hum, hum!" while the chief dikegrave rubbed his forehead as if he were concerned with an important decision. "Yes, my dear girl," he said at last, "but how is it with the matrimonial property rights here? I must confess I am not thoroughly at home in these complicated matters."

"That is not necessary, your Grace," answered the dikegrave's daughter, "I will transfer the property to Hauke before the marriage. I have my own little pride," she added, smiling; "I want to marry the richest man in the village!"

"Well, Manners," said the pastor, "I suppose that you, as godfather, will have no objection when I unite the young dikegrave and the daughter of the old one in marriage!"

The old man shook his head gently. "May God give them his blessing!" he said, devoutly.

But the chief dikegrave held out his hand to the girl. "You have spoken truly and wisely, Elke Volkerts; I thank you for your forceful explanations and I hope also in the future and on more joyous occasions than this to be the guest of your house; but—the most wonderful thing about it all is that a dikegrave should be made by such a young woman."

"Your Grace," replied Elke, who looked at his kindly

face again with her serious eyes, ''the right man may well
be helped by his wife!'' Then she went into the adjoining
parlor and silently laid her hand in Hauke Haien's.

It was several years later. Tede Haien's little house
was now occupied by an active workman with his wife and
children. The young dikegrave Hauke Haien lived with his
wife in what had been her father's house. In summer the
mighty ash rustled in front of the house as before; but on
the bench which now stood beneath it generally only the
young wife was to be seen in the evening sitting alone with
her sewing or some other piece of work. There was still no
child in this home and Hauke had something else to do than
to spend a leisure evening in front of the house, for in spite
of the help he had given the old dikegrave the latter had
bequeathed to him a number of unsettled matters pertaining
to the dike, matters with which Hauke had not liked to
meddle before; but now they must all gradually be cleared
up and he swept with a strong broom. Then came the
management and work of the farm itself, increased as it
was by the addition of his own property, and moreover
he was trying to do without a servant boy. And so it happened that, except on Sunday when they went to church,
he and Elke saw each other only at dinner, when Hauke
was generally hurried, and at the beginning and end of the
day; it was a life of continuous work and yet a contented
one.

And then the tongues of the busy-bodies disturbed the
peace. One Sunday after church a somewhat noisy gang
of the younger landowners in the marsh and upland dis-
tricts were sitting drinking in the tavern on the uplands.
Over the fourth or fifth glass they began to talk, not indeed
about the king and the government—no one went so high
in those days—but about the municipal officials and their
superiors and above all about the municipal taxes and
assessments, and the longer they talked the less they were
satisfied with them, least of all with the new dike assess-

ments; all the drains and sluices which had hitherto been all right now needed repairs; new places were always being found in the dike that needed hundreds of barrows of earth; the devil take it all!

"That's your clever dikegrave's doing," shouted one of the uplanders, "who always goes about thinking and then puts a finger into every pie."

"Yes, Marten," said Ole Peters, who sat opposite the speaker; "you're right, he's tricky and is always trying to get into the chief dikegrave's good books; but we've got him now."

"Why did you let them load him onto you?" said the other; "now you've got to pay for it."

Ole Peters laughed. "Yes, Marten Fedders, that's the way it goes with us here and there's nothing to be done. The old dikegrave got the office on his father's account; the new one on his wife's." The laughter that greeted this sally showed how it pleased the company.

But it was said at a public house table and it did not stop there; soon it went the rounds on the uplands as well as down on the marshes; thus it came to Hauke's ears too. And again all the malicious faces passed before his inward eye and when he thought of the laughter at the tavern table it sounded more mocking than it had been in reality. "The dogs!" he shouted and looked wrathfully to one side as if he would have had them thrashed.

At that Elke laid her hand on his arm: "Never mind them! They would all like to be what you are!"

"That's just it," he answered rancorously.

"And," she went on, "did not Ole Peters himself marry money?"

"That he did, Elke; but what he got when he married Vollina was not enough to make him dikegrave!"

"Say rather; he was not enough himself to become dikegrave!" And Elke turned her husband round so that he looked at himself in the mirror, for they were standing between the windows in their room. "There stands the

dikegrave,'' she said; ''now look at him; only he who can
exercise an office holds one!''

''You are not wrong there,'' he answered, thinking, ''and
yet * * * Well, Elke, I must go on to the eastern sluice;
the gates don't lock again.''

She pressed his hand. ''Come, look at me a minute
first! What is the matter with you, your eyes look so
far away?''

''Nothing, Elke; you're right.''

He went; but he had not been gone long when he had
forgotten all about the repairs to the sluice. Another idea
which he had half thought out and had carried about with
him for years, but which had been pushed into the background by urgent official duties, now took possession of
him anew and more powerfully than before as if suddenly
it had grown wings.

Hardly realizing where he was going he found himself
up on the seaward dike, a good distance to the south,
towards the town; the village that lay out in this direction
had long disappeared on his left; still he went on, his gaze
turned towards the water-side and fixed steadily on the
broad stretch of land in front of the dikes; anyone with
him could not have helped seeing what absorbing mental
work was going on behind those eyes. At last he stopped;
there the foreland narrowed down to a little strip along
the dike. ''It must be possible,'' he said to himself.
''Seven years in office! they shan't say again that I am
dikegrave only on my wife's account!''

Still he stood and his keen glance swept carefully over
the green foreland in all directions; then he went back to
where another small strip of green pasture-land took the
place of the broad expanse lying before him. Close to the
dike however a strong sea current ran through this expanse
separating nearly the whole outland from the mainland and
making it into an island; a rough wooden bridge led across
to it so that cattle or hay and grain carts could pass over.
The tide was low and the golden September sun glistened

on the bare strip of mud, perhaps a hundred feet wide, and on the deep water-course in the middle of it through which the sea was even now running. "That could be dammed," said Hauke to himself after watching it for some time. Then he looked up and, in imagination, drew a line from the dike on which he stood, across the water-course, along the edge of the island, round towards the south and back again in an easterly direction across the water-course and up to the dike. And this invisible line which he now drew was a new dike, new too in the construction of its profile which till now had existed only in his head.

"That would give us about a thousand acres more of reclaimed land," he said, smiling to himself; "not exactly a great stretch, but still——"

Another calculation absorbed him. The outland here belonged to the community, its members each holding a number of shares according to the size of their property in the parish or by having legally acquired them in some other way. He began to count up how many shares he had received from his own, how many from Elke's father and how many he had bought himself since his marriage, partly with an indistinct idea of benefit to be derived in the future, partly when he increased his flocks of sheep. Altogether he held a considerable number of shares; for he had bought from Ole Peters all that he had as well, when the latter became so disgusted at losing his best ram in a partial inundation that he decided to sell. But that was a rare accident, for as far back as Hauke could remember only the edges were flooded even when the tides were unusually high. What splendid pasture and grain land it would make and how valuable it would be when it was all surrounded by his new dike! A kind of intoxication came over him as he thought of it, but he dug his nails into the palms of his hands and forced his eyes to look clearly and soberly at what lay before him. There was this great dikeless area on the extreme edge of which a flock of dirty sheep now wandered grazing slowly; who knew what storms and tides might do to it even within the next few years; and for him it would mean a lot of work, struggle, and annoyance. Nevertheless, as he went down from the dike and along the foot-path across the fens towards his mound, he felt as if he were bringing a great treasure home with him.

Elke met him in the hall; "How did you find the sluice?" she asked.

He looked down at her with a mysterious smile: "We shall soon need another sluice," he said, "and drains and a new dike!"

"I don't understand," replied Elke as they went into the room. "What is it that you want, Hauke?"

"I want," he said slowly and stopped a moment. "I want to have the big stretch of outland that begins opposite our place and then runs towards the west, all diked in and a well-drained koog made out of it. The high tides have left us in peace for nearly a generation, but if one of the really bad ones should come again and destroy the new growth, everything might be ruined at one blow; only the old slip-shod way of doing things could have let it go on like that so long."

She looked at him in amazement. "Then you blame yourself!" she said.

"Yes, I do, Elke; but there has always been so much else to do."

"I know, Hauke; you have done enough!"

He had seated himself in the old dikegrave's easy-chair and his hands gripped both arms of it firmly.

"Have you the courage to do it?" asked his wife.

"Indeed I have, Elke," he said hastily.

"Don't go too fast, Hauke; that is an undertaking of life and death and they will nearly all be against you; you will get no thanks for all your trouble and care!"

He nodded: "I know!" he said.

"And suppose it doesn't succeed!" she exclaimed again; "ever since I was a child I have heard that that water-course could not be stopped and therefore it must never be touched.''

''That is simply a lazy man's excuse,'' said Hauke; ''why should it be impossible to stop it?''

''I never heard why; perhaps because it flows through so straight; the washout is too strong.'' Suddenly a memory came back to her and an almost roguish smile dawned in her serious eyes. ''When I was a child,'' she said, ''I heard the hired men talking about it once; they said that the only way to build a dam there that would hold was to bury something alive in it while it was being made; when they were building a dike on the other side—it must have been a hundred years ago—a gypsy child that they bought from its mother at a high price had been thrown into it and buried alive; but now probably no one would sell her child.''

Hauke shook his head. ''Then it is just as well that we have none, or they would probably require it of us!''

''They wouldn't get it!'' said Elke, and threw her arms across her own body as if in fear.

And Hauke smiled; but she went on to another question: ''And the tremendous expense! Have you thought of that?''

''Indeed I have, Elke; we shall gain in land much more than the expense of building the dike, and then too the cost of maintaining the old dike will be much less; we shall work ourselves and we have more than eighty teams in the parish and no lack of young hands. At least you will not have made me dikegrave for nothing, Elke; I will show them that I am one.''

She had crouched down in front of him and was looking at him anxiously; now she rose with a sigh. ''I must go on with my day's work,'' she said slowly stroking his cheek; ''you do yours, Hauke.''

''Amen, Elke,'' he said with an earnest smile; ''there is work here for both of us!''

And there was work enough for both, though now the

husband's burden became even heavier. On Sunday after-
noons and often late in the evening Hauke and a capable
surveyor sat together, deep in calculations, drawings and
plans; it was the same when Hauke was alone and he often
did not finish till long after midnight. Then he crept into
his and Elke's bedroom, for they no longer used the stuffy
wall-beds in the living-room, and so that he might at last
get some rest, his wife lay with closed eyes as if asleep
although she had been waiting for him with a beating heart.
Then he sometimes kissed her brow, whispering a word of
endearment, and laid himself down to wait for the sleep
which often did not come to him till cock-crow. During the
winter tempests he would go out on the dike with paper
and pencil in his hand and stand there drawing and making
notes while a gust of wind tore his cap from his head and
his long tawny hair blew across his hot face. As long as
the ice did not prevent it he would take one of the men-
servants and go out in the boat to the shallows and measure
the depth of the currents there with a rod and plumb-line,
whenever he was in doubt. Elke often trembled for him,
but the only sign she showed of it when he came home again
was the firmness of her hand-clasp or the gleaming light in
her usually quiet eyes. "Have patience, Elke," he said
once when it seemed to him that his wife did not want to
let him go; "I must be perfectly clear about it myself before
I make my proposal." At that she nodded and let him go.
His rides into town to the chief dikegrave were no trifle
either, and they and all the work of managing the house
and farm were always followed by work on his papers late
into the night. He almost ceased to associate with other
people except in his work and business; he even saw less
of his wife from day to day. "It is a hard time and it will
last a long while yet," said Elke to herself and went about
her work.

At last, when the sun and spring winds had broken up
the ice everywhere the preparatory work came to an end.
The petition to the chief dikegrave to be recommended to

a higher department was ready. It contained the proposal for a dike to surround the foreland mentioned, for the benefit of the public welfare, especially of the koog and not less of the Sovereign's exchequer as, in a few years, the latter would profit by taxes from about one thousand acres. The whole was neatly copied, packed in a strong tubular case, together with plans and drawings of all the localities as they were at present and as planned, of sluices and drains and everything else in question, and was provided with the dikegrave's official seal.

"Here it is, Elke," said the young dikegrave, "now give it your blessing."

Elke laid her hand in his: "We will hold fast to each other," she said.

"That we will."

Then the petition was sent into town by a messenger on horseback.

"You will notice, my dear sir," the schoolmaster interrupted his tale as he looked at me with kindness in his expressive eyes, "that what I have told you up to now I have gathered during nearly forty years of activity in this district from reliable accounts from what has been told me by the grandchildren and great-grandchildren of enlightened families. Now in order that you may bring this into harmony with the final course of events I have to tell you that the rest of my story was at the time and still is the gossip of the whole marsh village when, about All Saints' Day, the spinning wheels begin to whirr.

About five or six hundred feet north of the dikegrave's farm, as one stood on the dike, one could see a few thousand feet out in the shallows and, somewhat farther from the opposite bank, a little islet called "Jeverssand" or "Jevershallig." It had been used by the grandfathers of that day as a sheep pasture, for at that time it had been covered with grass; but even that had ceased because several times the low islet had been flooded by the sea, espe-

cially in midsummer, and the grass had been damaged and
made unfit for the sheep. So it happened that, except for
the gulls and other birds that fly along the shore, and perhaps an occasional fishhawk, nothing visited it any more;
and on moonlight evenings, looking out from the dike, only
the foggy mists could be seen as they hung lightly or heavily above it. When the moon shone from the east on the
islet people also thought they could distinguish a few
bleached skeletons of drowned sheep and the skeleton of a
horse, though how the latter had come there no one could
explain.

Once, towards the end of March, late in the evening, the
day-laborer who lived in Tede Haien's house and the young
dikegrave's man Iven Johns stood together at that spot
and gazed out fixedly at the islet, which could scarcely be
distinguished in the misty moonlight; apparently something
unusual had caught their attention and kept them standing
there. The day laborer stuck his hands in his pockets and
shook himself. "Come on, Iven," he said, "that's nothing
good; let us go home!"

The other one laughed, but a shudder could be heard
through his laughter. "Oh, nonsense! It's a living creature, a big one! Who in the devil's name could have driven
it out there onto that piece of mud! Look! Now it's
stretching its head over towards us! No, it's lowering its
head, it's eating! I thought there was no grass there!
Whatever can it be?"

"What business is that of *ours*?" answered the other.
"Good night, Iven, if you won't go along; I'm going home."

"Good-night then," the day laborer called back as he
trotted home along the dike. The servant looked round
after him a few times, but the desire to see something
uncanny kept him where he was. Then a dark, stocky figure
came along the dike from the village towards him; it was
the dikegrave's stable boy. "What do you want, Karsten?"
the man called out to him.

"I?—nothing," answered the boy; "but the master wants to speak to you, Iven Johns."

The man had his eyes fixed on the islet again. "All right; I'm coming in a minute," he said.

"What are you looking at?" asked the boy.

The man raised his arm and pointed to the islet in silence. "Oh ho!" whispered the boy; "there's a horse—a white horse—it must be the devil who rides it—how does a horse get out there on Jevershallig?"

"Don't know, Karsten; if only it's a real horse!"

"Oh, yes, Iven; look, it's grazing just like a horse! But who took it out there; there isn't a boat big enough in the whole village! Perhaps after all it's only a sheep; Peter Ohm says, in the moonlight ten stocks of peat look like a whole village. No, look! Now it's jumping—it must be a horse!"

The two stood for a time in silence, their eyes fixed on what they could see but indistinctly over there. The moon was high in the sky and shone down on the broad shallow sea whose rising tide was just beginning to wash over the glistening stretches of mud; no sound of any animal was to be heard all around, nothing but the gentle noise of the water; the marsh too, behind the dike, was empty; cows and oxen were all still in their stalls. Nothing was moving; the only thing that seemed to be alive was what they took to be a horse, a white horse, out on Jevershallig. "It's growing lighter," said the man breaking the silence; "I can see the white sheep bones shining clearly."

"So can I," said the boy, stretching his neck; then, as if an idea had suddenly struck him, he pulled at the man's sleeve. "Iven," he whispered, "the horse's skeleton that always used to lie there, where is it? I can't see it!"

"I don't see it either, that's queer!" said the man.

"Not so very queer, Iven! Sometimes, I don't know in what nights, the bones are said to rise up and act as if they were alive."

"So?" said the man; "that's old wives' superstition!"

"May be, Iven," said the boy.

"Well, I thought you came to fetch me; come on, we must go home. There's nothing new to see here."

The boy would not move till the man had turned him round by force and pulled him onto the path. "Listen, Karsten," he said when the ghostly island was already a good bit behind them, "they say you're a fellow that's ready for anything; I believe you'd like best to investigate that yourself."

"Yes," replied Karsten, shuddering a little at the recollection, "yes, I'd like to, Iven."

"Are you in earnest?" asked the man after Karsten had given him his hand on it. "Well then, tomorrow evening we'll take our boat; you can go over to Jeverssand and I'll wait for you on the dike."

"Yes," replied the boy, "we can do that. I'll take my whip with me."

"Yes, do!"

In silence they went up the high mound to their master's house.

The same time the following evening the man was sitting on the big stone in front of the stable door as the boy came up to him cracking his whip. "That makes an odd whistle!" said Iven.

"To be sure, look out for yourself," answered the boy; "I have plaited nails into the lash."

"Come along then," said the other.

As on the day before the moon was in the eastern sky and shone down clearly from its height. Soon they were both out on the dike and looking over at Jevershallig that stood like a spot of fog in the water. "There it is again," said the man; "I was here after dinner and it wasn't there, but I could distinctly see the white skeleton of the horse lying there."

The boy stretched his neck. "It isn't there now, Iven," he whispered.

"Well, Karsten, how is it?" asked the man. "Are you still itching to row over there?"

Karsten thought for a moment; then he cracked his whip in the air. "Undo the boat, Iven!"

Over on the island it looked as if whatever was walking there raised its head and stretched it out towards the mainland. They did not see it any longer; they were already walking down the dike and to the place where the boat lay. "Now, get in," said the man after he had untied it. "I'll wait till you come back. You must head for the east shore, there was always a good landing there." The lad nodded silently and then rowed out, with his whip, into the moonlit night. The man wandered along the dike back to the place where they had stood before. Soon he saw the boat ground near a steep dark spot on the other side to which a broad water-course flowed, and a short, thickset figure sprang ashore. Wasn't that the boy cracking his whip? Or it might be the sound of the rising tide. Several hundred feet to the north he saw what they had taken to be a white horse, and now—yes, the figure of the boy was going straight towards it. Now it raised its head as if startled and the boy—he could hear it plainly—snapped his whip. But—what could he be thinking of? He had turned round and was walking back along the way he had gone. The creature on the other side seemed to go on grazing steadily, he had not heard it neigh; at times white stripes of water seemed to pass across the apparition. The man watched it as if spellbound.

Then he heard the grounding of the boat on the side on which he stood and soon he saw the boy coming out of the dusk and towards him up the side of the dike. "Well, Karsten," he said, "what was it?"

The boy shook his head. "It wasn't anything," he said. "Just before I landed I saw it from the boat and then, when I was once on the island—the devil knows where the beast went, the moon was shining brightly enough; but when I came to the place there was nothing there but the bleached bones of half a dozen sheep and a little farther on lay the horse's skeleton with its long, white skull and the moon was shining into its empty eye-sockets!''

"Hmm!" said the man; "did you look carefully?"

"Yes, Iven, I stood close up to it; a God-forsaken lap-wing that had gone to sleep behind the bones flew up shrieking and startled me so that I cracked my whip after it a few times."

"And that was all?"

"Yes, Iven, I didn't see anything else."

"And it's enough," said the man, pulling the boy to-wards him by the arm and pointing across to the islet. "Do you see anything over there, Karsten?"

"As I live, there it is again!"

"Again?" said the man; "I was looking over there the whole time and it never went away; you went right towards the uncanny thing."

The boy stared at him; a look of horror that did not escape the man appeared on his usually saucy face. "Come," said the latter, "let us go home; seen from here it is alive and over there it is only bones—that is more than you and I can understand. Keep your mouth shut about it; things like that must not be questioned."

So they turned and the boy trotted along beside him; they did not speak and the marsh lay in unbroken silence at their side.

But after the moon had declined and the nights had grown dark something else happened.

Hauke Haien had ridden into town at the time the horse-fair was going on, without however having anything to do with that. Nevertheless towards evening when he came home he brought a second horse with him; but its coat was rough and it was so thin that its ribs could be counted and its eyes lay dull and sunken in their sockets. Elke had gone out in front of the door to meet her husband. "For heaven's sake!" she exclaimed, "what's the old white horse for?" For as Hauke came riding up in front of the house and drew rein under the ash she saw that the poor creature was lame too.

But the young dikegrave sprang laughing from his brown gelding. "Never mind, Elke, it didn't cost much."

"You know that the cheapest thing is usually the dearest," his wise wife answered.

"Not always, Elke; this animal is four years old at the most; look at him more carefully! He has been starved and abused; our oats will do him good and I will take care of him myself so that he shan't be overfed."

During this conversation the animal stood with his head lowered; his mane hung down long over his neck. While her husband was calling the men Elke walked round the horse looking him over, but she shook her head: "We never had such a nag as this in our stable!"

When the stable boy came round the corner of the house he suddenly stopped with terror-stricken eyes. "Well, Karsten," said the dikegrave, "what's the matter with you? Don't you like my white horse?"

"Yes—Oh, yes, master, why not?"

"Well, then, take both the horses into the stable but don't feed them; I am coming over there in a minute myself."

Cautiously the boy took hold of the white horse's halter and then hastily, as if to protect himself, he seized the rein of the gelding which had also been trusted to his care. Hauke went into the house with his wife; she had warm beer ready for him and bread and butter were also at hand.

He was soon satisfied and, rising began to walk up and down the room with his wife. "Now let me tell you, Elke," he said, while the evening glow shone on the tiles in the walls, "how I happened to get the animal. I stayed at the chief dikegrave's about an hour; he had good news for me—some changes will undoubtedly have to be made in my plans; but the main thing, my profile, has been accepted and the order to begin work on the new dike may get here any day now."

Elke sighed involuntarily: "Then it is to be done **after** all!" she said apprehensively.

"Yes, wife," replied Hauke; "it's going to be uphill work but that is why God brought us together, I think. Our farm is in such good order now that you can take a good part of it on your shoulders; think ten years ahead— then our property will have greatly increased!"

At his first words she had pressed her husband's hand assuringly in hers, but his last remark brought her no joy. "Who will the place be for?" she said. "Unless you take another wife instead of me; I cannot bear you any children."

Tears rushed to her eyes; but he drew her close and held her tight in his arms: "Let us leave that to God," he said; "but now, and even then, we shall be young enough to enjoy the fruits of our labor ourselves."

She looked at him long with her dark eyes while he held her thus. "Forgive me, Hauke," she said, "at times I am a despondent woman."

He bent his face to hers and kissed her. "You are my wife and I am your husband, Elke! And nothing can change that."

At that she put her arms close round his neck. "You are right, Hauke, and whatever comes will come to us both." Then, blushing, she drew away from his arms. "You were going to tell me about the white horse," she said softly.

"Yes, I will, Elke. I've already told you that I was in high spirits over the good news that the chief dikegrave had given me; and just as I was riding out of the town, there, on the dam, behind the harbor, I met a ragged fellow; I didn't know whether he was a vagabond or a tinker or what. He was pulling the white horse on the halter after him and the animal raised its head and looked at me with pleading eyes, as if it were begging me for something; and at the moment I was certainly rich enough. 'Hello, fellow!' I shouted, 'where are you going with the old nag?'"

"He stopped and the white horse stopped too. 'Going to sell it,' he said and nodded to me with cunning in his eyes.

" 'To anyone else, but not to me!' I said merrily.

" 'Why not?' he answered; 'it's a fine horse and well worth a hundred thalers.'

"I laughed in his face.

" 'Oh, you needn't laugh,' he said; 'you needn't pay me that! But I can't use the beast; it would starve with me. It would soon look different if you had it a little while.'

"So I jumped down from my gelding and looked at the animal's mouth and saw that it was still young. 'How much do you want for it?' I asked, for the horse was looking at me again as if begging.

" 'Take it for thirty thalers, sir,' said the fellow, 'and I'll throw in the halter.'

"And so, Elke, I took the brown, clawlike hand that the lad offered me and it was a bargain. So we have the white horse, and cheap enough too, I think. Only it was curious; as I rode away with the horse I heard laughing behind me and when I turned my head I saw the Slovak standing there, his legs apart, his arms behind his back, laughing like the devil."

"Phew!" exclaimed Elke; "if only the white horse doesn't bring you anything from his old master! I hope he'll thrive for you, Hauke."

"He shall thrive for his own sake, at least as far as I can manage it!" And with that the dikegrave went out to the stable as he had told the boy he would.

But this was not the only evening on which he fed the horse; from then on he always did it himself and kept it under his eye all the time; he wanted to show that he had made a good bargain and at least the horse should have every chance. And it was only a few weeks before the animal began to hold up its head; gradually the rough hair disappeared, a smooth, blue-mottled coat began to show and when, one day, he led it about the yard, it stepped out daintily with its strong, slender legs. Hauke thought of the tattered, adventurous fellow who had sold it: "The chap was a fool, or a scoundrel who had stolen it!" he murmured to himself. Soon, whenever the horse heard his step in the stable it would throw its head round and whinny to him, and then Hauke saw that its face was covered with hair as the Arabs like to have it while its brown eyes flashed fire. Then he led it out of the stall and put a light saddle on it, but he was hardly on its back before a whinny of joy broke from the animal and off it flew with him, down the mound onto the road and then towards the dike; but the rider sat tight and once they were on top the horse quieted down and stepped lightly, as if dancing, while it tossed its head towards the sea. Hauke patted and stroked its smooth neck but the caress was no longer necessary; the horse seemed to be entirely one with its rider and after he had ridden out a bit on the dike towards the north he turned it easily and rode back to the yard.

The men were standing below at the entrance to the driveway, waiting for their master to come back. "There, John," the latter called, as he sprang from his horse, "take him and ride him down to the fen, to the others; he carries you as if you were in a cradle!"

The horse tossed his head and whinnied loudly out into the sunny open country, while the man unbuckled the saddle and the boy carried it off to the harness-room; then he laid his head on his master's shoulder and suffered himself to be caressed. But when the man tried to swing himself up onto his back he sprang suddenly and sharply aside and then stood quiet again, his beautiful eyes fixed on his master. "Oh ho, Iven!" cried the latter, "did he hurt you?" and tried to help his man onto his feet.

Iven rubbed his hip hard. "No, master, it's not so bad; but the devil can ride the white horse!"

"And so will I!" added Hauke, laughing. "Take the rein and lead him to the fen, then."

And when the man, somewhat ashamed of himself, obeyed, the white horse quietly allowed himself to be led.

A few evenings later the man and the stable-boy were standing together at the stable door; behind the dike the evening glow had paled, and on the inner side the koog lay in deep dusk; occasionally the lowing of some startled cow came from the distance or the shriek of a lark as a weasel or water rat put an end to its life. The man was leaning against the door-post smoking a short pipe, the smoke of which he could no longer see; he and the boy had not yet spoken to each other. The latter had something on his mind, but he did not know how to approach the silent man with it. "Look, Iven," he said at last. "You know the horse's skeleton on Iverssand?"

"What about it?" asked the man.

"It isn't there any more; not in the daytime nor by moonlight; I've been out on the dike at least twenty times."

"I suppose the old bones have fallen apart!" said Iven, and went on smoking calmly.

"But I was out there by moonlight too; there's nothing walking about over on Jeverssand!"

"Well," said the man, "if the bones have fallen to pieces I suppose it can't get up any more."

"Don't joke, Iven! I know now; I can tell you where it is."

The man turned towards him with a start. "Well, where is it then?"

"Where?" the boy repeated impressively. "It's standing in our stable. It's been standing there ever since it has not been on the islet. It's not for nothing that the master always feeds it himself. I know what I'm talking about, Iven."

The man puffed away violently for a while. "You're a bit off, Karsten," he said at last; "our white horse? If ever a horse was alive it's he. How can a bright lad like you believe in such an old woman's tale!"

But the boy could not be convinced: if the devil was in the horse why shouldn't it be alive? On the contrary, so

much the more for that! He started every time that he
went into the stable towards evening, where even in summer
the animal was sometimes bedded, when he saw it toss its
fiery head towards him so sharply. "The devil take it!" he
would murmur, then, "we shan't be together much longer."

So he began to look about him secretly for a new place,
gave notice, and on All Saints' Day entered Ole Peters'
service. There he found attentive listeners to his story of
the dikegrave's devil-horse. Ole's fat wife, Vollina, and
her stupid father, the former dike commissioner Jess
Harders, listened to it with pleasurable shuddering, and
later repeated it to everyone who had a spite against the
dikegrave or who enjoyed tales of that kind.

In the meantime towards the end of March the order
to begin work on the new dike had been received through
the chief dikegrave. Hauke's first step was to call together
the dike commissioners and they all assembled one day in
the tavern up by the church and listened while he read the
main points to them from the various documents: from his
petition, from the report of the chief dikegrave, finally
from the decision in which, above all, the profile that he
had proposed was accepted, so that the new dike would not
be steep like the other but slope gradually on the water-
side; but they did not listen with cheerful or even satisfied
faces.

"Yes, yes," said an old commissioner, "we are in for it
now and no protests can help us, for the chief dikegrave is
backing up our dikegrave."

"You're right enough, Dethlev Wiens," said another;
"the spring work is at the door and now we've got to
make miles of dike, so of course we must drop everything
else."

"You can finish all that this year," said Hauke; "things
won't move as fast as that."

Few of them were ready to admit it. "And your profile!" said a third, bringing up a new subject; "on the outside, towards the water, the dike will be wider than Law-

renz's child was long! Where are we to get the material?
When will the work be done?''

''If not this year, then next; that will depend mainly on
ourselves,'' said Hauke.

A laugh of annoyance passed through the company.
''But why all this useless work? The dike is not to be any
higher than the old one,'' shouted a new voice; ''and that's
been standing for more than thirty years I think!''

''That's right,'' said Hauke; ''the old dike broke thirty
years ago, then thirty-five years before that and again
forty-five years before that; since then, although it still
stands there steep and contrary to reason, the highest tides
have spared us. But in spite of such tides the new dike
will stand for a hundred and then another hundred years;
it will not be broken through because the gentle slope
towards the water offers no point of attack to the waves
and so you will gain for yourselves and your children a safe
and certain land, and that is why our sovereign and the
chief dikegrave are backing me up; and it is that, too, that
you ought to be able to see yourselves, for it is to your own
advantage.''

As no one seemed anxious to give an immediate answer to
this an old white-haired man rose from his chair with difficulty. It was Elke's godfather, Jewe Manners, who still
held office as commissioner at Hauke's request. ''Dikegrave Hauke Haien,'' he said, ''you are putting us to a
great deal of trouble and expense and I wish you had
waited for that till God had called me home; but—you are
right, no one with reason can fail to see that. We ought
to thank God every day that, in spite of our laziness, he has
preserved that valuable piece of foreland from storm and
water for us; but now it is the eleventh hour when we ourselves must take hold and try with all our knowledge and
ability to save it for ourselves without depending any more
on God's long-suffering. I am an old man, my friends;
I have seen dikes built and broken; but the dike that Hauke
Haien has projected, by virtue of the understanding that

God has given him, and that he has succeeded in getting
our sovereign to grant—that dike no one of you who are
alive here today will ever see break; and if you yourselves
will not thank him your grandchildren will one day not be
able to refuse him the crown of honor that is his!''

Jewe Manners sat down again, took his blue handkerchief
from his pocket and wiped a few drops from his forehead.
The old man was still known for his thoroughness and in-
violable uprightness, and as those assembled were not ready
to agree with him they continued their silence. But Hauke
Haien took the floor and they all saw how pale he had
grown. ''I thank you, Jewe Manners,'' he said, ''for being
here and for speaking as you have spoken; the rest of you,
gentlemen, will please regard the new dike, for which indeed
I am responsible, at least as something which cannot be
changed now. Let us accordingly decide what is to be
done next!''

''Speak,'' said one of the commissioners. Hauke spread
the plan of the new dike out on the table. ''A few minutes
ago,'' he said, ''one of you asked where we should get all
the necessary earth. You see here that as far as the foreland extends out into the shallows there is a strip of land
left free outside the line of the dike; we can take the earth
from there and from the foreland that runs along the dike,
north and south from the new koog. If we only have a good
thick layer of clay on the water side, we can fill in, on the
inside or in the middle, with sand. But now we must find a
surveyor to stake out the line of the new dike on the foreland. The one who helped me to work out the plan will
probably suit us best. Further, we must make contracts
with several cartwrights for single tipcarts in which to haul
the clay and other material. In damming up the water-
course and on the inner sides, where we may have to do with
sand, we shall need, I can't say now how many hundred
loads of straw, perhaps more than we shall be able to spare
here in the marsh. Let us consider then, how all this is to
be obtained and arranged; and later we shall also want a

capable carpenter to make the new sluice here on the west side towards the water."

The commissioners had gathered round the table, looked indifferently at the map and now gradually began to speak, but, as it seemed, more for the sake of saying something. When they came to discuss the engaging of a surveyor one of the younger ones said: "You have thought it out, dikegrave; you must know who would be best fitted for the work."

But Hauke replied: "As you are all under oath you must speak your own, not my opinion, Jacob Meyen; and if you can do better I will let my proposal drop."

"Oh well, it will be right enough," said Jacob Meyen.

But one of the older men did not think so. He had a nephew who was a surveyor, such a surveyor as had never been seen here in the marsh country; he was said to know even more than the dikegrave's blessed father, Tede Haien!

So the merits of both surveyors were discussed and it was finally decided to give the work to them both together. It was the same thing when they came to consider the tipcarts, the straw supply, and everything else, and Hauke arrived home late and almost exhausted, on the gelding which he still rode at that time. But he had no sooner sat down in the old easy chair which had belonged to his predecessor, who, though more ponderous, had lived more lightly, than his wife was at his side. "You look so tired, Hauke," she said, stroking the hair away from his forehead with her slender hand.

"I am, a little," he answered.

"And how is it going?"

"Oh, it's going," he said with a bitter smile; "but I must turn the wheels myself and I can be glad if somebody else does not hold them back."

"But they don't all do that, do they?"

"No, Elke; your godfather, Jewe Manners, is a good man; I wish he were thirty years younger."

A few weeks later, after the dike-line had been staked out and most of the tip-carts delivered, the dikegrave called a meeting in the parish tavern of all those who had shares in the koog which was to be surrounded by the new dike, and also of the owners of land that lay behind the old dike. His object was to lay before them a plan for the distribution of labor and expense, and to hear any objections they might have to make. The latter class of owners would have to do their part, too, inasmuch as the new dike and the new drains would diminish the cost of maintenance of the older ones. This plan had been a difficult piece of work for Hauke, and if, through the kind offices of the chief dikegrave, a dike messenger and a dike clerk had not been assigned to him he would not have finished it so soon, although every day for some time he had been working late into the night. Then, when, tired out, he sought his couch, he did not find his wife waiting for him in pretended sleep as formerly; she too had now such a full measure of daily work that at night she lay in imperturbable slumber as if at the bottom of a deep well.

When Hauke had read his plan and spread out again on the table the papers which had already lain in the tavern for three days so that they might be examined, it appeared that there were serious men present who regarded this conscientious diligence with deference, and after calm deliberation submitted to the dikegrave's just demands. Others, however, whose shares in the new territory had been sold either by themselves or their fathers or other former possessors, protested against being made to bear part of the cost of the new koog, in which they no longer had any interest, without considering that the new works would gradually disburden the old territory. And others again who were blessed with shares in the new koog shouted that they wanted to sell them, that they would let them go at a low price; for on account of the unjust demands made of them they could not afford to hold them. But Ole Peters, who was leaning against the doorpost with wrath in his face, called out: "Think it over first and then trust to our dike-grave! He knows how to figure! After he already had most of the shares he persuaded me to sell him mine, and as soon as he had them he decided to build a dike around this new koog."

After he had spoken there was dead silence in the meeting for a moment. The dikegrave stood at the table on which he had spread out his papers before; he raised his head and looked at Ole Peters. "You know well, Ole Peters," he said, "that you slander me; you do it nevertheless because you know, as well, that a good deal of the mud with which you pelt me will stick! The truth is that you wanted to get rid of your shares and that I needed them at that time for sheep breeding; and, if you want to know more, I can tell you that it was the abusive words that you used in the tavern, when you said that I was only the dikegrave on my wife's account, that aroused me; I wanted to show you all that I could be a dikegrave on my own account, and so, Ole Peters, I have done what the dikegrave before me should have done long ago. And if you bear me a grudge because at that time your shares became mine—you hear yourself that there are men enough here who are offering theirs at a low price now, merely because this is more work than they want to do."

A murmur of applause broke from a small part of the men assembled and old Jewe Manners, who stood among them, shouted: "Bravo, Hauke Haien! God will give you success in your undertaking."

They were not able to finish, however, although Ole Peters was silent, and they did not disperse till supper time. A second meeting was necessary before everything could be arranged, and then only because Hauke took it upon himself to provide four teams for the following month instead of the three that would properly have fallen to his lot.

Finally when the bells were all ringing through the country for Whitsuntide the work had been begun. Unceasingly the tip-carts moved from the foreland to the dike-line where they dumped their loads of clay, while an equal number were already making the return trip to the fore-land for new loads. At the dike-line itself stood men with shovels and spades to shovel the clay into place and level it; tremendous wagons of straw were brought and un-loaded; the latter was used not only to cover the lighter material such as the sand and loose earth on the inside of the dike, but also, when portions of the dike had been finished and covered with sod, a firm coat of straw was laid over that to protect it from the gnawing waves; overseers were appointed who walked hither and yon, and, in time of storm, stood with wide-open mouths shouting their orders through the wind and weather. Among them rode the dike-grave on his white horse, which he now used exclusively, and the animal flew here and there with its rider as he gave his short, dry orders, praised the laborers or, as sometimes happened, dismissed a lazy or incompetent man without mercy. "It's no use!" he would say at such times; "we can't have the dike spoiled on account of your laziness!" While he was still far away as he rode up out of the koog they heard his horse snorting and all hands began to work with a better will: "Look alive! Here comes the rider on the white horse!"

While the workmen were stretched off on the ground in groups eating their lunch Hauke rode along the deserted works and his eyes were keen to discover spots where careless hands had handled the spade. If, however, he rode up to the men and explained to them how the work must be done, they did indeed look up and went on chewing their bread patiently, but he never heard a word of agree-ment or any other remark from them. Once at that hour, it was already late, when he found a place in the dike where the work had been particularly well done; he rode up to the next group of lunchers, sprang from his horse, and asked pleasantly who had done such good work there, but they merely looked at him shyly and sullenly and named

slowly a few men as if they did it against their will. The
man whom he had asked to hold his horse, which was
standing as quiet as a lamb, held it with both hands and
looked, as if in fear, at the animal's beautiful eyes which,
as usual, were fixed on its master.

"Well, Marten," said Hauke; "why do you stand as if
you had been struck by lightning?"

"Your horse is as quiet, sir, as if it were thinking of
some mischief."

Hauke laughed and took hold of the rein himself, when
the horse at once began to rub its head caressingly against
his shoulder. A few of the workmen looked fearfully over
at horse and rider; others, as if all that did not concern
them, continued to eat their lunch in silence, now and then
throwing a crumb to the gulls which had remembered this
feeding-place, and, balancing on their slender wings, tipped
forward almost onto their heads. The dikegrave stood for
a while, absently watching the begging birds as they caught
the pieces thrown to them in their bills; then he sprang
into the saddle and rode away without looking round at the
men; the few words which they now spoke sounded to him
almost like mockery. "What is it?" he said to himself;
"was Elke right when she said they were all against me?
Even these servants and small owners for many of whom
my new dike means added prosperity?"

He spurred his horse so that it flew down to the koog
like mad. He himself knew nothing, to be sure, of the
uncanny nimbus that his former stable-boy had thrown
about the rider on the white horse; but if only the people
had seen him then as he galloped along, his eyes staring out
of his lean face, and his horse's red nostrils cracking!

Summer and autumn had passed by; the work had gone
on till near the end of November; then frost and snow had
called a halt; the men had not been able to finish and it
was decided to leave the koog lying open. Eight feet the
dike rose above the level of the ground; only to the west
towards the water where the sluice was to be laid a gap

had been left; also above, in front of the old dike, the water-course was still untouched. Thus, as for the last thirty years, the tide could flow into the koog without doing much damage there or to the new dike. And so the work of men's hands was consigned to the great God above, and placed under his protection until the spring sun should make its completion possible.

In the meantime preparations had been made in the dikegrave's house for a happy event; in the ninth year of their married life a child was born to him and his wife. It was red and shriveled and weighed its seven pounds as new-born children should when, like this one, they belong to the female sex; only, its cry had been strangely muffled and did not please the midwife. But the worst was that on the third day Elke lay in a high fever, wandered in her speech and did not know either her husband or the old nurse. The wild joy that had seized upon Hauke at the sight of his child had turned into tribulation. The doctor had been fetched from the town; he sat beside the bed, felt Elke's pulse, wrote prescriptions and looked helplessly about him. Hauke shook his head; "He can't help; only God can help!" He had figured out a kind of Christianity for himself; but there was something that prevented his praying. When the old doctor had driven away he stood at the window staring out into the winter day and, while the patient screamed aloud in her delirium, he clasped his hands together tightly; he did not know himself whether it was an act of devotion or due to his tremendous fear of losing control of himself.

"Water! The water!" whimpered the sick woman. "Hold me!" she screamed; "hold me, Hauke!" Then her voice died down; it sounded as if she were crying; "into the sea, out into the ocean? O, dear God, I'll never see him again!"

At that he turned and pushed the nurse away from the bed. He dropped on his knees, put his arms round his

wife and held her close: "Elke! Elke! Oh, know me,
Elke, I am right here with you!"

But she only opened wide her eyes burning with fever
and looked about her as if helplessly lost.

He laid her back on her pillows; then, twisting his hands
together, he cried: "Oh Lord, my God, do not take her
from me! Thou knowest I cannot be without her!" Then
he seemed to recollect himself and added softly: "I know,
indeed, Thou canst not always do as Thou wouldst, not
even Thou; Thou art all-wise; Thou must do according to
thy wisdom—Oh Lord, speak to me if only by a breath!"

It was as if a sudden stillness had fallen; he heard nothing but gentle breathing; when he turned to the bed his
wife lay there in calm slumber; only the nurse looked at
him with horrified eyes. He heard the door move: "Who
was that?" he asked.

"The maid, Ann Grete, went out, sir; she came to bring
the child-bed basket."

"Why do you look at me so confusedly, Mrs. Levke?"

"I? I was frightened at your prayer; such a prayer will
never save anyone from death!"

Hauke looked at her with penetrating eyes: "Do you
too, like Ann Grete, go to the conventicle where the Dutch
jobbing tailor Jantje is?"

"Yes, sir; we both hold the living faith!"

Hauke did not answer her. The dissenting conventicle
movement which was in great vogue at that time had also
put forth blossoms among the Friesians; artisans who had
come down in the world, or schoolmasters who had been
dismissed for drunkenness, played the chief part in it, and
girls, young and old women, loafers and lonely people
assiduously attended the secret meetings in which anyone
could play the priest. Of the dikegrave's household Ann
Grete and the stable-boy, who was in love with her, spent
their free evenings there. Elke, to be sure, had not failed
to express her misgivings about this to Hauke; but it had
been his opinion that no one should interfere in matters

of faith; the conventicle would not hurt anyone and it was
at least better than the tavern!

So it had gone on, and therefore too he had kept silence
this time. But others did not keep silent about him! The
words of his prayer circulated from house to house; he
had denied God's omnipotence, and what was a God without omnipotence? He was an atheist; perhaps the affair
of the devil-horse might be true, after all!

Hauke heard nothing of this; in those days he had eyes
and ears only for his wife; even the child had vanished
from his mind.

The old doctor came again, came every day, sometimes
twice, then he stayed all night, wrote another prescription,
and the man, Iven Johns, galloped off to the apothecary's
with it. And then his face lost something of its serious-
ness, he nodded confidentially to the dikegrave: "We'll
pull through! With God's help!" And one day—was it
that his art had triumphed over the disease or, after Hauke
had prayed, had God been able to find another way out
after all—when the doctor was alone with the patient he
spoke to her and the old man's eyes beamed: "Mrs. Haien,
now I can tell you confidently, today the doctor has his
holiday; things were bad with you, but now you belong to
us again, to the living!"

At that a flood of joy broke from her dark eyes: "Hauke,
Hauke, where are you?" she cried, and when in response to
her clear call he rushed into the room and up to her bed,
she threw her arms around his neck: "Hauke, my husband, I'm saved! I'm going to stay with you!"

The old doctor drew his silk handkerchief from his
pocket, passed it over his forehead and cheeks and went out
of the room nodding his head.

On the third evening after this day a pious orator—it
was a slipper-maker who had been dismissed from work
by the dikegrave—preached in the conventicle at the Dutch
tailor's, and explained to his hearers God's qualities:
"But whoever denies God's omnipotence, whoever says:

'I know Thou canst not do as Thou wouldst'—we all know the wretched one; he lies like a stone upon the community —he has fallen away from God and seeks the enemy of God, the lover of sins, to be his comforter; for man must reach out for some staff. But you, beware of him who prays thus; his prayer is a curse!''

This too was carried about from house to house. What is not in a small community? And it also came to Hauke's ears. He did not speak of it, not even to his wife; only at times he embraced her vehemently and held her close: "Be true to me, Elke! Be true to me!" Then her eyes looked up at him full of astonishment: "True to you? To whom else should I be true?" But after a little while the meaning of his words came to her: "Yes, Hauke, we are true to each other, not only because we need each other." And then he went about his work and she about hers.

So far that would have been well; but in spite of all his absorbing work there was a feeling of loneliness round him, and defiance and reserve towards others crept into his heart; only towards his wife did he always remain the same, and morning and evening he knelt by his child's cradle as if that were the place of his eternal salvation. With the servants and laborers however he grew stricter; the awkward and careless whom formerly he had reproved quietly were now startled by the sudden harshness of his rebuke and Elke sometimes had to go softly and put things right.

When spring approached work on the dike began again; the gap in the western line of the dike was now closed by a cofferdam dike, in the form of a half-moon both towards the inside and towards the outside, in order to protect the sluice which was now about to be built. And, like the sluice, the main dike grew gradually to its height, which had to be attained by more and more rapid labor. The dikegrave, who was directing the work, did not find it easier; for in place of Jewe Manners, who had died during the winter,

Ole Peters had been appointed dike commissioner. Hauke had not wanted to try to prevent it; but, instead of the encouraging words and affectionate slaps on his left shoulder that went with them, which he had so often received from his wife's old godfather, he met with secret resistance and unnecessary objections from his successor, which had to be battered down with unnecessary reasons; for Ole did indeed belong to the men of consequence but, as far as dike matters were concerned, not to the wise men; and moreover the "scribbling farm-hand" of before was still in his way.

The most brilliant sky again spread out over sea and marsh, and the koog grew gay with strong cattle whose lowing from time to time interrupted the wide stillness; high in the air the larks sang unceasingly; one did not hear it till, for the length of a breath, the song was silent. No bad weather disturbed the work and the sluice already stood with its unpainted timber-structure without having needed the protection of the temporary dike even for one night; God seemed to favor the new work. Frau Elke's eyes also laughed to her husband when he came riding home from the dike on his white horse; "You've grown to be a good horse, after all," she would say and pat the animal's smooth neck. But Hauke, when she held the child, would spring down and let the tiny little thing dance in his arms; and when the white horse fixed its brown eyes on the child he would say perhaps, "Come here, you shall have the honor too!" Then he would put little Wienke—for so she had been christened—on his saddle and lead the horse round in a circle on the mound. Even the old ash-tree sometimes had the honor; he would seat the child on a springy bough and let it swing. The mother stood with laughing eyes in the door of the house, but the child did not laugh. Its eyes, on either side of a delicate little nose, looked rather dully out into the distance, and the tiny hands did not reach for the little stick that her father held out to her. Hauke did not notice it and of course he knew nothing

of such little children; only Elke, when she saw the bright-
eyed girl on the arm of her work-woman whose child had
been born at the same time as hers, sometimes said sor-
rowfully: "My baby isn't as far along as yours, Stina!"
and the woman, shaking the sturdy boy whom she held by
the hand, with rough love, would answer: "Oh, well, children are different; this one here stole the apples out of
the pantry before he had passed his second year!" And
Elke stroked the curly hair out of the fat little boy's eyes
and then secretly pressed her own quiet child to her
heart.

By the time October was coming on the new sluices on
the west side stood firm in the main dike, which closed on
both sides, and now, with the exception of the gaps at the
water-course, fell away with its sloping profile all round
towards the water sides and rose fifteen feet above the
ordinary tide. From its northwest corner there was an
unobstructed view out past Ievers Islet to the shallows; but
the winds here cut in more sharply; they blew one's hair
about and anyone who wanted to look out from here had to
have his cap firmly on his head.

At the end of November, when wind and rain had set in,
there only remained the opening close up to the old dike to
be stopped, on the bottom of which, on the north side, the
sea-water shot through the water-course into the new koog.
On both sides stood the walls of the dike: the gulf between
them had now to be closed. Dry summer weather would
undoubtedly have made the work easier but it had to be
done now in any case, for if a storm broke the whole construction might be endangered. And Hauke did his utmost
to carry the thing to a finish now. The rain streamed
down, the wind whistled; but his haggard form on the fiery
white horse appeared, now here, now there, out of the
black mass of men who were working above as well as
below, on the north side of the dike, beside the opening.
Now he was seen down by the tip-carts which already
had to bring the clay from far out on the foreland, and of

which a compact body was just reaching the water-course
and sought to dump its load there. Through the splashing
of the rain and the blustering of the wind were heard from
time to time the sharp orders of the dikegrave, who wanted
to be the sole commander there that day; he called up the
carts according to their numbers and ordered those who
pushed forward back; "halt" sounded from his lips and
the work below ceased. "Straw, a load of straw down
here!" he called to those above, and from one of the carts
on the top a load of straw plunged down onto the wet clay.
Below, men jumped into it, tore it apart and called to those
above not to bury them. And then new carts came and
Hauke was already above once more, and looked down
from his white horse into the gulf, and watched them
shoveling and dumping; then he turned his eyes out to
the sea. It was blowing hard and he saw how the fringe
of water crept farther and farther up the dike and how the
waves rose higher and higher; he saw too how the men
were dripping and could scarcely breathe at their hard
work for the wind, which cut off the air at their mouths,
and for the cold rain that streamed down over them.
"Stick to it, men! Stick to it!" he shouted down to them.
"Only one foot higher, then it's enough for this tide!"
And through all the din of the storm the noise of the workmen could be heard; the thud of the masses of clay as they
were dumped, the rattling of the carts and the rustling of
the straw as it slid down from above went on unceasingly.
Now and then the whining of a little yellow dog became
audible, that was knocked about among the men and teams,
shivering and as if lost; but suddenly there sounded a
piteous howl from the little creature, from down below in
the gulf. Hauke looked down; he had seen it being thrown
into the opening from above; an angry flush shot up into
his face. "Stop! Hold on!" he shouted down to the carts,
for the wet clay was being poured on without interruption.

   "Why?" a rough voice from below called up to him;
"surely not on account of the wretched beast of a dog?"

"Stop! I say," shouted Hauke again; "Bring me the dog! Our work shall not be stained by any outrage!"

But not a hand moved; only a few shovels of sticky clay still flew down beside the howling animal. Thereupon he put spurs to his horse, so that it shrieked aloud and dashed down the dike, and all stood back before him. "The dog!" he shouted; "I want the dog!"

A hand slapped him gently on the shoulder as if it were the hand of old Jewe Manners; but when he looked round it was only a friend of the old man's. "Take care, dike-grave!" he whispered to Hauke. "You have no friends among these men; let the dog be!"

The wind whistled, the rain streamed; the men had stuck their spades into the ground, some of them had thrown them down. Hauke bent down to the old man: "Will you hold my horse, Harke Jens?" he asked; and the man had scarcely got the reins into his hand before Hauke had jumped into the chasm and was holding the little whining creature in his arms; and almost in the same instant he was up again in the saddle and galloping back up the dike. His eyes traveled over the men who were standing by the wagons. "Who was it?" he called. "Who threw the creature down?"

For a moment they were all silent; for anger flashed from the dikegrave's haggard face and they had superstitious fear of him. From one of the teams a bull-necked fellow stepped up to him. "I did not do it, dikegrave," he said and biting a little end off a roll of chewing tobacco he calmly stuffed that into his mouth before he went on; "but whoever did it did right; if your dike is to hold, something living must go into it!"

'Something living? In what catechism did you learn that?"

"In none, sir," replied the fellow and an insolent laugh came from his throat; "even our grandfathers knew that, who could certainly have measured themselves with you in

Christianity! A child is still better; if that can't be had, a dog probably does instead!''

"Be silent with your heathenish doctrines!" Hauke shouted at him; "it would fill it up better if you were thrown in!''

"Oh ho!'' The shout rang out from a dozen throats and the dikegrave found himself surrounded by wrathful faces and clenched fists; he saw that these were indeed no friends; the thought of his dike came over him with a shock; what should he do if they should all throw down their shovels now? And as he looked down he saw again old Jewe Manners' friend going about among the workmen, speaking to this one and that, laughing to one, tapping another on the shoulder with a friendly smile, and one after the other took hold of his spade again; a few moments more and the work was once more in full swing. What more did he want? The water-course would have to be closed and he hid the dog securely enough in the folds of his cloak. With sudden decision he turned his white horse towards the nearest wagon: "Straw to the edge!'' he shouted commandingly and mechanically the teamster obeyed; soon it rustled down into the depths and on all sides the work stirred anew and all hands took hold busily.

The work had gone on thus for another hour; it was after six o'clock and already deep dusk was descending; the rain had ceased. Hauke called the superintendents to him as he sat on his horse: "Tomorrow morning at four o'clock,'' he said, "every man must be at his place; the moon will still be up; with God's help we shall be able to finish then! And one more thing,'' he called as they were about to go. "Do you know this dog?'' and he took the trembling animal out of his cloak.

They replied in the negative; only one of them said: "He's been running about begging in the village for days; he doesn't belong to anyone!''

"Then he is mine,'' said the dikegrave. "Don't forget —tomorrow morning at four o'clock!'' and rode away.

When he got home Ann Grete was just coming out of the door; she was cleanly and neatly dressed and it passed through his mind that she was just on her way to the tailor in the conventicle: "Lift up your apron!" he called to her and as she involuntarily obeyed he threw the little dog, covered with clay as he was, into it. "Take him to little Wienke; he shall be her little playfellow! But wash and warm him first, thus you will be doing a deed that is pleasing to God, for the creature is almost benumbed."

And Ann Grete could not refuse to obey her master, and so on that evening she did not get to the conventicle.

And on the following day the last touch of a spade was put to the new dike; the wind had gone down; now and again the gulls and avocets hovered above the land and water in graceful flight; from Jevershallig resounded the thousand-voiced honking of the barnacle geese that even at that time of year were enjoying themselves on the coast of the North Sea, and out of the morning mist, which hid the broad expanse of marsh, a golden autumn day gradually rose and illumined the new work of men's hands.

A few weeks later the chief dikegrave came with the government commissioners to inspect it. A great banquet, the first since the funeral repast at the time of old Tede Volkerts' death, was given in the dikegrave's house. All the dike commissioners and the men having the largest holdings of land in the new koog were invited. After dinner the dikegrave's carriage and all those of the guests were got ready. The chief dikegrave put Elke into the gig, before which the brown gelding stood stamping; then he jumped in himself and took the reins; he wanted to drive his dikegrave's clever wife himself. So they drove off merrily from the mound and out into the road, up the way to the new dike and along the top of that round, recently reclaimed koog. In the meantime a light northwest wind had sprung up and the tide was driven up on the north and west sides of the new dike; but it could not fail to be noticed that the gentle slope broke the force of the waves. The government commissioners were loud in their praise of the dikegrave, soon drowning the doubts that the local commissioners now and then hesitatingly uttered.

This occasion too passed by; but there was still another satisfaction in store for the dikegrave one day when he was riding along the new dike sunk in quiet self-congratulatory thought. The question might well occur to him why the koog, which never would have been there but for him and in which the sweat of his brow and his sleepless nights were buried, had now been named "the new Caroline Koog," after one of the princesses of the ruling house; but it certainly was so: in all the documents pertaining to it that was the name used, in some of them it was even written in red Gothic letters. At that point he looked up and saw two laborers with their farm implements coming towards him, one some twenty paces behind the other: "Wait for me, then," he heard the one that was following call; but the other, who was just standing at the path that led down into the koog, called back: "Some other time, Jens! It's late; I've got to dig clay here!"

"Where?"

"Why here, in the Hauke-Haien-Koog!"

He called it aloud as he ran down the path as if he wanted the whole marsh that lay below to hear. But to Hauke it was as if he heard his fame proclaimed; he rose in his saddle, put spurs to his horse and looked with steady eyes across the broad scene that lay at his left. "Hauke-Haien-Koog!" he repeated softly; that sounded as if it could never be called anything else. Let them be as obstinate as they would, his name could not be downed; the princess' name—would it not soon exist only in mouldy old documents? The white horse galloped on proudly and in Hauke's ears the words continued to ring: "Hauke-Haien-Koog! Hauke-Haien-Koog!" In his thoughts the new dike almost grew to be an eighth wonder of the world; in all Friesland there was none to equal it! And he let the white horse dance; he felt as if he stood in the midst of all Friesians; he towered above them by a head and his keen glance swept over them with pity.

Gradually three years had passed since the building of the new dike; the latter had proved successful and the expense of repairs had been but slight. In the koog white clover was now blooming nearly everywhere and when you walked across the protected pastures the summer breeze wafted a whole cloud of sweet scent towards you. It had been necessary to replace the nominal shares with real ones and to assign permanent holdings to each of the men interested. Hauke had not been slow in acquiring a few new ones himself, before that; Ole Peters had held back stubbornly; no part of the new koog belonged to him. Even so it had not been possible to make the division without vexation and dispute; but it had been done nevertheless, and this day too lay behind the dikegrave.

From then on he lived a lonely life, devoting himself to his duties as a farmer and a dikegrave, and to his immediate family; his old friends were no longer alive and he was not fitted to make new ones. But under his roof was peace which even his quiet child did not disturb; it spoke little; the continual questioning that is peculiar to brighter children seldom came from its lips and when it did it was usually in such a way that it was difficult to answer; but the dear, simple little face almost always wore an expression of content. The little girl had two playfellows and that was all she wanted: when she wandered about the mound the little yellow dog that Hauke had saved always accompanied her, jumping and springing, and whenever the dog appeared little Wienke was not far away either. The dog was called "Perle" and her second comrade, a peewit-gull, was "Klaus."

It was a hoary old woman who had installed Klaus at the farm; the eighty-year-old Trien' Jans had no longer been able to make a living in her cottage on the outside dike, and

Elke had thought that the worn-out servant of her grand-father might still find with them a few peaceful hours at the end of her life and a comfortable place to die. So half by force she and Hauke had fetched the old body to the farm and settled her in the little northwest room of the new barn, which the dikegrave had been obliged to build when he enlarged his place a few years before. A few of the maids had been given their rooms next to hers so that they could look after her at night. All round the walls she had her old household goods; a strong box made of red cedar, above which hung two colored pictures of the prodigal son, a spinning wheel which had long since been laid aside and a very clean four-post bed in front of which stood a clumsy foot-stool covered with the white skin of the deceased Angora cat. But she also still had something living, and had brought it with her: this was the gull Klaus that had stuck to her for years and been fed by her; when winter came, to be sure, it flew south with the other gulls and did not come again till the wormwood exhaled its sweet odor along the shore.

The barn lay somewhat farther down the mound; from her window the old woman could not see out over the dike to the sea. "You've got me here like a prisoner," she murmured one day when Hauke came in, and pointed with her gnarled finger to the fens which lay spread out below. "Where is Jeverssand? Out there above the red or above the black ox?"

"What do you want with Jeverssand?" asked Hauke.

"Oh, never mind Jeverssand," grumbled the old woman. "But I want to see where, long ago, my lad went to God!"

"If you want to see that," replied Hauke, "you must go and sit up under the ash-tree; from there you can look well out over the sea."

"Yes," said the old woman; "yes, if I had your young legs, dikegrave!"

For a long time such were the thanks for the aid that the dikegrave and his wife had given her; then all at once there was a change. One morning Wienke's little head peeped in at her through the half-open door. "Well!" called the old woman, who was sitting on her wooden chair with her hands clasped, "what message have you got to tell me?"

But the child came silently nearer and looked at her unceasingly with indifferent eyes.

"Are you the dikegrave's child?" asked Trien' Jans, and, as the child lowered her head as if nodding, she continued: "Sit down here on my footstool then! It was an Angora tomcat—as big as that! But your father killed him. If he were still alive you could ride on him."

Wienke looked at the white skin dumbly; then she knelt down and began to stroke it with her little hands as children do a living cat or dog. "Poor Tomcat!" she said, and continued her caresses.

"There," exclaimed the old woman after a while, "now it's enough; and you can still sit on him today; perhaps your father only killed him for that!" Then she lifted the child up by both arms and set her down roughly on the stool. But as Wienke sat there silent and immovable, only looking at her all the time, she began to shake her head: "Thou art punishing him, Lord God! Yes, yes, Thou art punishing him!" she murmured; but pity for the child seemed to come over her after all: she put out her bony hand and stroked the little girl's sparse hair and an expression came into the child's eyes as if she liked the touch.

From now on Wienke came to see the old woman in her room daily. Soon she sat down of her own accord on the Angora footstool and Trien' Jans gave her little pieces of meat or bread of which she always kept some on hand, and let her throw them on the floor; then the gull shot out of some corner, screeching, with outstretched wings, and fell upon them. At first the child used to be frightened and screamed at the big flapping bird; but soon it was like a game they had learnt, and as soon as she stuck even her head through the crack of the door the bird shot out

towards her and lighted on her head or shoulder till the old
woman came to her aid and the feeding could begin. Trien'
Jans, who in general could not bear even to have anyone
stretch out his hand towards her Klaus, now looked on patiently while the child gradually won the bird entirely away
from her. It let Wienke catch it willingly; she carried it
about and wrapped it in her apron, and, when, on the
mound, the little yellow dog sometimes sprang about her
and jumped jealously at the bird, she would cry out: "Not
you, not you, Perle!" and would lift the gull so high in her
little arms that it would free itself and fly away shrieking
across the mound, and the dog would try to secure its place
in her arms by jumping and rubbing against his little
mistress.

When Hauke's or Elke's eyes chanced to fall on this odd
group, like four leaves all held fast on one stem by only a
common lack, a tender glance would indeed fly towards
their child; when they turned away there remained in their
faces only pain which each bore for himself, for they had
never yet unburdened their hearts to each other about the
child. One summer morning as Wienke was sitting with the
old woman and the two animals on the big stone in front of
the barn door, her parents, the dikegrave with his white
horse behind him, the reins over his arm, passed by; he
was going out on the dike and had fetched his horse from
the fens himself; on the mound his wife had slipped her
arm through his. The sun shone down warmly; it was almost sultry, and now and then there came a puff of wind
from the south-southeast. The child must have found it
tiresome where she was: "Wienke wants to go," she
called, shook the gull from her lap, and reached for her
father's hand.

"Come along then," he said.

But Elke exclaimed: "In this wind? She'll be blown
away!"

"I'll hold on to her; and the air is warm today and the
water merry; she can see it dance."

So Elke ran into the house and fetched a little shawl and a cap for her child. "But there's going to be bad weather," she said; "see that you hurry and go and get back again soon."

Hauke laughed: "That won't catch us!" and lifted the child up to his saddle in front of him. Elke remained out on the mound for a while and, shading her eyes with her hand, watched the two trotting out on the road and over to the dike; Trien' Jans sat on the stone and mumbled something incomprehensible with her faded lips.

The child lay without moving in her father's arm; and it seemed as if, oppressed by the thundery air, she were breathing with difficulty. He bent his head to her: "Well, Wienke?" he asked.

The child looked at him for a while. "Father," she said, "you can surely do that! Can't you do everything?"

"What ought I to be able to do, Wienke?"

But she was silent; she seemed not to have understood her own question.

It was high tide; when they came up on the dike the reflection of the sun on the great expanse of water shone in her eyes, a whirlwind drove the waves up high in an eddy, and others followed and beat splashingly against the shore; she clasped her little hands so fearfully about her father's fist in which he held the reins that the white horse bounded to one side. Her pale blue eyes looked up in confused terror to Hauke: "The water, Father, the water!" she cried.

But he freed himself gently and said: "Be quiet, child, you are with your father; the water won't hurt you!"

She smoothed the pale blonde hair away from her forehead and ventured to look out at the sea again. "It won't hurt me," she said trembling; "no, tell it not to hurt us; you can do that and then it won't hurt us."

"I can't do that, child," replied Hauke seriously; "but the dike on which we're riding protects us and it was your father who thought that out and had it built."

Her eyes looked at him as if she did not quite understand

that; then she hid her strikingly small head in her father's loose coat.

"Why do you hide yourself, Wienke?" he whispered to her; "are you still frightened?" And a trembling voice came from the folds of his coat: "Wienke doesn't want to see; but you can do everything, can't you, Father?"

A distant clap of thunder rolled up against the wind. "Oh ho!" exclaimed Hauke, "there it comes!" and turned his horse to go back. "Now we'll go home to Mother."

The child drew a deep breath, but not until they had reached the mound and the house did she raise her little head from her father's breast. Then in the room when Elke had taken off the little shawl and the cap she remained standing like a little dumb ninepin in front of her mother. "Well, Wienke," said the latter and shook the little girl gently, "do you like the great water?"

But the child opened her eyes wide: "It speaks," she said; "Wienke is frightened."

"It doesn't speak; it only roars and surges."

The child looked off into the distance. "Has it legs?" she asked again; "can it come over the dike?"

"No, Wienke, your father takes care of that, he is a dikegrave."

"Yes," said the child and clapped her hands with an idiotic smile; "Father can do everything—everything." Then suddenly, turning away from her mother, she cried: "Let Wienke go to Trien' Jans, she has red apples!"

And Elke opened the door and let the child out. After she had shut it again she looked up at her husband, and an expression of the deepest sorrow lay in the eyes which hitherto had always brought consolation and courage to his aid.

He held out his hand and pressed hers as if there were no need of any further word between them; but she said softly: "No, Hauke, let me speak: the child that I have borne to you after waiting for years will always remain a child. O, dear God! She is feeble-minded; I must say it before you once.''

''I have known it a long time,'' said Hauke, and held tight the hand that his wife wanted to draw away from him.

''And so we are still alone after all,'' she said.

But Hauke shook his head: ''I love her and she throws her little arms around me and presses herself close against my breast; I would not do without that for any treasure!''

The woman looked darkly ahead of her: ''But why?'' she said; ''What have I, poor mother, done to deserve it?''

''Yes, Elke, I too have asked that, asked Him who alone can know; but, as we both know, the Almighty gives men no answer—perhaps because we should not understand it.''

He had taken his wife's other hand and drew her gently to him: ''Don't let yourself grow disturbed and be hindered in loving your child, as you do; you can be sure she understands that.''

At that Elke threw herself on her husband's breast and wept her fill and was no longer alone with her sorrow. Then suddenly she smiled at him; after pressing his hand vehemently she ran out and fetched her child from old Trien' Jans' room, and took her on her lap and fondled and kissed her till the little girl said stammeringly: ''Mother, my dear Mother!''

Thus the people on the dikegrave's farm lived quietly together; if the child had not been there much would have been lacking.

Gradually the summer went by; the birds of passage had passed through, the air was empty of the song of the larks; only in front of the barns where they picked up grains of corn, while the threshing was going on, occasionally one or two could be heard as they flew away screeching; everything was already hard frozen. In the kitchen of the main house old Trien' Jans sat one afternoon on the wooden step of a stairway that led up from beside the range to the attic. During the last few weeks it seemed as if she had returned to life; she came gladly into the kitchen some-

times, and saw Elke at work there; there could no longer be
any question of her legs not being able to carry her there,
since one day when little Wienke had pulled her up there
by her apron.   Now the child knelt at her side and looked
with her quiet eyes into the flames that flickered up out of
the stove-hole.   One of her little hands clasped the sleeve
of the old woman, the other lay in her own pale blonde
hair.   Trien' Jans was telling a story: "You know," she
said, "I was in your great grandfather's service as a house-
maid and then I had to feed the pigs; he was cleverer than
them all—then, it is terribly long ago, but one evening, the
moon was shining and they closed the outer sluice and she
could not get back into the sea.   Oh, how she screamed and
tore her hard shaggy hair with her little fish-hands! Yes,
child, I saw it and heard her screaming myself!   The
ditches between the fens were all full of water and the
moon shining on them made them sparkle like silver and
she swam from one ditch into the other and lifted her arms
and struck what were her hands together so that you could
hear it a long way off, as if she wanted to pray; but, child,
those creatures cannot pray.   I was sitting in front of the
door on a few beams that had been brought up there to be
used in building, and looking far out across the fens; and
the water-woman still swam in the ditches, and when she
raised her arms they too glittered like silver and diamonds.
At last I did not see her any more and the wild geese and
gulls that I had not heard the whole time began to fly
through the air again, hissing and cackling."

The old woman ceased; the child had caught up one word.
"Could not pray?" she asked.   "What do you say? Who
was it?"

"Child," said the old woman, "it was the water-woman;
those are accursed creatures who can never be saved."

"Never be saved," repeated the child and her little breast
heaved with a deep sigh as if she had understood that.

"Trien' Jans," came a deep voice from the kitchen door
and she started slightly.   It was the dikegrave Hauke Haien

who was leaning there against the post. "What are you
saying to the child? Haven't I told you to keep your
legends to yourself or to tell them to the geese and hens?"

The old woman looked at him with an angry glance and
pushed the little girl away from her: "Those are no
legends," she murmured half to herself, "my great-uncle
told me that."

"Your great-uncle, Trien'? Why just now you said you
had experienced it yourself!"

"It's all the same," said the old woman; "but you don't
believe, Hauke Haien; I suppose you want to make my
great-uncle out a liar." Then she drew nearer to the range
and stretched her hands out over the flames in the grate.

The dikegrave threw a glance towards the window; it
was scarcely dusk as yet outside. "Come, Wienke," he said
and drew his feeble-minded child to him; "come with me;
I want to show you something from out on the dike! Only
we shall have to walk; the white horse is at the black-
smith's." Then he went with her into the living-room and
Elke tied thick woolen shawls about the little girl's throat
and shoulders; soon after her father took her out on the
old dike towards the northwest, past Jeverssand, to where
the flats lay broad before them almost farther than the
eye could reach.

Part of the time he carried her, part of the time he led
her by the hand; the twilight deepened gradually; in the
distance everything disappeared in mist and vapor. But
there, where one could still see, the invisibly swelling currents of the shallows had broken the ice, and, as Hauke
had once seen it in his youth, smoking fog now rose from
the cracks along which the uncanny, impish figures were
once more to be seen hopping towards one another and bowing and suddenly stretching out wide, in a terrible fashion.

The child clung to her father in fear and covered her
little face with his hand: "The sea-devils!" she whispered
tremblingly between his fingers; "the sea-devils!"

He shook his head: "No, Wienke, neither water-women

nor sea-devils; there are no such things; who told you about them?"

She looked up at him dully but did not answer. He stroked her cheeks tenderly: "Just look again," he said; "those are only poor hungry birds. Just see how the big one spreads his wings now; they are catching the fish that come into the steaming cracks."

"Fish," repeated Wienke.

"Yes, child, all those creatures are alive like us, there *is* nothing else. But God is everywhere!"

Little Wienke had fixed her eyes on the ground and held her breath; she looked as if she were gazing into an abyss terrified. Perhaps it only seemed so; her father looked at her long; he bent down and looked into her little face, but no feeling of her imprisoned soul was visible in it. He lifted her in his arms and stuck her benumbed hands into one of his thick woolen gloves: "there, my little Wienke," and the child probably did not hear the tone of intense tenderness in his words—"there, warm yourself close to me! You are our child after all, our only one. You love us——" The man's voice broke, but the little girl pressed her head tenderly into his rough beard.

Thus they went home full of peace.

After the New Year, trouble once more entered into the house; the dikegrave was seized with a marsh fever; it went hard with him too, and when, under Elke's nursing and care, he recovered, he scarcely seemed to be the same man. The languor of his body also lay upon his mind, and Elke was worried to see how easily content he was at all times. Nevertheless towards the end of March he was moved to mount his white horse and ride out again for the first time along the top of his dike. It was on an afternoon and the sun, which had been shining earlier in the day, had long since been concealed by the haze.

A few times during the winter there had been high tides but they had done no serious damage; only over on the other bank a herd of sheep on an islet had been drowned and a bit of the foreland had been washed away; here on this side and in the new koog no harm worth mentioning had been done. But in the previous night a stronger gale had raged and now the dikegrave himself had to ride out and inspect everything with his own eyes. He had already ridden all along the new dike, beginning below at the southeast corner, and everything was in good condition, but as he came towards the northeast corner where the new dike ran up to the old one, the former was indeed uninjured, but where before the water-course had reached the old one and flowed along beside it, he saw that a great strip of the grass-line had been destroyed and washed away, and a hollow had been eaten in the body of the dike by the tide, which moreover, had thus laid bare a whole maze of mouse-passages. Hauke dismounted and inspected the damage from near-by: the destructive mouse-passages seemed unmistakably to continue on beyond where they could be seen.

He was seriously frightened; all this should have been thought of and prevented at the time the new dike was built; as it had been overlooked then it must be taken care of now! The cattle were not yet out on the fens, the grass was unusually backward; in whatever direction he glanced it all looked bleak and empty. He mounted his horse and rode back and forth along the bank: the tide was low and he did not fail to perceive that the current from outside had bored a new bed for itself in the mud and had come from the northwest against the old dike: the new one however, as far as it was involved, had been able to withstand the onslaught of the waves owing to its gentler profile.

A new mountain of annoyance and work rose before the dikegrave's mental vision: not only would the old dike have to be strengthened here but its profile would also have to be approximated to the new one; above all, the water-course, from which danger now threatened again, would have to be diverted by new dams or brush hedges. Once more he rode along the new dike to the extreme northwest corner

and then back again, his eyes fixed on the newly channeled
bed of the water-course, which was plainly to be seen at
his side in the bared mud. The white horse fretted to go
on, and snorted and pawed the ground, but Hauke held him
back; he wanted to ride slowly and he wanted also to
master the inner disquietude which was fermenting and
seething within him with ever-increasing strength.

If a storm should come bringing with it high tides—such
a one as in 1655, when men and property were swallowed
up uncounted—if it should come again as it had already
come several times!—a hot shudder trickled over the rider
—the old dike, it could never stand the violent attack that
would be made on it! What, what could be done then?
There would be one way, and one way only, to save perhaps the old koog, and the property and life in it. Hauke
felt his heart stand still, his usually strong head whirl; he
did not speak it aloud, but within him it was spoken clearly
enough: your koog, the Hauke-Haien-Koog, would have to
be sacrificed and the new dike broken through.

Already he saw in imagination the rushing flood breaking in and covering grass and clover with its salt seething
froth. His spur gashed into the white horse's flank, and
with a cry it flew forward along the dike and down the
path that led to the dikegrave's mound.

His head full of inward alarm and confused plans, he
came home. He threw himself into his armchair and when
Elke entered the room with their daughter he stood up
again, lifted the child up and kissed her; then he drove the
little yellow dog away from him with a few light blows.
"I've got to go up to the tavern again!" he said and took
his cap from the peg on the door, where he had only just
hung it.

His wife looked at him troubled: "What do you want
to do there? It's already growing dark, Hauke."

"Dike affairs," he murmured. "I'll meet some of the
commissioners there."

She followed him and pressed his hand, for by the time
he had finished speaking he was already outside the door.

Hauke Haien, who hitherto had made all his decisions alone, now felt anxious to hear a word from those whose opinions he had formerly regarded as scarcely worth considering. In the inn he found Ole Peters sitting at the card table with two of the commissioners and a man who lived in the koog. "You've come from out on the dike, I suppose, dike-grave," said the former picking up the half-dealt cards and throwing them down again.

"Yes, Ole," replied Hauke; "I was out there; it looks bad."

"Bad? Well, it will cost a few hundred sods and some straw work I suppose; I was out there too this afternoon."

"We shan't get off as cheap as that, Ole," answered the dikegrave. "The water-course is there again and even if it doesn't strike against the old dike from the north now, it does from the northwest."

"You ought to have left it where you found it," said Ole dryly.

"That means," replied Hauke, "you're not concerned in the new koog and therefore it should not exist. That is your own fault. But if we have to plant brush hedges to protect the old dike the green clover behind the new one will more than make up for that."

"What do you say, dikegrave?" cried the commissioners; "hedges? How many? You like to do everything the most expensive way!"

The cards lay on the table untouched. "I'll tell you, dikegrave," said Ole Peters leaning his arms on the table, "your new koog that you've foisted on us is eating us up. Everyone is still suffering under the cost of your broad dike; now it's consuming the old dike too and you want us to renew that! Fortunately it's not so bad; it held this time and will continue to do so. Just mount your white horse again tomorrow and look at it once more."

Hauke had come to the tavern out of the peace of his home. Behind the words he had just heard, which after all were fairly moderate, there lay—he could not fail to recognize it—an obstinate resistance. It seemed to him

that he lacked the strength he had formerly had to cope
with it. "I'll do as you advise, Ole," he said: "only I'm
afraid I shall find it as I saw it today."

A restless night followed this day; Hauke tossed sleep-
lessly about on his pillow. "What is the matter?" asked
Elke, kept awake by worry about her husband; "if there
is anything on your mind tell it to me; we have always
done that."

"It is not of any consequence, Elke," he replied; "there
are some repairs to be made to the dike, to the sluices;
you know that I always have to think such things out in
my mind at night." He said nothing further; he wanted
to keep himself free to act as he chose. Without his being
conscious of it his wife's clear insight and strong mind
were an obstacle to him in his present weakness and involuntarily he avoided it.

On the following morning as he came out onto the dike
he saw a different world from the one he had found the
day before; it was indeed low tide again but the day was
growing and the rays from the bright spring sun fell almost
perpendicularly on the shallows which extended as far as
the eye could reach; the white gulls glided calmly hither
and thither and, invisible above them, high under the azure
sky the larks sang their eternal melody. Hauke, who did
not know how nature can deceive us with her charm, stood
on the northwest corner of the dike and sought the new
bed of the water-course which had given him such a shock
the day before; but with the sunlight darting directly down
from the zenith he could not even find it at first; not until
he shaded his eyes with his hand from the dazzling rays
did it show itself unmistakably. Nevertheless the shadows
in the dusk of the evening before must have deceived him;
it was outlined but very weakly now; the mouse-passages
that had been laid bare must have been more responsible
for the damage done to the dike than the tide. To be sure,
it must be changed; but by careful digging and, as Ole
Peters had said, by fresh sodding and a few rods of straw
work the damage could be repaired.

"It wasn't so bad, after all," he said to himself with relief, "you made a fool of yourself yesterday!" He called the commissioners together and the work was decided upon, for the first time without any objection being raised. The dikegrave thought he felt a strengthening calm spreading through his still weakened body; and in a few weeks everything was neatly carried out.

The year went on but the older it grew the more clearly the newly laid grass shot up green through its covering of straw, with the more agitation did Hauke walk or ride past this spot. He turned away his eyes, he rode close along the inside of the dike; several times when he would have had to pass the place and his horse was ready saddled for him to start he had it led back into the stable; then again, when he had nothing to do there, he would suddenly hurry out there on foot just so as to get away quickly and unseen from his mound; sometimes too he had turned back, he had not been able to trust himself to examine the dismal place anew; and finally he had felt as if he would like to tear everything open again with his hands; for this bit of the dike lay before his eyes like a prick of conscience that had taken form outside of him. And yet his hand could not touch it again and he could speak of it to no one, not even to his wife. Thus September had come; in the night a moderate wind had raged and finally had shifted to the northwest. On the following dull morning, when the tide was low, Hauke rode out on the dike and a start ran through him as he let his eyes rove over the shallows; there, coming from the northwest he suddenly saw it again and cut through more sharply and deeply, the new spectral bed of the water-course; exert his eyes as he might, it refused to disappear.

When he came home Elke took his hand; "What is the matter, Hauke?" she asked, looking into his gloomy face; "surely there is no new misfortune? We are so happy now; I feel as if you were at peace with them all."

In the face of these words he could not express his confused fear.

"No, Elke," he said, "no one makes an enemy of me; only it is a responsible office to protect the community from God's sea."

He freed himself so as to avoid further questioning from the wife that he loved. He went into the stable and shed as if he had to inspect everything; but he saw nothing around him; he was only intent on quieting his prick of conscience, on trying to convince himself that it was a morbidly exaggerated fear.

"The year of which I am telling you," said my host, the schoolmaster, after a while, "was the year 1756, which will never be forgotten about here; in Hauke Haien's house it brought with it a death. At the end of September the almost ninety-year-old Trien' Jans was found dying in the room which had been given up to her in the barn. According to her desire she had been propped up against her pillows and her eyes looked through the little leaded panes into the distance; there must have been a thinner over a denser layer of air lying there along the sky for at this moment there was a clear mirage and the sea was reflected like a glistening strip of silver above the edge of the dike so that it shone dazzlingly into the room; the south end of Jeverssand too was visible.

At the foot of the bed crouched little Wienke and held her father's hand tightly in one of hers as he stood close by. Death was just engraving the Hippocratic face on the dying woman and the child stared breathlessly at the uncanny, incomprehensible change in the plain countenance with which she was so familiar. "What is she doing? What is it, Father?" she whispered fearfully and dug her finger nails into her father's hand.

"She is dying," said the dikegrave.

"Dying," repeated the child and seemed to fall into confused thought.

But the old woman moved her lips once more: "Jins! Jins!" a shrill cry of distress broke from her and she stretched out her bony arms towards the reflection of the sea that glistened outside: "Help me! Help me! You are above the water. * * * God have mercy on the others!"

Her arms sank, there was a slight cracking of the bedstead; she had ceased to live.

The child drew a deep sigh and raised her pale eyes to her father: "Is she still dying?" she asked.

"She has finished!" said the dikegrave, and took the child in his arms. "She is far away from us now, with God."

"With God," repeated the child and was silent for a while as if she were thinking over the words. "Is it good to be with God?"

"Yes, best of all." But in Hauke's heart the dying woman's last words tolled heavily. "God have mercy on the others!"—the words sounded softly within him. What did the old witch mean? Can the dying prophesy?

Soon, after Trien' Jans had been buried up by the church, there began to be ever louder talk of all kinds of misfortune and curious vermin that were said to have frightened the people in northern Friesland. And it was certain that on the Sunday in Mid-Lent the golden cock had been thrown down from the top of the tower by a whirlwind; and it was true too that in midsummer a shower of large insects fell from heaven like snow so that it was impossible to open one's eyes and they lay nearly as high as a hand on the fens and no one had ever seen anything like it. But after the end of September when the head-man and the maid Ann Grete came back from town where they had driven with grain and butter for the market, they climbed down from their wagon with faces pale with fear. "What is it? What is the matter with you?" cried the other maids, who had come running out when they heard the sound of the wagon.

Ann Grete in her traveling dress stepped breathlessly into the roomy kitchen. "Oh, hurry up and tell us!" called the girls again, "where is the misfortune?"

"Oh, may our dear Jesus protect us!" cried Ann Grete. "You know from the other side, across the water, that old Molly from Siegelhof—we always stand together with our

butter at the corner near the apothecary's—she told me
about it and Iven Johns said too, 'that means a misfortune,' he said, 'a misfortune for the whole of northern
Friesland; believe me Ann Grete!' And"—she lowered her
voice—"perhaps after all it's not all right with the dikegrave's white horse."

"Ssh! Ssh!" said the other maids.

"Yes, yes; what does it matter to me! But over there,
on the other side, it's going on worse than with us! Not
only flies and vermin, blood too has fallen like rain from
heaven; and on the Sunday morning after that when the
pastor went to his washbasin there were five death's-heads,
the size of peas, in it, and they all came to see it; in the
month of August horrible red-headed caterpillars went
through the land and ate up the grain and flour and bread
and whatever they could find and no fire was able to destroy
them!"

Ann Grete suddenly ceased; none of the maids had noticed that their mistress had come into the kitchen. "What
tales are you telling there?" she asked. "Don't let your
master hear that!" And as they all wanted to begin to
tell her she went on, "It's not necessary; I heard enough
of it; go about your work, that will do you more good!"
Then she took Ann Grete with her into the sitting-room to
go through her market accounts with her.

So in the dikegrave's house none of the family paid any
attention to the superstitious gossip that was going about;
but it was different in the other houses and the longer the
evenings grew the more easily did it find its way in.
Everyone lived as if in an oppressive atmosphere and secretly people said to themselves that a misfortune, and a
heavy one, would fall on northern Friesland.

It was in October, before All Saints' Day. A strong wind
had blown from the southwest all day; in the evening the
crescent moon was in the sky, dark brown clouds drove
past and a medley of shade and dull light flew across the
earth; the storm was growing. In the dikegrave's room the

empty supper table still stood; the men had been sent into the stable to look after the cattle; the maids were busy in the house and in the attics seeing that the doors and windows were securely fastened so that the storm should not gain an entrance and do damage. Hauke stood beside his wife at the window; he had just swallowed down his supper; he had been out on the dike. He had gone there on foot early in the afternoon; here and there, where the dike looked weak, he had had pointed stakes and sacks of clay or earth piled up; everywhere he had left men to drive in the stakes and make dams with the sacks in front as soon as the tide should begin to damage the dike. The largest number he had placed at the corner towards the northwest at the intersection of the old and new dikes; their instructions were not to leave the places assigned to them except in case of necessity. That was what he had left behind him and then, scarcely a quarter of an hour ago, he had come back to the house wet and disheveled and now, his ear fixed on the gusts of winds that rattled the leaded panes, he gazed out absently into the wild night; the clock behind the pane of glass in the wall was just striking eight. The child, who was standing beside her mother, started and buried her head in her mother's dress. "Klaus!" she called, crying, "where is my Klaus?"

She might well ask, for this year, as indeed the year before, the gull had not flown away for the winter. Her father did not heed the question, but her mother lifted the child in her arms. "Your Klaus is in the barn," she said, "he has a warm place there."

"Warm?" said Wienke, "is that good?"

"Yes, that's good."

The master still stood at the window. "It won't do any longer, Elke," he said; "call one of the girls, the storm will break in the panes; the shutters must be screwed on!"

At her mistress's word the maid had run out; they could see from the room how her skirts were blown about; but when she unfastened the catch the wind tore the shutter out of her hand and threw it against the window so that a

few broken panes flew into the room and one of the lights
flared and went out. Hauke himself had to go out to help
and it was only with great difficulty that the shutters were
at last got into place. When they opened the door again
to come into the house a gust of wind followed them that
made the glass and silver in the cupboard shake and clatter; upstairs in the house above their heads the beams
trembled and cracked as if the gale were trying to tear
the roof off the walls. But Hauke did not come back into
the room. Elke heard him walking across the floor towards
the stable. "The white horse! The white horse, John;
quick!" She heard him call the order; then he came into
the room, his hair tumbled but his gray eyes sparkling.
"The wind has shifted!" he cried, "to the northwest, at
half spring-tide! No wind; we have never experienced
such a storm!"

Elke had grown as pale as death: "And you must go
out there again?"

He seized both her hands and pressed them convulsively:
"That I must, Elke."

Slowly she raised her dark eyes to his and for a few
seconds they looked at each other; but it was like an eternity. "Yes, Hauke," answered the woman; "I know well
that you must!"

There was a sound of trotting before the front door.
She flung herself on Hauke's neck and for a moment it
seemed as if she could not let him go; but that too was only
for a second. "This is *our* fight," said Hauke; "you are
safe here, no tide has ever come up to this house. And pray
to God to be with me too!"

Hauke wrapped himself in his cloak and Elke took a scarf
and wound it carefully round his neck; she wanted to say
a word, but her trembling lips refused to utter it.

Outside the white horse neighed so that it sounded like
a trumpet in the howling storm. Elke went out with her
husband; the old ash creaked as if it were being split
asunder. "Mount, master," called the man, "the white
horse is as if mad; the rein might break." Hauke threw

his arms round his wife: "I shall be here again at sunrise!"

Already he had leapt onto his horse; the animal reared; then, like a war-horse rushing into battle, it charged down the mound with its rider out into the night and the howling of the storm. "Father, my Father!" cried a child's plaintive voice after him: "my dear Father!"

Wienke had run out after them in the dark; but she had not gone more than a hundred steps before she stumbled against a heap of earth and fell.

The man Johns brought the crying child back to her mother; the latter was leaning against the trunk of the ash, the boughs of which lashed the air above her, staring out absently into the night in which her husband had disappeared; when the roaring of the gale and the distant thunder of the sea ceased for a moment she started as if frightened; she felt as if everything was trying just to destroy him and would be dumb instantly when it had got him. Her knees trembled, the wind had blown her hair down and now played with it at will. "Here is the child!" John shouted to her; "hold her tight!" and he pressed the little girl into her mother's arms.

"The child? I'd forgotten you, Wienke!" she exclaimed; "God forgive me." Then she hugged her to her breast as closely as only love can and dropped on her knees: "Lord God, and Thou, my Jesus, let us not become widow and orphan! Protect him, Oh dear God; only Thou and I, we alone know him!" And there was no more interruption to the gale; it resounded and thundered as if the whole world were coming to an end in one vast reverberation of sound.

"Go into the house, Missis!" said Johns; "come!" And he helped them and led the two into the house and into the sitting-room.

The dikegrave, Hauke Haien, flew forward on his white horse towards the dike. The narrow path was like a mire, for excessively heavy rain had fallen in the preceding days; nevertheless the wet sticky clay did not seem to hold the horse's hoofs, it moved as if treading on a firm dry road. The clouds drove across the sky in a mad chase; below, the wide marsh lay like an unrecognizable desert filled with agitated shades; from the water behind the dike came an ever-increasing dull roar as if it must swallow up everything else. "Forward, my white horse!" cried Hauke; "we're riding our worst ride!"

At that moment a sound like a death cry came from under his mount's hoofs. He pulled up and looked round; at his side, close above the ground, screeching mockingly as they went, moved a flock of white gulls, half flying, half tossed by the gale; they were seeking protection on shore. One of them—the moon shone fleetingly through the clouds —lay crushed on the path: it seemed to the rider as if a red ribbon fluttered from its neck. "Klaus!" he cried. "Poor Klaus!"

Was it his child's bird? Had it recognized horse and rider and tried to seek shelter with them? He did not know. "Forward!" he cried again, and the white horse had already lifted his hoofs for a new race when suddenly there was a pause in the storm and a deathlike silence took its place; it lasted but an instant, then the gale returned with renewed fury; but in the meantime the rider's ear had caught the sound of men's voices and the faint barking of dogs and when he turned his head back towards the village he distinguished, in the moonlight that broke forth, people on the mounds and in front of the houses busy about wagons that were loaded high; he saw, as if in flight, still other wagons driving hurriedly towards the upland; the lowing of cattle being driven up there out of their warm stables, met his ear. "Thank God, they are saving themselves and their cattle!" his heart cried; and then came an inward shriek of terror: "My wife! My child! No. No; the water will not come up to our mound!"

But it was only for a moment; everything flew by him like a vision.

A fearful squall came roaring up from the sea and into its face horse and rider stormed up the narrow path to the dike. Once on top Hauke halted his steed with force. But where was the sea? Where Jeverssand? Where lay the opposite shore? Nothing but mountains of water faced him, rising up threateningly against the night sky, seeking to overtop one another in the dreadful dusk, and beating, one over the next, on the shore. They came forward with white crests, howling, as if the roar of all the terrible beasts of prey in the wilderness were in them. The white horse pawed the ground and snorted out into the din; but it came over the rider as if here all human power were at an end; as if night, death, chaos must now set in.

Still he considered: after all it was a storm-tide; only he himself had never seen such a one as that; his wife, his child, they were safe on the high mound, in the solid house; but his dike—and pride shot through his heart—the Hauke-Haien-Dike, as the people called it; now was the time for it to prove how dikes must be built!

But—what was this? He was at the angle between the two dikes; where were the men whom he had ordered here, whose work it was to watch this spot? He looked north up the old dike; for he had sent a few up there too. Neither here nor there could he see a soul; he rode out a piece; but still he was alone: only the soughing of the storm and the surging of the sea that filled the air to an immeasurable distance smote deafeningly on his ear. He turned his horse back; he came again to the deserted corner and let his eyes pass along the line of the new dike; he saw distinctly, the waves rolled up here more slowly, less violently; it almost seemed as if there were other water there. "It will stand, all right!" he murmured and felt a laugh rise within him.

But his inclination to laugh soon passed as his eyes glanced farther along the line of his dike: on the northwest corner—what was that? He saw a dark swarm of moving beings; he saw how industriously they stirred and hurried—there could be no doubt, they were men! What were they trying to do, what work were they doing on his dike now! And already his spurs were in the white horse's flanks and the animal was flying with him thither; the gale came from the broad side, at times the gusts came with such force that they were almost swept down from the dike into the new koog; but horse and rider knew where they were riding. Hauke already perceived that probably a few dozen men were working industriously there together and already he saw distinctly that a gutter was cut right across through the new dike. Violently he reined in his horse. "Stop!" he cried, "stop! What devil's work are you doing here?"

The men had ceased shoveling with a start when they suddenly perceived the dikegrave among them; the wind had carried his words to them and he saw that several were trying to answer him; but he only caught their vehement gestures, for they all stood at his left and what they said was carried away by the gale which was so violent out here that it hurled them against one another so that they were obliged to crowd together. Hauke measured with his quick eyes the gutter that had been dug and the height of the water which, in spite of the new profile, dashed up almost to the top of the dike and spattered horse and rider. Only ten minutes more work and then—he saw it distinctly —then the high tide would break through the gutter and the Hauke-Haien Koog would be buried by the sea!

The dikegrave beckoned one of the laborers to the other side of his horse. "Now, speak," he shouted, "what are you doing here, what is the meaning of this?"

And the man shouted back: "We've got to break through the new dike, sir! So that the old dike doesn't break."

"What have you got to do?"

"Break through the new dike!"

"And flood the koog? What devil ordered you to do that?"

"No, sir, no devil; the commissioner Ole Peters has been here; he gave the order!"

Anger flamed up into the rider's eyes: "Do you know me?" he shouted. "Where I am Ole Peters has no orders to give! Away with you! Back to your places where I left you."

And as they hesitated he dashed into the group with his horse: "Away, to your own or the devil's grand-mother!"

"Be careful, sir," shouted one of the group and struck at the madly careering animal with his spade; but a kick from the horse knocked the spade from his hand, another fell to the ground. At that moment there suddenly arose a shriek from the rest of the group, a shriek such as only deathly terror wrests from the human throat; for a moment all, even the dikegrave and the horse, stood as if paralyzed; only one of the laborers had extended his arm like a sign-post; he pointed to the northwest corner of the two dikes, where the new one ran up to the old one. Only the raging of the wind and the surging of the water could be heard. Hauke turned in his saddle: what was that there? His eyes grew large: "By God! A breach! A breach in the old dike!"

"Your fault, dikegrave," shouted a voice from the group. "Your fault! Take it with you before God's throne!"

Hauke's face, first red with anger, had grown pale as death; the moon which shone on it could not make it whiter; his arms hung limp, he scarcely knew that he held the rein. But that too only lasted for a second; already he drew himself up, a hard groan broke from his mouth; then dumbly he turned his horse and with a snort it raced away with him to the east along the dike. The rider's glance flew sharply in all directions; thoughts were whirling in his head: What blame had he to bear before God's throne? The break through the new dike—perhaps they would have accomplished it if he had not called "stop!" But—there was another thing and his heart grew hot, he knew it only too well—the summer before, if only Ole Peters' evil mouth had not held him back then—that was where it lay! He alone had recognized the weakness of the old dike; he should have pushed on the new work in spite of every-thing: "Lord God, I confess it," he cried out suddenly aloud into the storm. "I have discharged my office badly."

At his left, close to his horse's hoofs, raged the sea; before him, now in complete darkness, lay the old koog with its mounds and homes; the moon's pale light on the sky had disappeared entirely; only at one spot did light shine through the darkness. And something like comfort crept into the man's heart; it must be shining over from his own house, it seemed to him like a message from his wife and child. Thank God, they were safe on the high mound! The others, certainly, they were already in the upland village; more light glimmered from there than he had ever seen before; yes, even high up in the air, probably from the church-tower, light shone out into the night. ''They will all have gone away,'' said Hauke to himself; ''to be sure, on more than one mound a house will lie in ruins, bad years will come for the flooded fens; drains and sluices to be repaired! We must bear it and I will help, those too who have done me harm; only, Lord, my God, be merciful to us men!''

He turned his eyes to the side, towards the new koog; about it foamed the sea; but in it lay the peace of night. Involuntarily triumphant rejoicing rose in the rider's breast: ''The Hauke-Haien-Dike, it must stand; it will hold after more than a hundred years!''

A roar like thunder at his feet roused him from these dreams; the white horse did not want to go on. What was that? The horse jumped back and he felt how a piece of the dike in front of him plunged down into the depths. He opened his eyes wide and shook off all meditation: he had stopped close to the old dike, the horse's front feet had been on it. Involuntarily he jerked the horse back; at that moment the last veiling of clouds swept from the moon and the mild planet illumined the horror that seething and hissing rushed down before him into the old koog.

Hauke stared at it senselessly; it was a deluge, come to swallow up man and beast. Then a light shone again into his eyes; it was the same one that he had seen before; it was still burning on his mound; and now as, encouraged, he looked down into the koog he perceived that behind the confusing whirl that dashed down clamorously before him, only a breadth of about a hundred feet was inundated; beyond that he could clearly distinguish the way that led up from the koog. He saw still more: a carriage, no, a two-wheeled gig came driving madly up towards the dike; a woman, yes, and a child too, were sitting in it. And now —was not that the shrill bark of a little dog that was borne by on the wind? Almighty God! It was his wife, his child! They were already coming quite close and the foaming mass of water was rushing towards them. A shriek, a shriek of desperation broke from the rider's breast: "Elke!" he shouted; "Elke! Back! Back!"

But wind and sea were not merciful, their raging tossed his words away; only the wind had caught his cloak and nearly flung him from his horse; and the approaching vehicle flew on steadily towards the rushing flood. As he looked he saw his wife stretch out her arms as if up towards him: had she recognized him? Had longing, had deathly anxiety about him driven her out of her secure house? And now—was she shouting a last word to him? These questions shot through his mind; they remained unanswered: all words from her to him, from him to her were lost; only an uproar as if the world were coming to an end filled their ears and excluded all other sounds.

"My child! Oh Elke, Oh faithful Elke!" cried Hauke out into the storm. Another large piece of the dike in front of him gave way and thunderingly the sea plunged in after it; once more he saw below the horse's head the wheels of the conveyance rise up out of the chaotic horror and then disappear in a whirl. The fixed eyes of the rider who stood so solitary on the dike saw nothing further. "The end!" he said softly to himself; then he rode to the edge of the abyss where, below him, the waters rushing uncannily were beginning to flood his home village; he still saw the light shining from his house; he felt that the soul had gone out of it. He raised himself high in the saddle and drove his spurs into the white horse's flanks; the animal reared and nearly fell over backwards; but the man's strength forced it down again. "Forward!" he cried once more as he had so often urged it on to a steady ride. "Take me, God; spare the others!"

Another pressure of the spurs; a shriek from the white horse that rose above the gale and the roar of the waves; then from the plunging stream below a dull splash, a brief struggle.

The moon looked down from above and illumined the scene; but on the dike beneath there was no longer any life save that of the savage waters which soon had almost completely covered the old koog. But still the mound where stood Hauke Haien's home rose up out of the swelling flood, the light still shone from there; and from the upland where the houses gradually grew dark, the solitary light from the church steeple threw its wavering beams across the seething waves.

The narrator ceased; I reached out for the filled glass that had long been standing before me; but I did not put it to my mouth; my hand remained lying on the table.

"That is the story of Hauke Haien," my host began again, "as I had to tell it according to my best knowledge. Our dikegrave's housekeeper, of course, would have made another tale; for this too people have to report: after the flood the white skeleton of the horse was to be seen again in the moonlight on Jevershallig as before; everyone in the village believed he saw it. So much is certain: Hauke Haien with his wife and child went down in that flood; I have not been able to find even their graves up in the churchyard; the dead bodies were undoubtedly carried back through the breach by the receding water out to sea, at the bottom of which they gradually were dissolved into their original component parts—thus they had peace from men. But the Hauke Haien Dike still stands now after a hundred years, and tomorrow if you ride to town and don't mind going half an hour out of your way you will have it beneath your horse's hoofs.

"The thanks Jewe Manners once promised the builder that the grandchildren should give have not come, as you have seen; for thus it is, sir: they gave Socrates poison to drink and our Lord Jesus Christ they nailed to the cross! It is not so easy to do such things as that any longer; but—to make a saint of a man of violence or a malicious bull-necked priest, or to make a ghost or a phantom of night of an able fellow just because he is a whole head above the rest of us—that can be done any day.''

When the earnest little man had said that he got up and listened at the window. "It is different out there now," he said, and drew the woolen curtain back; it was bright moonlight. "See," he continued, "there are the commissioners coming back, but they are separating, they are going home; there must have been a break over on the other side; the water has fallen."

I looked out beside him; the windows upstairs, where we were, lay above the edge of the dike; it was as he had said. I took my glass and finished it: "I thank you for this evening," I said; "I think we can sleep in peace!"

"That we can," replied the little man; "I wish you a good night's sleep from my heart!"

In going down I met the dikegrave below in the hall; he wanted to take home with him a map that he had left in the tap-room. "It's all over," he said. "But our schoolmaster has told you a story of his own, I suppose; he belongs to the rationalists!"

"He seems to be a sensible man."

"Oh yes, certainly; but you can't mistrust your own eyes after all. And over on the other side, just as I said it would be, the dike is broken!"

I shrugged my shoulders: "We will have to take counsel with our pillows about that! Good night, dikegrave!"

He laughed. "Good night!"

The next morning, in the most golden of sunlights, which had risen on a wide devastation, I rode along the Hauke Haien Dike down to the town.